WINNING THROUGH

WINNING THROUGH

The Chadwick Family Chronicles
The Later Years

Marcia Willett

HEADLINE

First published in 2000
by HEADLINE BOOK PUBLISHING

10 9 8 7 6 5 4 3 2 1

British Library Cataloguing in Publication Data

Willett, Marcia
Winning through
I. Title
823.9'14 [F]

ISBN 0 74722 1855

Typeset by Palimpsest Book Production Limited,
Polmont, Stirlingshire
Printed and bound in Great Britain by
Clays Ltd St Ives plc

HEADLINE BOOK PUBLISHING
A division of the Hodder Headline Group
338 Euston Road
LONDON NW1 3BH
www.headline.co.uk
www.hodderheadline.com

To Paula

Acknowledgements

In this, the final book of the trilogy, I should like to mention those people who have been especially helpful. My gratitude to Dr John Halliday, Phil and Jeannie Higgins, Yvonne Holland, Bob and Maya Mann and Michael and Carolyn Winterton for generously and patiently making available to me their specialised knowledge. My thanks also to Charles Keay and Hannah Leach for their invaluable assistance with research. I should also like to thank Father Iain Matthew OCD for his permission to use his translation of St John of The Cross's Prayer of a soul in love.

THE CHADWICK FAMILY

Edward Chadwick (1788–1881)
married 1847
Elizabeth Chadwick (1826–1887)

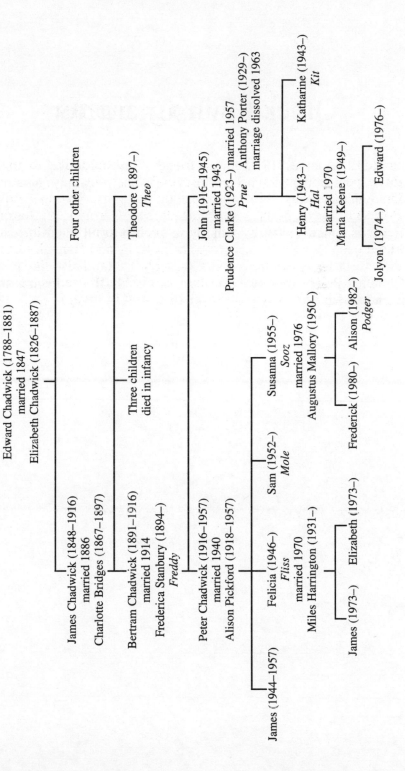

James Chadwick (1848–1916)
married 1886
Charlotte Bridges (1867–1897)

Four other children

Bertram Chadwick (1891–1916)
married 1914
Frederica Stanbury (1894–)
Freddy

Three children
died in infancy

Theodore (1897–)
Theo

Peter Chadwick (1916–1957)
married 1940
Alison Pickford (1918–1957)

John (1916–1945)
married 1943
Prudence Clarke (1923–) married 1957
Prue   Anthony Porter (1929–)
                marriage dissolved 1963

Henry (1943–)
Hal
married 1970
Maria Keene (1949–)

Katharine (1943–)
Kit

Felicia (1946–)
Fliss
married 1970
Miles Harrington (1931–)

Sam (1952–)
Mole

Susanna (1955–)
Sooz
married 1976
Augustus Mallory (1950–)

James (1944–1957)

James (1973–)   Elizabeth (1973–)

Frederick (1980–)   Alison (1982–)
                     Podger

Jolyon (1974–)   Edward (1976–)

Other Main Characters

CAROLINE James (1928–) was a friend of Prue Chadwick (Caroline's elder sister being at school with Prue). She became nanny to the Chadwick orphans.

Cynthia Janice Tulliver – otherwise known as SIN – Kit's closest friend

Clarence Prior – otherwise known as CLARRIE – neighbour and friend to Kit

Book One
Summer 1986

Chapter One

The golden brilliance of the summer twilight was fainting into quiet shadowy evening; thick sweet scents were drifting in the warm air; a thrush was singing in the orchard.

The old man leaned back a little in his chair, stretching out his cramped legs, removing his spectacles and massaging the bridge of his nose between thumb and forefinger. In his late eighties, Theo Chadwick was still a big man, tall and wide-shouldered, but his once black hair was now grey, though still thick, and his naturally lean frame was thin almost to the point of gauntness. His article for the *Quarterly Defence Journal* lay on the battered leather-topped desk before him. It was nearly finished, several pages covered with his small clear writing, but this evening he was distracted and finding it difficult to concentrate. The thrush's glorious song, the liquid succession of lyrical phrases, was excuse enough for inattention to a complicated subject but Theo knew that the thrush was not to blame.

It was Fliss's return from London which had sown the seeds of this distraction. His great-niece had been away for a few days, staying with her husband, Miles, who had newly arrived from Hong Kong. Their two years of separation were over and the decision as to whether she should join him permanently in Hong Kong must now be made. All through the fourteen years of their married life Miles had been firmly in control. When he had accepted the job as a manager with an import/export firm in Hong Kong without discussing it with her, Fliss had known that she must make a stand. She did not want to leave her family or her country and settle permanently in Hong Kong. In her view, their twins, at eleven, were too young to be left behind in boarding school and she'd been deeply hurt – though not particularly surprised – that her feelings had not been considered by him for a single moment. After several long, painful scenes Fliss moved back to The Keep, the Chadwick family home near Totnes in Devon, back to her Great-Uncle Theo and her Aunt Prue, and to Caroline who had been nanny to Fliss and her siblings.

After he'd been only a few months in Hong Kong, at Miles's request, Fliss had flown out to stay for two weeks, and the following Christmas she had travelled there once more, taking the twins, Jamie and Bess, with her. In the autumn, after eighteen months of separation, she'd made another trip.

'There's a woman,' Fliss had told Theo, privately, after this third visit. 'Well, I might have guessed it, I suppose. After all, why not?'

Watching her small face, Theo had tried to guess at her reaction. He wondered if he simply imagined that she was growing more and more like her grandmother, his sister-in-law Freddy Chadwick, whom he had loved so much. Fliss lacked Freddy's height but that unconscious tilt of the chin, the way she squared her shoulders, the thick fair hair bundled at the back of her neck, all these things could make him catch his breath. He knew that Fliss still considered herself morally tied to Miles and that it must have been a shock to her to learn that he did not consider this period of separation in the same light. Theo was rather shocked, too, but he'd waited for her to work out her feelings and presently she'd grinned at him.

'I'm cross,' she told him honestly. 'Not really jealous or hurt. Just cross. Oh, they were fairly discreet, of course, but neither of them could *quite* disguise that tiny air of triumph. D'you know what I mean? He needed me to see that another woman wanted him even if I didn't, and she simply couldn't resist a little show of possessiveness. "*Oh, it was such fun, wasn't it, Miles? Do you remember, Miles? Oh, we did laugh*," and so on.'

Her unexpected imitation – the braying voice and coy yet sly expression – brought the unknown woman clearly before him. He saw her – glossy, hard-faced, immaculately presented, plumped up with confidence, yet uneasy in the presence of the legitimate wife – and felt a stab of anger on Fliss's behalf.

'I pretended utter indifference just tinged with a faint disgust,' said Fliss. She'd jerked her chin at the memory – slightly hurt, despite her protestation – and once again he was reminded painfully of Freddy. 'That showed 'em.'

'I'm sure it did,' he'd answered cautiously. 'Did she . . . this woman cause any real problems?'

'It helps,' she'd answered with pleasurable recollection, 'that I'm a good fifteen years younger than she is. She's Miles's age, you see. In her fifties and rather looks it. She's a naval widow.'

Now, the separation period finished, it appeared that Miles was giving Fliss an ultimatum: either she joined him at once or he would seek a divorce in order to marry the widow.

Theo pushed his chair right back, stood up and wandered over to the window. Hands in pockets, he stared down into the shadow-filled courtyard, wondering just how much of this was bluff on Miles's part, and wishing – not for the first time – that Freddy was still alive to advise him. He knew that in almost any other situation Freddy would have unhesitatingly talked of the sanctity of the marriage vow but in Fliss's case there was a complication. After the murder by Mau Mau of their parents and elder brother, Fliss and her younger brother and sister had returned from Kenya to their grandmother at The Keep. Fliss's affection for her big cousin Hal had developed into an unswerving love. Freddy and Hal's mother, Prue, on discovering this love – their word for it was 'infatuation' – had immediately used their authority to separate them. First cousins, especially when their fathers had been identical twins, should not marry. It was only later that Freddy had begun to question whether she should have encouraged Fliss into her marriage with Miles. Fliss had been influenced by her grandmother's approval of this sensible, reliable, older man. Only Theo had voiced his dissension but even he – to his lasting shame – had allowed himself to be convinced that Miles would make Fliss happy.

Now the marriage was under threat and it was clear that, though she had never allowed it to affect her loyalty to Miles, Fliss still loved Hal, whose own marriage was being strained with different complications . . .

Sitting down upon the window seat, Theo closed his eyes, emptied his mind, and took refuge in his own particular brand of support: the secret, quiet inflowing of God.

Directly below his window, on the bench in the courtyard, Fliss was listening to the thrush in the orchard and watching the roses dim into pale, insubstantial shapes, ghostly upon the high stone walls. She was still trying to come to terms with the fact that the Miles she'd just met in London had become an unknown quantity: someone she did not quite recognise. Out in Hong Kong, with memories flooding back, the paintings and ornaments from the Dartmouth house arranged about the flat, looking up one or two friends, there had been a familiarity which eased the tension so that her shyness with him had dissipated fairly quickly. They'd managed to have quite a lot of fun and she'd been reminded of those early days of marriage, before the twinnies came along. Even so, there had been a certain amount of strain. Miles had approached that first visit with an affectionate 'so now you can see what you're missing, silly girl' attitude, which had aroused her worst instincts. Yet she had been aware that beneath this quite genuine feeling – he *did* think she was being obstinate and rather silly – was a very real desire to impress and win her on to his side. The overcrowded streets and neon lights, the bustle and noise and smells, the busy waters of the harbour and the familiar green Star ferries chugging back and forth to Kowloon – all these brought back poignant memories but . . .

'But it is not my *place*,' she'd cried in despair, towards the end of her first stay. 'Can't you understand that, Miles? I don't fit in here. I'd feel like . . .' she cast about for some image he might possibly understand and gave up '. . . like a dislocated limb. Uncomfortable and awkward. Miserably out of place.'

He'd shaken his head, smiling impatiently, insisting that if only she would *try* . . .

'I lived here for two years,' she'd reminded him. 'It's not as if I don't know what life is like out here. I'm not criticising it, not judging it. It's simply not for *me*.'

He'd grown surly then – she'd noticed he was drinking more heavily – accusing her of ingratitude and selfishness, and she'd reminded him that he hadn't been obliged to take this job without consulting her or thinking about the twinnies. At the mention of Jamie and Bess his face had become blank, intractable, and she'd felt the old desperate drag of despair. Fighting the urge to give up the whole thing there and then she'd suggested that she and the twins return at Christmas and he'd brightened a little, no doubt hoping that the children might fall in love with the place, giving weight to his own pressure. The eleven-year-old twins had been excited at the plan – not only at the thought of seeing their father, but also at the idea of actually visiting their birthplace . . .

Fliss stirred on the bench, shivering a little in the cool evening air, remembering. What sixth sense had alerted the twinnies to the awareness that they were being manipulated? Was it their father's unusual affability towards them, his strange anxiousness to entertain and impress them that had made them wary? First they were flattered, then they became puzzled; their natural excitement and enthusiasm gradually waned into a kind of polite, obedient tolerance to his enthusiasms which irritated him, and the old antagonisms flared up until his natural indifference to them re-established itself. Since then they'd seen their father on only two brief occasions when he'd flown to London for a few days. Miles had refused to travel down to The Keep and the meetings at the hotel were rather strained although they'd all tried hard to pretend that they were still a viable family.

Fliss thought: I can't really blame him for taking up with Diana.

We've all hurt his pride, one way or another. He'd probably be much happier with her . . . but it was a bit of a shock all the same.

She wondered now if her answer to his ultimatum was a foregone conclusion and Diana was already primed to step into her, Fliss's, shoes. After all, she'd given him very little encouragement to hope for a reconciliation. These last few days in London had been almost humiliating. Miles had been friendly in a brusque, cheerful way, patting her arm or her shoulder as he had been used to doing in the past, treating her with an odd mix of tolerance and impatience. Once again he'd refused to travel down to Devon, making it clear that now the two years were up he had come to receive an answer, not to waste time in idle pleasantries with her relatives. He was in no mood for delaying tactics and made no attempt at finesse. It mortified her when she realised that he expected her to share his bed within an hour or two of her arrival – although she had done so in Hong Kong – and she saw at last that he had become . . . what?

Fliss drew her heels up on to the edge of the bench and hugged her knees. It wasn't true, now she thought about it, that Miles had become a stranger. He was more like a distant, rather difficult relative; a little-known uncle perhaps? Nevertheless it was odd that he seemed less familiar to her in London than he had in Hong Kong. His faintly brutal, almost amused, approach to the physical side of their relationship had shocked her and, unable to pretend so immediately to an intimacy which was so clearly absent, she'd told him that for this first evening at least she would stay with her cousin Kit, Hal's twin sister, at her flat in Hampstead. He'd shrugged with an air of 'well, it's no more than I expected' and had let her go. She'd felt like a schoolgirl – but that at least was nothing new in their relationship – and had fallen into her cousin's arms with a relief which bordered on the hysterical. Kit, surprised at such emotion from her usually reticent cousin, had poured her a large drink and settled down to cross-question her. For once Fliss's natural instinct for oyster-like privacy had given way before Kit's obvious anxiety and affection, and she'd answered her questions with an almost devastating candour.

'Perhaps,' Kit had mused at last, 'you've been subconsciously waiting for him to give way. You know? To suggest that he might move back to England and find a job here so that you can all be together again?' She saw the expression of alarm on her cousin's face and raised her eyebrows. 'And then again,' she'd murmured drily, 'perhaps not.'

'It just feels so different this time,' Fliss had mumbled inadequately.

'Naturally it does, little coz,' Kit had answered patiently. 'That's because it's make-up-your-mind time. Your freedom's just run out, honey.'

Neither of them had mentioned Hal.

In the end, when Fliss had gathered up her courage and told Miles that her answer must be 'no', he'd refused to accept it, saying that he had another fortnight in London before he returned to Hong Kong and that he would speak to her again at the end of that time. Confused by his reaction, irritated by his stubbornness, she'd caught the train back to the West Country with the sinking sensation that it was all to be done again, assailed by the familiar demons of guilt and self-doubt, trying to analyse her true feelings for Miles . . .

Someone was calling her name. The light shone out suddenly from the hall windows, stretching rectangular shapes, black-barred, across the flagged path, and climbing stiffly to her feet she went quickly into the house.

Chapter Two

Miles lay on his bed, listening to the noises of London outside his hotel bedroom window, a generous tumblerful of whisky within reach. Arms behind his head, ankles crossed, he stared up at the uninspiring ceiling and cursed briefly from time to time beneath his breath. He'd taken an enormous gamble which had not paid off and he was trying to decide how best to retrieve what was left of an unpromising situation. Why had he ever been fool enough to attempt to bluff Fliss, to try to rouse her jealousy and so bounce her into giving way? He remembered her cool little look which slid over Diana like cold water: the tiny, nearly contemptuous glance when the older woman had attempted intimacy with him; the faintest sketch of an indifferent shrug when he'd hinted that he was attracted to this middle-aged widow. He'd felt equal measures of shame and anger at her response yet some evil demon had driven him on to greater lengths – encouraged by Diana – in an attempt to rouse a more positive reaction. What, he wondered now, had ever made him think that an ultimatum might work the miracle?

Groaning aloud as he remembered Fliss telling him that her answer must be 'no', he hauled himself up, punching the pillows into a support for his back, reaching for his glass. Despite her antipathy to Hong Kong or, rather – he strove to be absolutely fair – her refusal to settle permanently away from her own country and her family, he'd felt that she was still very fond of him. There were many occasions during the last two years when they'd slipped back into the familiar intimacy of companionship. She'd spontaneously taken his hand, smiled at him with her own particular warmth, done small wifely things which pertained to his comfort and happiness. Miles set his teeth together. He could not let her go. He would not allow it. The tenacity that was characteristic of him refused to admit a scenario in which he might lose her. His love for her was not in question, never had been, despite her accusation that he did not love her enough to give up the job in Hong Kong. How well he remembered the scene in the house in Above Town; how

9

like old Mrs Chadwick she'd looked: autocratic, unapproachable, determined. It was the first time in fourteen years of marriage that she'd openly opposed him. Oh, there had been moments of . . . Miles caught himself up sharply – he'd damned nearly used the word 'insubordination'. Sipping thoughtfully he allowed himself to admit that he'd often been high-handed with her. She'd been so much younger that it had seemed right to take care of her; to relieve her of any anxiety. It was natural that he should know what was best. The arrival of the twins had thrown a spanner in the works of their closeness and freedom and he was prepared to accept that it might have been tactless, even hurtful, to look forward quite so openly to the time when the children were grown up and he and Fliss could start a new life together. If he were pressed he would agree that it had been unrealistic to expect Fliss to take the same view. She loved Jamie and Bess much too dearly and had clearly enjoyed their childhood. Still, it was an undeniable fact that many men were not natural fathers and found it difficult to take a deep interest in small children. No shame in that. He'd tried never to let this . . . he instinctively dismissed the word 'indifference' but found it hard to think of a substitute . . . very well, let it stand, dammit. He'd tried not to let this indifference show, tried not to create situations in which Fliss had to choose between him and the twins, although when it came to the Hong Kong job she'd made it damned clear where her loyalties lay . . . Miles bit his lip, wondering if a sense of grievance might be creeping into his retrospective glance at their relationship.

Cradling the glass on his midriff, recrossing his ankles, he made a real attempt to review his marriage honestly. There had been moments of doubt . . . He gave a mental shrug, defending himself. Well, that was fair enough. Surely every married person, if they were absolutely honest, had the odd twinge of uncertainty. The point was that he'd never stopped loving her. He was prepared to admit that she'd irritated him occasionally, that he'd have preferred her to make a little more of her natural attributes . . . He had a sudden flashback of Fliss and Diana standing together. Fliss, not quite forty, slender, natural, uncluttered, casual; Diana, rigidly controlled to the last tinted hair and varnished nail, eager, alert, coiled for action. He closed his eyes against his own embarrassment. What a fool he'd been. Never mind. That could all be forgotten, now: put aside. There hadn't been much in it, after all, and the talk of marriage was pure bluff. If Diana had any hopes of it *he* had by no means encouraged them. No, forget all that, the point was: what should he do now?

It occurred to him that during these last two years Fliss had grown up. The confrontation – and her refusal to allow him to continue to control her life – had been the turning point. He searched his memory, trying to remember if there had been serious signs of rebellion before the Hong Kong row. Had he, during those fourteen years, actually allowed her room to grow? She'd been so young, so charming and vulnerable, when he'd first met her, back in the Dartmouth days when he'd been Hal's divisional officer. How old had she been – eighteen, nineteen? To him it was as if she'd never changed, had been sealed like a fly in amber into his first romantic image of her. Swallowing more whisky, he relived the jubilation which had flooded him when at last, after five years of waiting and hoping that she might see him in a light other than that of a friend, she'd telephoned. She'd felt suddenly lonely, she'd said, dreading the weekend, wanting someone to talk to . . . Even now he had no idea why she'd chosen him and not some member of the close-knit Chadwick clan.

Swallowing back the unfamiliar sensation of emotional tears, Miles placed the glass on the bedside cabinet and reached for the telephone. He knew now exactly what he must do to begin the long siege which might win her back to him. If it took another five years then he'd sit it out. He'd done it once; he could do it again.

The garden was full of the sounds of early summer; an invisible cooing, droning, rustling murmur of quiet activity. Rex, the golden retriever, had taken refuge from the afternoon sunshine in the shade afforded by the towering branches of the rhododendron bushes. Now flowering into their annual breathtaking glory of crimson, cream and rose, banks of heavenly blossoms edged the lawn, hiding the kitchen garden behind them. Stretched on the dry, barren earth beneath them, Rex was unaware of all this beauty. Nose on paws he was watching the group on the lawn – and Podger in particular.

It was a peaceful scene. Fliss lay as if she were pegged to the tartan rug, arms and legs flung out as though abandoned, her face upturned to the golden sunlight. She remained quite motionless yet alert, listening to her Aunt Prue, who was kneeling by the herbaceous border, wrestling with a particularly obdurate buttercup whose roots had spread stealthily but deeply. Prue knew that Freddy would never have allowed such anarchy to have flourished so extensively but Prue – who had come to gardening late in life – had none of the ruthlessness or dedication of her formidable late mother-in-law, who had lived for more than sixty years here at The Keep, most of them as a widow. Prue herself had been a widow for over forty years, and, like Freddy, had been left to bring up her twins alone.

Prue, having connived with Freddy over Fliss's infatuation with Hal, was struggling with her own sense of guilt where Fliss was concerned. As she dug deep into the earth about the buttercup's roots she tried to guess what advice Freddy would now be giving her granddaughter. In some ways Fliss was very much like Freddy, and Prue, easy-going, gentle, overgenerous, hesitated to guide her. Aware of her own inadequacies, not to mention a rather unimpressive track record when it came to wise judgement, nevertheless she knew that this time she must speak out. Now was an opportune moment: Caroline was making a cake for tea and Theo was closeted in his study. Only Podger, Fliss's niece was with them and, at not quite four, it was doubtful that she was old enough to be interested in Fliss's dilemma. Prue put down the trowel on the grass and grasped the stubborn, earthy tentacles, bracing herself to speak, reminding herself that Fliss had broached the subject first a short while before.

'I know it is quite wrong to interfere,' she said rather breathlessly, knowing that she was about to do just that, 'but I simply have to say that I think that the fact that Miles refuses to take no for an answer shows that he still loves you. No, not that trowel, Podger. See how sharp the edges are? Where is that very nice little fork we bought for you? Ah, here it is. That's better. Good girl. That's not to say that I think you should go to Hong Kong – I think he behaved very badly about that – but perhaps he might now be prepared to be more flexible. Oh, Fliss, I just want you to be absolutely certain . . .'

Podger rested on her haunches, twiddling her hair thoughtfully whilst she regarded her Great-Aunt Prue. Her own small plastic fork had been cast aside contemptuously and she was awaiting another opportunity to seize the larger, heavier tool which a little earlier had produced such satisfactory results in the flowerbed. She'd managed a quite deep hole in the soft crumbly earth in which she'd buried Rex's ball and now she'd set her mind on making a few mud pies. Meanwhile she was content to sit here in the warm sunshine keeping an eye on Rex, who had now risen from his refuge beneath the rhododendron bushes and was busily quartering the lawn, feathery tail waving, in search of his ball. She listened idly to the conversation that ebbed about her. After Mummy, Aunt Prue was her very favourite person and she could see that, today, she was . . . Podger frowned, sucking her thumb thoughtfully. For some reason, whenever she looked at Aunt Prue this afternoon, Mrs Tittlemouse came to the forefront of her mind.

'"Tiddly, widdly, widdly, Mrs Tittlemouse",' she murmured round her thumb, and Aunt Prue beamed at her, forgetting her worries for the moment, giving her a quick hug.

'Yes, darling. We'll have a story after tea, shall we? You shall choose. Don't think I can't imagine how you feel, Fliss, but love is such a very precious commodity. Oh dear.' Prue sat back on her heels, pushing the soft wispy grey hair back from her forehead. Earth clung to her hands and left a smear upon her cheek. 'I *promised* Caroline I wouldn't interfere.'

Fliss, still lying flat upon the tartan rug, stretched almost languorously.

'I'd rather you said what you thought,' she murmured. Slowly she rolled over, resting her cheek on her folded arms. 'After all, it's not a secret.'

'Well then.' Prue abandoned the obdurate buttercup root with relief and plumped down on the rug beside her. 'I know that I have no qualifications as a marriage counsellor but . . . oh, Flissy darling, *do* think twice about divorcing Miles. It's such a huge step and it's not easy to be alone, you know, without a man. I know you have all of us, and we all love you, but it's not the same. It's probably old-fashioned to say that women need men but I think it's true.'

'Caroline seems to have managed perfectly well,' murmured Fliss, 'not to mention Grandmother. And you, too, come to that.'

Prue settled herself more comfortably and, seeing them thus absorbed, Podger stealthily reached for the trowel, pushing it behind her, her eyes fixed guilessly upon her older relatives lest they should suddenly remember her.

'I *knew* you'd say that,' Prue was almost enjoying herself, 'but it's not quite the same thing. Caroline has never been married, never had children and Freddy more or less cut herself off from the world. Of course, hers was a different generation. Remarrying wasn't always easy.'

'But neither did you,' protested Fliss. 'Remarry, I mean. Well, except for Tony . . .'

'I missed Johnny so terribly.' Prue was remembering, her eyes grieved. 'I thought that Tony could take his place, you see, but it simply didn't work. It was almost a relief when he left me.'

'But I thought you said that women need men.'

'They do.' Prue paused to marshal her confused thoughts. 'What I'm trying to say is that if there is still love between you then you shouldn't let it slip away. Especially when there are children involved. There was no real love between me and Tony. Johnny was my first and only love and no one else ever quite measured

13

up to him. It was wrong of me to marry Tony when I still loved Johnny, even though he was dead. Tony was always second best.'

She paused, remembering Fliss's love for Hal. Had her first love also been her only love? Had Miles been second best? There was a long silence. Hal's shadow lay between them as clearly as if he had been standing on the lawn. There, amongst the sounds of the summer afternoon, Prue faced the fact that she was anxious lest Fliss's freedom might present Hal with a very good reason to leave his ailing marriage; to divorce his rather tiresome and selfish wife, Maria. Prue didn't want this to happen. Of course she wanted her son to be happy but there were the boys, Jolyon and Edward, to consider, not to mention Hal's career as a naval officer . . .

Presently Prue reached for Fliss's hand and held it tightly. 'Forgive me,' she said humbly. 'Caroline is quite right. I have no right to interfere. We're all biased, one way or another.'

Fliss squeezed her hand warmly. 'It's quite all right. Honestly. I know you're trying to help me. I wish I knew what to do. I go round and round in circles. Each time I make up my mind I think about a different aspect of it, which throws everything back to square one.'

Sensing that their attention was centred firmly elsewhere, Podger seized the opportunity to climb to her feet, the trowel clasped awkwardly behind her back. Watching the two on the rug, she began to back cautiously away.

'Don't let him bully you,' Prue cautioned anxiously. 'Give yourself time to think.'

Fliss began to laugh. 'I've had two years in which to think,' she reminded her aunt. 'The trouble is that I haven't really thought at all. I've postponed it until the twelfth hour. To be honest, I'm scared stiff.'

Before Prue could answer, a cheerful hooting sounded from the courtyard and a car door slammed.

'Susanna,' she announced, almost with relief. 'Fred will be ready for some tea. Now where on earth has Podger disappeared to and what*ever* is Rex doing digging in the border?'

She scrambled up, flapping at Rex, calling for Podger, and Fliss, following more slowly, crossed the lawn to greet her sister. Caroline appeared at the garden-room door.

'Oh, there you are,' she said. 'Susanna and Fred have just arrived. Tea's all ready in the hall and I'm sure that Podger's hands need washing. Start pouring, will you, Flissy, dear . . .'

Presently the garden lay deserted in the afternoon sunshine. Rex, having fended off Prue's wrath and retrieved his muddy ball, had returned to his place beneath the rhododendrons. As he lay licking the earth from his paws it occurred to him that there would be cake and scones for tea in the hall. He brooded thoughtfully. Podger's tendencies towards mischief often caused problems for him, and adult retribution usually resulted in guilt offerings from the real culprit. Today she might be feeling particularly repentant. Rising, Rex padded towards the garden room, shouldered through the half-open door, and crossed the courtyard. Only Podger saw him enter the hall. Taking a generous piece of scone from her plate she surreptitiously put it on the floor beside her. Lying down close to her feet, feeling her small hand on his head, Rex sighed contentedly and began to eat.

Chapter Three

'And do you still love him?' asked Susanna curiously. She looked closely at the photograph of the twinnies with their father and then replaced it on the bureau, glancing about the first-floor sitting room which had once been Grandmother's private domain. 'I can still see her here, can't you? Sitting there writing her letters or listening to some concert on the Third Programme.'

Relieved that Susanna had been distracted from her first question, Fliss looked around her.

'It was rather unnerving to begin with,' she admitted. 'But Uncle Theo and Prue were so determined that her rooms should be used. It was like a kind of sacrilege to begin with but very soon it was a tremendous comfort. It was important to be able to come home once Miles had gone to Hong Kong . . .'

She hesitated, wondering if Susanna would be reminded of her earlier query but her younger sister was concentrating on the past, their conversation about Miles temporarily forgotten. Fliss watched her. Large with child she still had all the qualities which had defined her childhood: positive, cheerful, vitally alive, yet possessed of an inner serenity. She stood gazing up at the Widgerys which flanked the fireplace, her jaw-length, shiny, dark hair thrust negligently behind her ears and her bare legs and arms already tanned a warm brown.

'The thing was,' Susanna was saying, 'she had to be a mother to us. It must have been a terrible shock for her, mustn't it? Not only to hear about Mummy and Daddy and Jamie dying so dreadfully but to be suddenly landed with the three of us. She can't have been all that young, after all.'

'She was in her sixties.' Fliss sat down on the window seat. 'And you were barely two and there was Mole, being quite unable to speak with the shock of it all . . .' She fell silent remembering those terrible weeks of terror, of the relief at being back at The Keep, the feeling of safety. 'Of course, Ellen and Fox were just brilliant. Can you remember anything about it, Sooz?'

Her sister sank into one of the deep, comfortable armchairs with a sigh.

'Not really,' she said. 'I try to remember them – you know, Mummy and Daddy and Jamie – but I don't know how much is true remembering or whether it's what people have told me. I was the luckiest one, really. This was my childhood. Here with Grandmother, and Ellen and Fox looking after us all, and Uncle Theo. It was only later, when I went away to college, that I realised that my background wasn't quite the same as that of the people of my own age. I was quite upset about it for a while. Someone said that our life here was an anachronism, being brought up by Grandmother's generation, and I hated not being normal.'

Fliss snorted derisively. 'So what's normal?'

'I sometimes wonder if we're a bit of an odd family, though,' insisted Susanna. 'The Chadwicks seem to be very good at living alone, don't they? Well, not so much alone as without partners. Grandmother, Uncle Theo, Mole, Kit, Prue. Even you seem to have been perfectly happy during these last two years.'

'Prue was saying something similar earlier.' Fliss pushed up the sleeves of her blue denim shirt and twined some stray blonde hairs back into the loose knot on her neck. 'You and Gus seem to be the only happily married couple in the whole family. So there you are. You're normal at last.'

'I notice you don't count Hal and Maria,' observed Susanna idly. 'It's been great having Hal based at Devonport, hasn't it? What a pity Maria won't move down, although I can understand her wanting to be near Edward whilst he's still so young. Perhaps she'll let him board now he's settled in. It must be two years since he started, isn't it?'

'Two years,' agreed Fliss. 'He's not a probationer any more. He's been made up to a full chorister and everyone's delighted.'

Susanna pushed a cushion into the small of her back. 'Including Jolyon?'

'Including Jolyon,' said Fliss firmly. 'Jolyon's never been jealous of his brother, you know that. He's a dear.'

'Oh, Jo's all right,' said Susanna casually. 'But he must get a bit miffed occasionally with all the attention his little brother gets. I'm so pleased that he's really happy at Herongate with Bess. I always thought it was a bit hard that he should be sent away to school so that Maria could go and live in Salisbury to cater to Edward's needs.'

'It was difficult to get it right for everyone,' said Fliss, after a moment. 'But the scholarship was too good to turn down, and it's all worked out quite well.'

'I did wonder whether Maria might come down a bit more often, what with Hal here when the ship was in and Jo coming home for exeats with the twinnies. Still, she's a naval wife and she must be used to the separation.'

'I think they did the best they could for both children.' Fliss made an effort to sound calmly judicious. 'Hal went back to Salisbury for all his leaves. It was only when the ship was alongside for just a couple of days that he stayed here. He *is* the captain, after all. Very often he had to stay in the port area anyway. It was lovely for Prue to have him here so that she could really spoil him without putting Maria's back up.'

Susanna chuckled. 'She's the original mother hen. It's been such fun, hasn't it? Especially with Mole's submarine based at Devonport, as well. Janie was in seventh heaven. She was really miserable when he was posted to Northwood.'

'It would be wonderful if he and Janie could get together,' admitted Fliss. 'But I can't see it. Not after all this time. He's known her for years, since you were at college.'

'He can't bring himself to make the commitment.' Susanna frowned a little. 'It all goes back to the Kenya thing. He's terrified that something frightful will happen to the people he loves when he's not there to protect them. He hates it when I have the babies in case I die in childbirth, and he worries about the children because they're so vulnerable. It's so odd given that he's a submariner. You'd think he'd want a nice safe job, wouldn't you?'

'I think it's more complex than that. If it hadn't been for our family tragedy he'd probably have been a perfectly ordinary sort of chap. But our parents and Jamie dying so violently made him aware of the fragility of life when he was far too young to deal with it. He's so much better than he was but the shadow is still there. It's been something he's continually fighting to control. Chadwicks have always gone into the Navy and it was terribly important to him to prove that he could do it, too. Anyway, I don't think that he's in love with Janie. He's very fond of her but Mole will need some great passion to push him over the edge.'

'I know.' Susanna sighed regretfully and then shrugged. 'It would just be so very convenient, apart from everything else, what with her working with Gus and being such a chum, but I fear that you're right. It's no good marrying just for convenience. And speaking of that . . .'

'Shouldn't we go down and see what the children are up to?' Fliss glanced at her watch and stood up, holding out a hand to her sister.

19

'I can take a hint,' said Susanna placidly, allowing herself to be heaved to her feet. 'I just thought you might want to talk about it.'

'I do, really,' Fliss confessed. 'But when I start I get even more muddled. Do you know what I mean?'

'I think so.' They wandered out on to the landing together. 'The trouble is, we all want to put in our two penn'orth and you just need someone to confirm what you think about it yourself.'

'If only I knew what that was,' murmured Fliss. 'Anyway, never mind all that. I hope it's another girl you've got in there, Sooz. This new generation of girls are outnumbered two to one already.'

'Could I cope with another Podger?' mused Susanna. 'What a sobering thought! Ah well. I must get them home to bed and make Gus some supper. Do I hear singing?'

'You could call it that.'

Several voices – Podger's squeak and Fred's husky growl, blending with Prue's light, pretty soprano – could be heard drifting up from the hall below and the two women went down the stairs to find them.

Later that evening, as Fliss walked on the hill behind The Keep with Rex, Susanna's question echoed in her head. *And do you still love him?* Long shadows, indigo and purple, were stretching across the hill and two rooks flapped homeward with a steady, rhythmical beating of wings. The sun sank gently into an armada of curded, cushiony clouds, towering up from the west, and suddenly, as she watched, molten, brilliant, dazzling gold streamed along their fluffy, fluted edges, flooding and drenching them in colour. Fliss, who had seized Caroline's padded jacket from the peg by the back door, slid her arms into the sleeves, and sighed with pleasure. She had watched the sunset from this hill on countless occasions but the endlessly changing pageant, season by season, year by year, never ceased to enthral her. This was her place, this ancient hill fortress where her ancestor had built The Keep from the granite of the old fort; this was where she belonged. Now, when it was too late, she knew that she should never have married Miles – that she had turned to him as a reaction to the news of Hal's engagement – but what was so clear with hindsight had seemed so different at the time. *And do you still love him?*

Fliss thrust her hands deep into her pockets and followed Rex down to the river. Surely the question should be 'Did you *ever* love him?' Instinctively she shrank from admitting that she had married without love – and, anyway, would it be true? She did not love him

20

as she loved Hal but there were many different kinds of love and who was to say that one kind should not succeed as well as another? She *had* loved Miles – oh, not with the overwhelming passion which she had given to Hal, but with an altogether gentler, calmer love. Miles had been strong, comforting, determined, and she had leaned against his strength and been grateful for his protection. His love had allowed her to keep her pride. At the time it had been the only thing that mattered. '*And do you still love him?*'

This was what mattered now. If Hal were free, if there were no children involved, she knew that her decision would be an easier one. After all, her own children were not likely to be much affected if she were to divorce Miles. Too late she'd realised that children were not a part of his plan and he had never been able to exert himself in their direction. He had been generous, strict, aware of his responsibility, but he had not loved them. Now, after two years of separation, it would be easy to allow things to drift wider so that the total separation was more or less painless as far as Jamie and Bess were concerned but . . . But Hal was not free and they both knew that Jolyon and Edward would suffer terribly if their parents were to separate. Jolyon especially would feel it. He had willingly agreed to go away to school – frightened though he was at the prospect – if it made life easier for his mother and Edward and kept the family as a unit. Hal had promised Jolyon then that there was no danger of divorce, that he and Maria loved each other, that there was nothing for him to fear. Hal would not go back on his word to his son.

Following the well-worn sheeptracks that wound down the side of the hill, Fliss crushed down a familiar sense of resentment. Her cousin Kit, Hal's twin, had told her in confidence that Maria was having an affair with a former boyfriend, her father's junior partner. This was part of the reason she had so readily moved back to Salisbury when Edward had been offered his scholarship to the cathedral school. Her father's architect's practice was situated in Salisbury, where this Adam Wishart now lived, and Maria had made the most of her opportunities during these last two years with Hal at sea. However, Adam's wife would not give him his freedom and Maria had no intention of leaving Hal whilst she had no other protector available.

Fliss thought: It's because she's getting away with it that I feel so cross. She's cheating on Hal, manipulating the boys, and getting off scot-free while Hal and I try to behave as though we're just good friends. It's sickening.

'You're a pair of idiots,' Kit had announced roundly. 'I simply can't believe that you don't grab the opportunity to let off steam. Oh, I can see that it would be impossible down at The Keep with

Ma and Uncle Theo pottering around – pretty nerve-racking, I grant you. But why don't you come here? Dear old Sin spends most of her time downstairs with Andrew these days and I could bugger off for a weekend. Just say the word. Honestly, honey, it's crazy. Everyone knows that if Grandmother and Ma hadn't shoved their oars in, you and Hal would be together. You've loved each other for years. OK, I know all that about cousins having funny children and I know that our fathers were identical twins but it doesn't matter any more. You and Hal aren't going to want more children now. So what's stopping you grabbing a few hours of happiness?'

'I promised Uncle Theo,' Fliss had mumbled – and Kit had shaken her head in despair, rolling her eyes in disbelief.

'I don't *believe* this,' she'd cried, frustrated in her attempt to help her brother and her cousin. 'Is this the eighties or have I slipped a decade or three?'

'It's different for you.' Fliss had attempted to defend herself. 'Prue was never so strict with you as Grandmother was with us. You're a child of your generation, a sixties child. You do as you please. I probably *am* three decades behind you but I can't help myself. Hal feels the same, anyway. He's promised Jo that he and Maria will stick it out. I think we both feel it would be dangerous to give way even for one afternoon. Once we started neither of us might be able to stop.'

'Suit yourselves but don't blame me if you both go off bang one of these days,' grumbled Kit. 'What masochistic bastard invented love anyway? It's like some terrible disease for us Chadwicks, isn't it? We get it once and we're immune for ever. It's just that we never get over that one first agony.'

'And do you still love him?'

Now, standing by the river, watching the midges in their eternal, shimmering twilight dance above the fast-running water, Fliss wondered if Kit might be right. In which case, was it sensible for her, Fliss, even to think of trying again with Miles? Was it fair to him? Or to her? Putting Hal right out of the picture, if that were possible, what was the right thing to do for Miles and herself and their children?

Rex pushed against her leg, dropping a sodden, dripping piece of branch at her feet. He stared at it, ears cocked, tail waving, and then looked up at her, his tongue lolling expectantly.

'OK, then,' she muttered. 'Here it goes. Watching?'

She flung it as far as she could in the direction of the spinney and then slowly followed in his wake. So many memories were bound up in this hill, the river that wound its way through the valley down towards the sea, and the spinney with its lofty trees and its dim, mysterious interior; memories that stretched back for thirty years. One thing was certain: she could not settle permanently in Hong Kong. No, she must remain firm. She had given Miles her answer and she must stand by it.

A voice, calling to her, rippled out over the hill, and, turning to look up towards the house, she saw Caroline descending towards her, waving. Fliss, waving back, was seized by an unexpected clutch of fear. No reason to believe that Caroline hadn't merely come out to join her as she sometimes did, yet even while acknowledging that, Fliss found that she was hurrying up the path to meet her, anxieties crowding into her head. Were the twinnies OK? Or was it Uncle Theo? Or Hal . . . ?

'What is it?' she asked breathlessly as they met together on the narrow path. 'Sorry.' She tried to laugh away her panic. 'Just for a moment, I thought . . .' She stared at Caroline. 'What's happened?'

'Nothing terrible,' said Caroline quickly. 'Of course not. Sorry. I didn't mean to frighten you. Just something a little odd, that's all. Miles telephoned just now and has asked if you will call him back.'

'That's OK,' said Fliss, relaxing. Miles was less alarming than those brief imaginings. 'I thought he probably would. I've been half expecting it.'

'Yes,' said Caroline, as they climbed the path together, Rex panting in the rear. 'I guessed as much. But the odd thing is that he's not in London any more. It seems that he's come down to Dartmouth and he's hoping that you'll go over to see him.'

Chapter Four

Miles woke suddenly in his room at the Royal Castle Hotel. He lay quite still, watching the patterns made by the sun on the wall, listening to the crying of the gulls. It was odd to be back in Dartmouth yet not in the narrow house in Above Town which he'd owned for more than twenty years. Excitement curdled in his gut. Today he would see her; today he would begin again. This excitement, mixed with apprehension and optimism, confused him. He'd felt rather like this two years ago when he'd heard about the job in Hong Kong but at that time these emotions had all been tied up with the challenge of a new career after twenty-five years in the Navy. To be fair, he reminded himself, he had also looked upon it as the beginning of a new life together for him and Fliss but he realised now that he had been taking a great deal for granted. He had assumed that the two of them would simply start again where they'd left off when the twins were born. No allowances had been made for the fact that Fliss might have changed or have other needs; he'd expected her to be as delighted as he'd been himself, ready to support him in his new role. How angry he'd felt when she'd questioned his right to take decisions which affected them jointly without consulting her; how hurt when she'd refused to consider the future in the same light; how shocked when she'd decided not to accompany him and had suggested her plan for a two-year moratorium. It was true that he would have been able to find a job in the United Kingdom but he was too absorbed, too engrossed by the plans for his new career, to be prepared to consider alternative ideas. She was his wife and her place was at his side. His anger and resentment refused to allow him to back down, although he'd secretly hoped that at the last moment she would relent. Even then, despite the pain of leaving her behind, the excitement of this new life had dulled his unhappiness. It had only been a matter of months, however, before he'd written to her, asking her to visit him. To do her justice she'd always been ready to respond instantly to his need. He cast his mind back, trying to remember how he'd felt when she'd come out to Hong Kong on those fleeting visits during the last two years. His reaction had been different then: excitement, yes, but overlaid with the calming sense of his own importance. He could admit that now.

He thought: Subconsciously I was trying to bully her into submission. To bludgeon her senses with what I had achieved and the great life we could have together out there. I always believed that sooner or later she'd give in and join me.

He pushed back the bedclothes and sat for a moment on the edge of the bed, yawning. At fifty-five he'd lost none of his broad-shouldered, thickset strength and, although the rumpled brown hair showed plenty of grey, his keen glance and air of command lent a youthfulness to his appearance. None of these benefits weighed with him for a moment. Miles was not a man to waste time considering how he might set himself off to the best advantage physically. His whole will was bent on dealing with the difficulties before him: his mind doubling back and forth, examining weaknesses and strengths, determining strategy. Fliss, he knew, would be unmoved by anything less than a genuine change of heart and a re-evaluation of the situation. During the last few days in London he had thought long and hard, trying to be as honest as he could, suspending self-justification and self-pity in favour of truth. It had been a painful, humbling business – and he still had a very long way to go – but he was working at it. His marriage was on the line and the shock of Fliss's answer to his ultimatum had jerked him out of years of complacency.

Miles stood up and pottered over to the coffee-making equipment, mourning the passing of good old-fashioned room service and examining with dislike the usual display of milk substitutes. Since he always drank his coffee black this was simply habit, a gesture of rebellion against the lowering of standards, but he liked to go through the motions whilst he tore open the sachet and tipped the instant coffee powder into the cup. As he waited for the kettle to boil, he stood at the window looking out at the town.

The tide was out. In the boatfloat the small vessels rested untidily on the pale soft mud, forlorn, useless until the water returned. On the wall above them a swan preened herself, heavy-bosomed and clumsy, broad-splayed feet awkward and in-turned. She too was waiting for the life-bestowing tide. Outside a shop door, where bright flowers trailed from hanging baskets, a girl was standing on some folding steps watering the plants with a long-spouted watering can. Soon the locals would be about their daily business; stepping round the visitors who dawdled on the pavements; hurrying past them as they drifted across the narrow medieval streets. As he watched the girl pausing to exchange greetings with a friend, Miles felt a sense of shock that he, too, might be considered a visitor and was surprised by a deep and unexpected need to be accepted, to belong in this town where such roots as he had were buried. Dimly he recognised Fliss's similar attachment to The Keep, her allegiance to her own small part of Devon, and allowed it to influence his new, painful humility.

The kettle was boiling behind him and he made his coffee, carrying it back to the window, watching the town coming alive below him. He suddenly needed to be out there, walking along the embankment, feeling the soft warm breeze on his face. Reaching for his watch amongst his possessions on the bedside table, he saw that there was time for a stroll before breakfast. Between gulps at the hot black liquid, he dragged clothes from the wardrobe and the small chest, flinging them on the bed until, with one last glance at the river, he put the empty cup on the tray and disappeared into the shower.

The bar was empty when Fliss opened the door and looked inside. It surprised and irritated her to feel her hand tremble slightly on the handle and she stood quite still for a moment, swallowing down her nervousness. It was that quiet hour between the departure of late lunchers and the appearance of those in search of tea, and there was a languid atmosphere, as if the staff were all putting their feet up somewhere else, leaving the hotel temporarily deserted. As her eyes grew accustomed to the dimness, rather a shock after the brightness of the sunny afternoon, she saw that someone was, after all, behind the bar at the far end by the coffee-making machine. She hesitated, unwilling to ask if there might be a message for her. It hadn't occurred to her that Miles would not be here to meet her and she instantly suspected that this was, despite his conciliatory words, all set to be another battle of gamesmanship. Perhaps he was hoping that she'd be obliged to go up to his room.

Turning abruptly she dragged the door open and, hurrying out, barged into Miles as he came hurtling into the bar.

'Sorry,' he gasped. 'Really I am. I bumped into Jeff Burns. Had no idea he was at the college now and I couldn't get away.' He peered into her face, and, reading her expression rightly, bundled her back into the bar lest she should escape and disappear. 'Please. Don't be angry. I only went out because the waiter was trying to clean round me and I walked straight into Jeff. He would drone on. I thought I might have to knock him out so as to get away. The

Ancient Mariner could take his correspondence course and learn a few new tricks.'

He looked so distraught, so un-Miles-like, that she was obliged to laugh, albeit unwillingly. His relief was patent and he laughed with her, still holding her wrist, keeping her close. Embarrassment made her glance away from the strange blend of tenderness and fear on his face and he released her quickly, glancing round him.

'It's silent as a churchyard in here at this time of the day,' he told her. 'That's why I suggested it. I felt we needed to meet on neutral ground. Tea?'

'Yes.' She fumbled with the strap of her bag, unwilling to look at him again. 'Yes, please.'

'I don't quite know the form here.' He jingled the loose coins in the pocket of his cords, staring towards the bar. 'A scone, perhaps? Cream cake?'

'No.' She shook her head quickly. 'No thanks. Tea will be great.'

He wandered away from her, along the length of the bar, and she looked about, trying to decide which table would afford most privacy. She sat by the window, watching the passers-by, until Miles came back and sat down opposite.

'So . . .'

Once again she was embarrassed by his scrutiny but this time she met his gaze squarely, eyebrow raised a little.

'Thanks for coming, Fliss. It's good to see you.'

Various sentences formed and re-formed in her head but in the end she opted for the direct approach.

'I'm not absolutely certain what this is all about.' She tried to keep a light, friendly tone. 'I haven't changed my mind, you know.'

'I'm sure you haven't. I can see that there's no reason why you should but I wanted to talk to you. To explain that since our last meeting I've been doing a lot of thinking.'

She waited, unwilling to make any contribution, sitting back in the upholstered chair. He was frowning, assembling his thoughts, and she felt a fleeting sympathy for him.

'The trouble is,' he said, looking at her with a rueful anxiety, 'I can see now that over the years I've been rather high-handed.'

She laughed then, spontaneously and genuinely, and he smiled as he watched her.

'Oh, Miles,' she said, shaking her head, 'honestly . . .'

'I know.' He was ready to enjoy the joke against himself. 'It's taken long enough, hasn't it? But I can't do much about that except to say that I'm sorry. No, no,' he correctly interpreted her quick little frown, 'I know that it's not anywhere near that simple. That's just the beginning. When you said "no" in London, I realised that I'd never really accepted that you truly meant to leave me. Not deep down. In my arrogance I believed that you'd come back to me. It's been a funny two years, learning the ropes out there and finding my feet. It wasn't that different from a foreign posting in the Navy, and I could easily pretend that when the two years were up we'd be back together again.'

'Except,' said Fliss slowly, as he paused for breath, 'except that if it had been a naval posting you'd have been coming back home. Not staying out there.'

'I realise that.' The waiter was arriving with the tray of tea and Miles leaned back in his chair, waiting until they were alone again. 'That's perfectly true.' He bent forward eagerly as the waiter departed and Fliss prepared to deal with the tea. 'So what would your answer have been if that were now the case?'

She stared at him, puzzled, her hands stilled amongst the cups and saucers. 'How do you mean?'

He shrugged. 'Just that. If this had been a naval posting and I was coming home how would you feel about it?'

Confused, wary of some kind of trap, she frowned impatiently. 'But you're not. What's the point in dealing with hypothetical situations?'

'I'm trying to discover whether it's Hong Kong you have an antipathy to or whether it's me? Do you see?'

'I suppose so.' She began to pour the tea. 'But it still isn't relevant, is it?'

'It could be.'

She suppressed a tremor of fear as she passed him his tea. 'How so?'

He dropped several lumps of sugar into the white china cup and stirred the tea slowly, his eyes fixed on the swirling liquid.

'Do you remember that day you telephoned from the school you were teaching at in Gloucestershire? You were lonely. Remember? I drove up and fetched you back here and we had a wonderful weekend together . . .'

'Don't do this, Miles,' she said angrily. She sat back in her chair, shoulders squared. 'It's not fair. I shan't be affected by sentimental memories. It's actions that count. Apologies and promises mean nothing if they aren't followed up by deeds. Oh, I know that sounds a good old-fashioned thing to say, doesn't it? Worthy of my Victorian grandmother? Perhaps so, but it's how I feel . . .'

'Please.' He was shaking his head, trying to recapture her

29

attention. 'Just wait a minute. I'm not trying to sweet-talk you. It's just that I want us to see the whole picture. From the very beginning I wanted to protect you – and what could be more Victorian than that in this modern world? – and you seemed to accept it. No, hang on a minute, I'm *not* trying to justify my actions, just trying to find out where it all went wrong, and I can see I gave you no room to grow up. I resented the twins because they came between us and realise that I was simply marking time, waiting to pick up the threads. I told you on the telephone last night that I've been doing an awful lot of thinking, Fliss, and it's not before time. I'm just hoping that it's not too late.'

She watched him, trying to guess at his purpose, refusing to be drawn.

'So what are your conclusions?' she asked at last, hating herself for being unresponsive, terrified that he might overwhelm her by appealing to the ever-present demon of guilt.

He sighed, smiling at her, touching the back of her hand with his finger.

'You were right to accuse me of not loving you,' he said gently. 'I wanted to go to Hong Kong and I risked our marriage to do it. It's impossible to hope that you might understand how I felt. I suppose after all those years in the Navy I simply expected you to pack and follow, except this wasn't the Navy. You were quite right about that. If you marry a sailor you expect disruption and separation but I didn't have to go to Hong Kong. I had choices and I chose Hong Kong rather than you, only I didn't, or wouldn't, see it like that. I always loved you but not enough to jettison all my plans and the excitement of a new career. But I truly think that it was simply because I never believed you'd leave me.' He shrugged. 'I'm an arrogant bastard, Fliss, but you knew that, didn't you?'

There was silence until Fliss unclenched her fists, which were clasped in her lap, and relaxed a little.

'Yes,' she said. 'I knew that. But at the beginning it was what I needed. It's not your fault that I grew up.'

He exhaled a great breath of relief.

'Bless you,' he said. 'I missed all the signposts, you see, blundering on, Johnny-head-in-air, and now here I am at the crossroads and everywhere I look it's saying "No Through Road".'

'Oh, Miles,' pity fought with exasperation, 'try to see that I can't go backwards. I couldn't help growing up. Even if I wanted to, and I don't, I can't go back to the way we were sixteen years ago.'

'I'm not asking you to,' he said quickly. 'I'm only asking you not to give up just yet. I've been thinking things through. Supposing

30

I work out my contract and come home? I'd probably be able to transfer to the London office. Supposing I could, what then?'

She stared at him, too shocked to speak. He smiled involuntarily at her expression and bit his lip. The silence lengthened painfully.

'Well,' he said at last, with an attempt at cheerfulness, 'that was a bit of a conversation stopper. At least tell me that you'll think about it. Please?'

'Are you serious?'

'Perfectly serious. I love you, Fliss. My ultimatum was so much hot air. Another attempt to bounce you into coming back to me. Diana means nothing to me. It was a crass attempt to make you jealous but I didn't even succeed at that, did I? You just despised me for it and quite right, too. Please just think about it. It would mean more years of separation but you could come out now and again, perhaps, and then we could think about things after that. I could weekend from London if you wanted to stay in Devon and you could come up to the theatre and things like that . . .'

He fell silent, swallowing back his lukewarm tea, suddenly deflated, his energy spent. She felt a spasm of affection for him, a longing to please, and crushed it down. She needed to believe that he was utterly sincere, that it wasn't simply talk which might end in nothing except to put her back into a submissive role.

'Of course I'll think about it,' she began cautiously – and he looked at her with such joy and gratitude that she was momentarily silenced.

'Bless you,' he said, 'oh, bless you, my dear girl. I'll look into things my end and see what can be done. Oh, Fliss . . .'

She let him take her hand and hold it to his cheek but all the time her senses were reeling with terror and her thoughts were chaotic. Seeing this, he drew back a little, allowing her to go, promising not to rush things, agreeing that she needed plenty of time to think. Back in his room he hurried to the window, watching the straight slender figure crossing the road, disappearing into Mayor's Avenue. Resisting an urge to burst into tears, he rested his forehead against the cool glass and stared down at the scene below. The tide was in now and the boats, restored to life, rocked quietly at their moorings whilst, elegant and transformed, the swan glided sedately amongst them.

Chapter Five

Up in his eyrie on the top floor of the Hampstead house, Clarence Prior was cooking breakfast. The house in South Hill Park had been in his family for generations, used as a staging post by those members of it who were passing through London or coming up to visit the dentist or the theatre. Some years after the war, when the elderly resident Prior died, the family decided to turn the house into flats. The ground-floor flat was to be retained for family use whilst the two other floors could be let to family friends or like-minded people with good references. Clarrie's cousin Andrew, who was now the legal owner, used the ground-floor flat as a bolt hole, regularly coming to London to sit on several different boards of which he was a director, and to go to the opera, of which he was a devotee. He had been glad to offer the top-floor flat to Clarrie when he'd returned from India as a widower in the early sixties and Clarrie, in due course, had introduced Kit and Sin into the household, suggesting that they should apply for the first-floor flat when it became empty. Now, nine years on, it was as if they'd all been together for ever.

The kitchen was a cheerful place, its window looking down upon the twisting lanes and huddled roofscapes of Hampstead. Clarrie enjoyed cooking and lived most of his life in the kitchen so that there was a comfortable, busy atmosphere in the big square room: books leaning together on shelves and toppling from the big, deal table; a dog lead coiled round a large ashtray on the dresser; a bowl of dried fruit soaking on the draining-board, standing beside a pot of geraniums waiting to be watered. This Sunday morning he and Fozzy, the large, wire-haired dachshund, had already been for their walk on the Heath and Fozzy now lay curled in his basket next to the armchair by the window.

Clarrie, breaking an egg carefully into the frying pan, sighed heavily. The past nine years had been the happiest since he'd been a young married man in the Indian Army. He was very fond of his cousin Andrew, a quiet, gentle man tied to the insensitive

33

and domineering Margaret, who'd avoided the responsibilities of motherhood, preferring the company of animals. Clarrie had nicknamed her the Memsahib, disliking the way she manipulated and humiliated Andrew. She rarely came to London, much to everyone's relief, preferring to remain in Wiltshire with her donkey sanctuary, chickens and two elderly Labradors, but she'd made it clear that she disapproved of Kit and Sin to the extent that Andrew had required all his peace-making skills to wear down her dislike thus allowing them to remain. Clarrie adored both of them. He'd worked with Sin at the British Museum, becoming extremely fond of her as the years passed, and he'd been delighted to give her the opportunity to take over the first-floor flat when it fell empty just as he was due to retire. He and Kit had taken to each other very quickly; soon she was driving him down to meet other members of the Chadwick family at The Keep and he was quite used to meeting Hal or Mole on the stairs when they had jobs at the Ministry of Defence or were in London to see the Appointer. Self-reliant and independent though he was, Clarrie enjoyed being part of this group of people, ranging from the charming, elderly Theo to the small, delightful Podger, who had stayed at the house just before Christmas, with her brother, Fred, and her mother, Susanna, so as to be taken to see *Peter Pan.*

When Andrew and Sin had discovered that their friendship had slowly warmed into love both Kit and Clarrie had been delighted for them, and for two years their love had continued to grow until it was now almost impossible for them to be apart. Andrew, after more than thirty years of a miserable, if loyal, existence, blossomed into a grateful joyfulness which was utterly disarming whilst Sin, whose love affairs had never materialised into anything permanent, was so happy that it was almost frightening. For the last six months, however, it had become increasingly apparent that something must be done about Margaret: but what? In his calmer moments, Andrew could see that a man of sixty, passionately in love, might well be an object of derision, and knew that she would never take him seriously. A private, cautious man, he shrank from showing his feelings to the insensitive Margaret who, as his wife, was the last person who could be expected to be sympathetic to them.

'Doesn't matter what she thinks,' Clarrie had pointed out impatiently. 'Better that you should tell her than she finds out for herself. Get it over with, man, and have done.'

'We have to consider her feelings, too,' Andrew had replied. 'She's no longer young. We have to think about that. We don't want to take our happiness at her expense.'

34

Clarrie had snorted derisively into his thick white moustache. He had little patience with these chivalrous sentiments and no benevolence at all towards the Memsahib. 'Can't think why not. She's been taking her happiness at your expense for the best part of thirty-five years. It's about time the boot was on the other foot.'

Andrew had prevaricated, fearing that this precious, last-minute happiness should be desecrated, and Sin had agreed with him. Never one to bother about conventionalities, she was perfectly happy to let things drift, spending more and more time with Andrew in the ground-floor flat but trying to behave circumspectly when they were out in public together. Clarrie tried to reason with them, to convince them that it was best for everyone if Andrew told his wife the truth, but they were too absorbed, too happy to listen to him.

'Of course they can't see themselves,' Clarrie had said bitterly to Kit. 'The poor things genuinely think they look like good friends and nothing more. Might as well try to hide the Eiffel Tower under a candle snuffer.'

'And anyway, arc you sure that Margaret would care?' Kit had asked. 'She doesn't give a damn about Andrew as far as I can see.'

'She will if she thinks some other woman wants him,' he'd answered cynically. 'He belongs to her, like those smelly Labs and the broken-down old donkeys. He's there to be managed and bullied, and woe betide anyone who tries to take him away from her. Dog in the manger, that's Margaret. You take away her bone and just watch the fur fly.'

'What a delightful picture you paint of her,' she'd said, trying to make him smile, but he'd hunched an irritable shoulder and switched on the tiny portable television so as to watch *Sesame Street*. He adored the Muppet-like characters – and Oscar the Grouch, who lived in a dustbin, just suited his present mood. Alarmed by this uncharacteristic gloom, Kit had tried to persuade Sin to insist that Andrew should have it out with Margaret but nothing had come of Kit's attempt and the affair continued to drift on.

None of them knew how it was that rumours finally filtered back to Wiltshire, nor who had alerted Margaret, but she'd arrived unannounced at the house late on Friday evening. Fortunately, Sin and Andrew had just come in from the opera and were able to make a reasonable show of innocence but, left alone with her, Andrew was unable to brazen it out. A fearful row had ensued and various objects and garments left about his flat by Sin had fuelled Margaret's suspicions. She'd demanded that Sin and Kit be turned out of the house and that Andrew should return with her to Wiltshire. Here he'd stood firm, however, and the next morning, after telling Sin exactly what she thought of her and, promising retribution through the channels of a letter from her lawyer, Margaret had left. The rest of the day had passed in a hushed shock and this morning there was still no sign of life from the other occupants of the house.

Clarrie thought: We were too complacent, taking it all for granted. Well, the cat's out of the bag now.

As he emptied the contents of the frying pan on to a large plate, Fozzy stirred from his sleep, raising his head, listening intently before padding out into the small hall. Clarrie listened to the murmurings of greeting and was pouring coffee when Kit put her head round the door. He picked up a mug, eyebrows raised.

'May I come in? Oh, yes please.' She nodded at his unspoken question. 'I'd love some coffee. Oh, Clarrie, what a dust-up. Whatever are we going to do?'

Clarrie sat down to his breakfast, fighting the desire to say 'I told you so' and Kit, for the first time for twenty-four hours, couldn't help smiling. She knew exactly what he was thinking.

'It's no good being holier than thou at this late stage,' she pointed out. '*I* always agreed with you that they should tell Margaret. Well, it's too late now to worry about that. We've got to be ready for her. Sin's still asleep. She's exhausted after all the traumas and Andrew's in a state.'

'In a state!' Clarrie forked up some bacon contemptuously. 'No point in being in a state. That woman's poison. Told him so, over and over again. Begged him not to marry her but no, he knew best. Not that he had much chance once she'd got her claws into him.' He munched meditatively. 'He's got to have a plan. She'll do her best to get him away from Sin but when she comes to her senses it'll be the property she'll be after. He'll have to do a trade. Let her keep the house in Wiltshire while he stays here.'

Kit brightened up a little. 'Do you really think she'll agree to that?'

'Not all at once.' Clarrie still sounded grumpy. They were like children, the three of them, refusing to listen to advice but expecting everything to be put right at the wave of a wand. 'She'll want to make as much trouble as she can first. "Hell hath no fury" and all that sort of thing. She'll probably telephone the British Museum and put the boot in there. Try to make things unpleasant for Sin.'

'She wouldn't?' Kit stared at him, distressed. 'Oh, surely not?'

Clarrie swiped some fried bread irritably round his plate. 'Let's try to be realistic, shall we? You've known the Memsahib for how many years now? Nine, is it? You've heard the stories, seen how

36

she treats Andrew? Do you really see her taking it all quietly? Retreating back to Wiltshire and agreeing to Andrew's demands without a fight? You heard her screaming at Sin yesterday. She's probably already decided what she's going to go for but she'll want her pound of flesh first. Andrew mustn't give in too easily. With a really good lawyer he'll come out of it without too many bones broken but he's got to be prepared to put up a fight. He's used to the Memsahib getting her own way, d'you see. It's become a habit. We'll have to brief him.'

'Oh, Clarrie, you are such a comfort.' Kit sipped her coffee, feeling the usual lightening of anxiety that his rotund presence always imparted. 'Poor old Sin was absolutely knocked sideways. I've never seen her so utterly overwhelmed.'

'The Memsahib was on particularly good form,' admitted Clarrie reflectively, pushing his plate aside and reaching for his pipe. 'I could hear her right up here, y'know. Mind, I had the door open, listening. It's a good many years since I heard anyone being called a whore. Real Restoration stuff, wasn't it? I thought she had a very good line in invective for someone who runs a donkey sanctuary. My old colour sergeant had a pretty impressive vocabulary but the Memsahib could have taught him a thing or two.'

'Honestly.' Kit began to laugh in an involuntary but horrified kind of way. 'It was terrible, wasn't it? She refused to come into our flat but insisted on standing out on the landing screaming at the top of her voice. And when Andrew tried to restrain her she said she'd have him arrested for assault.'

'Thought we'd have the neighbours round.' Clarrie grinned unwillingly. 'Made a right spectacle of herself, if you ask me. And dear old Sin maintaining a dignified silence, all white and proud and backed up against the doorpost.'

'She said that she was speechless with terror,' explained Kit. 'And she was hanging on to the doorpost for support. Andrew did quite well, didn't he? Managed to maintain his dignity while standing up for Sin. I was terrified he might give in and disown her.'

Clarrie looked at her indignantly. 'He's a Prior, I'll have you remember. He won't let Sin down now. He'll try to sort things out as peaceably and fairly as he can but he'll stick by her. I just hope that this house won't have to go. We've all been so happy here.'

'That would be terrible.' Kit no longer felt like laughing. 'Oh, Clarrie, we simply mustn't let that happen. How upset will Andrew be if he has to lose the house in Wiltshire?'

Clarrie drew down the corners of his mouth, shrugging a little. 'Can't see him being too miserable. He owns all sorts of bits and pieces, a few cottages here and there and some town property. It won't break his heart to see the house go.'

'And it's not as if he likes being in the country, is it? He'd rather be here in London with us than down there with the donkeys.'

Clarrie smiled at her eagerness, her anxiety to be convinced. With her ashy-fair hair standing up in spikes, the baggy sweatshirt pulled on over black leggings, she looked far younger than her forty-two years and he wondered, not for the first time, if the emotions he had known for his child, truncated so tragically at her early death, had been revived in his love for Kit. He pushed down his private anxieties and tried for a more encouraging note.

'If it's handled sensibly there might not be too much to fear. She mustn't be allowed to be top dog. Andrew's in the wrong, no doubt about it, but there are plenty of extenuating circumstances. He'll have to swallow his finer feelings of loyalty and pride, and be prepared to spill the beans.'

'Talk to him,' urged Kit. 'Make him see it all properly, won't you? He'll be waiting to hear from her lawyer, I expect, rather than getting on with his own defence. You must make him see sense, Clarrie.'

'That's all very well,' he began testily – but hesitated when he saw the real fear and misery in her face. 'Don't worry. I'll sort him out. Course I will. The Memsahib won't beat us, I promise. Let's not meet trouble halfway. We'll have some more coffee, put on our thinking caps and make a plan. Present old Andrew with a *fait accompli*.'

Feeling more cheerful at the thought of some positive organisation, encouraged by her faith in him, Clarrie scraped the remains of his breakfast into Fozzy's bowl and went to fill the kettle.

Chapter Six

Hal Chadwick replaced the telephone receiver but continued to remain for some moments lost in thought, gazing unseeingly out of the kitchen window. It was the first Sunday of a fortnight's leave but he was possessed of none of that light-hearted anticipation which generally characterises the beginning of a holiday. He had been unable to synchronise his leave with the boys' half term – although the two schools never had exactly the same dates anyway – and this oversight always irritated Maria, who considered that Hal, as the captain of HMS *Broadsword*, should be able to have his leaves to suit his family. It was odd that after sixteen years of being a naval wife, Maria was still capable of such peculiar ideas. He'd tried – patiently in the early days of their marriage – to explain that the Royal Navy didn't exist for the benefit of the men who served in it but she'd always shrugged aside such reasonable approaches, implying that he could do better if only he would try. In those early years she had hated it when he went to sea, missing him terribly, fearing that he might be tempted into infidelity. The depth of her jealousy had been the measure of her lack of confidence and he had tried hard to deal with it compassionately. His own easy-going, generous, friendly character made it difficult sometimes for him to respond to her demands and it had been easier when the longed-for babies had at last arrived. Looking back, Hal wondered at what point her passion for him had been poisoned by the resentment which now had taken hold with just as great a tenacity.

Still sitting there, in the basement kitchen of the town house in Salisbury, Hal wondered which of the signposts along the road of their marriage he had ignored or misread. Several events stood out clearly in his memory: taking Rex, their golden retriever, down to Caroline at The Keep when Maria began to ill-treat him; overlooking her suspiciously close relationship with Keith Graves; persuading Jolyon into going off to boarding school so that Maria could concentrate on his younger brother, Edward. These had been important diversions but Hal suspected that the really significant signpost had been the one which had 'The Keep' written upon it. Maria had believed Hal to be his grandmother's sole heir and confidently expected to become the mistress of the family home after her death. The house had been left in trust, however, with the funds from shares in the family's china clay business to provide for its upkeep. His grandmother had always hoped that Hal would move in but she'd made it clear that the house should remain a refuge for the Chadwick family. When she'd realised that Hal had no intention of dispossessing his great-uncle or his mother – not to mention Caroline, who had shouldered so much of the responsibility of the running of The Keep once the children had grown up – Maria's resentment increased further. Her mother, Elaine, had encouraged her to move to Salisbury and connived at the renewal of her relationship with Adam Wishart, her father's junior partner. So Hal had spent the last two years between Salisbury and the base at Devonport, trying to balance his time fairly and to see as much as he could of his two boys, but Maria was indifferent to his efforts.

Hal's expression grew grim. He knew that she was having an affair with Wishart. With Edward installed happily at the cathedral school and Jolyon away at boarding school at Herongate in the New Forest, Maria had plenty of opportunity to pursue her own desires. It was she who suggested that Jolyon should accompany his cousins, Jamie and Bess, to The Keep for exeats and half terms. Since they were all at Herongate together it seemed quite natural that Jo should have some holidays in Devon, especially if the ship were in for a few days so that he could see his father. It was so silly to drag Hal up to Salisbury, and there frequently seemed to be some difficulty which prevented her from collecting Jolyon. To Hal's immense relief Jo enjoyed being with his cousins, who had helped him to settle in quite happily at school, and there was so much more to do at The Keep than in the small walled garden of the house in Salisbury. His grandmother spoiled him outrageously, Caroline took care of the practical side of his life and Fliss took all three children on outings to the beaches and the moors.

Fliss had been one of the reasons for Jo's almost painless transition. She'd eschewed the motherly role, leaving that to Prue and Caroline, and had attempted a more elder-sisterly approach which made it possible for Jo to talk openly about his anxieties, to feel that he had a friend in whom he could confide. It had been tremendously successful and Jo had settled happily. Hal's face lightened as he remembered the happy times the five of them – he and Fliss and the children – had spent during weekend exeats and the longer half-term breaks. There had been a deep, instinctive

40

sense of rightness which had informed the whole relationship so that sometimes he'd had to remind himself that he and Fliss were not married, not the joint parents of these three children. He made a noise which was part sigh, part groan. Perhaps the most important early warning sign should have borne the legend 'Fliss'. Ever since he'd been fool enough to tell Maria of their youthful infatuation she'd feared Fliss.

Hal thought: Why did I tell her? Was it because she was such a jealous girl and I felt it was only fair to forewarn her? What idiots we are when we're young. But she was so pretty, so loving . . .

'Who was that on the phone?' Maria stood in the doorway, eyebrows raised questioningly.

Hal looked at her thoughtfully. She'd lost weight recently and her thick dark hair had been layered into a jaw-length bob, held in place by a velvet band. Her striped shirt with its pie-crust collar was tucked into a full, long, denim skirt and she wore flat leather loafers. Just after the move to Salisbury a friend had lent her a copy of *The Official Sloane Ranger Handbook* and Maria's life had been changed overnight. It was as if she'd suddenly found her niche in life; her existing wardrobe had been jettisoned for the Sloane uniform and a Barbour now hung by the back door. She'd even insisted that the family car be exchanged for a large Volvo estate.

'Rather pointless, isn't it,' Hal had suggested idly, 'now that wc live in the town and we don't have a dog?' but Maria had ignored him. The fact that Jolyon needed to be taken to or fetched from school with his tuckbox and trunk was all the excuse she required. Hal had actually feared that she might buy another dog – a black retriever, of course, so as to comply more fully with the image – but his fears had proved groundless. Maria was not prepared to go so far as to adopt the Sloanes' ability to cohabit happily with mud and dog hairs . . .

She was still staring at him, frowning slightly, fiddling with the crucial pearls – her mother's – which she always wore now. Hal pulled himself together.

'It was Kit,' he told her. 'In a bit of a stew.'

'What's new?' snapped Maria. 'Your sister should consider the possibility of growing up sometime. She and Sin are like two adolescents. It ceases to be funny when you pass twenty, let alone when you're in your forties.'

'Perhaps it's being married and having children that grows one up,' said Hal lightly. 'Gives one a sense of responsibility, wouldn't you say?'

41

She glared at him, suspecting that he was getting at her. 'Kit doesn't know the meaning of the word. As for Sin . . .'

'Oh, I'm tempted to agree with you about Sin,' he said. 'I don't think any woman – or man – who sets out to undermine a marriage could be called responsible, do you?'

He watched the colour rising in her cheeks, realising that he disliked himself intensely, wondering if he could ever put things right between them . . . wondering if he even wanted to try. Jolyon's image rose in his mind and the question with which he always greeted him sounded in his ears. *'Hi, Dad. Is everything OK?'* They both knew, he and Jo, what the question implied. At nine, Jo had been wise enough to see the warning signs – and had been ready to go away to school so as to avert disaster – and Hal had promised Jo that all would be well.

'Are we going to Evensong?' he asked, getting up, smiling at her. 'Shall I make some tea? I expect Ed's starving as usual.'

She hesitated, knowing she'd been let off the hook, ready to accept his offer but refusing to show any sign of backing down.

'I wish you wouldn't call him Ed.' This was an old grievance. 'But yes, you could get things started. I want to finish the ironing.'

She went out, leaving him feeling defeated, despising himself – and her – but determined to hold his marriage together as long as he could. He'd been half expecting Maria to pull the plug, to tell him that she was leaving him for Wishart, but he was beginning to realise that Liz Wishart had no intention of surrendering her husband to Maria; it seemed that she, too, was prepared to play the waiting game. Hal, who was obliged to meet his wife's lover socially, had already judged that he was not a man who considered all was well lost for love. Salisbury was a small place and he had his reputation to consider. Maria's father would be retiring soon and the architect's practice would then be his. It was clear that he had no wish to rock any boats just yet. Stalemate: a particularly apt word, given the circumstances.

Hal cleared the table of the Sunday papers and went in search of Edward, to discover what he might like for tea, hoping for company.

Mole, watching television in an almost deserted Mess, decided that one of these days he must start thinking about getting married. This thought was not a novel one but usually occurred to him on just such afternoons as these when the pleasant image of a happy hearth and home superimposed itself on his rather bleak, lonely surroundings.

Settling more comfortably in his armchair, his attention wandering from the usual Sunday afternoon war film, he allowed himself to enjoy the fantasy of a young, pretty wife – sexy in a restrained kind of way, fun but practical, too – with one or two small children in the background, just toddling perhaps, but definitely beyond the wrinkled, screaming stage. He closed his eyes the better to see this delightful family group and to imagine himself a part of it. He saw now that his wife had a distinctly Meryl Streep-ish appearance with *Out Of Africa* overtones – tanned skin and a khaki shirt – and the children were jolly little moppets with fair hair, just like their mother. They were playing together on a sunlit lawn whilst he himself was sitting further back, on a verandah, perhaps, a hat tilted forward over his eyes against the brightness of the sun. It was very warm and he felt pleasantly drowsy so that the little group kept moving out of focus as he dozed. It was the singing that roused him, a familiar song but one that awoke faint echoes of fear.

> *I had a cow and the cow pleased me,*
> *I fed my cow by yonder tree.*
> *Cow goes moo-moo,*
> *Cat goes fiddle-i-fee . . .*

The children were singing with high happy voices but the danger was coming closer and he knew that he must warn them of the menace which lurked under the trees and was now creeping over the bright grass. Other voices were making themselves heard, drowning out the childish song, echoing in his ears.

'. . . *They were hiding in the trees, just waiting, still and dark as shadows . . . The blood was everywhere . . . they just beat and chopped them down. The boy's shirt was soaked with blood . . .*'

Mole struggled to wake, to make himself heard above the children's voices which were still singing, oblivious to the terrible danger.

> *I bought a horse, the horse pleased me,*
> *I fed my horse by yonder tree.*
> *Horse goes neigh-neigh,*
> *Cow goes moo-mooo . . .*

Gasping, sweating with terror, he fought to rouse himself, knowing he must save them, knowing that he couldn't.

'*They had machetes, axes, sticks . . . They'd smashed his head to pulp and nearly severed it from his body . . .*'

43

He could see the sunlight glancing off the blades, the blood on the grass, and with one last, immense effort he cried out.

'Are you OK, sir?'

One of the stewards was standing beside him, looking down at him anxiously. Mole swallowed in a dry throat, glancing about him, seeing the comforting emptiness of the Mess, the black-and-white film still flickering on the screen. He breathed deeply, his heart still hammering in his side.

'Sorry, Chief. Must have dropped off. I was having a bloody awful nightmare.'

'Not surprised, sir, watching that rubbish. Seeing Noël Coward in Her Majesty's uniform would give anyone bloody awful nightmares. Letting him loose amongst a couple of thousand sailors and calling it *In Which We Serve* . . .'

Mole knew that the man was giving him the chance to pull himself together and he was grateful. He laughed obligingly and nodded in response to the unspoken question.

'Perfectly OK now. Perhaps a cup of tea . . . ?'

'Oh, I think we can do a bit better than that, sir. I was just about to open the bar. Would a horse's neck hit the spot?'

'It would indeed. Thanks, Chief.'

He sat quite still, deliberately forcing down the hideous memories of his parents' and older brother's murder, slowly regaining his composure. No. Pretty wives and children weren't for him, not yet, perhaps not ever. Not while this nightmare vision and crippling fear could strike so unexpectedly . . . Death striking suddenly out of a bright day.

'There you are, sir. Put yourself outside that.'

He sipped the brandy and dry ginger, listening to the steward moving about behind him, feeling steadier. Presently he would telephone Susanna, the companion of his childhood, his beloved younger sister, and have a chat; find out how young Fred and Podger were and ask after the family at The Keep. Susanna would make him laugh. Of course, the new baby was due at any moment . . . He had to steel himself to remain in his chair, to stop himself from leaping up to find a telephone so as to reassure himself that all those whom he loved were still safe. His hand clenched on his glass, he reminded himself that it was . . . how long? . . . a year? eighteen months? since the last attack. He was winning. One day he would overcome it utterly.

Swallowing back the last of the brandy, Mole stood up, put the empty glass on the bar and with a nod to the steward went off to his cabin.

Chapter Seven

Just outside the French windows at the west end of their converted barn, Gus Mallory sat reading the score of Mozart's *Requiem* in preparation for the first rehearsal by the Dartington Community Singers in a few days' time. He was always drawn to this spot at this time of a summer's day when the sun was beginning to sink and the humped high shoulders of the moor appeared to move closer, standing out from the shimmering blue haze of afternoon heat, clearly defined against the brilliant sky. Again and again his eyes were drawn from his sheet music, following the line of the vivid turf down to the new beech hedge beyond which the neat fields began to rise towards the foothills of the moor. During the six years in which he and Susanna had lived here his eye had become used to the shapes and contours of the countryside so that now he could instantly identify the slightest change, however small. A dark object moving across a distant field might be a fox or a dog; the hunched shape amongst the bare branches of a tree in winter was probably a buzzard hoping for a meal in the frozen furrows below; he rejoiced when the cows, released after the long imprisonment of dreary winter months, were let out into the lush, green fields, kicking up their heels with the dizzy sense of freedom; he waited impatiently for the first sighting of Lux-white woolly lambs springing uncertainly at their mothers' ambling heels, the air echoing their thin, plaintive, bleating cries. The landscape was as familiar as the sitting room behind him, and just as dear.

How hard he and Susanna had worked, first on the barn itself and then on the garden, to achieve this fulfilment of their plans. Gus heaved a sigh of gratitude, offering up a quick prayer of thankfulness. From the first days in the small flat above their graphic art studio in Totnes, until now, with their third child about to make its appearance, he and Susanna had known the deep contentment which comes to those who are in perfect accord, one with the other. Generous, hospitable, confident, their home was open to their friends and a place of security for their children. Neither he nor Susanna was weighted down with the fears that pursue the overimaginative nor weakened by the terrors of the insecure. Susanna didn't panic when their small business suffered the usual setbacks regarding cash flow, or occasional loss of clients, and Gus remained calm when Susanna had sudden frights about the various members of her family. She had begun to recover from the death of her grandmother, although she still missed her quite dreadfully at times, but he knew that her real anxiety was for her brother, Mole.

A sheet of music fluttered to the flagstone beneath the garden chair and Gus bent to retrieve it. He, too, worried about Mole, sensing the dark undercurrents that flowed deep beneath the Chadwick charm and capability. It was clear that the early tragedy had affected him more deeply than his two sisters although he'd seemed more at peace with himself in the last two years. It was a pity that he couldn't have fallen in love with Janie. Her easy-going temperament, much like Susanna's, would have gone a long way towards healing his pain and preventing those headlong swoops into 'black dog', as Susanna called it. Silently Gus saluted Mole's courage. To risk exposure amongst the fighting force of the Royal Navy must demand iron self-control.

Gus thought: And the trouble with that kind of bottling-up is that sooner or later it comes out somewhere else.

He had a private theory that such rigid refusal to allow or admit to anger, fear, jealousy, resentment, ultimately led to terrible outbreaks of disease. He believed that what was mentally suppressed eventually made itself known in physical ways, destroying the body's health. He breathed another prayer, brief but heart-felt, expressing thankfulness for his happy, uncomplicated children and hoped that this third child would be just such another. Susanna came out of the house behind him and lowered her bulk carefully into the chair beside him.

'That was Mole,' she said – and he looked at her quickly, questioningly. She made a face. 'So-so. Quite cheerful but I know him too well to be taken in, even on the end of the telephone. There was that note in his voice. You know?'

She turned her face towards the west and sat brooding.

'The thing is . . .' began Gus carefully, and paused.

'But we thought he was better, didn't we?' she asked sadly, longing for some kind of comfort.

'He *is* better,' he answered quickly. 'There's no question about that. I'm sure that the time is getting longer between these bouts. You said so yourself.'

'I know I did.' She shifted uncomfortably. 'But there might be times we know nothing about. When he's at sea and he can't get to a telephone.'

'I think that's very unlikely.' Gus spoke firmly. 'I suspect that when he's fully occupied it doesn't happen at all. It's during idle moments that these things strike. Honestly, Sooz, I'm sure he's coming out of it. Slowly but surely. He's got some leave coming up, hasn't he? Did you tell him to come down?'

'Of course I did. I gave him all the news and told him I was about to pop. He said he'd come down ready to catch the pieces.' She smiled rather reluctantly. 'Poor old Mole. He hates it really. It would be hell for him to be around just at the moment.'

'Rubbish.' Gus spoke with more confidence than he felt. 'Much better to be on the spot than feeling helpless miles away. He can lend a hand with the gruesome twosome. Speaking of which . . . ?'

'Putting away the Lego, which is scattered all over the courtyard.' Susanna grinned, happier now. 'It'll probably take all night. They should have been in bed but it's such a perfect evening I hadn't got the heart to shut them away from it.'

He reached a hand towards her. 'How are you feeling?'

'Fat.' Susanna laced her fingers between his. 'I'm bored of it, as Fred would say. I'm fed up with looking like the Fat Lady at the circus.'

'You look beautiful.' Gus looked at her lovingly. Pregnancy suited her; her tanned skin glowed with health and her brown eyes were serene. Her thick dark hair was held back from her face with combs and her loose long dress was made of a faded red Indian cotton. 'So what's it going to be?'

'Another girl,' Susanna answered promptly. 'We'll call her Louise and I shan't let Kit anywhere near her for the first two years.'

Gus chuckled. 'Poor old Podger. Even *I* hardly remember that we christened her Alison after your mother. I expect that things will change when she goes to school.'

'Possibly. At the moment she doesn't mind a bit but we'll all have difficulty when the time comes.'

She glanced round as Fred came out through the French doors, Podger trailing behind him. Fred climbed on to his father's lap and immediately began to wrestle with him. Gus rescued his score, dropped it beside his chair and began to tickle Fred who, panting with exertion, began to shriek with helpless laughter. Podger watched silently, thumb in mouth, leaning against her mother's knee. Susanna touched the rosy cheek with her finger, smoothed

47

the shining dark hair, and suddenly Mole's anxieties brushed her own serenity with shadowy wings of fear. Was Podger jealous of the coming baby? Did she see the baby as an intruder who might usurp her special role as youngest? Susanna leaned forward as best she could and gathered Podger closer. The child turned to look at her with merry eyes and a mischievous smile and Susanna felt a rush of relief.

'How about some supper before bed?' she suggested, almost as if she were rewarding Podger for being happy.

'Cake,' said Podger at once, never a child to let an opportunity slip, and attempting to assist her mother to her feet. 'Cake and beans on toast.'

'If you must,' shuddered Susanna.

'Cake,' shouted Fred, dropping his head back so that his hair brushed the flagstones, his knees gripped round his father's waist. 'Lots of lovely chocolate cake.'

Gus swung him up and got to his feet, Fred's legs still round his waist, his arms about his neck; Susanna took Podger by the hand and they all went into the house together.

Some miles away, Jolyon was standing at the edge of the lake, making the most of the last moments of freedom before bedtime. This was his favourite spot, protected from the playground by the dense rhododendron bushes and offering privacy and peace. He had several friends of his own now but he treasured these rare moments when he could be alone and think about things. He'd been much happier at Herongate than he could have possibly imagined, helped by Jamie and Bess in those early days when he missed being at home with Mummy and Edward, waiting for Daddy to come back from sea.

He frowned a little, bending to pick up a grey feather which lay on the shingly shore and drawing its pearly silkiness gently through his fingers. One of the difficult things was not being able to keep his eye on things at home. He'd always been able to tell when things were not quite right, to see that Mummy was in a bate or that Daddy was feeling edgy, and he'd try to stop them arguing. It had been almost a relief to know that Daddy was hardly ever going to be able to get back to Salisbury for a while because of being captain of *Broadsword*, so that the chance of anything going wrong was lessened. It was a bit disappointing that, although they were settled now into the house in Salisbury and Ed was quite happy at school, Mummy was still sort of edgy. Jolyon tried to be as helpful as he could when he went home for holidays. He was old enough to be

48

really useful now and he was quite happy to do washing-up and hoovering and the things that seemed to make Mummy irritable. There was always so much for her to do that he felt guilty that his being at home added to it. Sometimes she was out for hours in the evening when Ed was in bed, at meetings or something she told him, and when she came back she was happier in a funny sort of way, laughing and singing and dancing about. He'd wait up ready to make her a cup of tea, the kettle having been boiled a dozen times, and sometimes she'd hug him and he could smell the delicious scent that was so much part of her.

Jolyon closed his eyes, trying to conjure up the smell. Those were the best times, when she was really nice to him and talked to him as if he were grown up like Daddy. Sometimes her words came out oddly and she'd laugh and say that she was tired but he didn't mind, although he knew now that it was best to get her bath going before she grew too tired because then she became a bit grumpy and sometimes even tearful. Once or twice she'd started to say things, not very nice things about Daddy, and he'd felt frightened although he couldn't quite say why. He knew he had to shut her up and he'd dropped the sugar bowl accidentally on purpose to stop her. She'd been really cross and sent him to bed but he didn't really mind because he knew that it was better than the other thing; the thing he couldn't control.

He stopped to watch a heron with its slow, stalking walk, its head sunk on rounded shoulders. Great twiggy platforms measuring several feet across could be seen in the trees beside the lake and there were plenty of young birds perched high in the boughs or wading hopefully in the shallow waves. Leaning forward carefully, Jolyon placed the feather as far out on the water as he could reach and watched it drift gently away. He would miss the lake when he went on to Blundell's School next year but it would be good to be with Jamie again. He missed old Jamie. Bess was really nice but being a girl and that much older she didn't have so much in common with him, and he was glad that Mummy had agreed that he could go to Blundells. With Jamie there it wouldn't be so strange and they'd already got lots of plans made. Not only that, he'd be able to go down to The Keep so easily. He loved being at The Keep. It was as if it was the one place on earth where he really and truly belonged and it wasn't just because Granny Chadwick was there to spoil him and Fliss was such fun. No, it was the whole place: the house and the hill and that special bit of Devon. Jamie agreed with him. They liked reading the books and playing with the toys that had been bought or made for years-ago Chadwick children and they liked

49

making up games in the little stone house in the orchard which Daddy's cousins, Mole and Susanna, had used when they were children. Bess wasn't so bothered, and anyway she was usually stuck in the drawing room, playing the piano, but he and Jamie never tired of hearing stories about Ellen and Fox and all the dogs that had lived at The Keep before Rex. As for Rex . . .

Jolyon let his breath out in a big gasp. It was just brilliant about Rex. He'd been their dog once and lived with them in Hampshire but when Mummy couldn't cope, Daddy had taken him down to The Keep to be looked after there. Oh, how he'd missed Rex; how he'd cried when no one could see him, wriggling right down under the bedclothes so Mummy wouldn't hear. At the same time he'd been almost glad because poor old Rex got into trouble so often and was locked in the garage so much that it was terrible and he'd hated to hear him whining, all lonely and cold out there in the dark all by himself. Now he'd been reunited with Rex and they'd had a simply brill time with him down on the beach at Bigbury or Torcross and up on Dartmoor. It was easy to see that Rex was really happy and so he should be. If he, Jo, could spend all his life at The Keep with Granny Chadwick and Caroline and Uncle Theo, as well as Fliss and Daddy and the twins, then he'd be really happy, too.

He allowed himself to think about the next big treat, the thing he was really looking forward to more than anything. In two weeks' time there was an exeat and he and Bess were going down to Devon for the weekend. Daddy would be there on his way back from leave and they'd have a simply great time. Daddy had written to him, telling him he was sorry that his leave hadn't worked in with the holidays but that wasn't Daddy's fault. You had to do what the Navy told you, even he, Jo, knew that. Anyway, Daddy was driving over on Tuesday for the cricket match and Mummy was coming, too.

Excitement wormed about inside him and he suddenly longed to run and shout, to churn up the shingle with his feet and frighten the herons. Too happy to be alone any longer, Jolyon turned back along the path, heading for the playground. After a few steps he began to run.

Chapter Eight

In the drawing room Theo sat quietly, his book held lightly upon his knee, his eyes closed. It might have been Freddy at the piano – a young Freddy, with her square shoulders and small, poised head – playing the Schumann *Kinderszenen*. In his mind's eye he could picture the familiar scene; lamplight gleaming softly on polished mahogany, glancing brightly off the heavy brass fender; the pale bulky shape of the high-backed sofa; the portraits of long-dead Chadwicks making dark oblongs on the walls. Beyond the long windows the garden was wrapped in a cool, soft mist, the aftermath of a dripping, dismal day. He and Fliss had been shooed from the kitchen, sent off to the drawing room with their coffee, so that Prue and Caroline might wash up together. This had happened several times lately and there was an air of conspiracy between the two women, the inference that some special consideration was due . . .

Theo shifted uneasily, the spell fading slightly as these uncomfortable thoughts pressed in upon his consciousness. In the six years since Freddy had died there had been great changes at The Keep. The formality which had been so much a part of her generation had passed with her and now Prue and Caroline ran the house between them, achieving a comfortable, if occasionally erratic, routine which embraced the needs of the elderly Theo as well as the demands of the younger generation. Up in the nursery wing on the top floor the thirteen-year-old twins were allowed to listen to their pop music whilst two floors down Podger and young Fred played riotous games in the playroom which had once been a rather gloomy study. Prue and Caroline shared the responsibilities of these two disparate generations whilst enjoying their own particular pleasures and taking comfort from each other's company. Fliss moved between them all, a kind of very special guest, not quite a permanent resident, nevertheless utterly at home. Her role was indistinct, unsettled.

Theo thought: She must make up her mind. There will be no true peace for her until she does.

He opened his eyes. Fliss had stopped playing and had turned on the piano stool, watching him. How like her grandmother she was . . .

'Your coffee's cold,' she said. 'Prue will be cross with you.'

He noticed that she'd begun to drop the prefix of 'Aunt'. It was the effect, no doubt, of living in such close proximity but he couldn't see that it mattered much.

'I was listening to you,' he admitted, 'and thinking about the past.'

'Woolgathering, Ellen would have called it,' said Fliss cheerfully. 'Although I could never see why. I used to think it had something to do with all those skeins of wool I used to hold for her while she wound them into balls. Goodness, my arms used to ache sometimes. How shocked she'd be to see us all eating in the kitchen together. "Whatever next, I wonder," she'd say.'

'It was a different world,' admitted Theo, putting aside his book and drinking the cold coffee lest Prue's feelings should be hurt. 'There were certain rules and codes of behaviour which have long since vanished.'

'Do you mind?' asked Fliss curiously. 'It must be rather difficult for you at times. For you more than the rest of us.'

'You must remember that I lived with sailors for thirty years,' he reminded her, 'and I was alone for quite a long time after that. I know how lucky I am, believe me.'

As she watched his slow, sweet smile, which started in his eyes but barely touched his mouth, Fliss felt her heart contract with terror and love. It was impossible to imagine life without his strength at her back. Subconsciously she braced herself against that future time, squaring her shoulders, raising her chin, whilst Theo watched her, guessing at her fear.

'Did you feel that we were being got out of the way this evening?' she asked lightly – and he silently saluted her attempt to recover her self-possession. 'Not allowed to wash up or make the coffee. I have this odd sensation that it's my birthday or something. It's a bit like Sooz with Podger now that the baby's due any moment, if you know what I mean.'

'They think that you need cosseting because you have a difficult decision to make,' he answered. 'You're right in saying that they're treating you like a child, assuming that special treats and privileges will soften the ultimate blow.'

She was silent, unprepared for such an honest appraisal of the situation.

'You make it sound as if there's something pathetic about it,' she said at last. 'As if you disapprove.'

'Not necessarily. Only if it should weaken you.'

'But why should it?' she asked anxiously. '*How* could it?'

He hesitated, half regretting his direct reply, determined that she should remain strong.

'It is easy to adopt another person's viewpoint,' he said slowly. 'Not immediately or consciously even. Through the pores, as it were. You begin to react slightly differently under such an influence.'

She was frowning, trying to understand him.

'You mean that by fussing over me Caroline and Prue might influence the way I feel about Miles?'

He nodded. 'Something like that. You are already changed, wouldn't you say? By Miles himself?'

She stood up, folding her arms across her breast, and went to stand by the fireplace, leaning her shoulder against the high mantelpiece.

'I *do* feel different,' she admitted carefully. 'He's being so sweet, you see. It reminds me of when we were very first married. He was so much older and it was so easy to push everything on to him and he wanted desperately for it to be wonderful. But then the twinnies came along and he withdrew somehow . . . You know,' she interrupted herself, 'there's a tremendous feeling of power when you're very young and a much older, successful man falls in love with you.'

Theo felt a sense of real fear. The idea of power always terrified him; he had seen its insidious effect.

'But you did not use your power,' he said quickly. 'Did you?'

Fliss considered the question, thinking it over carefully.

'He had power, too,' she said at last. 'He was determined and strong-willed and his career was important to him. His power overbalanced mine, I suppose. He was stronger. Remember how he planned his job in Hong Kong and refused to give it up for me?'

'And now?'

'Now,' said Fliss slowly, 'I am no longer young. I am not grateful because he loves me. I know I can be alone if I have to be.' She was feeling her way along, attempting to analyse her feelings. 'He is prepared to make tremendous sacrifices now. I'm rather overwhelmed, to tell you the truth and . . . He so badly wants us to start again that it's terribly touching and . . . well, he is my husband,' she finished rather lamely.

'And the idea of being the stronger partner is attractive?'

53

Fliss began to fiddle with a pretty little Staffordshire group, her back half turned to him, but he could see her down-turned face in the big gold scallop-framed looking-glass.

'It's not *quite* that,' she murmured. 'He used to be so bossy. I was never allowed to know anything and he would always assume that he must know best because he was older. I don't feel that any more. It's a different kind of power but you're right. The balance has changed.'

'But not equalised?' he asked sharply.

She turned the china group in her fingers. It was true that she was experiencing a sense of great power. Miles was treating her with deference; respect informed his love and it was a new and heady experience. She felt a great affection for him but her true love, her sense of belonging, was still Hal's. That had never changed. However, Hal belonged to Maria and he would never leave her whilst the boys needed the security of their marriage. Meanwhile, Miles was prepared to do everything he could to give their relationship a new start and she was allowing him to hope whilst enjoying her new status.

'No,' she said. 'Not equalised. Does it matter?'

He was silenced by the naïve question. Was it possible that she could not see the danger?

'Miles married you because he loved you,' he said. 'He loved you and he wanted you and he was prepared to wait and hope. You married him for different reasons—'

'You think I shouldn't have married him,' she interrupted. 'You said as much at the time.'

'I think that you *needn't* have married him,' he corrected her gently. 'You used his strength and his love to help you over the difficult time of Hal's engagement to Maria, although you denied it at the time. I believed that you had quite enough strength to manage by yourself. You were seduced by *his* strength and flattered by his love and you were too young and too hurt to attempt to deal with your pain by yourself. I like Miles very much but his use of his power nearly destroyed your marriage. I shouldn't like to see it happen again.'

'You mean that I might use *my* power this time?'

'He is placing the weapons in your hands. He is showing you that he needs you. Needs you so much that he is prepared to come back to England. He asks only that you will continue to be his wife on your own terms. You asked for a moratorium to give you both time to discover your true feelings. It seems that Miles has discovered his and is prepared to act upon them but in doing so he is passing the power to you.'

'You make it sound as if you don't think I should agree to a reconciliation.' She was watching him now, frowning defensively. 'I thought you'd be in favour of it.'

He closed his eyes, praying for guidance, ignoring his own sense of inadequacy.

'I want you to see it clearly. I don't want you to start again because Hal is not available or because you are being offered a new, interesting position of power. I want it only if it is the right thing for you and for Miles, because you love each other enough to care for each other's happiness. Not because you feel that you deserve his love as some kind of right or a prize to be awarded for your condescension in agreeing to returning to him. All love, excepting only the love of God, is fraught with danger. I don't want you to be confused by it.'

There was a long silence; long enough for Theo to wonder if he'd ever learn not to interfere in things he couldn't hope to understand. What did he know of love between husband and wife or the pitfalls of the married state? Yet here he was, giving advice . . .

'I don't love Miles,' Fliss said in a low voice. 'I've never loved him. Not as I love Hal. Oh, I've tried to stop loving Hal, truly I have, but it won't go away. It's been wonderful and terrible these past two years having him around. We both know that it's hopeless but what am I to do? I know that Hal intends to stick with his marriage but I still couldn't face the thought of living in Hong Kong with Miles. I'd just decided that my first answer to his ultimatum must stand when he turned up in Dartmouth and everything changed. He is prepared to move heaven and earth if necessary and I'm back to the old question: have I the right to say "no"? Can second best ever be good enough? Prue thinks it should be if there are children involved but then Prue is nervous at the thought of me being free. It might prove a threat to Hal's marriage.' She smiled bleakly at him. 'I'm not quite such an idiot as to be unable to see what's behind her special little kindnesses. She's fattening me up for the sacrifice.'

'My dear Fliss.' Theo stood up and went to her, taking her cold hands in his. 'Forgive me.'

'No, you're right.' She laughed a little. 'I needed to hear the words. It's true, I've been enjoying my moment of power but I see the danger now. No point in going through it all over again only to find that it comes apart at the seams for a second time.' She returned the pressure of his fingers and let them go, wandering over to the window. 'So what am I to do?'

'Are you quite certain that you don't love him?' he asked diffidently.

55

'I'm not certain about anything.' She stared moodily out at the drifting mist. 'I don't love Miles the way I love Hal but there so many different kinds of love, aren't there? The question is: can we be happy together? If we think that there's a chance of it then I suppose we should try. Divorce is so easy these days, it's almost fashionable, but then I never was much of a one for following fashion. But I don't want to be a sacrifice either.'

'I think we agreed once before that martyrdom generally leads to resentment and self-pity. As for divorce . . .'

Fliss turned back into the room. 'How could I divorce him?' she asked almost desperately. 'On what grounds? He's prepared to work out his contract and come back as soon as he can. How can I *not* agree to give it a try?'

Theo remained silent.

'I do love him, I suppose, otherwise I wouldn't care whether I hurt him or not. I'm just so afraid that once I give in it'll be just as it was before. That's why I'm hanging on to my power. I don't want to use it against him, only to protect myself, but you're right to show me the danger. I find that I *do* use it from time to time just to test him.'

Theo tensed against the flicker of fear. 'And?'

'And it works. And it's exciting.' She shrugged, shaking her head at his expression. 'Don't worry. You've ruined it for me now. When I think of trying it in future I shall see your face and it'll all be dust and ashes.'

'I hope that it is so,' he said soberly, refusing to laugh with her. 'Never underestimate its danger.'

'It will probably be two years before he's back in England,' she said. 'It gives us a bit longer to see how it's working. I shall go out for visits but it will definitely be make-or-break time when he moves back. Silly to get worked up just yet, really.'

'You should try to be wholehearted.' He hated himself but she was too dear to him to hold back. 'Another two years of limbo will be detrimental to your peace of mind. You set your marriage a test and Miles accepted your terms. Now he is prepared to make every effort to make it work. You can't go back on your word. You must tell him yes or no and if it is yes, then your actions should be positive and your heart committed even if he is thousands of miles away. If it is no then you have a new life ahead.'

She was staring at him. 'What you're really saying is that if I say yes I should go back with him to Hong Kong. Oh, I can't.'

'You fear that he might trick you? That he'd get you back there and then let matters slide?'

She shook her head. 'I don't know. He's never suggested that I might go back with him. He seems content to wait. But supposing it's a bluff?'

Theo opened the French windows and stepped out into the cool damp air. Fliss followed him, anxious and confused. They stood together, staring down the garden, and she took his arm, holding it tightly.

'Why don't you bring him over?' he murmured. 'Would he come, d'you think? Perhaps we'd have things clearer in our minds after a meeting. Do us all good, perhaps. Open it all up and let some fresh air in. What do you say?'

'He's mentioned it,' she admitted, 'but I didn't feel ready. Everyone fussing and Miles being all defensive.' She chuckled softly beside him. 'And I shall do that brittle thing, you know? Cold and unapproachable. I can feel it already.'

He pressed her hand against his side. 'If you could bear it, I think it might be well worth trying. If he's bluffing he'll find it hard to hide it here amongst your family. I think it's most encouraging that he's suggested it himself. He hasn't wanted to see any of us for a very long time.' He thought about it, testing it, knowing it to be good. Releasing his arm he slipped it about her shoulders, holding her close. 'Be brave, Fliss. I think the time has come to make another move forward.'

Chapter Nine

'Children are such a terrible worry,' said Prue plaintively. 'It's bad enough when they're very small, throwing sudden temperatures and going down with all those awful infectious diseases. And then they go off to school, little white faces going in through the gate and you spend the day sick with anxiety in case no one will play with them or that they'll be teased. After that it's waiting to see if they've been picked for the part in the school play or chosen for the first fifteen, and then there's the pressure in case they don't pass exams or get good jobs. But you *do* feel that once they're grown up then all this nightmare of worrying about them will stop.'

Caroline, who was driving them both through the narrow lanes on the way to Totnes, slowed down behind a tractor and opened her window. Warm air and the scent of honeysuckle mingled with diesel fumes drifted into the car.

'Which particular children do you have in mind?' she asked cautiously.

'All of them,' answered Prue with a kind of tragic generosity. 'There's poor Fliss unable to make up her mind what to do about her marriage, and Susanna having a baby. And then there's Hal. It's no good telling me he's happy because he isn't. Oh, he is with us down here but it's very different when he's with Maria. The last time I visited them she could hardly bring herself to be polite to me and as for the boys, well, I know that Edward is lucky to be a chorister and all that but there's a peaky look to him and his hair is sort of stiff and lifeless. And they were so much in love, weren't they? Do you remember, Caroline? I thought it was going to be just like me and Johnny all over again. I can't understand what must have gone wrong. As for Kit, well I've almost given up there. She's forty-three in the autumn. *Forty-three . . .*'

Prue fell silent and shook her head, as if the contemplation of so great an age was beyond her.

'Forty-three isn't very old,' said Caroline consolingly. 'Not these days. Women do so much more now. The pressure to marry and settle down has gone and women can fulfil themselves in other ways.'

'What other ways?' demanded Prue. 'In what ways is Kit fulfilling herself? Fooling about with Sin like they did when they were twenty and being looked after by darling old Clarrie? Oh, I know she's done well on the business side but a job isn't everything. If you ask me she's still in love with Jake. What with her and Mole . . . Oh, what is the *matter* with our family?'

'Nothing's really wrong.' Caroline edged out a little as the lane widened but pulled back in behind the tractor as a car appeared over the brow of the hill. 'Blast! I shan't be able to get past for miles now. Anyway, Mole's only thirty-three. Plenty of time for him to get married. Honestly, Prue, it's no worse than any other family. Everyone has problems. Perhaps the next generation will do better.'

Prue snorted. 'If children are brought up in unhappy homes it's bound to have an effect on them. They lose their self-confidence.'

'Well, the twinnies seem perfectly normal and there's nothing unconfident about young Fred or Podger. Oh, *do* look at the dog rose, Prue. Isn't it pretty?'

Prue bent her head unwillingly to peer at the trailing delicate blooms. '"*Unkempt about those hedges blows. An English unofficial rose*",' she quoted morosely.

Caroline glanced sideways at her in surprise; Prue wasn't given to reciting poetry.

'Well,' she said admiringly. 'Get you! That's rather nice actually. "*An English unofficial rose.*" Who wrote it?'

'Search me.' Prue sighed. 'Theo said it the other day when we were going to Dartington and it just sort of stuck.'

She sat up straighter and gave herself a little shake, winding down her own window and leaning out as the tractor slowed in front of the car. Charlock and ox-eye daisies gleamed, gold and white, amongst the tall feathery grasses beneath the hedgerow, and two meadow brown butterflies fluttered round the wild parsley. A small vole scurried along secret ways, half hidden by the glossy, heart-shaped leaves of the black bryony, twining and scrambling its way through the hawthorn, whilst somewhere above his head a yellowhammer sang its single cheerful note.

Prue's spirits lifted a little and, as the tractor turned in through a field gateway, she put her hand on Caroline's arm.

'I've had an idea,' she said. 'Let's not go and do boring old shopping. Let's go to Dartington. The gardens are looking so wonderful at the moment and there won't be too many tourists about yet. Not until the schools break up. Shall we?'

'Why not?' answered Caroline. She was always glad to fall in with anything that lifted Prue out of the depressions that assailed her. 'Fliss is over in Dartmouth and Theo is having lunch with the Rector so I don't see why we shouldn't have a bit of a jolly.'

'Neither do I.' Prue settled back contentedly. 'We'll have a wander round and then I'll treat you to lunch in the White Hart.'

'You're on,' said Caroline. 'We should be able to manage for supper. We've got the cold beef from Sunday's roast left and plenty of lettuce in the kitchen garden. There should be enough new potatoes to go round . . .'

'I'll make a gooseberry pie,' promised Prue, knowing that Caroline would be unable to concentrate on enjoying herself until these culinary anxieties were laid to rest, 'and Fliss is bringing back some of that nice cheese she found in Cundells the last time she went to see Miles.'

'Well then.' Caroline took a deep breath, her hands relaxing a little on the wheel. Although Theo and Prue treated her exactly as if she were a member of the family, she never quite forgot her responsibilities. 'We shan't starve. I can dash in and do the shopping tomorrow.'

'Splendid.' Prue was feeling much better. Her mind dwelled pleasurably on the idea of a glass of chilled white wine with her lunch, two glasses, perhaps. She wondered why the thought was such a comforting one; dulling fear and banishing unhappiness, temporarily, at least.

Caroline, guessing accurately at what she was thinking, wondered if she should be worried about Prue's propensities for consuming alcohol. For herself it only increased her hot flushes and gave her headaches but Prue seemed to find the effect most beneficial. Caroline shrugged away her anxieties; after all, she was hardly at the alcoholic stage and if it chased away the terrible blackness of depression then what did it matter if Prue relied on it rather heavily at present?

Caroline thought: Once a nanny always a nanny. I'm nearly as bad as Prue worrying about the children.

As the car swung left into the lane which led to Dartington Hall both women were feeling cheerful at the prospect of the treat in store: the quiet pathways through the noble trees; a moment in the sun on the bench beside the herbaceous border; lunch prepared by somebody else and no washing up afterwards . . .

'And I could always pop into the food hall at the Cider Press on the way back,' said Caroline, following her own train of thought, 'and pick up a few bits, just in case.'

Prue smiled at her affectionately. 'If you like,' she said comfortably, 'and we'll have a pot of tea in Cranks and perhaps a piece of their delicious lemon sponge.'

She thought: How strange life is. I was so miserable a few minutes ago and now I feel so happy. It's going to be a perfectly lovely day . . .

In Bayards Cove, sitting on the seat outside the Dartmouth Arms, Fliss waited for Miles to bring their drinks and sandwiches out into the sunshine. A cool breeze plucked fitfully at the surface of the bright water and, out at sea beyond the entrance to the river, white horses pranced. Fliss pressed her hands between her thighs nervously, mentally preparing her invitation to The Keep, wishing that she knew what was truly right for Miles, for herself, for the twinnies.

'Good sailing breeze.' Miles set a tray beside her on the seat; plates of sandwiches, a glass of wine, a pint of beer in a tall glass. He straightened up and looked down river. 'Some of the college boats went out just before you arrived. *Martlet* and *Seahorse*. And the picket boats are out in force.'

There was a wistful note in his voice and she wondered just how much he missed the Navy, how difficult the adjustment had actually been in Hong Kong, despite his brave words. Guilt prodded her; she had not been there to help him. He'd had to adjust to that, too, to being alone at a major upheaval in his life. She lifted her chin, as if defying this charge of neglect she brought against herself. It had been his choice to go, after all. He was smiling at her and she realised with a tiny shock that this was Miles, not the stranger which he became once he was no longer before her but someone whom she knew very well and – most of the time – liked very much.

'Hungry?' he asked. 'Dig in.'

'Thanks.' She picked up a sandwich and stared at it. Miles sat down with the tray between them and took a pull at his beer. He was quite as nervous as she was but he'd had a long tough training when it came to hiding weakness, disguising fear. He was used to taking charge even when he, too, felt sick with fright – and this was so important to him. During the long evenings alone in Dartmouth he'd thought things through very carefully, looking back over the years of their marriage, acknowledging his mistakes. He knew now that the first mistake had been to switch off when the twinnies were born. He'd been so delighted to get that first posting to Hong Kong, the command of his own ship, that the birth of his children had seemed of minor importance. He hadn't wanted children, he'd admitted it quite openly, but only now did he realise how deeply that admission had hurt Fliss. He'd believed that he could sit it out, waiting for the children to grow up, assuming that he and Fliss could pick up their relationship where they'd left it off, before the children were born in Hong Kong. He'd wondered if it might have been this which had given her such a dislike of the place but he knew that it wasn't quite that simple. She was so English, his Fliss, so rooted in her own land and amongst her own people. He slid a glance sideways at her. Her long fair hair was gathered loosely back and she wore a blue denim shirt which accentuated her tanned skin and deepened the grey of her eyes. She was thin, too thin, and as he appraised the clear line of her jaw his heart ached with love.

'Don't you like the sandwich?' he asked gently, and she turned to him with a quick, polite smile which was like a blow. 'Don't,' he said involuntarily – and shook his head at his own foolishness. Why shouldn't she treat him like a stranger? How could she understand that his love for her had never ceased but merely been put into a kind of cold storage until the right moment should come for it to thaw again, warming into passion? He had isolated her, leaving her alone with her children whilst he immersed himself in his career, staying on the periphery of her life until he chose to enter in again. How angry he'd been when she'd refused him entry.

'It's good,' she was saying, eating the sandwich, swallowing with difficulty. She took a gulp at her wine and looked at him again. 'I've a message from Uncle Theo. He's asked if you'd like to come over to lunch.'

'How very kind of him.' Miles selected a sandwich whilst he considered this suggestion. Was the invitation merely a formality from Fliss's great-uncle as the head of the household but embracing a welcome from them all, or was it a more personal request? Self-assured though he was Miles would never be foolish enough to underestimate Theo Chadwick, who would prove a formidable adversary if you were unlucky enough to come up against him. Miles had avoided The Keep for two years, punishing the Chadwick family for taking Fliss's side, for giving her sanctuary. Miles shuddered inwardly. How Theo must despise him!

'Does that mean that the answer is yes?' She was watching him curiously, surprised at his expression of self-loathing, at the shame in his eyes. A pang of affection touched her heart. She could not feel for him a tenth part of all that she felt for Hal but in a different way she *did* love him. Her love for Hal went deep into her roots, back into their shared past; 'one flesh', that's how marriage would have been with Hal, but then what of Jamie and Bess or even darling

Jo who had become so very dear to her? Nor could she deny those early years with Miles nor forget how he had rescued her from loneliness and from the humiliation of Hal's engagement to Maria. How restful it had been to lean against his strength, to feel cherished by his devotion. Oh, the different kinds of love . . .

'I'd like that very much.' He selected another sandwich, longing to ask if she'd managed to come to a decision, but some instinct held him back. Not usually sensitive to the workings of other people's minds he nevertheless felt a sympathy between them, a new kindliness which, though far from the feelings he hoped to arouse, was stronger than anything he'd felt so far. Declarations of love or self-pitying appeals tended to throw her back into a self-defensive brittleness. Any insistence now might destroy these fragile beginnings. Best to let the delicate roots take a firmer hold. Crushing an urge to fling the tray into the river and drag her into his arms, Miles finished his sandwich and picked up his glass.

'What about a drive along to Torcross?' he suggested. 'Or a walk at Blackpool Sands?'

She felt the usual instinctive withdrawal which rose in her breast each time she suspected that he might be using some tender memory to influence her present thinking. He looked so relaxed, however, so open, that she absolved him of deviousness and felt ashamed of herself. After all, where else was there to go where they might walk in glorious surroundings and so be together without strain?

'Your car or mine?' she asked lightly – and saw him smile.

'I'm surprised that the old thing's still going,' he said. 'We should have . . . You could have . . .'

He floundered to a halt, knowing that he had no right to suggest what she might do with the car she'd kept once he'd gone to Hong Kong. Guessing what he was thinking, Fliss felt a stronger surge of affection for him.

'It's going perfectly well,' she said, 'and it'll keep going for a good few years yet. It was built to last. Not like that modern tin can you've hired.'

He laughed gratefully, delighted to feel a current of familiar ease flowing between them.

'Your car it is,' he said, standing up. 'I'll take this lot in and then we'll be off.'

She turned, laying her arm along the back of the seat, watching him go, experiencing the familiar confusion of emotions: affection, pity, resentment, fear . . . and love?

Fliss thought: Oh, the different kinds of love.

Chapter Ten

A deep pall of gloom hung over the house in Hampstead. The Memsahib had wasted no time in apprising her lawyer – an old family friend – of the situation in South Hill Park and Andrew had been given a warning shot across the bow: Sin's tenancy must be terminated and Andrew must remain at home in Wiltshire and cease all contact with her. If he refused to accede to her wishes then she intended to sue him for adultery. She made it clear exactly how she intended to proceed, should this be the case, and on what grounds her case would rest.

'There's something so beastly about it,' Kit told Clarrie. 'It gives the impression that Sin is a kind of call-girl, leading Andrew astray and making him do the dirty on the dear loyal little wifie and we *know* it isn't like that.'

'Mmm.' Clarrie puffed thoughtfully on his pipe.

'Don't say "mmm" like that,' she cried indignantly. 'It makes it sound as if you think it's all rather grubby, too.'

'My dear girl,' said Clarrie testily, 'what *we* think doesn't matter a jot. It's what the court thinks that will count. From the outside it *will* look grubby. Sin is twenty years younger than Andrew and very pretty with it. Here's this old chap sneaking up to London on the pretext of attending a few board meetings and going to the opera and all the time he's with this sexy piece a fraction of his age whom he's installed in the flat above his.'

Kit stared at him, shocked into silence. He knocked his pipe out in the large glass ashtray and heaved an exasperated sigh.

'For goodness sake, woman! Don't look at me as if I've just grown an extra head. *I* don't see it like that. Good grief, you *know* how I loathe the Memsahib. I'm just showing you what it will look like to people who don't know Sin and Andrew. The Memsahib's holding all the cards, don't you see? The faithful old wife, stuck down in the country making a home for this philanderer.' He broke off to laugh bitterly. 'Of course she would run a donkey sanctuary, wouldn't she? Plenty of mileage there. Animal lover and so on. Oh, hell and damnation!'

'What shall we do?' Kit looked frightened. 'I can't bear it for Sin. She's gone all silent and her face is sort of white and pinched, as if it might shatter if someone shouted at her. It's horrid.'

'Is it possible that you might get her down to The Keep for a few days? Just while the preliminaries are sorted out? It might just distract her for a moment and give Andrew time to think without worrying about her all the time.'

'I suppose so.' Kit thought it over. 'Of course they're all in a bit of a state down there about Fliss and Miles. You know, whether they're going to stay together or split up.'

'Well, it'll give them something to think about when they see Sin,' said Clarrie callously. 'Make 'em sit up a bit. Divorce isn't nice. And it's even worse when there are children involved.'

Kit cast about for the words which might show that it was different for Fliss and Miles, too, and gave up. 'We could go down for the weekend. If Sin will leave Andrew, that is.'

'See if she can't get a few days off and make it a long one, if the world of interior decorating can spare you,' advised Clarrie. 'She'll need to be well equipped for the days ahead. Get her batteries recharged and so on. It's going to be messy.'

'It's so unfair,' burst out Kit. 'It's not as if Sin has asked for anything out of it.'

'Only another woman's husband,' Clarrie pointed out drily.

'Oh, it's no good feeling holier than thou just because you told them to tell the Memsahib ages ago,' said Kit crossly. 'It's too late now.'

'Quite. In which case it's no good, either, kicking against the pricks. If Andrew had told her openly and asked for a legal separation then she wouldn't have this hole-in-the-corner business to play on. It's her strongest suit. However, as you rightly say, it's too late to dwell on the rights and wrongs of it all. Let's just cope with what has to be done now.'

'Sorry,' said Kit. 'I didn't mean to snap. It's just so frustrating. Dear old Andrew is the last person in the world to be a philanderer. And as for Sin, I think she still hasn't got over all those terrible names the Memsahib called her. I've never seen her like this. Nobody who knows her could believe such awful things.'

'It won't matter much in the end,' said Clarrie philosophically. 'People will take sides but I don't think that Andrew or Sin will be the losers. Not in terms of friends, anyway. Andrew will probably find that he's a great deal lighter in the pocket but he'll have to put up with it. Freedom costs.'

Kit shivered. 'How right I was not to get married. How on earth can you be sure that you can live a whole lifetime with just one person? It's such a terrific gamble.'

'You didn't think so once,' he reminded her – but his voice was gentle.

Her face grew sad. 'Jake was different,' she said. 'Jake was a once-in-a-lifetime person.'

Clarrie shook his head. 'That's what we all think at the time. That's the trick Mother Nature plays on each of us.'

They sat in silence for a moment as the twilight gathered in corners and the room grew dimmer, each deep in thought. As he brooded over the situation, reviewing their conversation, an idea occurred to Clarrie. He grew very still, his eyes thoughtful, conning the idea, turning it this way and that and finding it good. Fozzy sat up suddenly and began to scratch himself and Clarrie glanced at his watch.

'Where's Sin now?'

'She went downstairs to see Andrew after supper.' Kit slid on to her knees beside Fozzy and began to stroke him, murmuring to him quietly whilst Clarrie drummed his fingers in a silent tune upon the table.

'Let's go out,' he said suddenly. 'Let's take old Foz for a run on the Heath and then drop into the pub for a drink. What d'you say?'

'Great,' said Kit, her face lightening with relief. 'Oh, that would be nice. We'll knock on the door as we go past so that Sin knows where I am.' She scrambled up and dropped a quick kiss on Clarrie's white fluffy hair. 'Bless you. What would I do without you?'

'You'd manage,' he said. 'Come on, old chap. Where's your lead? Good boy, then.'

'I'll grab a jacket,' Kit said, 'and see you down in the hall.'

She disappeared and Clarrie moved about the kitchen, collecting his pipe, shrugging himself into a disreputable old cardigan, picking up Fozzy's lead. His instinct was to clear the two girls out of it until the dust settled but he knew that it simply wasn't possible. Both of them had jobs and, anyway, it was old-fashioned to believe that women needed looking after.

'But then I *am* old-fashioned,' he murmured to Fozzy, who pricked up his ears expectantly. 'Pre-war and out of date. Never mind, we still have our uses, don't we, boy?' and they went out together and down the stairs, to where Kit was waiting for them in the hall.

Maria stood at an upstairs window watching Hal mowing the lawn. She was feeling sorry for him. This emotion, as she knew from past experience, was a transitory one and would last only until he became an irritant again, an obstacle in the path which led to her desires. This morning, however, faint stirrings of pity for Hal had enabled her to resist Adam's urgent request that they should meet later on. He hadn't seen her properly since Hal had returned on leave, he'd said, and he couldn't wait another moment. She loved it when he talked like that, feeling the power she had over him pulsing and muscling inside her, almost enjoying the opportunity to refuse his pleas legitimately, secretly glad to get her own back at him for his misguided loyalty to that bitch of a wife of his. After all, she'd reminded him gently, she couldn't absolutely ignore Hal and it *was* only for two weeks – unlike your wife, she might have added, who's around all the bloody time. Adam had taken the hint. He'd been very sweet and said he'd be glad when Hal had gone back to sea. Well, of *course* it was much easier when Hal was away, although it sounded a bit hard when you put it like that . . . It wasn't her fault, she told herself quickly, that she'd fallen madly in love with Adam again so that she could barely think about anything else but the need to be with him. Not that it was Hal's fault either, of course, but Adam *had* been her first love. In fact, when you came to think of it, you could almost say that it was *Hal* who had been the one to cause all the trouble. He had come between them, dazzling her with his tall, fair, good looks and his habit of carrying all before him, impressing her parents and making the struggling, younger Adam look raw beside him. The disquieting thought that she should never have encouraged him in the first place made her feel slightly uncomfortable and she hastened to justify herself. She'd been so inexperienced, brought up to do as her parents thought best for her.

Resting one knee on the window seat, she watched Hal collecting the cuttings into a rubbish bag. He missed his compost heaps and bonfires and fretted at the lack of scope in this tiny, high-walled garden but she had no intention of moving to The Keep, to be an unpaid worker for the set of geriatrics who inhabited it. Her new friends who lived in the surrounding Wiltshire countryside had been impressed by descriptions of The Keep – which she hinted would be Hal's one day – and had accepted her more readily into their circle, imagining that she was looking forward to the day when Hal should take up his inheritance, but she knew now that she could not leave Adam. She should never have been persuaded to give him up in the first place. Looking back, she could remember now that her parents had been far keener about Hal than she had, that they had pushed her into his arms, influenced by his family background as well as his career in the Navy. It was unreasonable, she persuaded herself, to expect that the young girl she'd been then – cosseted, watched over, carefully guided – could have had the confidence to go against her parents' wishes.

It was faintly irritating to be obliged to acknowledge that she might have stood by Adam, to admit that she'd given in without a fight. Try as she might, and she tried very hard, it was difficult to remember a single confrontation. No comforting memories of tearful protestations or proud determination came to bolster this image of martyrdom; indeed, she was obliged instead to force back insistent images of happy times with Hal and a disturbing reminder of a love which had caused many painfully jealous moments.

Maria subsided into the corner of the window seat, resolutely denying the early years of shared love: their delight when at last the children had arrived; Hal's endless patience with her unreasonable possessiveness. It was clear, now she thought it through, that if she'd really been in love with Hal she'd never have been jealous at all. In her heart she'd always known that the whole relationship was wrong and so she'd become uncertain, unhappy, unconfident. No wonder she'd felt jealous. No one could blame her for that. She'd been barely twenty – and a sheltered, naïve twenty at that – and too ready to do what her parents decided was best for her. Hal had been so strong and sure of himself, pressing and hurrying her, almost *bullying* her into marriage with him. Would her mother be so keen to promote the renewal of her relationship with Adam if she wasn't feeling guilty about her own earlier, misguided behaviour? It was because she realised now that her daughter and Adam should never have been parted that she was doing all she could to make amends. The fact that they all knew now that Hal was merely a trustee and executor to the Chadwick estate had nothing to do with it. After all, he couldn't make them go and live in Devon and it was perfectly reasonable that Maria and Edward – and Jolyon, of course, when he was around – should want to be near their own family rather than with the overbearing Chadwicks. This was quite natural. Edward, certainly, was much more of a Keene than he was a Chadwick; he had her own dark attractiveness and was a gentle, quiet little boy, so devoted to his mummy and to his Keene grandparents. He'd never cared much for going to The Keep or for his Chadwick relations. Jolyon, on the other hand, was the image of Hal and already a favourite down in Devon. They spoiled him terribly and had made him dissatisfied with his home in Salisbury. He could be sweet, of course, when there was nobody else around to influence him – in fact he was far more aware of her feelings than Edward was . . . but surely this was because Edward was younger. When he was Jolyon's age he'd be just as anxious to please, if not more so. Let's face it, Jolyon had gone away to school happily enough, no fuss, no tears. Whereas poor darling little Edward would *die* if he had to leave his mummy.

Glancing down sideways, she saw Hal fix the grass-catcher to the front of the mower, swipe his sleeve across his forehead and set off again across the lawn. What was so special about the Chadwicks anyway? Years behind the times, all of them. There was something scary about old Uncle Theo, and Hal's grandmother had always been so hard and distant. His sister, Kit, was most peculiar, no doubt about that, and his wretched mother did nothing but spoil the boys at every opportunity. As for Fliss . . . Maria felt a kind of hardening inside. There was no doubt at all that this was where the whole problem had its roots. Before they were even married, Hal had admitted that he was in love with Fliss. Oh, he'd said it was all over, naturally enough – well he would, wouldn't he? – but looking back it was all so obvious. There had probably been some opposition because they were cousins, not to mention their fathers being identical twins, and they'd had to separate just as she and Adam had been forced apart. Hal had never loved her, Maria knew that now. She'd always been second best and this instinctive knowledge had been the cause of her jealousy. After all, she never felt jealous of Adam, did she? Well, only of the cow of a wife of his, of course, but that was perfectly natural. The woman had no right to hang on to Adam now that she knew he didn't love her, no right at all. It wasn't as if there were any children to worry about . . . No, she was just a selfish, bloody-minded cow.

The thought of her being with Adam intimately made Maria feel sick although Adam promised that there was nothing physical between them any more. She clenched her hands into fists, forcing her mind away from the pictures this thought evoked, and wondered if Hal and Fliss had been together like that during the last two years down at The Keep. There had been plenty of opportunities, no doubt about that. Recalling Hal's straight, cool look when she'd hinted at it – to be honest, he'd looked just like old Mrs Chadwick for one awful moment – she experienced again the crawling sensation of shame that she'd felt then . . . but now she wondered whether it had been bluff. After all, he was hardly likely to admit it, was he?

70

The more she thought about it the more possible it became and, that being the case, he had no right at all to sit in judgment on her and Adam. Not that he did, if she were to be absolutely fair. He never said a word about it and was always very polite to Adam when they met publicly so that it was she and Adam, who felt just the least bit . . . well, what? What did she and Adam have to feel guilty about? Absolutely nothing except that they'd allowed themselves to be misled by those whom they'd trusted most when they were very young. Her parents had ruined her early life and Hal had used her, pretending to love her whilst all the time he'd remained in love with Fliss.

Maria breathed deeply, absolutely determined to meet Adam this evening after all. Her feelings of pity for Hal were now quite done away with and she only wondered that she'd ever had them in the first place. It was she who deserved the pity, she and Adam were the ones who'd been betrayed, and to think that she'd very nearly been ready to refuse her lover's request simply because her husband was home for two weeks' leave. She must be mad. Hadn't she made quite enough sacrifices already? Always so sweet-tempered and ready to give in to the wishes of others, that was her trouble. Well, now it was her turn; hers and Adam's. The thought of him, of his love for her, of how it might be later, made her heart speed and her hands tremble with her need for him. Standing up, she went into the bedroom, wondering what she should wear this evening, everything forgotten except this choking, weakening, necessary excitement.

Chapter Eleven

As Theo led Miles out into the garden after lunch he was conscious of a great sense of relief and guessed that Miles was feeling it, too. It had been Prue who, seeing the pitfalls ahead, had suggested that Fliss should drive over to Dartmouth to fetch Miles.

'Nothing worse,' she'd said, 'than us sitting about waiting and you feeling all scratchy and nervous and then biting his head off when he arrives. And poor old Miles will be feeling like Daniel, bearding us all in our den. It will take ages before we all calm down and behave naturally, don't you think?'

'Well, yes.' Fliss had sounded doubtful. 'I see what you're getting at, and I think you're absolutely right, but what about afterwards?'

'Afterwards there would be that horrid sense of anticlimax,' said Prue promptly, 'with you feeling guilty and Miles having to go back all on his own, wondering what we're saying about him and kicking himself when he remembers all the daft things he said because he was so nervous when he arrived and you were looking all distant and proud, just like Freddy used to look.'

At this point Caroline had burst out laughing and Prue had beamed round at them all with such happy confidence in her suggestion that Fliss had accepted the wisdom of her plan with the only proviso that Miles should also agree to it.

Theo suspected that Miles had agreed to it very readily. By the time he and Fliss arrived they were both quite relaxed, although there was a slight feeling of tension whilst the greetings took place and everyone tried not to observe how long it was since Miles had been with them last. Prue's generosity with the pre-lunch drinks had helped enormously here and, though there had been several awkward moments, they had passed over smoothly enough. Now, with Caroline and Prue clearing the table and Fliss making some coffee, Theo suggested that a stroll in the garden might be rather pleasant.

As they wandered out into the courtyard, Rex at their heels,

73

Theo was aware of an unwelcome sensation elbowing out his relief. In the past it would have been Freddy who was deftly engineering a private interview with Miles, making her feelings known to him whilst deviously eliciting such information as might be useful with regards to the wellbeing of her granddaughter. Now, as head of the family, it was he who had received her mantle along with certain responsibilities towards its younger members. Theo suffered a spasm of panic and self-doubt. Who was he to play the inquisitor? Miles and Fliss were adults and their marriage was their own affair. It was sometimes necessary to give advice when pressed but rather different to intrude upon another soul's privacy. Leaning on his stick, Theo gazed about the courtyard and wished, not for the first time, that Freddy was still alive.

'I expect that Fliss has told you,' said Miles abruptly, 'that she is thinking of giving our marriage another go. I just want to say, sir, that if she gives me the chance I intend to make a better shot of it than I did last time.'

Theo sighed deeply. It was, after all, he who had suggested this lunch so that they might test the depth of Miles's commitment, but now, with Miles beside him, all his feelings of inadequacy flooded back. Talking to Fliss, attempting guidance from a spiritual standpoint, was one thing; interfering and making judgements upon other lives quite another.

Miles watched him anxiously. Despite his height the old boy looked very frail and his breathing wasn't too good. He was leaning so heavily on his stick that Miles feared he might topple over altogether.

'Shall we sit down, sir?' he suggested quickly. 'Rather warm, isn't it? Very sheltered with these high walls . . .'

Talking easily lest the poor old fellow should feel he was being patronised, Miles headed for the wooden seat. They sat down together and there was a short silence. Miles felt rather inhibited. Unable to decide whether he should continue where he left off or simply leave the subject alone, he couldn't think of anything intelligent to say at all. He sat in tongue-tied frustration, completely unaware of the beauty of the afternoon. Presently, Theo looked at him with an almost comical dismay.

'I'm so glad that you've told me,' he said, 'but these kind of reassurances are rather pointless, aren't they? We can all say things, and mean them, too, at the time, but it's what happens afterwards which counts.'

Both his honesty and his distress were so unexpected and so absolutely genuine that Miles was obliged to press down an almost irrepressible urge to burst into hysterical laughter. He realised that he'd been waiting for some polite but stern formulaic reply which acknowledged his good intention whilst hinting that he wasn't going to be let off the hook too easily, followed perhaps by a short homily. Clearly nothing less than the truth was good enough for the eldest of the Chadwick family.

'You mean,' said Miles, when he'd recovered his poise, 'that I could be pulling the wool over your eyes? Doing the earnest-younger-man-with-the-head-of-the-family stuff, hoping to earn your approval so as to get my own way but with no intention of changing at all?'

He stopped, wondering if he had gone too far, but Theo was smiling at him, delighted at his ready grasp of the situation.

'Exactly that,' he said with undisguised relief. 'I couldn't help thinking about Toad, you know. The poor dear fellow, weeping remorsefully and ready to swear anything to the upright and noble Badger – although I always had a sneaking feeling that he was a *touch* self-righteous concerning Toad – but as soon as he was freed from Mr Badger's influence he was back to his old ways. How terrible a thing it is to betray oneself, to deliberately blind oneself to the truth. Self-deception is so dangerous, much more dangerous than taking the risk of deceiving another person by promises and smiles. So much is at stake. Once you become a priest, you know, you learn that people behave most oddly when they are with you. They seem to imagine that a belief in God dulls the senses and blinds you to reality.'

Miles began to laugh. 'So how am I to convince you?' he asked. 'Since none of us can see into the future you only have my word for it that I intend to change.'

At that moment, Fliss came out of the house carrying a tray. The two men watched her approach, suddenly aware of the sun on their backs and the birds singing amongst the woody stems of the Albertine on the wall outside Theo's study.

'I've brought your coffee,' she said, balancing the tray on the broad wooden arm of the chair. 'We're still clearing up and we thought that you might be gasping. We shan't be long.'

'I love her,' said Miles, watching her going away from them, disappearing into the shadowy hall. 'I really do, although it hasn't always seemed like it. That's why it's so difficult to convince people. That I could take the job in Hong Kong without giving her a thought, I mean, and then say that I love her. I've spoken to my boss out there and it's possible that he could transfer me to their London office, not wait for my contract to end. The pay won't be so good but we'd get by. Of course they'd have to find a replacement for me, so it would all take time if I decide that it's what I want. It depends on Fliss. If she says no then I'd rather stay out in Hong Kong.'

'And if she says yes,' said Theo slowly, 'no doubt you'd want her to go back with you until it's all sorted out.'

'On the contrary,' said Miles at once, 'I think that would be a mistake. I'd rather wind things up out there and make a new start back here. Oh, I hope she'd come out to visit me, of course, but I wouldn't expect her to come back with me. It could take more than a year, you know. I wouldn't even ask her to live with me permanently in London. Fliss is a country girl and I know that her heart is here. She did it my way for fourteen years and now it's her turn. Perhaps her way will be more successful than mine was.'

'She must make up her mind soon. There is nothing worse than indecision.'

Miles looked at Theo quickly. 'And you won't be against it?'

'Fliss will make her own decision,' he answered. 'My opinion isn't important.'

Miles laughed rather bitterly. 'You underestimate yourself, sir.'

'You misunderstand me,' Theo said gently. 'Fliss is like her grandmother. She will consider everything, listen to advice, weigh the evidence, but in the end she will make up her own mind. That is as it should be, don't you think? Fliss, after all, knows more about you and your marriage than any of us. It would be wrong to interfere.'

'I must admit that I hoped I'd have you on my side.' Miles shrugged, hiding his disappointment. 'I think it would give me confidence to know that you believed that I am capable of change.'

Theo watched him. 'As far as it is of any use to you,' he said after a moment, 'you have my support. I believe that you are capable of change and growth and I think you will make the most of this opportunity if Fliss agrees to it.'

Miles took a deep breath, throwing back his shoulders, stretching mightily. The intensity of his relief showed how very important this old man's support was to him, more important, even, than he'd first suspected.

'Thank you for that, sir,' he said. 'I can't tell you what your good opinion means to me. You have my word that, if I am given the chance, I shall do my best for us both.'

Theo bowed his head, alarmed by so much responsibility. Freddy would have been better equipped to deal with this sort of thing; she would have handled it so much more wisely, basing her judgement on facts rather than on intuition.

'So that's settled,' he said, thankful in his turn that the matter was closed. 'Shall we drink our coffee before it gets cold?'

'And did you feel like Daniel in the lions' den?' Fliss asked Miles lightly, as she drove him back to Dartmouth.

He hesitated, guessing at her meaning, wondering how to answer. 'Prue's more like a cuddly old pussycat,' he answered with the same lightness of tone. 'Your Uncle Theo is a force to be reckoned with, though. Mrs Chadwick was daunting enough, a bit like my old headmaster now I come to think of it, but Theo has a rather different quality.'

'What do you mean?' she asked sharply.

Miles, sitting beside her, his arms folded across his chest, tried to get his thoughts into some sort of order. He wasn't accustomed to deep analytical exercises but he attempted to define his feelings.

'Your grandmother,' he said slowly, 'could make you feel awkward. Schoolboyish. You'd remember that you needed a haircut and wonder if your shoes were clean. She had that clear, cool look – you do it sometimes, Fliss – which keeps you up to scratch. It puts you at arm's length, sums you up and lets you know that you're found wanting, but at the same time, though you dread her retribution, you'd put it at the same level as the rest of it. A caning that would make your hands smart, perhaps? Standing in front of the class and feeling ashamed?' He laughed. 'I'm not doing this very well, am I?'

'Go on,' Fliss said.

'But your uncle is in a different league. He gets down there and suffers with you and you feel that if you let him down you'd be endangering something far more precious than your skin or your pride. In fact you know that you'd be letting down this vital thing inside yourself, not him at all, and he'd be alongside you in the gutter, holding your hand while you wept with the grief and the pain of it.'

There was a long silence. Miles blinked a little, frowned, and looked at Fliss. She drove very well, efficiently and with anticipation, always ready to back up for nervous tourists who hovered mid-lane, fearing to scratch their shiny, clean cars on the sharp-twigged hedges or the unforgiving stone walls. Chin up, lips closed, her fair hair blowing in the breeze from the open windows, she looked like some young seer, proud, isolated, not of this world . . .

Miles pulled himself together and became his usual prosaic self.

'Sorry if that sounded high-falutin. Something came over me. I love you, Fliss. Out of all the things I've said since I returned to England I can't remember now whether I've actually told you.'

She smiled then, a mischievous smile which made his heart move in his breast.

'I think you may have mentioned it,' she said. 'Once or twice.'

She swung the car left off the Kingsbridge road, taking the short cut through the back lanes which would bring them out at The Forces Inn. She was deeply moved by Miles's description of his feelings about Uncle Theo and in absolute agreement with him. She'd managed to have a moment alone with Theo when Caroline had carried Miles off for a walk with Rex on the hill. Whilst Prue was getting tea organised, Fliss and Uncle Theo had sat down together in the cool hall. She'd been too strung up to beat about the bush.

'What do you think?' she'd asked rather desperately. 'Is he sincere? Is it just his pride? You know what I mean, don't you? To have and to hold, come what may.'

'No,' he'd answered. 'I don't think it is. I think he truly loves you and genuinely means to try to adapt. He certainly has no intention of asking you to go back to Hong Kong with him. In fact he has already approached his superior to ask about being transferred to London should you agree. He wants a new start here in England and on your terms. He says that his way didn't work and now it's only fair to try it your way, if you'll allow it.'

'How frightening, Fliss had said soberly, after a moment or two.

'Only if you use the power he offers you.'

She'd shaken her head. 'It's very confusing,' she'd muttered anxiously. 'It's so easy to get it wrong. It always seems so natural to follow all one's baser instincts.'

He'd watched her compassionately, wondering how anyone ever dared to attempt anything without God's guidance. He'd remembered the prayer he'd copied out, intending to show it to Fox, but which somehow had fallen into Freddy's hands, to her great comfort. He'd murmured the first few lines aloud.

'Who can free himself from his meanness and limitations,
if you do not lift him to yourself, my God, in purity of love?
How will a person
brought to birth and nurtured in a world of small horizons,
rise up to you, Lord,
if you do not raise him by your hand which made him?'

'What is that?' she'd asked at last.

78

He'd sighed, wishing that he could help her. 'It's the prayer of a soul in love,' he'd answered. 'St John of the Cross.'

They'd sat together in silence and then Prue had come in and the moment had passed.

Now, as the tall grasses brushed against the car on both sides and the creamy heads of the meadowsweet leaned in at the open windows, dislodging tiny insects with shimmering, Cellophane wings, Fliss felt that she was standing at some vitally important crossroad in her life. The moment was now and must not be postponed. She could turn aside into safe, familiar byways or she could go forward into the terrifying unknown but any further procrastination would weaken and debase whatever was left to them.

'I love you, too,' she said and, taking her left hand from the wheel, she held it out to him.

Chapter Twelve

Margaret Prior wrote out the cheque for the butcher, hurried him off to his van and began to sort out the pile of meat on the kitchen table.

'One day,' remarked her friend Connie, treasurer of the donkey sanctuary, 'you're going to get confused and you and Andrew will be eating the ox cheek in the stew.'

'Wouldn't do that would we, boys?' Margaret edged an importunate Labrador away with one corduroy-clad knee as she stripped the bloodied greaseproof paper from the meat and tidied the chops and sausages into separate containers. 'Wouldn't eat your dinner, would we? It seems that I might not be able to get it much longer, anyway. New rules at the abattoir or something. So tiresome. We like our ox cheek, don't we, chaps? Right. Baskets. Did I say *baskets*? *Good* boys. You shall have a biccy. You'd like that, wouldn't you? Here we are. One each. Good boys.'

Connie watched the familiar ritual as each dog took his biscuit politely and gently from her fingers. They crunched eagerly, tails waving whilst they searched out the pieces which dropped from their soft mouths into the blankets lining their baskets.

'Nevertheless,' she said, returning to the conversation which the butcher had interrupted, 'I think you should take this letter seriously, Margaret. I really do.'

'Never been a one to let myself be bullied.' She clapped the last lid into place and carried the containers out into the utility room where the freezer lived. 'Only spoke the truth,' she shouted back over her shoulder. 'Not ashamed of that.'

Connie looked at the lawyer's letter she still held in her hand. 'But he's got a point, hasn't he? Can you *prove* that it's the truth?' Her eyes gleamed behind her spectacles and she looked at her friend with a grudging respect. 'Did you really say all these things? I had no idea you knew half these words.'

'I lost my temper,' said Margaret shortly, rinsing her hands at the sink and drying them with quick swipes on the striped roller

81

towel which hung on the back of the kitchen door. 'You know how I hate London. Train was late and I couldn't find a taxi and when I finally got to Hampstead there's the two of them just arriving home like a pair of young lovers.' She laughed briefly; a honking sound in which there was no trace of mirth. 'Andrew's face was a study.'

'And the girl?'

'She?' Margaret spoke witheringly. 'Oh, she tried to brazen it out. Only been to the opera and so on. Just good friends, that kind of rubbish. I soon got rid of her, I can tell you. Andrew caved in at once, of course. Well, what else could he do? There were her bits and pieces all over his flat.'

'Yes, you told me that.' Connie looked thoughtful. 'But we've got to be intelligent about this, Margaret. It's all a question of proof. What you saw doesn't matter, does it? The point is, can you prove it? No one will take your word for it. Isn't it called circumstantial evidence? They'll deny it, you see, so that it's your word against theirs.'

'Can't help that.' Margaret sat down at the battered refectory table and picked up her mug of cool tea. 'It's the truth. Andrew admitted it.'

'But that was before he got himself a lawyer.' Connie pushed aside several old newspapers, a half-finished packet of Polo mints and a Biro without a top, and rested her elbow on the table. 'Supposing he denies it in court, says they're just friendly neighbours who share a passion for the opera. What then?'

Margaret set her jaw stubbornly. The perm in her dry rough hair had gone frizzy in the earlier rain and her hands with their swollen joints looked red and raw. She was impervious to the cold and, apart from the kitchen where the Aga's heat penetrated the high, wide spaces, the house was gripped, even in high summer, by a deathly chill. Here in the kitchen, where she spent most of her time, the muddle was indescribable and Connie felt a fleeting pang of sympathy for Andrew.

'If it's my word against theirs,' said Margaret, 'why shouldn't they believe mine? They've only got to look at that little tart to get the measure of her. Sin by name and Sin by nature. And Andrew wouldn't lie under oath.'

'But suppose it doesn't get that far?' insisted Connie. 'This isn't from Andrew's lawyer. It's from the girl's. He's talking about slander here, not the other thing. Apparently she holds a very good position at the British Museum, very highly thought of and so on, and there's no basis whatever for your accusations. It seems that several people overheard you shouting at her and are prepared to come forward as witnesses.'

'What people?' asked Margaret contemptuously. 'That meddle-some old Clarrie? Who'd take *his* word for anything?'

'Well, it's up to you, of course.' Connie laid the letter aside. 'But I'd be very careful if it was me. I'd hate to lose all this, not to mention the donkey sanctuary.'

'How do you mean? Lose all this?'

Connie shrugged. 'If the fur starts flying you could just be the one who comes off worse. Clever things lawyers are. You could be shown as a jealous old woman, refusing to budge, staying down here with your dogs and devoted to your donkeys whilst poor old Andrew is neglected and driven out to spend most of his time alone in London. Why shouldn't he go to the opera with his neighbour? If push comes to shove Andrew might have to sell everything up. Oh, you'd probably get your share but it wouldn't be this house, more likely some tiny bungalow or a flat where there wouldn't be room for the dogs let alone the donkeys.'

'He wouldn't dare.'

'He might if he had a clever lawyer behind him.'

'But I'm in the right.'

'Oh, don't be so naïve, dear. Use your head. When did that ever matter in a court of law?'

Reluctantly, Margaret prepared to yield an inch or two. 'What are you suggesting?'

'Well, think about it. Never mind the rights or wrongs or the desire for revenge. Actually think it right through. To begin with, do you really want him back? Stuck here with nowhere else to go because you've insisted he can't use his Hampstead flat? Do you really want him under your feet all day long? You're always saying how pleased you are when he goes off for a while. Why be a dog in the manger?'

Margaret set her mug down. 'It goes against the grain to give in so easily, especially to that little tart.'

'I'm not advising you to give in. Just get in first. Say that you'll settle out of court and give him a divorce in return for this house and all the land and a decent income to go with it, and stick to it. If you try to fight it, well, you might just find that Andrew has clever ways of getting his own back. This is his house, remember, not yours. He doesn't have to ask you if he can sell it. In your shoes I should be *very* careful.'

'Give him a *divorce*?' Margaret spoke so sharply that the dogs sat up, alert, ears cocked. 'Are you mad?'

'Look,' said Connie patiently. 'Look, dear. Try to be honest with yourself. Forget all this upset for a moment. Let's pretend it hasn't happened. You don't really want Andrew, do you? You know he hates the country and he's not getting any younger, dear, is he? Supposing he comes home one day and tells you that he doesn't want to live here any more, all among the dog hair and the tack and the mud? Supposing he decides he wants to sell it all up for a nice comfortable town house, near his club and theatre-land? What then? You can't stop him. Don't you see that this could be an opportunity for you to get exactly what you want. He's played right into your hands. If it's all done legally and properly then no one could ever take it away from you.'

'Andrew wouldn't dare sell up without consulting me.'

'Have it your way, dear.' Connie shrugged. 'But you're braver than I am, that's all I can say. You might see another Andrew from now on and it's not going to be much fun for you, is it? Admitting in a crowded court that your husband prefers a young pretty girl and seeing the sniggers and the nudges. And hearing them read out all those words you used. Of course it'll be in the local papers. They'll have a field day, won't they? He's quite a bit younger than you, isn't he? Ah well.' She shook her head, laughing. 'You'll probably be glad to move away by the time they've all finished. Is there any more tea in the pot?'

Margaret didn't answer but her expression was grim and Connie stood up so as to peer into the teapot. She collected together several mugs containing cold tea or coffee dregs and placed them carefully in the crowded sink before rinsing out her own mug and washing a teaspoon.

'So how do you know so much about it?' Margaret asked grudgingly at last.

Connie chuckled. 'How do you think I got my nice little Georgian house in the village? I took advice and boxed clever. Hamish was sixty-three, his little tart was under thirty and he thought the world was well lost for love. She took him for everything he had and left him two years later. My dear mama used to say that there was no fool like an old fool and how right she was. Take my advice, dear, and get in first. He'll be so relieved he'll give you anything you want. Now, how about another cup?'

Searching through the airing-cupboard preparatory to packing his grip, Hal was quite suddenly overwhelmed by a sense of utter futility. He sat down on the edge of the bed, his hands full of folded shirts, and stared at nothing in particular. If he were to be honest with himself, he suspected that part of his depression was rooted in the knowledge that Fliss had decided to return to Miles. He knew that he was being selfish here – after all, he'd made it clear that he must hang on to his marriage for the sake of the boys, so why shouldn't Fliss feel exactly the same? – but admitting his selfishness brought no comfort. The truth of it was that during the last two years he'd become used to her being at The Keep, to finding her there when he got back from sea. It wasn't as if they were doing anything wrong – perhaps it would have been better for both of them if they had – and there had been something so satisfying, so natural about her being there.

It had come as a shock to him when she'd told him of her decision to return to Miles. He'd rung The Keep one evening when Maria was out and she'd answered the telephone . . .

'I feel that I must,' she'd told him. 'He's making such efforts and . . . well, he is my husband, after all, and it's not as if you and I . . . I mean . . .'

'No,' he'd agreed quickly, far too quickly. Had he hurt her? 'Oh, Fliss, you know how it is, don't you?'

'Yes,' she'd said sadly. 'I know how it is.'

'You're not going back with him?'

'He hasn't asked me to but I've decided that I shall go out for a month or two after the school holidays. He's trying to get transferred back to London but I feel I have to make an effort, too.' She'd laughed. 'You know how you get yourself all geared up to something and if you can't get on with it there's all that adrenalin washing about with nothing to do? Well, that's how I feel at the moment. Miles has gone back to Hong Kong and I'm left with all my good intentions and nothing to do with them.'

'Oh, Fliss . . .'

'I know,' she'd said at once. 'Oh, Hal, I *do* know but I can't not try. Do you see?'

'Of course I see. I'll be down next weekend, anyway.'

'The exeat, yes. I was surprised that Jo's coming here. I knew we were going to see you when you came back off leave but I thought you'd have Jo there with you for the weekend before you left.'

He'd told her then about Maria being busy and the various difficulties about getting Jo home but now, as he sat on Jo's bed, he knew that he'd made no effort when Maria had churned out the usual excuses. He had to admit that he'd been secretly pleased at the thought of the coming weekend with Jolyon down at The Keep. Jo, of course, had accepted it as he always did. He believed that his

85

father was doing what was necessary to keep the family together and trusted him.

Hal looked about the small bedroom. 'No point giving Jolyon a big room,' Maria had said, 'if he's going to be away at school,' so Jo had the boxroom. Since it contained the airing cupboard there wasn't much room for shelves and he'd reluctantly agreed that some of his books and toys – 'Honestly, darling, you're *much* too old to need these now' – should be packed away. Hal had stepped in here, however, and to Jo's delight had suggested that they should be taken down to The Keep.

'You've got a room there, too,' Hal had reminded him, shocked and furious by the expression of misery on Jo's face as he watched Maria's careless hands gathering up his beloved possessions. 'I'll take them down next time I go. They'll be waiting for you there,' and so they had been. It was sad that his son's room at The Keep should reflect his personality so much more clearly than this tidy, sterile little box, although it came to life during the holidays when Jo's battered tuckbox with its bright stickers stood beneath the window and his faithful old teddy sat on the small caned chair.

Hal put his shirts on the neat bed and stood up. The baseball cap bearing the legend HMCS *Assiniboine*, which Mole had coerced out of his Canadian Engineer Officer in *Opportune*, hung on the chair back, and Hal picked it up, turning it in his hands, feeling the thick black material, the rough gold lettering. Was he doing his absolute best for Jo or was he simply going along with the situation? How many times during the last two years had he stayed in Devon instead of making the effort to get home for a few days? How often had Jo travelled to The Keep for exeats and half terms which could have been spent here in Salisbury?

'I can't be half hearted,' Fliss had said on the telephone. 'If I'm honest, I suppose I hoped that Miles was going to let me off the hook. Stay in Hong Kong and say "Let's forget it" but he didn't. He wants to make a very real effort and what right have I to refuse it? The moratorium was to give us chance to see how we felt and now we know how he feels.'

'And you? How do you feel?'

He'd known that it was mean to ask her but he simply couldn't help himself. He'd heard her sigh.

'Nothing changes how I feel about you, Hal. Nothing ever will, I know that now. But I have no right to opt out of my marriage because of that. I knew it when I married Miles but I went ahead and did it anyway. So we'll give it another go and see what happens. And there are the twinnies to think of, too. I know they don't have the kind of relationship you have with your boys but he *is* their father. Actually, Bess is just beginning to show an interest in him. You know how reserved she is, so self-contained, but there's just a sign of, well, recognition, I suppose you'd call it. I think that Miles is much more likely to be effective now they're growing up and it's possible that they might be glad to have him around. We were lucky to come home to Grandmother and Ellen and Fox after Kenya but I know what it's like not to have your parents when you need them. It goes much deeper than you think. Look at Mole. I'm not pretending that it's going to be easy but . . .' the ghost of a chuckle here, '. . . I've started so I'll finish as Magnus Magnusson would say. You feel the same, don't you?'

'Oh, yes.' He knew he'd sounded resigned but it had been impossible to be cheerful about it. 'And don't forget that I know what it's like to grow up without a father. I don't want to be a part-time father for my boys. The truth is that neither of us should have married anyone but each other. Having done so I suppose we've got to make a go of it. I *do* love you, Fliss.'

'Perhaps it's wrong,' she'd said, 'but just knowing it helps me to carry on. Peculiar, isn't it?'

Now, standing in the late afternoon sunshine in Jolyon's bedroom, Hal put the baseball cap back on the chair and wandered over to the window which looked on to the garden. It *was* peculiar. He knew quite a few divorced couples now, men and women abandoning their long-standing partners and their children for people they hardly knew, and yet he and Fliss, who had loved each other for twenty-odd years, refused to make the ultimate break. Their love for each other *did* actually strengthen their ability to carry on with their partners. Perhaps it was sudden, forbidden attraction which rocked the foundations of a stable marriage; something new and exciting which overthrew people's normal good sense and caused such destruction? He knew that if Fliss set her hand to it she would do everything she could, now, to make her marriage work.

Hal thought: And that's what's making me depressed. I wanted her to be around, waiting for me.

Unwillingly he faced the unpalatable truth that he was hoping that Maria would be the one to make the break. If Maria were to leave him, then his conscience would be clear and if Fliss were free, too . . . '*I can't be half-hearted*', she'd said. Had he been half-hearted? He, too, had hoped that he would be let off the hook – but since he hadn't . . .

Abruptly he put his shirts back into the airing cupboard and went downstairs. Maria was in the kitchen, sitting at the kitchen table, reading the *Daily Telegraph* whilst Edward, perched on a stool, watched *Record Breakers* on the small black-and-white portable television on the breakfast bar. He glanced up as his father came in and they smiled at each other.

'Listen,' he said to both of them. 'I've been thinking. There's no reason at all why Jo shouldn't come home this weekend instead of going to The Keep. I can fetch him on Friday afternoon and drop him off on Sunday before driving down to Plymouth and we could have the weekend all together. Why don't we do that?'

Maria didn't look at him immediately but kept her eyes fixed on an article about the EEC summit calling for the release of Nelson Mandela and demanding recognition of the ANC. This did not interest her particularly but she needed time to think about this sudden threat to her plans. Liz Wishart had been summoned to Leicester. Her mother was seriously ill and she did not expect to be back for several days. Maria had been delighted by the news. The weekend was a wonderful opportunity for her and Adam to be together and she had no intention of sacrificing it.

'Well?' Hal's voice was slightly sharper now and she looked at him, frowning a little, as though she was having difficulty in tearing her mind away from the article she was reading.

'Sorry? Oh, the weekend. Honestly, Hal, I simply can't change things now. I've got all sorts of things lined up because I thought you were going back. I must say I thought it was a bit odd that you wanted to leave on Friday but I know how you enjoy your visits to The Keep. Fliss is still there, I suppose?'

She watched him, sensing his internal struggle, determined to do nothing to help him.

'Yes, she's there.' He lowered his voice, keeping his back to Edward. 'But I thought that the original plan was because there was the usual difficulty about fetching Jo. Or getting him back. Or both. Or am I wrong?'

'It's not that easy,' she began defensively, wondering how she could preserve her weekend without putting herself in the wrong.

'So you keep telling me.'

'You simply won't accept the problems caused by having to be in two places at once, will you?' She spoke so angrily that Edward glanced round anxiously. 'I've explained over and over again. Edward is too young to come home from school to an empty house.'

She looked at Edward, her exasperation so deliberate, so exaggerated that she might as well have said to him 'There, you see how I have to protect you from him? You see what I have to cope with

88

on your behalf? but he turned quickly away, pretending as much interest in Roy Castle as she had pretended in Nelson Mandela.

'I thought that one of the great advantages about living in Salisbury was that your mother was going to be at hand for exactly these moments.' Hal caught at his temper and tried to smile. 'Anyway, it doesn't apply in this case. I've told you I can pick Jo up on Friday and drop him back on Sunday before I drive down to the ship. It doesn't matter how late I get back.'

'Then you should have thought of that earlier. I have other plans now. Meetings and so on. I can't drop my commitments to order, you know. I have responsibilities, too. Oh, I know that you sneer at them but these charities do very important work.'

'More important to you than Jo?' he asked lightly. He turned to Edward. 'What do think, Ed? Wouldn't it be nice for the four of us to be together for the weekend? You'd like to see Jo, wouldn't you?'

Edward looked at his mother, biting his lip and hunching a nervous shoulder. 'Only if it's not difficult,' he mumbled.

'Of course it's difficult,' said Maria quietly. She looked at them with tight-lipped long-suffering. This time it was clear that she was deeply hurt, that she was about to be put upon, her good nature abused. 'It's not me I'm worrying about but you simply can't expect other people to fall in with sudden whims. I've already told you that I've got meetings booked.'

'I heard you,' said Hal gently, 'and I hoped that your *meetings*' – he deliberately emphasised the word, his eyes holding hers so that she should know that he knew the whole truth – 'were not more important than having a weekend with Jo. And me.' This last was an afterthought.

'My God!' she exclaimed, furious at being cornered. 'That's rich, coming from you. You've put the Navy first all our married life and expected me to manage on my own with the boys without complaining. How you've got the nerve—'

'OK,' he said. He waited for a moment, glancing at Edward who stared steadfastly at the screen, his back to them both. 'Well, never mind. It was just a thought.'

He went out, closing the door gently behind him, and returned upstairs to continue with his packing.

Chapter Thirteen

'The children break up from school next week,' said Susanna idly as she folded her shopping list and put it in her purse. 'Funny, isn't it, how these innocent words can strike such terror to the heart?'

'I wonder if Grandmother thought the same about us.' Mole waited patiently, staring out through the two big, partially glazed doors, whilst Susanna drifted to and fro collecting all the things which she needed to take with her to Totnes. 'Of course there was no playschool in those days. How would you have liked that? Podger would still be home with you now. No chance of getting rid of her three mornings a week.'

'But Grandmother had Caroline to help her,' his sister pointed out. 'And Ellen and Fox. Oh, Mole, I still miss them all, don't you?'

Mole hesitated. He hitched himself on to the edge of the enormous refectory table in the middle of the atrium – the name Gus and Susanna had given the great central living area of the barn whilst it was still an empty, unconverted shell – and, one leg swinging, hands in pockets, head bent, he thought about it.

'I do when I'm at The Keep,' he said at last. 'Not really when I'm at sea, I have to admit. When I get back here, though, the memories are all still waiting. The Keep is changeless somehow. You feel you've stepped out of time. Although the place is crawling with workmen at the moment. It's chaos.'

'It's all Fliss's fault.' Susanna put three library books into her big basket and looked about her vaguely. 'She decided that if she isn't going to be there quite so much this autumn the Aga should be converted to oil. She says that it's getting a bit grim for Caroline and Prue having to carry out the ashes and hump coke about. Fliss has been doing it for the last two years and she's worried about how they'll manage. Caroline took offence and said that she wasn't too old to be able to lift a bucket of coke but Prue thought that it was a very good idea. So Uncle Theo and Hal did their sums and decided that if they bought a new one then a few radiators could be run from it. The burning question was how they would cope whilst the old one was taken out and the new one was being fitted. Caroline raised all sorts of difficulties again and protested that she could manage with the old Aga and it was such a terrible expense . . .' She paused to peer in her bag, checking for her library tickets.

'So in a fit of excitement, to show her how easy it was going to be, Prue switched on that cooker which Grandmother bought but Ellen would never use and there was a huge bang and all the lights went out,' supplied Mole, who had already heard the story from Fliss. He began to laugh. 'Trust Prue. It must have been sitting there quietly corroding for years and years.'

'We tried to work it out. It was certainly there before Fliss went to Hong Kong the first time round. Anyway, there was pandemonium as far as I can gather. Everything fused and according to the electrician it's simply a miracle that they're not all dead. Apparently the original wiring is in a terrible state.'

'It's pretty depressing at the moment with floorboards being taken up and people crashing about in the attics but it could have been worse. It might have been the middle of winter. In a way it's a blessing that she did it before the old Aga was taken out. At least they can still cook and it supplies a certain amount of hot water.' Mole looked at his watch. 'Are you sure we're going to the market this morning? It'll be lunchtime soon and we'll have to fetch Podger.'

'I can't find Fred's library books. They must be here somewhere. Hang on a sec.' Susanna dropped heavily to her knees and fished the missing items from beneath the deep, comfortable sofa which stood on a raised step behind the big table. 'They *will* sit on the floor to read and then the books get kicked underneath the chairs.' She smiled at him as he hauled her to her feet. 'What were you thinking about?'

'I was thinking that your vision of this place was so absolutely accurate. It's exactly how you planned it. Just like the flat over the studio only much larger. Very clever of you both. I'd be hopeless at anything like that.'

They looked about the atrium together. The kitchen with its Esse and the old Welsh dresser was divided from the central living area by a long quarry-tiled working surface, whose high curved wooden back was an abandoned rood screen rescued from a derelict church, and, at the other end, three long, shallow steps led up to the snug. Armchairs were gathered round the fireplace with its brass hood, and the walls were lined with shelves for books and Gus's music. The long French windows looked west and the whole place was filled with light. The bedrooms with the bathroom and utility were contained in the short leg of the L-shaped barn, beyond the kitchen.

'We love it,' said Susanna contentedly.

'If you have many more babies you won't fit into it,' he said. 'By the way, I've got a message from Kit. Well, it's a list of names, actually. She wrote them down and said that I must be sure to give them to you.'

Susanna chuckled. 'She's going away, isn't she? She's afraid she won't be around to be consulted. I told her when she came down with Sin for that weekend that after Podger she hasn't got a hope. How is she?'

'They were in a state of great jubilation.' Mole picked up her basket and started edging her towards the kitchen. 'Apparently, Andrew's wife has offered to do a deal. She'll give him a divorce in return for the house in Wiltshire and a decent income.'

'Thank God,' said Susanna, rummaging in her bag for her keys. 'Kit was very low when I last spoke to her. She said that Sin was practically suicidal. What brought the miracle to pass?'

'It was Clarrie's idea.' Mole followed her out through the utility room and waited while she locked the door. 'He persuaded Sin to make her lawyer write a letter threatening to sue Andrew's wife for slander. Apparently she said some pretty terrible things to Sin. Anyway, she's taken the bait. Clarrie's like a dog with two tails. The joke is that she had no idea quite how well off Andrew is so he can settle the house on her without becoming destitute. Clarrie's taking the credit for that, too. He's been warning Andrew over the years to keep a few things under his hat and it's paid off. He said that it's the only thing Andrew's ever taken his advice about. Kit and Sin are tactfully clearing off for a couple of weeks while the arrangements are sorted out.'

'Where are they going?' asked Susanna. 'Bit tricky, going off suddenly at the end of July. Everywhere's booked.'

She paused to look at Mole's Alfasud: small, silvery, understated, but with a bite under its bonnet, she realised that this was much more suited to his character than some showy sports car.

'They've decided to go to Sin's friends in Viella.' He stood by whilst she carefully lowered herself into the passenger seat and then closed the door for her. 'It's just inside Spain, over the French border in the foothills of the Pyrenees. It's a great place.'

Susanna glanced at him sideways as he settled himself in the driving seat. 'She took you there, too, did she?'

'That's right.' Mole smiled without looking at her.

Susanna thought: His smile is just like Uncle Theo's.

As the car moved off a terrible thought occurred to her. 'You're not still in love with Sin, are you?'

'Don't be silly,' he said impatiently. He'd shared many things with Susanna but he still resisted any encouragement to talk about very personal emotions. 'It was over long ago. I'm delighted for her and Andrew. They're very happy together.'

'Sorry,' she said contritely as he drove slowly down the bumpy track. 'It's just that . . . Well, I wish you'd . . . Oh, you know.'

'Yes. I know.' He paused at the end of the track and then swung the car out into the road. 'Stop fussing. You and Gus are producing enough sprogs for me to be able to take my time. I shall wait until I'm forty and then marry some gorgeous young creature and have a dozen sprogs. By the way, there's a dit going round which says that I might be offered First Lieutenant in *Superb*.'

'Oh.' She looked at him with all the excitement and enthusiasm she'd felt in those early days of his career, her anxieties forgotten. 'That's brilliant, isn't it? And after that you'll be promoted and get another command.'

'Hang on,' he begged. 'Let's do this one first, shall we? Do you happen to know where *Superb* is based?'

'Of course not,' she began almost crossly – he must know by now that she never had a clue about those details – but his tone alerted her and she turned towards him as quickly as her bulk would allow. 'Oh, Mole. She isn't down here, is she? At Devonport?'

'She is indeed. It would be fun, wouldn't it? Only don't mention it to anyone until it's been confirmed. OK?'

'OK,' she promised – and grinned at him. 'Not even Gus?'

'No one,' he said firmly. 'I shouldn't have told *you*, really. Now, remember that you're the navigator and show me the best place to park. That's if we're lucky enough to find a place at this time on market day.'

Mole's leave was over and Susanna was heartily tired of being pregnant when Theo summoned Hal to The Keep in August. *Broadsword* was alongside for a few days and Jolyon had travelled down by train from Salisbury to spend the time with his father. The news was rather grim. The electricians had discovered something even more serious than dangerous wiring: there was dry rot in the roof timbers and in quite a number of the attic floorboards. Theo arranged for estimates and, whilst Fliss took the twinnies and Jolyon out to the beach or for picnics on the moor, Hal and Theo closeted themselves in Theo's study for two days running.

Both of them knew that there was only one answer: shares must be sold to pay the enormous bills. When Theo offered to put some of his own private money towards the cost as well as selling his shares, so as to relieve the younger generation of the burden, Hal refused firmly. The Keep belonged to all of them equally, he said, and they must all bear the expense of its upkeep.

'It won't really hurt us too much,' he pointed out. 'I've spoken to Mole and to Fliss. She's quite happy to have her allowance cut and so is Mole. People are living on far less than we earn and Miles can easily support Fliss and the twinnies. He took out masses of insurance for their school fees when they were babies and the Navy pays a substantial amount towards Jo's and Ed's, so we've all agreed to tighten our belts. Kit's managing OK and my mother is quite safe here. It's Susanna who will be the hardest hit. Old Gus doesn't earn that much but she'd want to be treated like everyone else. Fred's a bright little chap, and they're hoping that he might get a bursary to Gus's old school at King's, so I'm hoping that we might be able to cut her allowance as little as possible and let the rest of us take the strain.'

Slowly, carefully, they did their sums, leaving enough shares to continue to maintain The Keep as Freddy had wished, but Hal looked grim, knowing that his grandmother had always hoped that he would take over the reins, believing that he would be able to afford to use it as his own home and take a part of the financial weight. The house in Salisbury had been very expensive and he'd resented having to buy it when The Keep was here, waiting for him, but Maria had every right to resent the terms on which it was arranged . . .

'There is no reason to blame yourself,' Theo said as, the necessary steps taken, they relaxed on the wooden seat in the courtyard. 'The dead should never impose their wishes upon the living. The Keep isn't your sole responsibility. We all share in it together.'

'I know that.' Hal leaned forward, resting his forearms along his thighs. 'But I should have liked to have lived here, to let my sons grow up here. I sometimes wonder how the future generation will manage to support it, especially now that we shall have to sell off such a large parcel of shares . . .'

He refrained from adding that it probably didn't matter very much either way. He was unwilling to burden his great-uncle with his problems but he was still in the grip of the depression that had dogged him all summer, ever since Fliss had told him she was going back to Miles. When he'd arrived for that weekend, after tea the two of them had walked on the hill together. He'd put an arm about her and she'd leaned into him and he'd felt such happiness that he'd wanted to weep. Quite suddenly, in the shelter of the spinney, he'd put both arms round her and kissed her. She'd responded warmly, eagerly, and presently he'd looked down at her, holding her hands tightly.

'What are we doing, Fliss?' he'd asked desperately. 'Why are we wasting our lives? For God's sake, are we *mad*?'

'No,' she'd answered quickly, 'not mad. Well, probably . . .'

'We love each other,' he'd said urgently. 'Nothing else matters.'

'It's not just us. Other people matter, too,' she'd said. 'We don't live in a vacuum.'

'I don't care about anyone else,' he'd said angrily. 'It's our turn . . .'

'But you do,' she'd said. 'You love Jo and Edward. And you promised Jo you'd hold on. You'd hate being a weekend father, Hal. Driving to Salisbury and taking them out, wondering where to go when it's pouring with rain, having to put them back in through the front door at the end of the day or taking them to a hotel with a bleak empty evening ahead. That awful brittleness with Maria at the beginning and end of each outing and the boys miserable and awkward. Oh, Hal, you'd hate it and so would they.'

'But what will it matter in the long run?' he'd asked bitterly. 'We've sacrificed our youth, Fliss. We've given it all up. Wasted it. And for what? Maria despises me and is teaching Edward to do the same. What if *she* leaves *me*? What about Jo then? It will have all been for nothing.'

She'd held him tightly, trying to comfort him . . .

On the bench in the courtyard, his hands clasped on his stick, Theo sat in silence, sharing in Hal's silent pain, letting his love flow out to him. He tried to think of something to distract the poor dear fellow, to get him over this difficult moment, but as usual his mind remained obstinately blank. As he gazed out on the sunny grass rectangle an image came into his head. He was a small boy again, sitting in his maternal grandmother's summerhouse, looking across the lawn to the river, with her close beside him. He had loved her so much. His own mother had died giving him life and he had never been able to forgive himself, nor could he imagine that anyone else could forgive him. As he grew up he imagined that his father and elder brother must have considered him a poor exchange for the wife and mother they had known and loved, although they showed no outward sign of it. His grandmother had attempted to remove some of his burden of shame and he'd looked forward to those holidays each summer to the gracious house on the banks of the Tamar. He couldn't remember how old he was when she'd first begun to read poetry to him, sitting in the warmth of the summerhouse, but it had become a pleasant little ritual which occurred regularly at some point during each visit. Closing his eyes, Theo could hear again the rustle of her gown, smell the faint scent of verbena, feel her hand upon his shoulder. If he turned his head, just a little, he could see the great ruby on her thin, old finger, flashing in the sunlight. Her voice echoed down the years . . .

> *Beauty, strength, youth, are flowers but fading seen;*
> *Duty, faith, love, are roots, and ever green.*

He had no idea that he'd murmured the words aloud and Hal smiled bitterly to himself. To his jaundiced ears it sounded particularly moral and Victorian – but then the old boy *was* a Victorian and, after all, he was getting on a bit now and you had to make allowances . . . On the other hand, he'd been very glad that he'd been there when this latest crisis had broken. The memory of his great-uncle's ready grasp of the financial situation, of his wisdom quietly offered and his intelligent input and generosity, made Hal feel suddenly ashamed.

'Sorry,' he said. 'I was miles away. What were you saying?'

Theo opened his eyes. 'I was thinking of my grandmother,' he said. 'She lived in a house which looked over the river and on the lawn was a summerhouse. We used to sit there in the sun and she'd read me poetry.'

'And those words?' Hal tried to be interested, to put his own misery to one side. 'They were one of the poems?'

'George Peele. My grandmother read them to me until I was old enough to read them for myself. By then, of course, I knew them by heart.

> *Beauty, strength, youth, are flowers but fading seen;*
> *Duty, faith, love, are roots, and ever green.*

He repeated the couplet, realising now that he must have spoken them aloud.

Hal smiled at him. 'Very Victorian.'

Theo shook his head. 'George Peele was an Elizabethan. The lines are taken from a poem called "The Old Knight". I don't suppose anyone reads the Elizabethan poets any more but my grandmother loved them.'

97

Hal stared at him. 'Duty, faith, love,' he repeated cynically. 'Is anything really worth the sacrifice?'

'Oh, I think so,' answered Theo gently. 'The Keep is still a place of sanctuary as it has been so often in the past. For your grandmother with her boys after Bertie was killed. For me. For Prue and for Caroline. For Fliss and her children during this last two years. And for you, too, if I'm not mistaken . . .'

Hal sighed heavily, acknowledging the truth of this. 'Perhaps you're right.'

'*Duty, faith, love are roots, and ever green*,' quoted Theo thoughtfully. 'The poem is about service, you see. Of course, service might be to a place or to a person, to your country or to a child, but it's the usual question about dying to self so as to find life . . .'

He talked quietly, aware that Hal was hardly listening to him, but even as he spoke he was aware of a peculiar sensation of anticipation; as if he were half expecting someone; someone who would be the guardian of The Keep, coming forward to shoulder the burden for future generations. A tall fair boy was entering through the gateway between the gatehouses and Theo tried to focus on him, frowning against the sun. Behind him was another shadowy figure; a small boy, hardly more than three or four years old, one of the dark Chadwicks. He came running in, looking eagerly about him, unafraid and full of life. Theo felt his heart leap in his breast, acknowledging him, and Hal, still locked in thought, felt him start and sat up. He raised a hand to his son.

'It's Jolyon,' Theo was saying, 'but . . . is he alone?' He sounded puzzled and Hal glanced at his uncle quickly as Jo came up to him. He wrapped his father's arm about him and leaned against his knee, beaming at his great-great-uncle whom he adored.

'Hi, Dad,' he said, just as he always did. 'Everything OK?'

Hal thought: The old boy's right as always. Duty, faith, love. We'll have to hang on a bit longer.

'Everything's fine,' he said. 'Certain sure.'

The small boy had vanished. Theo laughed silently. Woolgathering, Ellen would have called it; quoting out-of-date Elizabethan poets and falling asleep in the sun. Well, he was past it, of course, senile and useless. Hal and Jolyon were smiling at him and he smiled back, grateful for their patience with him. Before anyone could speak, Prue came running out. They turned to watch her and Jolyon tensed with anxiety within his father's protecting arm.

He thought: Something terrible has happened to Mummy. Or Ed . . .

'Wonderful news,' Prue was calling. 'Susanna went into labour just after breakfast and didn't even give Gus time to get her to the hospital. She's had another little girl and they're both doing splendidly. Isn't it wonderful?' And, as they crowded round her, she burst into tears of happiness.

Book Two
Autumn 1990

Chapter Fourteen

'I know I was against it at the time,' said Caroline, standing up from the table and collecting bowls and plates together, 'but it is rather wonderful not to have to riddle out the Aga every morning and carry hods of coal to and fro. It makes me feel rather ashamed to admit it, remembering how hard Ellen worked.'

'She had Fox, of course,' said Prue, yawning mightily, 'but they were simply wonderful, weren't they? I still miss them. Oh, why do people have to die?'

'Anno Domini?' suggested Caroline. 'Fox was in his eighties, wasn't he? Remember the fuss when we moved him into the house? He missed Ellen so dreadfully, dear old boy. Poor Ellen. What a business that was. Having that fall and then contracting pneumonia. Of course, she was in her seventies but one didn't think of age in connection with Ellen and Fox. They seemed immortal somehow.'

'I shall be seventy in three years' time,' said Prue gloomily. 'It doesn't bear thinking about, does it? It's all such nonsense. I don't *feel* seventy.'

'That's because you're not seventy,' Caroline pointed out, practical as ever. 'You're sixty-seven. Don't meet trouble halfway, as Ellen would have said.'

Prue looked at her almost crossly. 'It's all right for you,' she said.' 'Sixty-five is the turning point. You just wait. That's when you really begin to feel old.'

'You said that at fifty and again at sixty and at every birthday since,' said Caroline cheerfully. 'Anyway, it isn't your birthday for ages yet. Not until February, so why all the gloom? At least you haven't got an incipient moustache like I have.'

'Oh, honestly, Caroline.' Prue was torn between a desire to pursue the cause of her own gloom and a need to comfort Caroline. 'What nonsense. You still look very young and pretty.'

Caroline smiled at her affectionately. 'Who cares?' she asked. 'Are you going to finish that toast or is it going out for the birds?'

Prue hesitated. She felt that it would indicate a more genuine depth of misery if she were to reject the toast, a lack of interest in food always indicating emotional disturbance, but she was feeling unusually hungry this morning. The crisp brown toast looked rather inviting in its white china rack, standing beside a pot of her own homemade – and particularly delicious – marmalade, and, after all, she had a busy morning ahead of her. Caroline watched her, amused at her dilemma but sympathetic, too. Prue did her best to struggle against the bouts of depression which continued to dog her life but the recent breakdown of Hal's marriage had brought her to new brinks of misery and Caroline was careful not to dismiss lightly Prue's moments of very real unhappiness.

'I suppose Jolyon's already out in the orchard.' Caroline edged the toast rack a little nearer to Prue's plate as she picked up the milk jug. 'He'd already had his breakfast when I came down. What an absolute blessing he's been this holiday. I can't imagine how we shall manage without him when he goes back to Blundell's.'

'He is wonderfully practical, just like Johnny was, you know.' Prue sat up a little straighter and reached absent-mindedly for the toast. 'He's so good with engines and mechanical things. He looks just like him, too. Well, so does Hal, of course, so it's not particularly surprising.' She spread marmalade lavishly and poured herself some more coffee. 'I think it's done him good to be here with us for most of the summer.'

'I'm sure it has.' Caroline skated carefully away from the thin ice which covered the dark, troubled waters of Maria's rejection of Prue's son. 'He loves it here, doesn't he? He reminds me of Hal when I first saw him, oh, more than thirty years ago. He's such a good-looking boy and it's so lovely to see them together. Hal looks happier than I've seen him for a long time.'

'Oh, Caroline.' Prue put her cup down, clouds gathering. 'But what a pity, isn't it? How can a mother treat her child in the way that Maria behaves to poor Jolyon? It's utterly inhuman.'

'It's probably because Jolyon *does* look so much like his father.' Caroline began to pile the breakfast dishes into the sink. 'Every time Maria sees him she must be reminded of how she's behaved to Hal – and to Jolyon himself, of course. She always had much more time for Edward, didn't she, and he fits in so easily with her new life in Salisbury? He's a dear little boy but he does rather take the line of least resistance. Poor old Jolyon was out on a limb, at school down here in Devon while Hal was at *Dryad*. Terribly easy for Maria to simply move in with Adam Wishart taking Edward with her.'

'How she could!' Prue had now genuinely lost her appetite.

104

'And poor Hal going back for the weekend and finding them gone.'

Caroline sighed inwardly, recognising Prue's need regularly to relive her son's betrayal but searching for some way of leading her on to happier thoughts.

'I think that once he'd recovered from the shock Hal was almost relieved.' Caroline had said this before but knew that it was necessary to repeat it as often as was required. 'It's not as if he didn't know what was going on. It's a terrible thing to say but I think it's a good thing for both of them. Poor Jolyon was like a cat on hot bricks with Maria blowing hot and cold and it's better for him to be settled. He'll have to come to terms with it all, of course he will, and I'm not saying that I think that's easy because I don't. But I *do* think it's always best to know where you are and then you can deal with the problems sensibly. As for Hal, well, he has the comfort of knowing that he did his best. He has nothing with which to reproach himself.'

'I suppose that's true.'

It was clear that this thought was not bringing Prue a great deal of comfort and, as she washed up the breakfast things, Caroline cast about in her mind for more encouraging ideas.

'Aren't you getting your hair done this morning?' she asked, knowing that an hour with Sheila at Town and Country would cheer Prue up. 'We'll have a cup of coffee in Anne of Cleves afterwards, shall we? And didn't I hear you saying that you need some tapestry wool? Not long to Fliss's birthday now, don't forget.'

Prue pushed back her chair, looking happier. 'Thank goodness you reminded me. I've nearly finished it but I mustn't waste any time. It's come out beautifully.'

'She'll be thrilled with it.' Caroline gave a sigh of relief. They were on to firmer ground now. 'I think you're so clever to make up your own pictures. She'll recognise it at once. The front door standing open with a glimpse of the hall inside and the light and shade done so realistically.'

'No cleverer than your lovely jerseys.' Prue returned the compliment, feeling more cheerful. 'What's the time? Oh, goodness, I'll have Sheila on the warpath if I don't get a move on.'

'I'll just see if Theo wants anything and then we'll be off.'

The two women went out together.

In his basket, next to the Aga, Rex stirred and stretched. At fourteen he was rather too old to enjoy the trips to Totnes in the car and his early morning walk on the hill had tired him. He rolled on to his side and shut his eyes.

Jolyon came in from the scullery and looked round the empty kitchen. He'd been busy since early morning, chopping logs from the remains of an oak tree which had been uprooted in the gales during last spring. It had formed part of the boundary hedge beyond the orchard and two ancient apple trees had been brought down with it, its great weight smashing them into matchwood. During the summer holidays, helped by young Fred, he'd gradually filled bags with twigs and the smaller branches for kindling and the huge trunk had been sawed up into manageable pieces which he was now chopping into logs. This work gave him a great sense of satisfaction as well as a good appetite and, although he'd had a big breakfast, he was beginning to feel hungry again. He lifted the lid and pushed the kettle over on to the hotplate. Rex sighed deeply and Jolyon bent to stroke him, murmuring to him, glad that he was there. Rex opened one eye whilst his tail thumped once or twice in recognition. Crouching beside him Jolyon remembered when Rex had been a fluffy puppy, always getting into mischief, and his eyes filled with the ready tears which humiliated him so often lately. He was dreading going back to school, knowing that everyone knew what had happened and that he was often unable to hide these treacherous emotions. Keeping his head low lest anyone should come in, Jolyon stroked Rex's soft ears, trying to come to terms with the bitter knowledge that his mother didn't love him. Rex settled contentedly, enjoying the attention.

Calmed alike by the mechanical process of stroking and the undemanding company of his old friend, Jolyon told himself that Mummy hadn't liked Rex much either. She'd shouted at him and locked him in the garage and he, Jo, had been powerless to defend him. He hadn't been able to defend Dad either, or himself, come to that. Dad had tried to make it work, he knew that, but it hadn't been enough. The painful truth was that Mummy simply didn't love either of them. Not as much as she loved Ed and Adam Wishart.

He sat right down beside Rex as the pain in his heart doubled him up. It was silly and girly to behave like this but he just couldn't help himself. He loved her so much and she just didn't care about him. Try as he might he couldn't see why she was able to love Edward but not him and Dad. Dad was simply great, much, much nicer than that boring Adam Wishart who looked as if his hair was sliding off backwards, like a quilt off a bed.

'I don't like him as much as Daddy,' Ed had said when he'd come down to The Keep for a few days at Easter. 'Of course I don't. But what can I do about it?'

The thing was, he didn't really know what Ed could do, either, but there was something, well, almost disloyal in the way Ed was so nice to Mummy and Adam. He'd been really uncomfortable here at The Keep during the Easter holidays.

'I don't belong here like you do,' he'd said at last. 'My home's in Salisbury now, with my friends and school. I don't feel right here, really.'

Jo knew that Dad had been really upset by the way Ed behaved and, when he'd taken him back to Salisbury, Jo had insisted on going too. That's when he'd seen how nice Ed was to Adam. There had been a really awful bit with Mummy and Adam and Ed all standing together like a proper family, staring at Dad as if he was an unwelcome stranger and he'd stood beside Dad and held his hand. Dad had held it terribly tightly and he'd been determined that he wouldn't show that it was hurting. He hadn't liked Adam's house and he knew that Mummy was cross because Dad was selling their old house. He'd overheard them talking when he'd been packing up some of his things at Easter and she'd called Dad a dog in the manger.

'You've got that big place down in Devon,' she'd said 'but you grudge me having this.'

'I've never grudged you having this house,' Dad had answered. 'But do you seriously suggest that not only should I stand by while Adam Wishart takes my wife and my son but that I should offer him my house as well? He's got a house of his own. You've moved into it, remember?'

'It's much smaller than this,' she'd said in a whining sort of voice – and Dad had said 'Bloody tough!' in a really frightening voice and he, Jo, had hurried into the room just in case they had a row.

She'd hugged him then, and he'd wanted her to, although he felt he was being really disloyal to Dad, and she'd pretended that he had a home with her and Adam and Ed even if there wasn't a bedroom for him. She'd said that if Dad hadn't wanted to sell the house they could have stayed in it and he could have kept his old bedroom, making it sound as if it was all Dad's fault, but he'd been really upset at the thought of Adam moving in and taking Dad's place and he'd said he didn't mind all his stuff going down to The Keep.

'You can always sleep on a Put-u-up in Edward's bedroom,' she'd said, and he could see that Dad was only just holding on to his temper so he'd said that he'd like that, just to keep the peace.

'I've let you down, Jo,' Dad had said later, driving down to Devon. 'I'm sorry, old son. It's not that Mummy doesn't love you just as much as Ed but he has to be there because of school . . .'

'It doesn't matter,' he'd said quickly. 'I'd rather be at The Keep anyway. There's more room and you'll be there, too, now.'

'Of course I will,' he'd said. 'Every spare minute.'

He was, too. Of course, he had to be at *Dryad* most of the time because he was the Principle Warfare Officer and, when he'd gone to stay with him at *Dryad* for half term, Dad had shown him the room where D-Day was planned and the map of the landings in Normandy and it was really great. Dad had booked some riding lessons for him at the stables in Southwick and afterwards he'd taken him to the Chairmakers for a pub lunch although he wasn't old enough to have a pint of beer. Dad had dropped him off in Salisbury for two days and it had been really good to see Ed, even if he did have to sleep on the Put-u-up, but Mummy had been all over Adam as if she wanted to make certain that he, Jo, knew just how happy she was. It was as if she was showing off all the time and Adam made a fuss of Ed, too, as if to prove that Mummy and Ed were happier with him than they'd been with Dad. They certainly didn't need *him*. He'd hugged Mummy tightly the morning that he was leaving and suddenly realised that he was as tall as she was, taller.

'You mustn't be so silly,' she'd said, laughing but impatient, too. 'And you mustn't be jealous of Edward. He's still only a little boy, remember. You'll be sixteen next Christmas. Try not to be a baby . . .'

The kettle was boiling. Scrubbing at his cheeks with his wrists, Jolyon climbed to his feet and fetched a mug. The door opened suddenly and Caroline dashed in.

'Lost my purse,' she said. 'No, here it is on the dresser. Just off to Totnes, Jolyon. Are you OK here or do you want to come?'

'No, I'll get on in the orchard,' he said, fiddling about with his mug and the jar of instant coffee, careful to keep his back to her. 'See you later.'

The door closed behind her and he sighed with relief. He was quite good at that now, making his voice quite bright and cheerful, even though his heart was a tight little ball of pain in his chest. He'd had this silly hope that Mummy might have discovered that she didn't like Adam so much after all, and that, this summer, things might have been put right between her and Dad, but he could see now that it was just wishful thinking. It was almost easier when Bess and Jamie weren't around, because he didn't have to pretend so much that he was fine, and he'd felt a kind of relief when Fliss had taken them up to London to stay with their dad for a few weeks, although they'd be back soon to get ready for school.

He stirred his coffee and sat down at the kitchen table, looking about him at the familiar scene: the gleam of china on the dresser shelves; the patchwork curtains which matched the cushions on the window seat; bright rugs on the worn flags; the geraniums on the deep windowsill. He liked to be alone here, listening to Rex snoring and pretending that at any moment Ellen or Fox might come in. Fox would have been chopping wood in the orchard, just like he'd been doing earlier, and Ellen would say, 'Sitting here drinking coffee at this time of the day. Whatever next, I wonder.' Ellen had died before he was born but he could just remember Fox. He felt he really knew them, though, because of all the things Fliss had told him about them. Fox had looked after The Keep, making sure that it was in good repair and that everything worked properly. It must have made him feel good, looking about and knowing that things were running smoothly because of his hard work. Ellen would have felt like that, too, taking care of all the people who lived in The Keep, cooking delicious meals for them and making them happy.

For a moment he felt that they were with him, there in the quiet kitchen – Ellen pottering at her tasks, Fox taking his ease in the rocking chair by the Aga – and he was part of them, part of a long human chain; another Chadwick looking after his home and the people who lived in it . . .

Feeling consoled, Jo slipped from his chair, rinsed his mug at the sink and, with a last pat for the somnolent Rex, he went back to his work in the sunny orchard.

Chapter Fifteen

Late on Friday afternoon Mole drove from the Royal Naval College at Greenwich across London to Lisson Grove where he kept a narrowboat moored on the Grand Union Canal. He had been promoted to Commander after his posting as First Lieutenant in *Superb*, and sent on the Staff Course at Greenwich but it was during his two years with *Superb* that one of the other officers had introduced him to the delights of the inland waterways. He had persuaded Mole to join him and his wife for a holiday because he was in need of a spare pair of hands. His wife was heavily pregnant and unable to deal with the locks but neither of them wanted to give up their plan to explore the Coventry canal. With a certain amount of reluctance Mole had agreed, only to find himself falling in love with the way of life and the boats themselves. During these last few years he'd spent several of his leaves on the canals and, earlier this summer, he'd bought a forty-foot narrowboat called *Dorcas* and put her on a mooring in the Lisson Wide.

It was not a particularly beautiful stretch of water, placed as it was between the St John's Wood sub station on the north bank and a housing estate and recreation courts on the south, but it was convenient for Whitehall and Northwood, and not too far from Greenwich. *Dorcas* was berthed against a finger pontoon, bow against the towpath, along with a score or so of other boats and, once on board, it was a pleasant enough outlook. Most of the owners worked locally and lived aboard, although some used their boats as weekend retreats, and had planted small flower borders at the edge of the towpath on the north bank beside their moorings. Trees hid the mesh fence on the opposite bank and the atmosphere was one of a quiet backwater. Mole had a few regular visitors – Kit and Clarrie often came down for a drink at weekends, and Fliss brought Miles and the twins along when they were in town – and he'd experienced all the pride and pleasure of the home owner when he first showed them over his boat, charming and traditional in her maroon and cream livery.

111

This afternoon he was lucky enough to find a parking space in Lisson Grove. The gates, which were locked at night, and to which the boat owners held keys, were still open and he ran down the steps and passed on to the towpath. He looked his *Dorcas* over with a critical eye as he approached her, feeling in his pockets for his keys as walked along the pontoon and stepped aboard. He unlocked the companionway and went below, passing along the whole length of the boat before dropping his briefcase by the folding table in the saloon. He opened the double stable doors into the cockpit, so as to allow the fresh air to circulate, and paused for a moment. Ownership of the *Dorcas* was still new enough to give him a small thrill as he looked aft, through the saloon to the galley and beyond to his nighttime quarters. It was a simple layout, cosy, comfortable and neat, and the bulkhead lining of light oak gave the whole area a feeling of warmth.

Leaving the doors open he went aft to change out of his uniform and have a shower. The time was approaching when he'd have to take some of the linen and his clothes ashore for the winter but he was hoping that the weather would be kind for a little longer. There was a solid-fuel stove in the saloon which, when lit, kept the boat as warm as he could possibly desire and he was looking forward to a time when he might live aboard for a while. Perhaps he should take her round towards Greenwich and try her out this winter . . .

Whistling softly to himself, he pulled on a faded twill shirt and his old jeans, and went to hang his uniform in the large full-height wardrobe which was built just inside the saloon door, opposite the stove. He knew that untidiness was disastrous in small living areas, although he had much more room on *Dorcas* than he'd ever had in a submarine, but boarding school and the Navy had reinforced his naturally tidy instincts and he had no difficulty in keeping his small craft shipshape.

He went back to the galley and took a bottle of Cabernet Sauvignon from his small wine cellar, thinking with cheerful anticipation – tinged with a small degree of apprehension – of the weekend ahead. He was having a bit of a thrash on Sunday morning and tomorrow he must go shopping in preparation for it. The U-shaped galley housed a hob with a separate oven and grill but it was difficult to cater for large numbers and he'd learned to keep his entertainments to drinks and small eatables which came ready prepared. Sometimes his guests – usually the wives – brought home-made pies and quiches, which could be easily sliced and eaten standing or sitting on lockers on the afterdeck, but the whole emphasis was casual. Just lately it had become a bit of a cult amongst his oppos to take a bottle down to the *Dorcas* and spend an evening or a Sunday morning with Sam Chadwick. Mole, who had never seen himself as an innovator, was secretly rather pleased with the idea of being a leader of fashion and his love life had definitely taken an upswing.

Wandering out on to the afterdeck, watching some moorhens, Mole told himself that it had taken long enough. At thirty-seven – well, very nearly thirty-eight – it was certainly time that he got his act together. He was beginning to attract divorcees and even young widows, finding that, on the whole, they simply required an escort to take them to the theatre or to dinner, followed by uncomplicated lovemaking. These relationships were rather like his affair with Sin and he was able to accept them, knowing that these women were no more ready for a commitment than he was.

Relaxing, drinking his wine, pondering on the subject of supper, Mole suddenly realised that it was years now since he'd had one of his nightmares; years since the assassin, blank-eyed with closed, smiling lips, had inspired helpless terror. He could almost laugh at those fears – almost but not quite – knowing that his self-confidence was now more solidly established, not something to be swayed or destroyed easily.

He thought: I must get Sooz and Gus up for a holiday. The sprogs would love it.

He tested himself for the once ready terrors regarding the safety of three small children on a narrowboat but found that he could regard the prospect with equanimity, apart from the problem of squeezing them all in. Wondering how the family was, Mole emptied his glass and went below. He would drink another glass of wine while he was preparing his supper and making a shopping list. The weekend stretched delightfully ahead.

The following Sunday was harvest festival and the whole family went to church. Caroline drove Theo and Prue whilst Fliss brought the twins and Jolyon. Susanna was already there with Gus and the three children and Fliss slipped in beside her whilst the others sat in the Chadwick pew in front of them. Prue turned round to smile at the three little ones: Fred sitting beside his father; Lulu on her mother's knee; Podger making sure that everyone was organised properly. She had already been very busy. On her arrival she'd found it necessary to rearrange the table display of tins and jars of goodies which would later be distributed amongst the house-bound and elderly. Podger wished to be absolutely certain that her own gift – a tin of baked beans and jar of home-made plum jam –

113

should occupy a central position and, too, Lulu's packet of digestive biscuits needed to be placed to advantage. Lulu – who was equally strong-willed as her older sister – was determined that she should be in charge of her own offering and a scuffle had very nearly broken out. Fred had peaceably shown them a second small card table with a very smart red and white check cloth, clearly reserved for any last-minute donations, and the girls had been able to take their time in making a creditable showing; although it must be said that, even as Lulu was borne away in her father's arms, Podger reached to give her sister's biscuits a last judicial twitch before following her mother up the aisle. Fred carefully stood his jar of coffee and packet of tea at the back of the table and collected his hymn book.

Now, he smiled contentedly at his Great-Aunt Prue as he leaned against his father and looked about the church. He loved it. There was something so deep-down peaceful and right-feeling about it. He liked to think of all the people who had kneeled here down the ages, worshipping and praising God, singing the same hymns that he himself sang. Sometimes when his mother or Fliss were putting flowers on Great-Grandmother's grave he would come into the dim, cool church on his own and feel the peace washing over him. It was like another home . . .

Today it was full of autumn flowers which burned like flame, purple and blue, against the backdrop of ancient granite, sheaves of yellow corn leaned in corners and a sack of earthy, knobbly vegetables sagged against the foot of the lectern. A mound of richly crimson Victoria plums stood in a raffia basket on the altar steps; a pyramid of bright green apples was balanced carefully on the bronze cover of the font. Whilst members of the congregation whispered quietly together and the organist played softly, hidden in his loft, Prue handed over the back of the pew a knitted dolly which Lulu had left at The Keep, and Jolyon turned to grin at his small cousins. Podger bustled importantly; passing the dolly to Lulu, checking that Fred had his hymn book open at the right page – *Come, ye thankful people, come, Raise the song of Harvest-home* – making sure that her mother had remembered the bag of books and toys to keep Lulu quiet should she become restless during the sermon.

Susanna showed her the bag and Podger sat down at last, riffling through her own hymn book. Susanna, with a tiny wink sideways at Fliss, reached into the capacious bag and pulled out a small book which she held so that only Fliss could see. It was Roger Hargreaves' *Little Miss Busy*, and Fliss gave a small mirthful snort. The two sisters leaned together, chuckling silently, utterly at one in this moment which stretched back into time and embraced years of sharing.

Theo dropped his stick with a clatter; Prue began to hunt feverishly for her collection; Lulu talked loudly about her dolly; and the twins rolled their eyes despairingly at each other, acknowledging the embarrassing behaviour of their family as a whole. They sat together at the end of the pew feeling all the superiority of their youth and health and wisdom. Standing between the childish ways of their small cousins and the outdated idiocies of the older generation they were aware of a superabundancy of confidence. They were now at the age which could fully appreciate a parent who was ready to put a flat in London at their disposal, and their relationships with their father had been resurrected. His earlier indifference had been transmuted into a kind of easy, friendly guardianship and, though they were careful not to overstep the bounds of his tolerance, they were beginning to enjoy this unusual friendship, which carried none of the usual parental stresses. He assumed that they could look after themselves and would behave like adults and, because he expected it, they found themselves responding to his expectations. They were allowed to invite one or two friends to stay and they enjoyed exploring London and visiting Bess's eccentric godmother, Kit, at her Hampstead flat. Bess, especially, enjoyed this. Kit bought tickets to concerts all over London and Bess, who was trying to decide whether she should go to university before taking up music professionally, liked discussing her future with Kit and the funny old buffer, Clarrie, who lived upstairs. They treated her like one of themselves, listened to her views, and argued companionably until the early hours. Bess loved this adult treatment. Her father was firmly on the side of university whilst her mother agonised over which might be best for her with an intensity which could be irritating. Jamie had no such problems. He was going to King's College, London, to the Department of War Studies and from there to a military think-tank or even MI6. He had no doubts about his future and his father was solidly behind him.

Jolyon, sitting beside Bess, envied their insouciance and determination. There was a polish about them, a sophistication which seemed light years away from his own insecurity. The twins' vision was fixed wholly upon their respective futures – and in their view London was the only place to be – whilst he could barely think further ahead than the beginning of the next term. He clenched his fists between his knees, determined not to show despair, and his grandmother, who had now found her collection, beamed at him. He smiled back at her, grateful for her boundless kindliness and affection, wondering why he wanted nothing more from life than to stay at The Keep.

Behind him, Fliss watched him sadly. She was aware of his general fears – and his more particular misery – and wished that he could acquire some part of Jamie's confidence. As Jamie grew up his Miles-like qualities showed ever more clearly, and she was glad that both twins were at last getting to know and like their father.

Despite good intentions and high ideals, the last four years had not been easy. Once Miles was back in England it had been more difficult than they'd anticipated to maintain their marriage at the level on which they'd set their sights. Miles sometimes slipped back into his old dictatorial ways and Fliss discovered that an excellent means of control was to constantly – if gently – remind him of her noble act of generosity. It wasn't long before she realised that this merely gave her the power against which Uncle Theo had warned her and which she tried not to use. Instead, resentment tended to surface. Miles, having willingly given up his job in Hong Kong and transferred back to London, occasionally felt that his own sacrifice should be appreciated rather more than was shown so that Fliss, travelling regularly between London and The Keep, sometimes wondered why she'd ever given up her chance of freedom – and especially now that Maria had left Hal.

Her glance travelled along the pew to Theo, who sat with his head bowed, his hands clasped loosely between his knees.

'I feel so resentful,' she'd told him, after one less than successful weekend in London. 'He was doing his old "I know best" thing about the twinnies. You know, patting me on the head. Oh, not literally. Figuratively speaking, as if I were about twelve. And I felt all this resentment rushing up inside me. Every time I think I've conquered it, back it comes as bad as ever.'

Theo had watched her thoughtfully and she'd felt ashamed of herself, remembering how strong and confident she'd felt when she'd told Miles that she was ready to give their marriage a second try. His delight and gratitude had made her feel positively saintlike . . . She'd started to laugh whilst he'd smiled his Theo smile, eyes crinkling.

'I was going to be so good,' she'd wailed.

'You sound rather like Podger,' he'd said reflectively, 'when Caroline found her eating the sugar.'

'I just wish I could forgive and forget,' she'd said more soberly. 'It's terrible, the way the past clings.'

'I've sometimes wondered,' he'd answered, 'if that's what Christ meant about forgiving our brothers – and sisters – seventy times

116

seven. That it's more to do with having to forgive the same hurt each time it comes back to haunt us than forgiving a succession of sins against us. Brooding over the past makes us less able to grow into the future. We have to learn to let things go. Not to bury them down but to truly let them go and trust ourselves to the future, generously and single-mindedly.'

'But how?' she'd asked almost desperately. 'How is it possible?'

He'd remained silent for a long time. 'Only God can make real change possible,' he'd said at last, almost reluctantly, 'and only then if we really want it. God will meet us at the threshold of our fear but we are too busy believing that He cannot manage without our tinkering and interfering to put our trust absolutely in Him. We cannot make that ultimate commitment which makes it possible to die to ourselves so as to receive our security, at last, for once, from Him.'

Now, looking at his broad shoulders and bent head, Fliss wondered why he so rarely talked about his faith or attempted to convince his family of his own beliefs. Terror moved within her. How could she live without him; without his love and wisdom and support? He was over ninety and might not survive another winter.

As the organ swelled and the choir entered from the vestry the family got to its feet and Jolyon, turning, caught her eye and smiled at her. Fliss thought that she might break down and weep. He looked like her brother Jamie as she remembered him before he was killed, like Hal as a boy, and her love for him was enormous. If Hal and she had married he might have been her own son – and now Hal was free and she was committed to Miles . . .

Susanna stood Lulu on the seat between them and Fliss pulled herself together, swallowing back frustration and anxiety, smiling at her small niece. Lulu missed her footing, gave a small squawk of fright and Fliss gathered her into her arm and held her tightly, quietly comforting her. Podger leaned out to frown quellingly upon them both, gave a brisk glance round to make sure that the rest of her family was behaving properly, and prepared to sing.

117

Chapter Sixteen

Hal, letting himself into Kit's flat, gave a shout of greeting, dropped his grip on the hall floor and went into the kitchen. A note was propped against the kettle and he picked it up in his left hand whilst he shook the kettle experimentally in the other. Feeling its weight and judging it fairly full, he set it down and switched it on.

Dashed out to see a client. Back soon.

At least she'd put a time on it. Four thirty was scribbled at the top of the sheet, ripped from an A4 pad. The message reminded him of Winnie-the Pooh for some reason – or was it Rabbit? – and, anyway, who the hell cared? He knew that he was lucky to have Kit's flat to use from Monday to Thursday now that he was back at the MoD. He could have found himself a bedsit or asked his oppos at Whitehall if anyone had a spare room going but, just at present, there was an odd comfort in being here in Hampstead where no one was likely to question him about his private life. Anyway, it was possible that none of his married friends would want him too close at hand. Sympathetic though they were there was a wariness about them, as if the wretched business was in some way infectious, and the usually relaxed camaraderie was just the least bit strained. Kit was different, of course. Kit was a kind of extension of himself and he need not pretend for her benefit. As for Clarrie, he'd been a tower of strength in an understated, comforting way. It was such a relief not to have to be brave about it all.

Hal rinsed a mug under the tap and opened the cupboard where the coffee and sugar lived. He knew that he'd been hell to live with since the early spring when Maria had finally taken the plunge.

Hal thought: After all, I was expecting it. Why is it so bloody difficult to deal with it rationally?

As he spooned coffee and sugar into the mug he tried to decide why he simply couldn't accept it and let it go. It wasn't as if he loved her any more and at least Jolyon was old enough to cope with it now. Hal snorted bitterly. If *he*, at nearly forty-seven couldn't come to terms with it, how the devil was a poor kid of fifteen supposed to

119

deal with the fact that his mother didn't care about him? He knew that he was merely attempting to comfort himself, to be grateful for the fact that it hadn't happened earlier when Jo was still a child. For Jo it was a straightforward case of loss, of knowing that his mother, whom he loved, no longer loved him. For himself it was far more complicated. Pride came into it, along with resentment and humiliation and frustration. His marriage had been taken out of his control and there was nothing he could do about it.

Hal sat down at the kitchen table and put his head in his hands. Before Maria had left him there had been a long period of limbo. He'd known about Adam yet the most important thing had been to keep going; to keep the thing together for the sake of the boys. Looking back, he couldn't quite see now why it had seemed so vitally important that everything should be sacrificed to this end; that he should swallow his pride and turn a blind eye in the hope that Maria would tire of Adam as she'd tired of Keith Graves.

'That's because you can't remember when Jolyon was small and vulnerable,' Kit had said when he'd asked this question. 'It's difficult to imagine it now that he's so tall and nearly as strong as you are. We should never judge the past. We forget what the true situation was. How we felt and whether we were worn out or depressed and simply couldn't hold on for one more day. We always feel we could have done so much more, gone the extra mile and then we feel guilty. It was right that you did everything you could. You'd never have forgiven yourself if you hadn't.'

'It's so much more satisfying to be the one who leaves,' he'd said, refusing to be comforted. 'The one who leaves takes the power. It's an active role. Being left is humiliating.'

'You need to talk to Uncle Theo about power,' she'd said. 'He has a very low opinion of it. But if you're honest, little brother, it's only your pride which is hurt. You don't love her any more. Be grateful for that.'

He'd begun to protest but had fallen silent, remembering Jake. He too had been the one to do the leaving; Kit had remained with nowhere to lay the burden of her love. Now Sin had gone, too, and Kit was alone.

'Sorry,' he'd mumbled. 'This sort of thing makes you selfish. You must have found it lonely when Sin and Andrew got married.'

'It was a bit of a shock,' she'd admitted. 'We'd been together for over twenty years, Sin and I. Remember the basement flat in Scarsdale Villas? And then Pembridge Square. We've been here for twelve years, for heaven's sake. Luckily I'd got used to her being off with Andrew an awful lot but it was odd to be completely alone. Of course they're only downstairs and old Clarrie's a great chum but it's . . . strange.'

'Do you ever hear from Jake?'

He couldn't think why he'd asked such a question but she'd given him an odd, brooding, almost secretive glance and returned an evasive reply.

Now, he wondered if he should have pursued it. He sat up straight and drank some coffee, thinking about Fliss. This was where the root of the resentment was buried. If only Maria could have left him when Fliss and Miles were having their moratorium how easy it would have been. Why did she have to wait until now, when Fliss and Miles were making every attempt to make their marriage work? The answer was very simple. She'd waited for Adam to be free, for his wife to get tired of waiting and, with the inheritance from her mother, take the final step. With Liz gone it was simply a case of moving in with her lover, taking Edward with her.

He could clearly recall Fliss's face when he'd told her that Maria had gone. She'd been playing the piano in the drawing room and she'd turned as he'd come in, staring up at him while he poured out all the feelings he'd pent up during the drive down from Salisbury. Suddenly she'd struck the keys with her clenched fist, silencing him. 'Oh Hal,' she'd cried furiously. 'What *bloody* awful timing!'

A memory of a conversation he'd had with his grandmother slid into his mind. She'd been near the end of her life, weak but still quite clear in her mind, and she'd talked about his love for Fliss, wondering if the family had overreacted against it. He'd replied – somewhat bitterly – that it was rather too late to be wondering and she'd reminded him that Maria had been his choice and that she was the mother of his children.

'I have no intention of leaving her,' he'd assured her – and she'd pointed out that there was a difference between merely doing one's duty and investing one's actions with a positive attempt at love. 'And suppose that *she* decides to leave *me*?' he'd asked.

'In that case you are absolved,' she'd replied, 'and you have the freedom to make your own happiness, assuming that it is not at the expense of *any* of the children . . .' Well, Maria had left him but now he and Fliss were trapped by their individual concepts of loyalty: her determination to make her marriage work; his own affection for Miles and a horror of hurting him. Then there were the twinnies to think about, starting their A level year, and Jo who'd just returned to school with a brave cheerfulness that wrung Hal's heart. Oh, the different kinds of love . . .

121

Voices were raised on the landing outside and he heard Kit's key in the latch.

'That was Clarrie,' she said, appearing in the doorway. 'He's at a bit of a loose end, poor old duck. He hasn't been the same since Fozzy died. Nor have I come to that. He's suggesting we all go to the pub for supper. I said that would be OK. You don't mind, do you?'

He shook his head. 'Fine by me. I've just made some coffee. Want some?'

'You say the nicest things,' she said. 'Pour me a cup while I check the answerphone and then I want to hear all the news from The Keep.'

Later, lying in the bath, eyes closed, Kit told herself that she knew now how people felt when they lived a double life. It was more than a week since she'd bumped into Jake in Dover Street. He was coming from the Royal Academy and she'd been lunching with a client at the Arts' Club. The shock had galvanised them into a moment of silent stillness. At last she'd stretched out her hand and grasped his sleeve.

'It *is* you?' It was partly question, partly disbelief, and he'd smiled with complete understanding, covering her hand with his own.

'If it's you, then it's me,' he'd said – and, at such a silly, Jake-like answer, they'd both dissolved into laughter.

As she lay in the steaming, scented water, idly pulling the foam about her as if it were a blanket, she examined the quality of that laughter. It exploded out of them, a bubbling issue of joy, buried for fourteen years and now bursting up from somewhere deep inside to greet the autumn sunshine. They clung to each other – though at arm's length – bound by convention, yet subtly acknowledging the danger of this unexpected meeting. She guessed that each would wait for the other to make the first move.

'Oh, Jake,' she'd said, 'you've hardly changed. How dare you look so good. You must be over fifty. Oh, I can't believe this . . .'

'But you *have* changed,' he'd answered teasingly. 'There's rather more Kit than I remember . . .'

'Don't!' she'd cried. 'Don't look at me. I'm old and haggy' – but inside she'd been singing a tiny prayer of thanksgiving that it should be today, when she was all dressed up for lunch, that they should meet.

His glance had travelled over her in the old Jake the Rake manner and she'd felt the long-missed gut-melting excitement weakening her as she took his arm, unable now to meet his eyes. They'd walked along together towards Piccadilly and he'd pressed her arm close to his side.

'It's suits you,' he'd murmured.

'What does?' She'd sounded almost aggressive, suddenly sullen, frightened by the strength of her emotions.

'Middle age.'

She'd felt him laughing silently, hugging her hand close, and she'd laughed too, the tension running out of her.

'Pig!' she'd said, without rancour. 'OK, so I've put on weight.'

'But I meant it.' He'd taken her hand from his arm and touched it briefly with his lips. 'You're beautiful. Not fat, no. Rounded, womanly, but not matronly, thank God. How thoughtless of you, Kit, to still be so attractive.'

'Oh Jake,' she'd said sadly. 'I've missed you so much . . . Where are we going?'

'Who cares? This looks OK,' and he'd steered her into a coffee bar and settled her at a corner table.

They'd sat there for hours – or so it had seemed – yet only briefly had they mentioned the present. He'd taken her left hand, running the ball of his thumb along the third finger.

'No one?' he'd asked softly, without looking at her, and she'd admitted it harshly, ashamed that he'd retained his power for so long whilst she had been displaced so completely . . . How had he managed?

'And you?' she'd asked reluctantly, cursing herself, wishing she could be proudly indifferent. 'Madeleine . . . ?'

'Oh, yes.' He'd nodded, almost absently, still staring down at their joined hands. 'Madeleine and four little girls.'

The silence had been full of bitter memories – she could almost taste the sharpness on her tongue – but when at last he'd looked at her she'd realised that, after all, none of it mattered. He was still Jake – and she was Kit; the two of them together as they'd always been, back in another life where Madeleine and her four little girls had no place. With that one long look the intervening fourteen years vanished into the smoky atmosphere that drifted about them.

'Sin's married, can you believe it?' she'd asked, leaning towards him. 'Honestly, it doesn't seem possible . . .'

How swiftly the old intimacy had been established between them. Heads together, chuckling away, destroying reputations, they'd drunk endless cups of coffee, until Jake glanced at his watch. Kit seized his brown wrist, covering it with her hand.

'Don't say you have to go.'

'A meeting,' he'd said. 'At the BNP. I shall be late. Are we going to do this again?'

The tension was back. Warily they'd watched each other, waiting. Neither could quite bear to say goodbye; neither wished to be the one to break the rules.

'When do you go back?' She'd tried to make the question casual.

'Madeleine is in Florence with the girls for another fortnight.' She'd translated it not as an answer but as an invitation. He waited.

'Perhaps lunch tomorrow, then?' It had been an effort – after all, she had her pride – but lunch still sounded respectable. Surely two old friends could have lunch together without suspicions being roused?

'Lunch?' He was laughing at her. 'Why not? Lunch would be good. Shall I pick you up?'

'No,' she'd answered quickly, much too quickly. 'No, I shall be with a client tomorrow morning. What about Le Caprice? At a quarter to one?'

He'd pulled back her chair, helping her into her jacket, barely touching her, but his proximity was disturbing, exciting . . .

The water was cooling into discomfort. Kit sat up, reaching for her Roger et Gallet, trying to calm her desperate neediness with rigorous soaping. Two lunches and two long afternoons in celibate, agonising intimacy had made her nervous. She suspected that each was waiting for the other to give way and she feared that it would not be Jake.

Kit thought: Either way I lose. Active or passive, I shall encourage him to be unfaithful and then I shall feel guilty. But why should I? He was mine first. We belong . . .

The sudden hammering on the bathroom door caused her to cry out with fright, the soap shot from her suddenly clenched fingers and her heart hammered in her side.

'You'll get waterlogged if you stay in there much longer.' Hal's voice was brutally cheerful. 'Get a move on, woman. Clarrie and I are starving to death out here.'

Kit closed her eyes, trying to control her trembling limbs, mocking herself for her foolishly fragile state.

'Coming,' she called – and pulled out the plug. 'Give me ten minutes and I'll be with you.'

On Friday she and Jake were going to the theatre, followed by a late supper – and then what? Kit's fingers shook as she dragged the towel about her. He'd suggested the theatre, booked the seats; he should be the one to make all the moves. It was at times like

124

these that she truly missed Sin, the old Sin who belonged to long, lazy weekends and idle companionship, who never judged nor condemned but listened and sympathised and who shared joys and sorrows equally. How pleasant and easy it would be to discuss this with her, to describe these disturbing feelings and explain the tiresome moral dilemma.

Kit hung the towel on the heated rail and shrugged into her dressing gown. There was no point in repining. Sin had joined the ranks of sensible married women and she might not look favourably on any plan which involved betraying one of her kind. Kit knew she mustn't risk it. She simply couldn't cope with Sin going all sanctimonious on her. It was for this same reason that she dare not tell Fliss, who would be back in London soon. Fliss and Hal had stuck it out and, whilst they would both be sympathetic, they were hardly likely to approve of her encouraging Jake to commit adultery.

Suddenly, as she cleaned the bath with vicious swipes, Kit felt as if everyone had grown up whilst she wasn't looking and only she was left – still curled up in the dog basket, listening to Ellen and Fox bickering, snuffing up the comforting odour of clean, warm dog – a careless yet insecure child.

'Shit,' she muttered, swilling off the cleaning solution, 'shit, shit, shit.'

Feeling ashamed and inadequate, she slipped into her bedroom and began to dress. She reached for the heavily chased silver locket, which she was rarely without, and paused, holding it in her hand. 'I always hoped it would be my morning gift to you,' he'd said on that terrible day when they'd finally parted. She closed her eyes, her hand clenched upon the locket, reliving the moment, hearing the music drifting from the café's kitchen: Roberta Flack singing 'Killing me Softly with his Song'. Despite her effort to regain control of her emotions Jake's face swam into her vision, the memory of his voice and touch blocking out every other sensation except her absolute need of him. 'My mother gave it to me on my twenty-first birthday,' he'd said, 'and told me that I should give it to the woman to whom I gave my heart although this might not be the woman I married.'

Sitting motionless, sunk in thought, Kit reminded herself that Jake had never been the physically faithful type; that there had always been other women, which is why they'd nicknamed him Jake the Rake. 'That's just sex,' Sin had said once. 'It's you he loves,' and Kit had known it to be true. This being the case, it was foolish to believe that Jake would have remained faithful to

125

Madeleine whom he had never truly loved. Clearly his marriage had survived his rakish tendencies so what did it matter if she took back to herself a little of his love?

So she reasoned and, by the time she was ready to join Hal and Clarrie, she was already able to justify any future actions which might assuage that pressing, overwhelming desire.

Chapter Seventeen

As soon as he woke, Theo knew that the weather had changed. His bedroom, which faced east, was filled with a soft dim light and the curtains were stirred by a cool breeze which touched his face and throat. He shivered a little and, resisting the urge to huddle lower under the blankets, pushed them aside and swung his long legs over the side of the bed. Reaching for his dressing gown but not bothering to look about for his slippers he crossed to the window and looked out at the familiar and well-loved scene. Tender blue skies shot through with the gold and crimson of the dawn were yielding before the soft grey clouds which billowed in from the west, dropping their moisture on the fertile land and wrapping the hilltops in mist.

Wrapping the warm folds of his dressing gown about his gaunt frame, Theo sat down in the chair by the window. Just lately he'd had the sensation that he was waiting for something; one last thing, as it were, before death. This was not far off now, and his heart speeded a little with joy at the thought of his imminent absolute union with God. Yet there was something more, it seemed, something to be dealt with before he could embark on the final journey. His family, held constantly in his thoughts and prayers, was his continual concern. He knew that his natural tendencies towards the contemplative life had made it difficult for him to force his beliefs upon them. His horror of proselytising, his awareness of his own inadequacies, both these held him back and he suffered now in the knowledge that he had failed them. Maybe he was to be given one last chance to put this right. The prayer which had comforted Freddy helped him as well. He was only too aware of his own meannesses and limitations but the last part of the prayer held him firm.

> *You will not take from me, my God,*
> *what you once gave me*
> *in your only Son, Jesus Christ,*

in whom you gave me all I desire;
so I shall rejoice:
you will not delay, if I do not fail to hope.

Just lately, as he prepared himself for that ultimate inflowing of God, he was aware of the presence of the small boy he'd first seen four years ago in the courtyard. He'd been sitting with Hal, he remembered, deciding what must be done to restore The Keep and talking about his grandmother's summerhouse. The boy had come running in, looking eagerly about him, unafraid and full of life. He'd seen him several times since, on the stairs and in the garden, and heard him singing in the hall – the song the children loved, a kind of American Old MacDonald's farm – and each time Theo felt his heart leap in his breast, acknowledging him, relieved that The Keep should be passing into his care.

Yet who was he? Sometimes Theo wondered if he was a shade of past Chadwicks, yet the whole impression he gave was of the future. He was a dark Chadwick, looking like he himself had looked as a child; like Susanna and Mole. When Prue had come rushing out, that first time, to tell them about Susanna's new baby, he'd been certain that it was a premonition and he'd been almost shocked when she'd told them that another girl had arrived. Lulu and Podger were dark Chadwicks, true enough, but young Fred was the image of his father and the other children were grown up now. The twins looked like Miles whilst Jolyon was a fair Chadwick in the making – which left Mole. Well, there was plenty of time for Mole to marry and have children, or Susanna and Gus might yet produce another boy . . .

Theo drew his dressing gown more closely around him as the chill, damp air rippled in through the open window. The Keep had survived its crisis – though it eventually proved a long and expensive business – and it would stand strong again. Within the family, however, there were still areas of disturbance. Saddened though he'd been by the breakdown of Hal's marriage, he guessed that it would be a relief to Hal that it was over. He'd seen it through for as long as he could but the effort had been very great and, once his hurt pride had healed, Hal would recover and make his home at The Keep as Freddy had always hoped. As for Jolyon . . . Theo frowned a little. The rejection of a parent could leave a deep, painful scar and Jolyon had a long way yet to go. At least, here with his grandmother and Caroline, his pain was eased and he drew great comfort from being busy and useful. He was a favourite with his smaller cousins – especially young Fred – and his relationship with Fliss was strong and necessary to them both. Jolyon would

128

be important to the future of The Keep if only because of his great love for it.

The twinnies, on the other hand, were already moving away. Physically and mentally they were like their father, determined and filled with a sense of purpose. They both had their sights fixed on achievable destinies and nothing would turn them aside. They would fight for what they wanted and, though youth might make them careless and selfish, yet, like Miles, they would be prepared to admit their faults and make amends. Theo wondered how Fliss felt as she saw them growing up, so like the father who had ignored them but whose company they now enjoyed. It was Jolyon who shared her love of The Keep, who understood her passion for the moors and beaches, who entered into her concern for the members of the family. How strange it all was, how incomprehensible.

He feared that Hal's freedom might undermine Fliss's efforts within her own marriage but he sensed that she had a very deep affection for Miles which had grown stronger and deeper in these last few years, despite their moments of exasperation with each other. Nevertheless it must be hard for Fliss to keep her energies concentrated on the relationship; to resist the temptation to throw it all away so as to seize the happiness with Hal which had always eluded her.

Sitting there by the window, Theo was aware of a creeping sense of premonition, as of some imminent disaster. Despite his innate humility, he was aware that the family looked to him as its head. He guessed that Hal would reach great heights in his career and knew that it would be some time before he could truly make his home permanently at The Keep. Who, then, would be at hand to bridge the gap between his own death and Hal's retirement? Anxiety edged with fear pressed in upon him, along with the sensation of waiting: but for what? How was he to deal with this unknown requirement, he who knew so well his meannesses and limitations? Presently he straightened his shoulders, smiling a little. He was also acquainted with the paralysing effect of worry, the draining numbness of fear.

> . . . *so I shall rejoice:*
> *you will not delay, if I do not fail to hope.*

Resolutely he emptied his mind and waited for guidance.

On Saturday mornings, the Mallory family divided itself into three parts. Podger went with her father to the studio; young Fred and Lulu were dropped at The Keep on the way; Susanna was able to have the morning to herself to indulge in whatever luxury might appeal to her. Being alone, she'd discovered, was a luxury in itself and often she did no more than a little quiet gardening or sit drowsing over the newspaper. Saturday lunch at The Keep had become a very pleasant habit and the little family would meet up again in the big warm kitchen, full of the morning's achievements.

On this damp and misty morning Susanna waved them off with the usual mix of pleasure and guilt, and returned to finish her breakfast in peace. It was not an outdoor sort of morning, so she made another pot of coffee and settled down to read Janie's letter. Nine months earlier, Janie who had worked so happily for Gus, had married one of Gus's clients who was selling up his pub and moving to Herefordshire to take over a country hotel. She wrote long letters describing her happiness, the hotel, its guests and, now, joy of joys, she wrote to say that she was expecting a baby and that David was delighted . . . Susanna smiled, glad for her friend, and made a note on her big pad to buy a special card to send. Janie regularly begged them to visit her but it was difficult to organise with three children and the business to be looked after. Since Gus had not yet replaced Janie, Susanna had started to go into the studio on the mornings that Lulu was at Brimhay playgroup. It was fun to be back at work and they were both wondering if they could manage without bringing in a new assistant. It would save on expenses, and they could let out the upstairs flat to make some extra cash, but the crunch would come during the school holidays.

Susanna sipped her coffee thoughtfully. Prue and Caroline were always delighted to have the children but there were limits to how much she could impose upon them. Maybe she and Gus should consider a compromise. It might be wiser to find someone to work part time, so as to share the load with her until the children were older; better than trying to do too much and none of it properly. Susanna enjoyed her children; she knew how quickly they grew, how precious those early years were, and she didn't want to miss any of it . . . Well, only Saturday mornings, anyway. After all, Lulu was only four; she was such a bright, quirky little girl, full of fun, although she could be stubborn and devious. She was probably driving her poor Aunt Prue to distraction at this very moment. Fred would be quietly getting on with his weekly tasks. He was big enough now to be useful although, being an impractical child, he needed a certain amount of guidance. How he had enjoyed being Jolyon's assistant during the summer holidays – and how he missed his older cousin now that Jolyon was back at Blundell's. Dear old

Fred was such an odd, dreamy child and so kind to his bossy little sisters. As for Podger . . . Susanna chuckled to herself. How Podger loved Saturday mornings; tidying the office, organising her father, questioning everything . . . Susanna yawned with contented idleness, poured some more coffee and returned to Janie's letter.

'Studio Graphics,' said Podger in her most businesslike voice. 'Who's calling, please? *Just* one moment.' She put her hand over the receiver. 'It's someone called Roger,' she told her father.

Gus held out a resigned hand. It was impossible to prevent Podger from answering the telephone, one of the things she enjoyed doing most, but he hesitated to teach her how to screen incoming calls. To put such power into her small capable hands made him feel oddly breathless. Meanwhile he was obliged to listen to a client who could waste hours chatting about nothing in particular. He relaxed in his chair watching Podger, who was now back in her seat, checking some advertising copy. Her legs swung and kicked as she bent over the page, a frown of concentration on her face, and he wondered if you were finally grown up when your feet could touch the floor . . .

She looked up at him, pulling a face, and presently, when he'd got rid of his client, he said, 'Got a problem?'

'It's just that this isn't true. It says, "Here in Devon, where the sun always shines . . ." Well, that's silly, isn't it?'

'You have to remember that the poor guy is trying to sell holidays,' explained Gus. 'He wants to fill his hotel up. No point in saying that it rains all the time, is it?'

'But when the people come for their holiday they'll see it isn't true,' argued Podger. 'Then they'll never come again.'

'You think they'll feel cheated?'

'Lied to,' she said uncompromisingly. 'You wouldn't want to stay with people who lie to you, would you? *I* wouldn't.'

'I suspect that most people will know it isn't true,' said Gus.

'Then they'll think he's stupid, which is just as bad as being a liar.'

Gus sighed. 'Take your pick,' he said. 'It's called advertising. How would *you* do it?'

'I'd list all the good things,' said Podger at once. 'There's lots of really good things in Devon. You don't have to lie. Or be stupid,' she added crushingly.

'It's the client's copy.' Gus felt the need to defend himself. 'He's written it himself and he doesn't want it changed.'

Podger snorted contemptuously. 'I hope no one comes to stay in his silly hotel. That'll show him,' she muttered.

'Then he won't earn any money,' Gus pointed out, 'and he won't be able to pay my bill and then I won't be able to feed you lot.'

Podger was silent, thinking this through, and Gus wondered if they were about to embark upon a discussion on the ethics of the business world.

'How about some coffee?' he suggested cunningly. 'Are you up to it, do you think? I hope we've got enough milk. You may have to dash over to the Happy Apple.'

She was off her chair immediately, vanishing into the kitchen, and he sighed with relief. He heard the gush of water and the clang of the kettle's lid; mugs were rattled and drawers banged. The telephone rang but, before he could reach it, Podger was out of the kitchen in a flash and had seized the receiver.

'Studio Graphics. Who's calling? *Just* one moment, please.'

At the same moment, Fred was earnestly discussing miracles with his Uncle Theo at the kitchen table at The Keep. They were all having a mid-morning break. Caroline was supervising Lulu's mug of milk, Fred was having orange juice and the grown-ups were drinking coffee. It was Prue who had reminded Fred of his recent Scripture lesson. She'd been pottering about, preparing lunch and talking jokingly about feeding the five thousand.

'Did the extra loaves and fishes just appear?' he mused. 'I wish I could have been there. Have you ever seen a miracle, Uncle Theo?'

'I think that it might be easy,' said Theo cautiously, 'to confuse miracles with magic. We can see miracles quite often if we're watching for them. Small human miracles.'

Fred looked puzzled. 'Human miracles?'

'It's how God works if we let him. Supposing the five thousand are a group of rather ordinary people. They've packed their small lunches and left their homes to go to listen to this Jesus, miles out in the hot dry desert, and when lunchtime comes they're all asked to sit down. Well, no one wants to be the first one to produce his lunch. He's going to feel a bit greedy eating it all by himself and he isn't sure that his neighbour has brought any. So he sits tight and waits. Presently a small boy, just like you, generously offers up his lunch to be shared amongst all those people. Can you imagine how those people felt who had brought food but weren't willing to share it?'

'They'd feel very small,' said Fred readily, 'and a bit embarrassed.'

'Quite right.' Theo nodded thoughtfully. 'And what do you think they might do?'

'I think they'd get out their own food,' said Fred, entering into the spirit of the thing, 'but they'd do it in a sort of casual and a bit of a surprised way. As if they'd just remembered that they'd brought some. You know? "Oh, *lunch*. Why didn't you say so before?" sort of thing. And then they'd share theirs, too, because they'd feel ashamed.'

'Quite,' said Theo. 'Don't you think that it's quite a miracle to get a crowd of selfish, hungry people to share their small rations? Remember that it was a poor country and these people had to work very hard to feed themselves. It was wonderful that one small boy's unselfishness should inspire such a crowd. It was a human miracle. It happens all the time.'

Prue, watching him, was suddenly moved to say that it was how Theo had influenced the entire family at one time or another. Unobtrusively, without even being aware of it himself, he had made them all want to be a little better. She tried out the phrases in her head, anxious lest she embarrass him, but before she could get her thoughts in order Lulu upset her mug of milk and the moment passed.

Chapter Eighteen

Clarrie shouted, 'Come in' and hauled himself to his feet as Sin came into the kitchen. He switched off the television, trying not to mind that he was missing the news, and greeted her cheerfully. He saw at once that something was wrong. Since her marriage to Andrew, Sin had visibly mellowed – 'She's like a contented cow,' Kit had observed rather waspishly – and she was clearly very happy. This evening however there was a *distrait* air about her, a preoccupation which allowed no room for the formalities. She cut short his enquiries as to her health and came straight to the point.

'I'm worried about Kit,' she said, pushing her fair hair behind her ears and sitting down on the sofa which he had just vacated. 'I've just been talking to her downstairs and there's something up.'

Clarrie waited. The arthritis in his knees made him cautious these days about carelessly getting up and sitting down. He was finding the two long flights of stairs to his eyrie very wearing and he tended to think ahead about unnecessary shopping trips.

'Would you like a drink?' he asked. 'Scotch, perhaps? Coffee?'

'No, no,' she said distractedly. 'Not for me, thank you. Have you noticed anything, Clarrie?'

Sighing a little, Clarrie painfully lowered himself on to the seat beside her.

'She's a bit taken up with Hal?' It was a suggestion rather than an answer. 'He's having a rough time of it, poor chap. And Fliss is in and out a bit, when she's up in town, that is. Kit's rather busy, one way and another.'

'It's not that.' Sin sat quite still, staring ahead of her. 'She's all evasive and touchy. You know how you are when you don't want to tell people the truth but you don't want to lie to them either?'

'My dear girl,' said Clarrie testily. 'It's many years now since my life was exciting enough for me to want to lie about it.'

'That's what I mean.' She looked at him with such intensity that he began to feel nervous. 'Kit and I have always shared

135

things. Why should she want to hide anything unless it was pretty important?'

'I accept that you are very close,' he said cautiously, 'but might it not be reasonable that she should occasionally want to keep a secret, even from you?'

Sin stared at him. 'No,' she said, flatly.

'Oh, really.' Clarrie began to laugh. 'Be realistic. You're a married woman, now. Perhaps Kit finds it difficult to be quite so open as when you were both single together.'

'That's why I'm suspicious,' said Sin at once. 'Don't you see, the only reason for Kit to be cagey is if she's messing about with a married man. Nothing else has changed. She thinks I shall disapprove of her, you see, now that I'm married.'

Clarrie looked at her, alarmed by such a devious and feminine calculation.

'Surely there could be many other reasons,' he began – but Sin was already her shaking her head.

'I don't think so. We still discuss everything, you know. Old habits die hard.'

'You terrify me,' murmured Clarrie. 'Does Andrew know that you . . . er, discuss everything?'

Sin smiled at him pityingly. 'Of course not,' she said. 'Don't be silly. But that's not the point. The point is that Kit more or less admitted it. I could tell at once that a man was involved. She's got that thin, sparkly look about her. D'you know what I mean?'

'No,' said Clarrie, out of his depth. 'I can't say I do.'

'I knew at once.' There was a certain satisfaction in her voice. 'But when she got all evasive I asked her outright.'

'And what did she say?' asked Clarrie, fascinated by these disclosures. He tried to imagine himself in such a situation with Andrew, say, or Hal, and felt a new depth of admiration for the female sex.

'She prevaricated,' said Sin grimly. 'So I taxed her with it. I said, "I bet he's married, isn't he?" and first of all she got confused and then she got cross.'

'Is that so unreasonable?' Clarrie shrugged. 'Bit personal, isn't it?'

'She said that I was bound to be on the side of the dear little wifie and then realised she'd given herself away and shut up like a clam.'

'Would it be too outrageous,' Clarrie suggested diffidently, 'if I were to say that it's none of our business?'

She frowned at him. 'Of course it's our business. Kit's such a

136

twit. The last thing she needs is to be involved with a married man. She'll think it's the great love of her life and then he'll drop her flat and she'll be devastated. Ever since Jake, each new man has been the one she's been waiting for. It's as if she never learns. It's like the first time every time for Kit. It's terrifying.'

'But what are we supposed to do about it? If she doesn't want to talk to *you* about it, she's hardly likely to confide in *me*.'

'Just keep an eye on her,' begged Sin. 'Andrew and I are going on holiday to Italy for a few weeks. Please, Clarrie. Look after her while I'm away. I'm really worried about her.'

'Of course I will,' he said tetchily. 'Naturally. But don't expect me to interfere, that's all. Not unless she asks me to.'

'Sorry.' Sin looked at him, as if she were only just seeing him properly. 'I know you look after her, Clarrie, especially since I moved downstairs, but I haven't seen her like this for, oh, years. I've got a horrid presentiment about it.'

'Fair enough.' He smiled at her, trying to soothe her. 'Who am I to deny a woman's intuition? I'll keep an eye on her, don't worry.'

'Bless you.' She leaned across and gave him a quick kiss. 'What would we do without you?'

'Sure you don't want a Scotch?' He didn't bother to answer the familiar question. 'Or coffee?'

'No, I must get back to Andrew. He'll wonder what's happened to me. Thanks, Clarrie. I'll see you before we go, anyway. Don't get up . . .'

She disappeared and Clarrie remained where he was, only too grateful to obey her injunction, brooding on what she'd been saying. It was true that he and Kit had drawn closer together since Sin and Andrew had married but it was odd how the formalising of the relationship had changed the atmosphere within the house. The balance had altered and the casual, easy-going feel of the place had disappeared. Having come to married love late, Sin and Andrew were making up for lost time and, whilst neither Kit nor Clarrie blamed them, it took time adjusting to having a very married couple on the ground floor. The bachelor-pad flavour had vanished, along with the informal get-togethers and the impromptu parties. Fozzy dying at the respectable age of fifteen hadn't helped. Clarrie missed him terribly. He still found himself talking to him, reaching down to pat him, listening for his deep-chested bark. The sight of his lead – with which he refused to part – could reduce him to unmanly tears, and walks on the Heath were simply not the same without him.

Kit felt exactly like that, and they comforted each other, although

Clarrie knew that it would be madness to attempt to replace Fozzy. As he pointed out to her, a top-floor flat combined with his arthritic knees were rather anti-puppy.

Sitting on his sofa, wishing that he had a remote control gadget for the television, Clarrie wondered about Kit. He hadn't seen her for a few days but had put it down to the fact that Hal was with her four evenings a week whilst he was at Whitehall. He tried not to let his own loneliness impinge on their privacy but sometimes it got the better of him. He was very fond of Hal. He stirred irritably. Sin had destroyed his peace of mind and he felt edgy and unsettled. Glancing at his watch, he decided that it was too late to do anything about Kit tonight – but the weekend was approaching. He'd suggest a potter down to the pub or he'd cook supper for her and perhaps, in his clumsy roundabout masculine way, he'd see if he could discover if there were any grounds for Sin's fear.

Groaning, Clarrie climbed to his feet and prepared to resume his evening's viewing.

'Where shall we go then?' asked Fliss, settling herself in the driver's seat. 'Are you certain you want to go anywhere at all? You don't have to, you know. It's only the first day and we've got a whole two weeks ahead.'

Miles watched her smilingly as she clipped on her seat belt and started the engine. It was good to be starting a fortnight's leave. He felt tired, terribly tired, and he'd been glad to come down to The Keep instead of going further afield. He was rather looking forward to being fussed over by Prue and pottering about generally but, now that the sun had broken through, he'd felt a sudden longing to be out in the fresh air.

'Nothing major,' he said, glancing automatically into the wing mirror as she reversed. 'Just a bit of a drive and a short walk somewhere. Not a hike or a scramble. Something civilised.'

'I know just the place.' Fliss drove carefully down the drive, avoiding potholes, and turned left into the lane. 'We'll go to Shipley Bridge. I don't think you've ever been there. It's wonderful in the early summer when the rhododendrons are out but it's lovely at this time of the year, too . . .'

He let her talk, leaning back comfortably, trying to relax. He didn't care much for being driven, excellent driver though Fliss was, but he was too tired today to cope with the narrow lanes.

He thought: I'm getting old. It's something we say so often but today I really feel it. I've been overdoing it . . .

Fliss was talking about her brother, now, repeating something

Susanna had said about Mole being a mole in more senses than one. She talked quite casually, perhaps hoping he might give her a small hint, but he remained silent. He knew that Mole had had at least one sensitive posting fairly early in his career, and he also guessed that he'd had one or two assignments of a risky nature since, but he had no intention of discussing it. He might be retired from the Navy now but the Official Secrets Act still held good.

He wound down the window and felt the afternoon sun, warm on his face. Fliss drove across the A38 at Dartbridge and continued on the back roads towards South Brent, evidently undismayed by his refusal to be drawn.

'Beats me how you know your way about,' he murmured.

'I've lived here for over thirty years, on and off,' she said cheerfully. 'Look how you know your way around London and you haven't spent nearly so much time there as I have in Devon.'

'I suppose that's true.' He watched the dappling fire and russet of the sun on the leaves, caught a glimpse of a field of golden stubble through an open gateway, and was surprised by an aching nostalgia. In the lane, beneath the thorn, billowy clouds of plumed seed adorned the dense clusters of willowherb; beyond their heads the purple shoulder of the moor rose into a chalk-blue sky where a buzzard circled lazily.

'Are you OK?' Fliss was glancing at him, puzzled, no doubt, by his long silence.

He stirred as if from sleep and nodded, folding his arms across his chest. 'I'm fine. How much longer is it to this place?'

'Nearly there.'

The car passed between high stony banks, through a small splashy ford, and stopped short of the little bridge.

'Hardly anyone here,' said Fliss with satisfaction, 'but I'll leave the car this side. Do you want your jacket?'

Shrugging himself into his Harris tweed, Miles strolled on to the bridge and stood leaning against the sun-warmed stone, watching the race of peaty sparkling water tumbling over the boulders.

'Good, isn't it?' Fliss stood at his shoulder, hands in pockets, smiling with pleasure. 'It's always impressive after a bit of rain. It's surprising how quickly the level drops, though.'

He followed her on to the metalled road which led up to the Avon Dam and she linked her arm in his.

'Civilised enough for you?'

'It's wonderful,' he admitted. 'All this natural beauty without having to get your feet wet. I approve.'

'I thought you would.'

139

She was laughing at him and he found her hand and held it. The last four years had been nearly everything he'd hoped for and he felt another pang of the unfamiliar nostalgia.

'I'm feeling sentimental,' he told her. 'It's the sort of day which encapsulates all the good moments of your life and you feel certain that you can make the future one long golden autumn afternoon.'

'Sounds good to me,' she said as they strolled forward together. 'I'm glad there have been some good moments.'

'Of course there have,' he said quickly – and hesitated. 'For you, too, I hope.'

She squeezed his hand. 'Lots,' she assured him. 'I'm sorry it hasn't always been . . . well, easy. You know. Giving up Hong Kong and things.'

'Oh, darling . . .' he began, distressed lest she should think that he might be regretting anything. 'It's been worth it. These last four years have been so good . . .'

'It's OK,' she said quickly. 'Honestly. Look at the robin in the rowan tree.'

He accepted her change of direction, watching the robin as he hopped amongst the scarlet berries and fluttered to the close-cropped turf below. White water thundered over a steep fall of rock and a sudden gust of wind fled down the deep-cut valley from the moors above, stirring the branches which leaned over the fast-flowing current. On the further bank yellow leaves sprinkled gently down, floating on the smooth skin of a deep, secret pool, drifting against the pitted stones. The dipper flew low and straight, speeding upstream, coming to rest on a flat rock. He bobbed, cleverly camouflaged against his background, and his sweet warbling song could be heard clearly above the tumult of the river. Miles and Fliss stood motionless until he took flight again, swift as an arrow, disappearing far upstream.

They drew apart, as if waking from a dream, and smiled at each other.

'We'll go as far as the gate,' she said, 'but next time we'll go to the bridge and after that it'll be the dam and no shirking.'

'How far is the bridge?' He didn't want to be a killjoy.

'Too far today,' she told him firmly. 'The gate's quite far enough and anyway we shall lose the sun soon.'

He smiled, reminded of her grandmother, and gave in meekly. Yet he feared to give the impression that he was an old man. He was barely sixty but he wondered if that seemed elderly to her forty-four years. He slid a glance sideways, wondering how much the age gap showed, but she always looked young to him. In the inevitable cords and guernsey, her fair hair hatless, golden strands whipping round her tanned cheeks, she looked like a slim, careless girl. Fear touched him and he slipped his hand into the pocket of her padded waistcoat, feeling for her fingers. She looked at him with that same quick anxiety and he shook his head.

'I told you,' he said, laughing at himself, 'I'm feeling sentimental. Make the most of it. I shall be my old cantankerous bossy self tomorrow.'

Hands linked they trod out on to the great flat slabs, almost into the river itself, where two grey wagtails fluttered and long shadows stretched across the shallows. Fliss put an arm about him and he hugged her gratefully and bent to kiss her cold lips.

'Come on,' she said. 'The wind's cold. Home to tea. It'll be easier going with the wind behind us.'

He was glad to step out again, back into the sunshine. He was surprisingly cold and he wished he'd remembered his cap. Back at the car he staggered a little, his leg collapsing beneath him and, discovering that suddenly, inexplicably, he had no use in his right arm, cried out to Fliss in alarm. She glanced up, across the car roof, and with an exclamation came running round to him. He tried to speak but couldn't frame the words and he was conscious of her lowering him into the passenger seat, lifting his numbed leg, before he blacked out completely.

Chapter Nineteen

Fliss sat for some minutes in the car park at Derriford Hospital, staring through the windscreen into the gathering darkness. It was as if a whirlwind had caught her up, battering and disorientating her, and had now dumped her into unfamiliar surroundings whilst the world settled back quietly around her. The lamps shed pools of orange light, showing her people hurrying to and fro. Some arrived at the hospital alone, others were in pairs or small family groups; some carried flowers and fruit, others had books and magazines. One woman came almost running into the car park; leaping into her car she fled away towards the main road. A man followed more slowly, his younger companion holding his arm. They stood for some moments in earnest conversation before the older man climbed into the passenger seat and the other – his son, perhaps? – backed the car carefully out of the parking space. As they passed in front of her, Fliss saw that the old man was wiping his eyes with a handkerchief.

Slowly, very slowly, she become aware of herself, of the chill that was icing her recently overheated skin; of the emptiness, as well as the sick sensation, in the pit of her stomach; of the strands of hair that hung stickily about her face. She took the tortoiseshell pins from her hair, combing her fingers through it, dragging out the knots. With a swift practised action she twisted the hair into a long rope, knotted it expertly and thrust the pins in with quick, impatient jabs. Her hands fell back on to her lap and she continued to sit, inert and exhausted. Presently, after some more time had passed, she attempted to rouse herself.

She thought: Miles has had a stroke and will probably never walk again. He might never speak to me again except in that slurred, groaning speech which I cannot understand.

Even thinking it through clearly did not make it more real. It was quite inconceivable that Miles – Miles of all people, so strong, so determined, so particularly articulate and controlled – should be lying in a hospital bed, half paralysed, making such

an appallingly harsh and desperate noise. As for his face . . .
Abruptly Fliss covered her own face with her hands. It was as
if a sculptor had suddenly dragged his hand down across the soft
clay, distorting one half of the statue's face. He had stared up at her
desperately whilst she hung over him, reassuring him, clutching his
live, warm hand which had held her own with such strength that
it seemed that all his energy had collected into that one member.
When the sedatives finally took hold and he'd fallen asleep, she'd
sat beside him, rubbing the life back into her own numbed hands,
watching his face, so strangely altered yet familiar, until the Sister
had beckoned her away.

'There's nothing more you can do this evening,' she'd said
kindly. 'He'll sleep now and the specialist will be here in the
morning. Go home now and get some rest.'

Exhausted though she was Fliss felt she would never be able to
sleep again. Tension twanged inside her, cramping her muscles,
knotting her gut. Between one breath and the next her life had
utterly changed; nothing would be the same again. She had left
The Keep as one person and would return as another.

She thought: This has happened to me before. When Daddy and
Mummy and Jamie were killed. When Hal told me that we could
never be together. When Miles took the job in Hong Kong. I've
come through these things before. I can do it again. It's a question
of holding on.

This only seemed worse because this was now: the present
problem. It was natural to think that those other things had been
easier to handle simply because they were in the past, because
she had contained them and come through them. She reminded
herself that, at the time, each of those catastrophes had seemed
insurmountable, too. Somehow she would find the strength to
manage this, to deal with it.

. . . *they that wait upon the Lord shall renew their strength*;
The text slipped unbidden into her mind. It was a favourite with
Uncle Theo. How did it go on? *they shall mount up with wings as
eagles; they shall run, and not be weary; and they shall walk, and
not faint.*

Thanks to Uncle Theo she had gradually moved beyond her early,
childish belief that God was some kind of avuncular old man, giving
presents if you were good, withholding favours if you displeased
Him. Nor was He some capricious deity, saving the life of this
person but not that, visiting this country with drought and another
with riches. She knew, in an as yet unformed, fumbling kind of
way, that God is a spirit who could, if one wanted Him enough

144

– which had to be, according to Uncle Theo, more than anything on earth – transform one's life.

'We trivialise God so that we can grasp Him,' he'd said once. 'We should try to live by faith, with hope, in love. Not just on Sundays or when a crisis strikes or when we've seen a magnificent sunset, but on a minute-by-minute basis. If we do this then we are experiencing God.'

Sitting there in the car, Fliss was surprised at how much of Uncle Theo's reluctantly proffered knowledge had penetrated her subconscious mind during the years. Perhaps it was because it *had* been reluctant, rather than loudly professed or rigidly enforced, that it had moved her and influenced her. Uncle Theo lived out his faith and by doing so had touched them all to a greater or lesser extent . . . He would be waiting for her at The Keep, with Caroline and Prue.

She rubbed her chilly hands together and reached forward to start the engine. The keys weren't in the ignition. Panic struck like a blow to the heart and she stamped down on it, forcing cold reason into her brain. She had let herself into the car. If the keys weren't in the ignition then they would almost certainly be in the pocket of her Puffa. She'd taken it off in the stuffy ward and when she'd come back to the car she'd flung it on to the passenger seat. As she lifted the jacket she shook it, hoping to hear the clink of metal, but when she reached into its pockets she discovered only some Kleenex. Someone knocked sharply on the window and she gave a tiny cry of fear. A tall shadowy figure was gesticulating, pointing. Winding down the window with trembling fingers, Fliss stared up at him in alarm.

'You've left your keys in the lock.' The voice was kindly, even amused. 'Thought I'd mention it. I do it all the time.'

He removed the keys, passed them into her and drifted away, not waiting for her thanks.

As she started the engine, managing a wry smile at her foolishness, a measure of calm returned. The moment of quiet reflection, her thoughts of Uncle Theo, had restored her balance. There was much to be done and she must plan ahead. To begin with she would have to be back here at the hospital first thing in the morning. As she drove out of the car park another disturbing thought occurred to her: she'd have to tell the twinnies . . .

Kit, searching through her catalogues for a particular kind of rocking chair required by an owner of a small craft centre, found that she'd looked up the same thing twice already, and pushed the book aside with an impatient sigh. She simply couldn't concentrate. Her small study was untidy: the sturdy pine worktable covered with samples of material, catalogues, price sheets; a length of striped ticking falling from its roll balanced on the only comfortable chair; her desk groaning beneath the weight of reference books. The carpet had almost disappeared beneath a selection of small Indian rugs, laid out fanwise, ready for inspection by the client from the craft centre. Usually Kit enjoyed the busy atmosphere of her study but this morning it irritated her. She stared out of the window, across to the pond and the Heath beyond, and thought about Jake.

Nothing was working out as she'd hoped and she simply couldn't understand why. Her plots and stratagems had come to nothing. After the theatre and their late supper – which had been such fun – he'd simply put her into a taxi and sent her home. Her pride had not allowed her to do anything but behave as though this was exactly what she was expecting. Back in the flat, however, she'd paced around, seething and frustrated, telling herself that it was perfectly reasonable that he should no longer fancy her; that, despite his flattering words and Jake-like glances, it was clear that he did not want her. She felt utterly miserable; deeply hurt and humiliated.

Watching the ducks on the pond, leaning her elbows on her cluttered desk, she wondered if she should have made her feelings more obvious. Jake was behaving as if they were two very dear friends, catching up on old times, sharing special memories, enjoying a small break from the usual routine. What was missing was the indication that it would lead on to anything else. He held her hand, kissed her cheek, laid his arm about her shoulders, but there was nothing more than deep affection in these gestures.

Kit thought: He's had other women since he's been married, I'm certain of it. So why not me? I can't bear it that he doesn't fancy me any more. And he used to be so fantastic in bed.

Studying him covertly when he was not aware of her – ordering drinks at the bar, paying a bill, talking to a waiter – she knew that he would have lost none of his talents. She saw, too, that other women watched him. Brown-skinned, casually elegant, his horn-rimmed spectacles lending him an academic air, he was very attractive. He had been hers and she had lost him. In chasing after the romantic shadow, she had lost the real live substance.

Kit stabbed her pencil into the blotter, breaking its point. How many times she'd imagined this very situation: Jake appearing out of the past and them both falling in love all over again. She'd invented several scenarios for Madeleine: sudden, but painless, death; a lover for whom she'd abandoned Jake; or even a simple breakdown of the marriage which left them amicable but indifferent. She hadn't, however, made any allowances for the four little girls. Jake did not speak about them but they presented more of a difficulty. He did not discuss his marriage nor did he show any signs of weariness with his family life. It was as if, for this moment in time, they had simply ceased to exist.

She remembered that Jake had always been capable of this: of living in the moment, accepting what came to pass.

Kit thought: But what about me? There has to be more to it than this.

Perhaps she had been less encouraging than she'd imagined. Although it was obvious that she wasn't married she'd allowed him to believe that there was no lack of men and that she had a very busy social diary. Maybe she should make it clear that she was willing to take him back into her life without making conditions or rocking any boats. After all, Paris wasn't very far away. Now that they'd met again it wouldn't be too difficult to maintain a relationship – despite Madeleine and the four little girls. This evening one of her clients was giving a party to celebrate the opening of his wine bar and she'd persuaded Jake to escort her. This time she must make more of an effort to convince him that they mustn't lose each other again. She'd made that mistake once already . . .

The telephone rang, making her jump. It was Jake. He broke straight through her delighted greeting, coming directly to the point.

'I'm at the airport,' he said. 'There's been an emergency. Gabrielle has been taken ill. Madeleine took her home to Paris and she's in hospital. I'm booked on the next flight.'

'Oh, but, Jake . . .' She hesitated, confused, bitterly disappointed, not wishing to sound heartless. 'But what shall we do?'

'Do?' He sounded puzzled.

'We can't just leave it at that.' She tried to say it lightly. 'Not after meeting up again after all these years.'

'Darling Kit,' he said gently. 'It's been such fun. But what else *can* we do? We can't go back, you know. Life isn't like that.'

'Not back,' she said quickly. 'Of course not. But can't we go forward?'

'I don't think we can.' He sounded sad but quite firm. 'I have a wife and four children whom I love. Forgive me, Kit, but there can't be any future for us. How could there be?'

'There must be something,' she cried. 'There has to be, Jake. I simply can't bear to say goodbye to you again. Don't tell me

147

you've been faithful to Madeleine because I shan't believe you. I know you've had other women.'

There was a silence and she could hear the clamour of the airport in the background.

'But you are not one of those women,' he answered at last. 'Not bored, lonely women who are glad to roll about in bed and ask for nothing more. You mean far more to me than that, Kit. You always did. Neither of us could be content with that.'

Only pride prevented her from screaming that she would be utterly content with just that, that she would agree to anything rather than lose him again. Instead she spoke from the heart.

'But I still love you, Jake.'

'I love you, too.' She could hear the smile in his voice. 'But our love has to be put where it belongs. It's been such fun remembering the way we were. But that's what it is. A memory. We have to live in the real world, Kit.'

'I can't bear it,' she said flatly – but she knew that he was no longer hearing her. She could tell that all his attention was strained away from her, concentrating on the quacking voice which echoed in the background. Suddenly he was back with her again.

'They're calling my flight, Kit,' he said. 'I must go.'

'Wait,' she said urgently. 'Jake. Don't go. Please. Just give me a second.'

'You have the locket,' he said. 'I know that you still wear it. You were my first real love, Kit. Nothing's changed that. But the locket should be a delightful keepsake, not an icon. Don't let it blind you to other kinds of love. I must go. Goodbye, my darling. God bless.'

The line went dead. Kit sat for some moments before she replaced the receiver on its rest but, as she did so, the telephone rang again immediately. She snatched it up.

'Oh, darling,' said her mother's voice. 'The most dreadful thing has happened. You'll never believe it. Miles has had a stroke. It happened yesterday afternoon. Oh, Kit. It seems that he'll never walk again . . .'

Kit could hear her sobbing quietly, all those miles away in Devon, and with an enormous effort she pushed aside her own grief and bitterness and attempted to comfort her mother.

'How perfectly appalling,' she said. 'Poor Fliss. Don't cry, honey. Calm down and tell me all about it. You know I'll do anything I can,' and, as her mother talked on and on, her words hurried and confused – sentences cut short repeating herself again and again – Kit sat silently, staring at the locket which she turned over and over in her hand.

*   *   *

148

Bess, fetched to the telephone by a friend, found Jamie waiting at the end of the line.

'Have you heard?' He sounded subdued, anxious, and the fear in his voice reignited her own sense of panic.

'He's not going to die,' she said quickly, as much to reassure herself as her brother. 'He might even recover. People do.'

'I know. Mum said it could be worse.'

It was clear that Jamie could hardly imagine how and Bess remained silent, pulling her brown hair forward and chewing an end of it. The silence troubled neither of them; awareness of the other's presence was comfort enough.

'Are you going down?' she asked at last.

'Mum says that since we're so near to half term it's better to wait until then. It's not as if Dad's in any danger or anything, and things are a bit chaotic apparently.'

'That's what she said to me. It only a fortnight. How's Jo?'

'He's in a bit of a state, actually. He got really upset when I told him. You'd have almost thought it was *his* father.'

'Well, it makes you think about things, doesn't it? When you're a kid you think everyone you love is immortal. When it's close like this it's different. Poor old Jo. He hasn't really got a mum any more and now he's suddenly realised that he easily might not have a dad either.'

'Sounds a bit morbid, put like that.'

'It *is* morbid. It's just . . . Well, I can't imagine Dad not . . . not . . . well, not like Dad,' she finished lamely.

'I know.' Jamie agreed so eagerly that it was clear that he'd already thought about this, too. 'He's so larger than life, isn't he? Always on the go and telling you things. I just can't imagine him . . . semi-paralysed.'

He said the words with a kind of reluctant horror and Bess had to summon up all her strength so as to block out her own terror at the mental picture of her father in such a condition.

'He's exactly the sort of person who would recover,' she said stubbornly. 'He won't give in, you'll see.'

'It seems so ironic.' Jamie sounded bitter. 'We were just getting to know him, weren't we?'

'I know. Poor old Dad. He won't be able to work again, Mum says. Not at the old job, anyway. She says that once they get him back to The Keep they're going to find him plenty to do.'

'Do you think she's OK?'

'You can never tell with Mum. She'll put a brave face on it.

I'm glad she's got the oldies. It would be awful if she was on her own.'

'And Susanna,' added Jamie. 'I expect she'll be OK with all of them but I wish we were there, too.'

'It's not long till half term. Will you be all right?'

'Yes. Sure. Will you?'

'Course I will. Look, I'd better go. There are people waiting.'

'OK. Give me a buzz.'

'I will. Love to Jo.'

'OK. Bye.'

Chapter Twenty

Caroline lit the first fire of the year in the hall just after lunch. She was lighting it as much for comfort as for warmth, mindful as she had always been of the natural balance between mental and physical requirement.

'We need it,' she murmured to herself, making a pyre of kindling in the vast, empty grate and lighting the firelighters beneath the scaffolding of twigs. There was a huge log basket in its own small alcove within the deep recess which housed the fireplace and Jolyon had filled it with dry logs before he'd gone back to school. While she waited for the flame to take hold she sat on the little stool, kept in the alcove opposite the log basket; a perch which was a favourite with the smaller children. Linking her hands round her knees, Caroline looked about the hall. She could never decide whether she liked it best in high summer, cool, shadowy, peaceful, with the door open to the courtyard, or in the depths of winter, with the curtains pulled against a wet afternoon and the fire leaping in the granite fireplace.

She'd always thought that the idea of making a room within a room was a good one. Two high-backed sofas piled with cushions faced each other across the low, long table. At the end of this table, opposite the fireplace, stood a deep, comfortable armchair. It was a cosy area within the vaster, draughty spaces of the hall and she could remember so many happy occasions which had taken place here, as well as much simpler everyday events. Tea, by tradition, was always eaten in the hall and Caroline could readily conjure up the memory of Mrs Chadwick, *The Times* open on the sofa beside her, pouring tea for Theo, cutting a slice of Ellen's delicious cake.

In those days she'd had her own tea in the kitchen with Ellen and Fox but now, with Prue resident at The Keep, she'd been drawn even more closely into the fabric of the family and she no longer felt slightly awkward when she had tea in the hall with whichever members of the family happened to be present. Unexpectedly she was visited by a memory of herself, returning from a shopping trip in

151

Exeter. Fliss had persuaded her into buying a winter coat in the sales: thick, brown, cut in a full swagger, its collar a long scarf with a black fringe at each end. Freddy and Theo had been having tea when she returned, and they'd persuaded her to share their tea and model the coat . . . Caroline smiled to herself, remembering. She'd flung the scarf about her neck and twirled on her toes and they'd laughed and clapped. There'd been something else, too. She frowned, cudgelling her memory, visualising a grey-green jersey dress with a crossover bodice and a gently flaring skirt. She'd bought the dress to wear at a dinner party to which Miles had invited her whilst the others were at a Ladies' Night. How strange it was to think that she'd believed herself in love with him. How long ago it seemed, those few short years when life had been full of naval parties and fun. She thought of Hal, tall and handsome in his uniform, and of Kit, sophisticated in her lovely London clothes; of Fliss, so young and in awe of life, and of Miles, strong, confident and so very much in charge of them all; Miles, who was now lying in Derriford Hospital, partially paralysed and helpless after his stroke . . .

The fire was taking hold now, the dry twigs already blazing and crackling whilst the flames licked greedily at the logs. It would take a while for a good bed of hot ash to build up but, with a couple of judicially placed logs and a few puffs from the bellows, the fire would remain alight now for most of the winter. Caroline glanced at her watch. By the time Fliss returned from the hospital the hall would be a cheerful haven in which to have her tea. Caroline put aside her memories, piled more logs on to the fire and hurried away.

Later in the afternoon, Theo was glad of its heat. One of the disadvantages of severe old age seemed to be that one never felt warm and even he, who had always been indifferent to the physical needs of his body, was grateful now for any means which held the cold at bay. He knew that the sight of the cheerful blaze would comfort Fliss, too, when she returned from the hospital. How quickly she'd reacted on that terrible afternoon: driving Miles straight to the surgery at South Brent, telephoning The Keep to tell them what had happened before following the ambulance to Derriford. Since then she'd spent most of her waking hours at the hospital.

Theo smoothed the soft folds of the tartan rug which lay on the arm of the chair, his face grave. He knew now why he had been waiting. This was the disaster for which he had been subconsciously preparing himself. As for Fliss . . .

'It's so awful,' she'd said when she'd finally returned on that shocking day. She'd been fed by a quiet Caroline and a tearful Prue in the kitchen and had then come up to his rooms. 'It's dreadful to see someone so positive and so strong reduced to helplessness.'

'Is he badly paralysed?' he'd asked. 'Is he conscious?'

'Oh yes. He's conscious.' She'd folded her arms beneath her breast, her hands clenched into fists. 'It's his right side that's affected. It would be, wouldn't it? And he can't speak properly. Only in a kind of groan. But he knew what was going on. We shall know more tomorrow when the specialist's examined him.'

She'd stared at him, tears threatening, and he'd realised that she was close to breaking point.

'He'd been so sweet,' she'd said before he could speak. 'On the walk. It was almost as if he'd had some sort of premonition. He held my hand and said he was feeling sentimental.' Her lips were shaking and she'd swallowed painfully. 'He said he didn't regret coming back from Hong Kong and the last four years had been so good . . . He was so nice. And I've been such a cow at times.'

Abruptly she'd burst into a storm of violent weeping and he'd gone to her and taken her in his arms.

'Keep a clear picture,' he'd murmured. 'I'm sure that there have been faults on both sides. And much generosity.'

She'd cried as wildly and uncontrollably as a child might, as Lulu might, and he'd held her closely, remaining silent. Presently she'd drawn away, reaching into her sleeve for a handkerchief, trying to smilc at him.

'Sorry,' she'd said. 'It's just such a shock. I'm OK.'

Now, staring into the flames, Theo wondered if this were true. She certainly seemed to have her emotions well under control, taking the news that Miles would never walk properly again with a composure which he could only admire but which also caused him anxiety. She flung herself into plans for his homecoming, making the preparations needed to convert the television room, which had once been turned into quarters for Fox, into an apartment for Miles.

'He'll need plenty of company,' she'd said firmly – and Prue had dissolved into tears, which she'd done at regular intervals since she'd first heard the news.

Caroline had been quietly positive. 'Of course he will,' she'd said. 'That's an excellent plan. Even in a wheelchair he'll have access to the whole of the ground floor. Thank God it's such a big old place and the doorways are so wide. There will be a few no-go areas but he needn't feel too restricted.'

Fliss had stared at her, one arm about Prue's shoulders, and Caroline had bitten her lip. Theo had guessed what they were both thinking. It was impossible that, if Miles were to be permanently confined to a wheelchair, he could feel anything but restricted.

'Relatively speaking,' she'd added, confused and apologetic.

Fliss had given her a tight smile, patted Prue comfortingly – if briskly – and had gone away to see what could be done about converting the downstairs cloakroom into a sensible bathroom.

'What a stupid thing to say,' Caroline had said wretchedly after she'd gone. 'I could have bitten my tongue out.'

'You're doing splendidly,' he'd told her. 'These are testing times and Fliss will know just how lucky she is to have you to support her.'

'Poor darling,' Prue had choked through her tears. 'And just when she and Miles were settling down again so happily. Oh, how terrible life is . . .'

He and Caroline had exchanged a glance and he'd put his arm about Prue, leading her out into the courtyard while Caroline hurried after Fliss.

It was true that Fliss was lucky to have the means at her disposal – how many people had to face such calamities with so much less! – nevertheless Theo's heart ached for her. As he leaned forward to reach for his cup of, by now, lukewarm tea, the door opened and Fliss came into the hall. He made to rise but she motioned him to stay as he was and bent to kiss him. He looked up at her, seeing the strain in her face, the deep grooves carved from nose to mouth, the wary almost blank expression in her eyes.

'Tea?' he asked. 'Caroline said to shout the moment you arrived. We decided not to wait.'

'I'm glad you didn't.' She sank down beside him and closed her eyes. 'No, not just yet. I don't want to talk to anyone for a moment.' She sat in silence for a while, eyes still shut. Presently she heaved a great sigh, almost a gasp, and opened her eyes, looking about her as if she wondered where she was. 'Who lit the fire?'

'Caroline. She thought we all needed the comfort of it.'

'She's right. Fire is so important. Didn't our ancestors kill the member of the tribe who let the fire go out? Something like that, anyway.'

She was talking for the sake of it and he turned a little in his seat so as to see her more clearly. Her profile was brittle as glass, her hair dragged impatiently back with little or no care. Her gaze was distant, preoccupied.

'How is he?' he asked gently.

154

'Frustrated.' She looked at him, almost shrugging. 'He wants to speak so much, you see, but he's unintelligible most of the time. It's fraught with difficulty. Him desperate to be understood and me desperate to understand him. Neither of us getting anywhere. He's fighting every inch of the way. Does everything he could possibly do for himself. He's terrific, really, but the strain is enormous. The nurses are absolutely brilliant.' Her thin fingers, laced tightly together, tensed and flexed rhythmically. 'I wonder how we'll manage when we get him home?'

She spoke lightly, almost conversationally, but he could feel the panic, fluttering and beating beneath her schooled, controlled exterior, and he cast about for inspiration, praying for guidance.

'It will be so difficult,' she was saying, 'to keep him calm. He's so restive. It's a pity he's never been a television watcher.'

'I shall read to him,' said Theo cheerfully. 'Now I do *like* that idea. My family have always refused, individually and collectively, to allow me to read to them but now I shall have a captive audience at last.'

She stared at him for a moment, surprised into stillness, almost affronted, and then she burst into genuine laughter. This unforced mirth, the first for several weeks, released her nervous tension and the happy sound of it brought tears of relief into his eyes.

'I shall get out all my John Buchans and Rudyard Kiplings and I shall work through the lot of them.' Encouraged, Theo elaborated on his plan. 'Your father and John resisted them. Hal rejected them. Mole refused them. Now I have an excuse for rereading them and no one shall deny me.'

She was still chuckling. 'Poor Miles,' she said – but her voice was full of warmth and ease. 'Actually he'll probably love them. He was reared on the *Boy's Own* paper and Baden-Powell.'

'Splendid fellow,' said Theo comfortably. 'We shall have a whale of a time together. It's a challenge. We shall play backgammon. Miles won't let a thing like this destroy him. He'll find a hundred ways to make up for his deficiencies.'

'Yes,' she said quietly. 'Yes, I'm sure that you're right. Miles is too stubborn – and too brave – to allow himself to be completely grounded.' She hesitated and then looked at him. The tension was gone but her face was full of sadness. 'But what about me, Uncle Theo? How will I bear it?'

'You'll bear it bravely, too,' he told her, 'because the other options aren't worth considering. You won't do it all at once. There will be good days and bad days but you can do this, Fliss.'

He saw that she was exhausted and that, now the tension had

been released, her strength had deserted her. Grim, frozen endurance was thawing, softening into patient forbearance, a more fruitful condition, and he felt his spirits rise a little.

'We shall come through this,' he said. 'Between us we shall survive it. Just don't think you're alone, Fliss. You haven't got to do it all by yourself. Resist false pride which cannot sustain you and let us all help you. We love him, too, you know.'

She gave another huge sigh but this time it was a gasp of relief, a willingness to share her burden, and he felt weak with gratitude.

'I know,' she said. 'I do know, really. It's just I was afraid to let go even for a second in case I shattered into pieces. It was as if I were receding into a kind of cocoon where nothing could reach me. I've felt so terribly isolated.'

'It's shock,' he said gently. 'And fear. It's over now. We're all in this together. And now I'm going to find Caroline and ask her to make you a cup of tea.'

Chapter Twenty-one

Hal stepped on to *Dorcas*'s stern deck and grinned at Mole, who was standing to attention, pretending to pipe him aboard.

'Welcome aboard, sir,' he said formally – and ducked, laughing, as Hal swung an open hand in the direction of his ear. 'Are you on your own? I thought Kit was coming.'

'It occurred to me that this was a good opportunity to have a talk,' said Hal, following him below, 'so I put her off.'

'Sounds serious.' Mole was opening some beer in the galley. 'Terrible about poor old Miles, isn't it?'

'Shocking. Doesn't bear thinking about.' Hal sat down at the table in the saloon and glanced about him. 'It's warm in here. Have you got the stove alight?'

'Thought I'd try it out.' Mole sounded nonchalant. 'With the wet weather coming in it seemed a good idea.'

'It's very cosy.' He took his beer. 'Thanks. I must say you've got it very homely.'

He paused and there was a moment's silence, neither of them quite certain how to deal with the subject that was at the front of both their minds. They spoke together – 'Have you heard how . . . ?' 'Are they all OK . . . ?' – and stopped. Mole indicated that Hal should go first.

He came straight to the point. 'Are you going down for the Birthday?'

'I thought I would.' Mole sat down opposite on the sofa. 'Fliss says that Miles isn't up to too many visitors yet but she's hoping that we'll all go down then, if we can.'

'Ma has been on the telephone pretty well nonstop, as you can imagine.' Hal's sympathetic expression took any sting out of the remark. 'She thinks that the Birthday will be a good excuse for a little jollity. Everything's been fairly bleak, as you can imagine. Kit and I are certainly going down, and Jo and the twins are home for half term. Apart from anything else, I think we may have to face the fact that this could be Uncle Theo's last Birthday.'

'It's impossible to imagine The Keep without Uncle Theo.' Mole stretched his legs out and crossed his ankles. 'It's odd, really, but Grandmother and Ellen and Fox have never seemed to be dead whilst he remains alive. Do you know what I mean?'

'I think so.' Hal smiled at his own memories. 'All the time he's there, you can imagine that the others are, too.'

'Yes, that's it. Out of sight but around somewhere.' Mole sighed and shook his head.

'He's asked me to have a word with you.' Hal stood his glass on the table and leaned forward, his forearms resting along his thighs, fingers clasped. 'He's wondering if you'd be prepared to be one of the Trustees when he . . . dies. There are three of us, as you know: Me, Fliss and Uncle Theo. Would you be happy with it, d'you think?'

'Well, yes.' Mole blinked. 'If . . . if there isn't anyone else.'

For a moment Hal was reminded of a younger Mole; a Mole who stammered badly and suffered nightmares, who had adored his big cousin to whom he had transferred – in part – the love he had once given his elder brother. Now he was a three-ringer and a submarine commander – and was getting the reputation for being a bit of a mystery within the Silent Service . . .

'No,' said Hal. 'There isn't anyone else. Uncle Theo would like you to succeed him. You know the rough outline of the Trust, don't you? Grandmother left enough shares to support and maintain The Keep, although that business with the roof and dry rot was a bit of a whammy. Because of that we've all lost our personal incomes. Well, except for Susanna—'

'We were all agreed on that, though, weren't we?' interrupted Mole. 'It seemed hard that her children shouldn't have the same advantages that the rest of the family have had, and she and Gus don't have the same level of income. It didn't hurt the rest of us to pull in our belts a little.'

'We came to the conclusion that it was what Grandmother would have wished,' said Hal. 'Of course Susanna hasn't a clue about it all, really. We decided that it was best not to explain it too carefully. I think she and Gus would have found it very hard to accept that they were being singled out for special treatment. As it is, Sooz and Gus are having to make quite a few sacrifices to send Fred and Podger to Herongate next year. They've held Fred back as long as they dared but he had brilliant results from his entrance examination. Sooz is praying that he'll get a scholarship when he moves on.'

'They'd heard so much about Herongate,' said Mole. 'What with Sooz telling them about her and me and then the twinnies and Jolyon raving about it. It would have been hard for them not to have done it, too.'

'Well, between us all we'll just about get the three of them through,' said Hal, 'but the next generation will have to fend for themselves.'

He emptied his glass and Mole passed him another can, wondering just how much Hal's loss of private income had influenced Maria's decision to leave him.

'I suppose Grandmother's vision was a bit romantic?' he suggested diffidently. 'It's a lovely idea but can it survive?'

'Another really expensive maintenance bill will probably mean that we'd have to cash in more shares and then there would be a serious problem. To be honest, The Keep needs someone who can put a good salary into it as well the income from the shares. Once the boys have finished school I shall be able to help but whether any of the next generation will want to do it, I've no idea.'

'The question is whether their partners will be prepared to agree to it, I suppose.' Mole refilled his own glass. 'They might not be so keen on supporting a place which can never truly be theirs.'

'Grandmother wanted the Trust to meet two objectives,' Hal told him. 'One was for The Keep to be a refuge for any member of the family should he or she need it. The other was to assist any beneficiary as determined by the Trustees. As we did for Susanna, for instance. When Grandmother died the three of us decided to continue to hold back enough of the income from the shares in the company so as to maintain The Keep and to divide the rest amongst the beneficiaries.'

'Who exactly *are* the beneficiaries?' asked Mole. 'I'm a bit woolly about it, I'm afraid. I know that our money comes from china clay but not much more than that, to tell you the truth.'

'The beneficiaries are the offspring of John and Peter Chadwick, which means that there are already seven of the next generation, let alone any that you're keeping hidden, young Mole.'

Mole beamed at him. 'I'm waiting for an appropriate moment to introduce them all,' he said. 'But perhaps there won't be that much to offer them, after all.'

Hal sighed. 'Another disaster like the last one and it might mean that the Trustees would have to sell The Keep. It would be the end of Grandmother's dream but it would provide some cash to meet her second objective. At least it would take care of the beneficiaries.'

'Perhaps your Jo will be the next candidate,' suggested Mole. 'If he loves it as much as you do, he might be prepared to help with its expense and use it as his home.'

159

Hal frowned. 'He loves The Keep,' he said, 'but just at the moment I'm not certain in which direction he's heading. He loves being there and working on the place but he shows no inclination for any particular career.'

'It's early days,' offered Mole gently, 'and your break-up with Maria has come as a bit of a shock to him.'

'Well, *she* certainly refused to have anything to do with Grandmother's hopes for The Keep,' said Hal. He shrugged. 'But who can blame her? She didn't want to share the kitchen with Caroline or put up with my old ma interfering and spoiling the children.'

'I can see that it needs a pretty special combination to make it work,' agreed Mole cautiously. 'I must say that I'm glad it's there for Fliss and Miles at the moment, though.'

'Well, this is the whole point of it, of course. A refuge. Fortunately Miles had various pensions and insurances so he won't be a burden on the Trust. And this is how The Keep works best – with a number of people, all with equal claims to shelter and protection supporting it and being supported by it, helping those who fall on hard times. Up until now Uncle Theo has been the head of the family and, since he has no dependants to make it difficult for him, it has worked.'

'You're much in the same position now.' Mole raised his eyebrows questioningly. 'Wouldn't you say?'

'I suppose so.' Hal nodded. 'I certainly think we'll get by for a bit longer. It's the next generation who might find it difficult. I have a strong feeling that the twinnies will very quickly spread their wings and fly the nest, and I suspect that Edward will never be interested. That leaves Jo and Fred and Podger and Lulu, who might conceivably want to make The Keep their home. I think that it's rather more difficult for one of the girls to bring a husband into this kind of setup than for one of the chaps to bring a wife home to it. Or am I being very old-fashioned?'

'Probably.' Mole grinned at him. 'Now that you're a hoary old four-ringer you're definitely past your best but never mind. Jo will probably become a millionaire and marry some generous warm-hearted girl who will be more than happy to look after us all in our dotage. Better make certain that he marries a nurse.'

'Motorised Zimmer frames?' mused Hal. 'Last one down the drive's a cissy?'

'And wheelchair polo,' assisted Mole. 'The courtyard will do splendidly.'

They burst out laughing – and then stopped, remembering how close to the truth their jokes were now.

'Poor sod,' muttered Hal. 'Poor old Miles. What a bummer.'

'People do recover.' Mole sounded doubtful.

'Well, if anyone can, Miles will,' Hal agreed. 'He's a fighter.'

'Poor Fliss,' said Mole sadly. 'They were just getting it together again, weren't they?'

Mole – along with Susanna – had been too young to know about Hal's and Fliss's early love. They assumed that the attachment which Fliss felt for her cousin had grown out of the same childhood need which had informed their own affection for him. He had no idea how bitter Hal might be feeling.

Hal thought: It's odd that I've never been able to dislike Miles. I ought to hate him but I can't. Now I have to pity him, too. Poor darling Fliss . . .

'Well, that's settled,' he said aloud. 'I'll tell Uncle Theo you've accepted his offer and we'll go through it all properly when we're down for the Birthday.'

'Sounds fine,' said Mole, glad to turn the conversation. 'So how's life as the Assistant Director in the Department of Naval Operations and Trade?'

Singly and in pairs the family arrived at The Keep for the Birthday. The tradition had begun quite simply. Freddy Chadwick's birthday had fallen at the end of October and, when her twin boys were small, a celebration had been made of it: home-made presents, carefully coloured cards and tea in the hall. Throughout their schooldays the date had coincided with half term and so, over the years, it had become an institution. Later, when Hal and Kit were born within a day of it, and again when Mole arrived on the very date itself, there was even more cause to celebrate. With the three children back from Kenya the Birthday had once again become an important date in the calendar: an opportunity for the family to gather together for a big party. After Freddy's death, and with the children grown up, it had been difficult to maintain the tradition but just occasionally everyone was in the right place at the right time.

Bess arrived first, travelling from Hampshire on the train. Fliss collected her from Totnes station on a bright blowy day with woolly clouds scudding before a south-westerly and crimson hawthorn berries gleaming in the hedgerows. Waiting on the platform Fliss thought of the many occasions when she had been met from the train here, usually by Caroline, and of other times that she had driven to meet members of the family arriving from up country: Kit from London, the twinnies from Herongate: Jolyon from Blundell's. Today there was a faint unreality about it all.

161

It seemed that it must have been another Fliss stepping from the train into Caroline's waiting arms; a different Fliss stooping to hug the twinnies, who were lumbered with overnight cases and coats, bursting to tell her the latest achievement, cheerful at the thought of the holiday ahead.

Fliss thought: And I thought those years were difficult enough. Loving Hal but unable to show it, trying not to mind that Miles wasn't interested in his children. I thought that it was just a question of holding on until one glorious day it would all somehow be resolved and I would come through into the sunshine.

The train was snaking round the curve in the track, grinding alongside, brakes screaming. Hands in pockets, Fliss scanned the compartments. Far along the platform she suddenly spied Bess, swinging herself off the train, hurrying to meet her, dark hair flying. Avoiding slower travellers, dodging embracing couples, they met at last and Bess caught Fliss in a bear hug.

'Oh, Mum,' she said breathlessly. 'I'm so sorry. How are you?'

She held her mother away from her and, looking into the glowing young face, Fliss felt a spasm of relief and recognition. The long years of love, of worry and caring, were yielding up an opportunity for friendship. There would be no need for pretence here, no being brave, no necessity to shield Bess with half-truths.

'Oh, darling, it's good to see you,' she said. 'It's so horrid when these things happen and you can't be on the spot, isn't it? Sometimes it's easier to be the one who is occupied and busy instead of the person who is worrying helplessly at a distance.'

Bess swung her sacklike bag over her shoulder and took her mother's arm.

'It's a no-win situation,' she said philosophically.

Hal and Kit arrived next, Hal driving. There had been the usual bickering about the rival merits of Eppyjay – Kit's convertible Morris Minor – and Hal's MGB. Eppyjay was now acquiring a certain rarity value, which Kit delighted to point out to him, quoting passages from a recent article in the *Observer*, nevertheless her usual verve was missing and, once out of London, she grew thoughtful and withdrawn. He attempted several topics, to which she responded with an effort, and after a while he, too, fell silent. It surprised him that she was quite so subdued – Miles had never been a particular favourite with his sister – and he wondered if she might be worrying about Fliss.

He thought: Poor old Kit's had a bit of a basinful lately. What with me draining down all over her about Maria and now Ma

162

pouring out her worries about Miles, she must be getting a bit depressed.

Clarrie had waylaid him earlier, suggesting that Kit needed a holiday, but dear old Clarrie had always been a bit mother hen-ish about Kit. Now, however, Hal began to wonder if there might be something else on her mind. He set himself to amuse her, and by the time they arrived at The Keep she was brighter and less apt to slip off into preoccupation.

Jolyon and Jamie arrived by train from Tiverton and were met by Caroline. She looked them over with an experienced eye, checking for any sign of ill health or overworking. She knew that Jamie must achieve very good grades to win a place at King's College in the Department of War Studies and she also recognised in him his father's determination to succeed. He was working very hard but he looked as if he were thriving on it and she guessed that his faintly anxious air was due to worry about Miles. Although over two years younger, Jolyon was now as tall as his cousin, and Caroline felt the usual warmth as she looked at him, seeing the Hal of thirty years ago in the adolescent features and slightly gangly gait. They approached her, laughing together, untidy, casual, and she opened her arms to them both, welcoming them home.

Mole arrived last, driving in between the gatehouses, getting out of the car, stretching. He paused for a moment, looking up at the castle-like building across the courtyard, the height of the surrounding walls and the comforting thickness of the tall wooden doors in the gatehouse, seeing it as he had thirty-three years ago. Grandmother had fetched the three of them from Staverton station and had brought them to this place of safety; to Ellen and Fox. The Keep offered him the greatest safety he could imagine but he'd had to learn that he could not live forever inside its walls.

'Look upon life as a river,' Uncle Theo had once said to him. 'We cannot walk beside it, watching it fearfully, clutching someone's hand. Sooner or later we must get in and learn to swim.'

Well, he'd done just that. He'd pushed himself beyond his limits again and again, determined to kill the corroding fear, to trample it underfoot – and he was winning.

Instinctively Mole glanced up at his uncle's window. Theo was there, watching him, and for a moment Mole felt that the old man had shared with him what had just passed through his mind.

Mole thought: However would I have survived without him? He's been like a shield and a buckler – or whatever it is in that psalm.

163

He raised his hand and Theo waved back, smiling down at him.

Then the front door opened and Susanna came out to meet him, Podger running ahead and Lulu tacking unsteadily in the rear, all wanting to be the first to welcome him back.

Chapter Twenty-two

'I haven't bought your present yet,' Fliss said to Kit. 'Shocking, isn't it? I thought we might have a browse in Totnes tomorrow. In Salago, perhaps? Any ideas?'

'None at all.' Kit sat down on the window seat and hitched her feet on the edge, wrapping her arms round her knees, looking about her. 'Do you realise that this room looks exactly as it did forty years ago when Hal and I used to come down for holidays from Bristol? I always feel as though I've been caught in a time warp. So how are you, little coz? Truth mind, no flannel.'

'I'm OK.' Fliss perched on the end of the bed. 'It sounds crazy but I can hardly remember life being any other way and yet it's only been a matter of weeks. Can you understand that? It's so weird.'

'Oh, yes, I can imagine that.' Kit rested her chin on her knees. 'It is the most dismal luck for both of you. What's the prognosis?'

Fliss shrugged. 'He'll probably be able to get about quite well with a stick, and his speech is improving a little, but his right arm is quite useless. He's learning to write with his left hand and doing very well. No more ciggies, of course, which can't be easy for him. Anyway, the outlook could be worse. They don't discount miracles but nor do they encourage me to hold my breath waiting for one.'

'So where does that leave you?'

'Exhausted.' Fliss tried to make a little joke of it. 'I shall be glad to get him home. All that travelling to and from hospital is very tiring.'

'But how will you cope, honey? After all, more than half of your life together has gone up in smoke, hasn't it? Finished. Kaput. How do you come to terms with something like that?'

Fliss was silent for a moment, faintly surprised by the almost brutal insistence of Kit's questioning. It occurred to her that there was something beneath the concern, something deeper which related to Kit herself.

'Speaking for myself,' she said slowly, 'everything happened so quickly that I haven't had time to think about how I shall survive it.

Oh, I had a really bad week or two at the beginning but Uncle Theo dragged me out of it. I asked him how I would bear it and he told me that I would be brave because the other options weren't worth considering.'

'Good stiff-upper-lip stuff,' said Kit drily. 'Did he give you any actual guidelines? You know? A manual on being brave? A tract on how to survive disaster through public smiling?'

Fliss chuckled. 'I don't think it's quite that easy. What really helped me was that he shook me out of my isolation. I was withdrawing, if you know what I mean. I'd shut myself off in my shock and fear. He told me that it was false pride and that I should allow myself to be helped. I didn't have to do it alone, he said. Other people loved Miles, too, and wanted to help. It was such a relief. I hadn't realised how terribly easy it is to isolate yourself.'

'No,' said Kit, after a minute or two. 'No, I can see that it might be . . . dangerous.'

'I think it is,' said Fliss, cautiously feeling her way forward and wishing that she had Uncle Theo's experience and wisdom. 'It's probably because you don't trust people to understand. Or there are aspects of the situation which you feel a bit ashamed to admit to, if you see what I mean. There's the selfish aspect, isn't there? That awful "what about me?" thing which will shove itself forward even in the most horrendous circumstances. You don't want to say that you're worried about yourself when someone else is in a far worse state. You get very confused and so, on top of all the other things, it becomes easier – and safer – to say nothing.'

'Yes,' said Kit. 'Yes . . .'

'Of course, I'm lucky.' Fliss pressed on valiantly. 'Having Caroline and Prue and Uncle Theo around to take the weight. And there's Sooz, of course . . . Kit, for heaven's sake, tell me what's wrong!'

At the sudden change in tone, Kit looked at her, startled but wary.

'I know there's something,' said Fliss, abandoning her attempt to adopt her uncle's approach. 'It reminds of that Christmas, oh, years and years ago, when you thought you were pregnant. Then your period started and you lay on this very bed and cried and cried. Remember?'

Slowly, painfully, Kit began to laugh. 'That dreadful Graham Thing,' she said. 'Oh, how I adored him. What fools we were. Still are, some of us. I've seen Jake again. He's still married to Madeleine and they have four little girls. And I love him just as much as ever.'

They stared at one another.

'Oh, Kit,' said Fliss at last, undeceived by her cousin's air of bravado. 'How perfectly wretched for you. What rotten luck that you should meet again. At least, it is if you still feel that way about him.'

'Why should I have changed?' asked Kit. 'You still love Hal.'

'Yes,' agreed Fliss slowly. 'Yes, I still love Hal. But I've been in constant contact with him over the last thirty years. Nothing Hal has done or become has made me fall out of love with him or changed how I think about him. It's been kept alive by proximity. But it must be twelve – fourteen – years since you saw Jake. I hoped that your love had died because it had nothing on which to feed.'

Kit shrugged. 'Well, it hasn't. I love him as much as I ever did and there is no future in it. He's left me all over again with nothing to hope for and I simply don't see how I can go through it all again.'

Fliss stood up and went to sit beside her on the window seat. She laid her hand gently on her cousin's hair as Kit sat, forehead on knees, quietly weeping. There was a knock at the door but, by the time Mole put his head into the room, Fliss was standing up, blocking any sight of Kit. He raised his eyebrows and Fliss shook her head, drawing down the corners of her mouth.

'It's only Mole,' she said quickly as Kit gave a gasp and tried to disappear behind the folds of the curtain. 'Nothing to worry about.'

Mole vanished, closing the door quietly behind him.

'Sorry,' said Kit, blotting her streaming eyes. 'It's just been . . . hell. It was like you said. Ma going on about poor old Miles and me thinking about myself and how I would survive. I felt such a cow. Oh, hell . . .'

Fliss stood beside her, smoothing her hand across Kit's back, staring down the garden, across the lawn and the orchard, to the three tall fir trees which the small Susanna had insisted were her friends. They had faces, she'd said, and guarded her bedroom. Now, as they swayed and shivered, their feathery outlines trembling in the wind, Fliss tried to make out features in the dense green foliage.

'Sorry,' said Kit again. 'What must you think of me? And you with all your problems . . .'

'Because I have problems doesn't mean that yours are any less terrible. I only wish that I could say something helpful. In some ways it's easier for me. It's all so . . . busy. So physically tiring. There's hardly a moment in which to think and in a way that's good. As soon as I sit down or lie down I immediately fall asleep.

Whereas you have plenty of time to feel miserable. Now that Sin's gone you're all alone, aren't you?'

'Clarrie's great.' Kit was sitting up straight, now, wiping her eyes. 'But I couldn't bring myself to tell even him. I felt such a shit when all this was happening down here. I thought he'd despise me.'

'I don't see Clarrie as the despising sort,' Fliss was saying, when the door opened again and Mole stood, half in, half out, with two mugs of coffee.

'I made them in the nursery kitchen,' he muttered as Fliss took them from him. 'Sorry to butt in but I thought you were having a bit of a crisis.'

He disappeared again and Kit took her coffee with an attempt at a smile.

'Dear old Mole,' she said. 'I don't mind him knowing I'm a cow.'

Fliss sat down beside her. 'Don't say a word,' she said, 'but Podger and Lulu are giving him a Tintin book for his birthday. It's the only one he hasn't got, according to Sooz, and she tracked it down specially as a joke. The girls are thrilled.' She began to laugh softly. 'And the thing is that Mole will be thrilled, too. He loves his Tintin books.'

Kit was laughing, too. 'He'll still be enjoying them when he's FOSM,' she said. 'Oh, Fliss, do any of us ever really grow up?'

'Only if we have to,' answered Fliss. 'Now come on. Get a grip and concentrate on birthday presents. There must be something you'd like – although I can't promise anything as good as Tintin.'

Miles, dressed and in his wheelchair, waited for the arrival of Fliss and the twins. His whole concentration was channelled towards the ward door, watching staff and visitors coming and going, intent, focused. Carefully he lifted his lifeless hand on to his lap, arranging it so that it looked natural, trying to will it into some sort of movement, however slight. There was nothing wrong with his brain, he was certain of that. Of course, occasionally he couldn't think of just the right word, forgot certain things, but who didn't? He'd done that before . . . before this damned thing had happened. He was determined to beat it, to get himself walking properly again. It would be easier when he got back to The Keep . . .

He let his breath go on a long sigh. Thank God for The Keep. Trying to prevent his eyes from glancing continually at the ward clock he deliberately set his mind to remember the pleasure he'd felt a few days ago – how many? Three? Four? Well, let it go – when Fliss had walked into the ward with Theo beside her. He'd told her that he'd like to see her uncle but had never imagined that the old boy could possibly make such an effort. All he could hope was that Theo had realised just how delighted he was. It was difficult to show emotion, with only a part of your face working, but he'd gripped Theo's hand with his own good one and they'd smiled at each another, still holding on.

Miles chuckled inside as he remembered how Theo hadn't attempted to pander to him. 'No, I didn't get that,' he'd say after listening intently to Miles's attempt at speech. 'Never mind. Write it down. Write it down.'

Fliss had wandered away and he'd been able to scrawl a few words so as to demonstrate his gratitude at the offer of hospitality at The Keep.

'It's your home, my dear boy,' Theo had said. 'It's where you belong now. We'll be glad to have you. I'm hoping you can play backgammon. The women of my family are hopeless. Quite hopeless. I'm counting on you.'

The weak tears, to which he was now prey, had poured down his cheeks, then, but Theo had found his box of tissues without a word and given him one.

'Sorry,' he'd muttered – only it didn't come out like that – and Theo had smiled that peculiarly sweet smile and waited in absolute serenity until Miles had recovered.

'You'll come through this,' he'd said, bending over him to say goodbye whilst Fliss had a few words with the Sister. 'Look how much you achieved in these last four years. You kept to your word and you were able to change and grow. Now you have another hurdle ahead. Mind you give it everything you've got.'

The words had jerked his memory – a fragment of a scene in the courtyard at The Keep – and he'd scrabbled for his pencil and his pad. He'd written laboriously, the pad wedged under his lifeless hand: 'No more Toad and Mr Badger?'

Theo had read the ill-formed words and burst into delighted laughter.

'No more Toad and Mr Badger,' he'd agreed. 'You've come through in the only way that truly matters. This—' a gesture put his disability in its proper place – 'has to be dealt with in the same way. So easy to use the power it will give you to blackmail others. Resist it if you can, dear fellow. Don't deny the inner man and don't give up.' He bent and kissed him lightly on the cheek. 'Goodbye, Miles.'

He'd watched them walk together down the length of the ward, Theo leaning heavily on his stick, his height dwarfing Fliss who looked so slight beside him. At the door they'd turned to wave, Fliss pantomimed a kiss, and then they'd gone. Fighting down the tears, he'd thought that it was so typical of Theo that, whilst he comforted and gave you his love, he also injected courage and showed you something hard on which to bite, something solid with which to wrestle and so grow strong. Physical recovery was not the only thing that mattered.

Now, renewed by the memory, he saw that Fliss and the twins were coming towards him. It was a shock to see that Jamie looked just like he, himself, had looked at the same age and that Bess was so pretty . . . Why had he wasted so much time? How had he dared to believe that he could put life on hold, to be picked up again when he chose so to do? Why should he expect anything but rejection from these two whom he had all but ignored for most of their lives? Bess was bending over him, kissing him: Jamie had taken his warm, lively hand and was holding it tightly. Across their heads Fliss smiled at him; chin lifted, eyes thoughtful, she watched him greet his children.

He thought: No self-pity, no trading on their sympathy. Theo's right. I mustn't cheat to win them back to me. This is where the real danger lies.

He smiled at her and then held out his pad to the twinnies. He'd already written his message as carefully and neatly as he could and they bent together to read it.

I can't tell you how much it means to have you here. Bless you both for coming. Tell me all your news and enjoy the fact that I can't pontificate as usual. Make the most of it. I shall return.

* * *

'Fifteen for tea,' said Prue with a kind of pleasurable horror. 'However shall we manage?'

'Susanna is making plenty of bits and pieces,' Caroline whisked a tray of scones from the Aga and turned them out on to the wire stand. 'I'm about to decorate the big birthday cake so it's just a question now of making masses of those sandwiches. Did we remember to buy extra orange squash for the children?'

'It's in the larder.' Prue put a few crusts from her sandwich making into Rex's basket – he loved it when the children were around, especially Jolyon – and watched him eat them up before returning to her task of spreading and filling. 'I know that Fliss and the twinnies have gone to see Miles but where have the others gone?'

'Hal and Mole are closeted with Theo. Business talks and so on. Jolyon's out in the grounds somewhere.'

'Making sure everything's in order.' Prue smiled reminiscently. 'Fox would have approved of Jolyon.'

'I'm not sure that Ellen would have approved of us this morning, though.' Caroline put a hand to her aching back and glanced about her. 'What a mess. "Tidy up as you go along," she'd be saying. "Leaving all this muddle behind you. Whatever next, I wonder." Never mind. We'll do a massive washing-up in a minute and make ourselves a cup of coffee.'

'Sounds good to me,' said Prue cheerfully. 'What did I do with the eggs?'

Later, the whole family gathered in the hall. Other chairs had been brought in to supplement the two sofas whilst the low table, as well as the two side tables under the windows, were covered with delicious food. Wrapping paper drifted on the flagstones and was tucked into the sides of the chairs whilst cards were propped in the most unlikely places. Mole was already reading Tintin's adventure to Fred, whilst Kit, looking happier than she had when she'd arrived, wore a huge cashmere shawl in gloriously subtle shades of blue. Every now and again she would run an appreciative hand over its comforting softness and then she would exchange a private smile with Fliss. Hal had tried on his new Aran sweater with a wink for Caroline, who beamed back at him, privately pleased with her handiwork. Other presents were unwrapped and exclaimed over and the food disappeared at a quite astonishing speed. Podger was everywhere at once, making certain that no one's cup or plate was empty, and everyone seemed to be talking together.

From his chair opposite the fire, Theo watched them affectionately. They were all very dear to his heart and, as his glance travelled between first this one and then another, his thoughts drifted back in time, to other Birthdays when Freddy had been there, too: tall, beautiful, elegant. How many dramas they had weathered together; how blessed they had been. He was beginning to realise that his recent anxiety had been groundless. The one last thing for which he had been waiting had been caught up and tied gently into the on-going pattern. They had all come through the shock of Miles's stroke and were back on course at last, prepared to deal with the future as best they could. It was quite clear to him now that, in these last few telling weeks, Fliss had moved forward into her rightful place. She had returned from the hospital earlier, with the twinnies full of admiration and praise for their father, and he had seen a new look of peace and confidence in her face. She would be here at The Keep permanently now, bridging the gap until Hal's retirement, so

171

that, between them, she and Hal would take joint place as head of the family. It was as it should be. Watching them, he saw the affection between them, that deep bond of sharing which he and Freddy had experienced, and knew that they would be safe with one another. Dear Mole was at hand to support them and Jolyon would be ready to take up the responsibility when the time came. As for the dark boy . . . Theo felt the familiar leap of the heart, the acknowledgement of his presence, but he knew that this was far beyond his knowledge; that he must trust to the future, give thanks for him and let it go.

Catching Hal's eye, he raised his eyebrows. Hal nodded and called for quiet whilst Fliss began to cut the birthday cake. As his uncle spoke a few words Hal slipped away and, by the time the little speech was coming to an end, he was back in the hall, passing round the glasses of champagne, ready for Theo's traditional toast.

'A happy birthday to the three of you and my good wishes to every one of you for the years ahead. God bless us every one.'

They raised their glasses, from the oldest to the youngest, and echoed his words.

'God bless us every one.'

Chapter Twenty-three

Out on the hill, Jolyon stood quite still, lifting his head to the south-westerly gale which roared above him. He could see the flash of the water far below, fast moving, gleaming in the pale shafts of sunshine which glanced down between the heavy clouds. Beside him Rex pottered, enjoying the change from the garden to which, because of his age and stiff joints, he was generally confined. Jolyon made no attempt to hurry him, pausing as he always did to pay tribute to the dogs buried here by the wall, so that Rex had time to sniff the air, ears alert, his tail waving gently as he remembered other days and other walks.

The twinnies were already far ahead. Their enjoyment of The Keep and its land was not hedged about with the thoughts and memories which were Jolyon's constant companions. The place was alive with past Chadwicks and their companions, their history bound up with his own, but, although the twinnies knew the stories as well as he did, as far as his cousins were concerned these tales had merged gradually with the past and had little to do with their own busy lives. They'd spent a great deal of their half term at the hospital with their father and, in between visits, were possessed of tearing high spirits and great vivacity. Watching them, Jolyon felt envious. It must be wonderful to have a twin, a ready-made friend who'd shared your past and with whom you could be utterly at ease. It didn't seem the same with the usual sibling relationship, although he couldn't quite decide why. Perhaps it was being the same age which was the key; neither twin could pull rank, so to speak.

They were running down the hill, shouting to each other above the wind, revelling in the wildness of the afternoon. As he watched, Bess made a leap and straddled Jamie's back, her arms about his neck in a stranglehold, whilst he almost buckled beneath her unexpected weight. Instead of shaking her off, however, he grabbed her legs and began to run with her, jogging and leaping down the narrow sheep tracks at such a speed that it seemed impossible that he didn't stumble and bring them both down. They reached the shelter of the spinney and Jolyon saw Bess slide to the ground and set off towards the river. Jamie doubled up for a moment, as if he had a stitch, and then straightening, he glanced back up the hill. Jolyon raised his arm and Jamie waved back. They both knew that Jolyon's walk would be dictated by Rex's pace.

Rex was already a little way ahead, on the trail of a long-gone rabbit, and Jolyon followed him slowly. Tomorrow they would be back at school but he held on to the thought that before him lay years of exeats and holidays until, one day, he would live here all the time and never have to leave. He didn't quite know yet how he would accomplish it but he felt strangely certain of it and the knowledge comforted him and made the on-going pain of rejection more bearable.

Dad had already returned to London with Kit but whilst he was at Whitehall he'd promised to come down every weekend and, after all, it wasn't too long until the next exeat. Perhaps that would be the moment to tell him about the plan which was forming in his mind. He still didn't quite know whether it was a good idea or not but Uncle Theo had thought it was quite exciting, although they'd agreed not to tell anyone else just yet.

'Why don't we grow more vegetables?' he'd asked idly, as they'd sat together one afternoon in the sunshine. 'There's so much ground going to waste in the kitchen garden.'

'It's difficult to find help,' his uncle had told him. 'We can't afford a full-time gardener as we once did, and poor Caroline doesn't have the time or energy she used to have. She and your grandmother have the rest of the garden and all the house to look after, too. Anyway, I'm not sure that the three of us could eat too many vegetables, although there will be a few more of us here now.'

'But you could sell them,' he'd argued. 'We could clear out the old stableyard and do all sorts of things. Dad and I were looking at it yesterday. He says that we need space for more cars now that there's lots of people coming and going, so we went to see if it could work. It's quite dangerous with everything falling down and he said that Great-Grandmother had forbidden him to go there when he was little. It was out of bounds.'

'That's quite true,' Uncle Theo had replied. 'That was many years ago now. I'd almost forgotten the stables were there.'

'There's plenty of room for machinery.' Jolyon could see rows and rows of fresh, healthy vegetables and flowers, all being cut ready for market and going off in little vans. 'We could grow all sorts of things. It's a pity there isn't more room, if you ask me.'

174

'Of course there's the land to the south-west, beyond the stables,' his uncle had said thoughtfully. 'We let it out for grass keep. Seventeen acres or so. Not much but you could probably make a living out of it.'

His uncle had looked at him strangely then, as if he was not quite seeing him, but looking at something in the distance, and then they'd smiled at each other. Uncle Theo had said that he'd like to have a word with Dad about it next time he was home and they'd agreed that they wouldn't mention it to anyone until then. It had made Jolyon feel excited in a quiet, contented sort of way and he felt fairly able to deal with going back to school.

He could hear the twinnies' voices carried faintly above the roar and bellow of the wind and he saw that Rex was now some way ahead. Putting his hands to his mouth, he shouted back, and slithering and jumping he began his descent towards the spinney.

'You're looking better,' Clarrie said, bringing Kit a drink, unable to disguise his pleasure at having her back with him. 'I missed you. What with Sin and Andrew in Italy, and you off in Devon, I felt pretty lonely.'

'I told you to come with us.' Kit looked at him affectionately. 'Everyone would have been delighted to see you. You shouldn't be so stubborn.'

'It was a family occasion,' he said. 'It wouldn't have been right. But it's good to see you looking more like your old self. I was beginning to worry about you. I know all that business with Miles has upset you – well, of course it has – but I've never seen you quite so low before.'

'Oh, Clarrie.' Kit put her drink down and held out a hand to him. 'You are such a chum. The truth is that it wasn't just that. It knocked me off my perch, I must admit, but the real problem was that I met up with Jake again.'

He took her hand. 'I suppose I should have guessed,' he said. 'You were behaving so oddly. And Sin—' He stopped.

'And Sin what?' she asked sharply. 'I might have realised that she'd guessed. She came in one evening while Jake was in London and it was terribly difficult to act normally. She tried to worm things out of me but I simply couldn't cope with her knowing. She came straight up here and gave you the third degree, I suppose?'

'She said that she was worried about you,' he answered cautiously, 'and I said I'd try to look after you whilst she and Andrew were away. I didn't get very far, I'm afraid. She suspected that it was a married man but neither of us thought about Jake.'

'I felt so selfish, you see.' She picked up her glass again. 'There was poor old Fliss, coping with this perfectly appalling thing that's happened to Miles, and all I was worried about was that Jake was going back to Madeleine for the second time in my life. I've been almost suicidal. Why can't I simply put him out of my mind?'

'It's a bit like me with old Fozzy,' said Clarrie sadly. 'Oh, I know he was only a dog but life simply isn't the same without him. I've tried to pull myself together but it doesn't work. We're a pair, aren't we? Life seems to have gone stale on us somewhere along the line.'

'I think it started with Sin and Andrew,' said Kit reflectively. 'It's lovely that they're together but it was a major upheaval, wasn't it? It's as if they've gone swimming off down some great waterway on a lovely new adventure and we're left high and dry in a backwater.'

'That sums it up rather neatly,' he agreed. There was a small silence. 'But we don't have to be, do we?'

'Have to be what?'

'Left high and dry. We have freedom of choice. We're not without resources. Perhaps we should find our own lovely new adventure.'

She looked at him, a smile beginning. 'How do you mean?'

He shrugged. 'You name it,' he said. 'We could take a holiday. Buy another dog. Move house.'

'Move *house*?'

'Why not? You're quite right. Things aren't the same here any more. Sin and Andrew are wrapped up in each other, and that's splendid, but why should we sit around here waiting for them to come back from their lovely long holidays? I'm finding the stairs a bit tricky and I'd like another dog. Why shouldn't we go in together with a little house somewhere? Try something new and different. A market town or somewhere like Oxford. With your contacts you could work anywhere and I've got plenty put by. We could do it sensibly and legally so that if it didn't work out we weren't tied to each other. What do you say?'

Kit was staring at him with an amazed awe. 'It sounds . . .' She shook her head and tried again. 'It sounds amazing. Brilliant. Really exciting. But could we? Isn't it a bit . . . risky?'

He shrugged again. 'I'm seventy-two,' he said. 'You're forty-seven. We're not young any more. And think about what's just happened to Miles. Do we have time to waste?'

Kit shivered. 'Don't,' she said. 'Oh, Clarrie, do you think we could? It sounds such fun. But where would we start?'

176

'Anywhere you like,' he said, grinning at her. 'The world is our oyster. Let's have another drink and we'll go from there.'

'It feels so strange now that everyone's gone back, doesn't it?' Caroline heaved the washing out of the machine and picked up the heavy basket with an effort. 'Are you off to the hospital?'

'Any minute now.' Fliss finished her coffee and began the usual hunt for car keys. 'I can't tell you how glad I shall be to have him home.'

'I think it's lovely that he'll be home in time for Christmas.' Caroline rested the basket on the edge of the table for a moment. 'It must have done him a power of good to hear that.'

'Oh, it has. He's getting about quite well now with his stick.' Fliss discovered the keys on the dresser and slipped them into her jacket pocket. 'I just wish I could understand him better. Well, you know what I mean.'

'Mmm.' Caroline nodded. 'I find that it's best to make a serious attempt but if it doesn't work then I give in and let him write it down. He exhausts himself so quickly otherwise, doesn't he?'

'I think that it's a relief in a way to write things on his pad,' agreed Fliss. 'A relief for him as well as for us, I mean. But on another level it frustrates him because he feels he's not making progress. It's a fine line to walk. I'm beginning to recognise certain sounds now and he is so thrilled when I can understand him. The expression on his face is terribly touching that I feel guilty when it doesn't work.'

'It'll be easier when he's home with us all,' said Caroline consolingly. 'We'll be able to share the burden of it all and he'll be more relaxed. There will be a great improvement, you'll see.'

Fliss smiled at her. 'I'm sure you're right,' she said. 'The nurses are just brilliant but it's not an ideal environment. Just keep your fingers crossed that there are no setbacks when the assessment team come round to check us out. I'd better be off. See you later.'

Setting off down the drive, Fliss felt the now familiar sense of peace descend upon her. The car had become a kind of sanctuary. In this little metal box she was alone, unapproachable, detached from the whirl of daily life. No demands were made upon her as she drove carefully through deep, quiet lanes or sped down the A38. She had a collection of tapes which she selected according to her mood. Sometimes she listened to Sibelius, sometimes to Nina Simone; sometimes to Thomas Tallis, sometimes to Gilbert and Sullivan. This morning she chose Sibelius's First Symphony. When she was very young this piece of music, along with his Seventh Symphony, had symbolised the relationship between herself and Hal: romantic, poignant, stirring, they contained all that was essential to accompany those turbulent, passionate emotions. Now, privately, she laughed at herself, accusing herself of sentimentality; nevertheless the association persisted. She no longer accused herself of disloyalty. Hal's love strengthened her, held her steady, enabling her to give Miles all the support that he needed.

These precious moments in the car also gave her the chance to let off steam. Here she was able to let her imagination run riot, to feel free; neither mother nor wife but only herself. She was allowed to weep or to laugh, or even simply to sit quietly at the wheel, empty and relaxed. It was only after the twinnies had returned to school that she realised how great a load had been lifted from her heart by Miles's approach to them and their attitude to him. It was hard that his stroke should have happened just when they were beginning to know each other but it was clear that all three of them intended to keep trying even harder. They had been impressed by his determination, whilst his cheerfulness, as well as the complete absence of self-pity, had released in them a flood of unforced affection for him.

Fliss heaved a great sigh and gave herself up to the music. Memories flooded into her mind; memories of those special moments which she and Hal had shared during more than thirty years. Now, at least, they would be under the same roof – although Hal would continue to be away for much of the time – and it was a tremendous comfort to know that there would be times when they could be together. For Fliss the prospect of Hal's company was like a beacon, lighting the dark corners of whatever might lie ahead. He was as much hers now as he could ever be and, after the years of separation and loneliness, this knowledge was enough to ease her heart and give her courage.

Chapter Twenty-four

It was almost a month later when Hal arrived late on Friday night for the weekend. A tyre puncturing just outside London had delayed him, and an accident on the M5 had resulted in serious tailbacks. It was good to drive in between the gatehouses, grab his grip and go into the cosy, welcoming hall; good to see Fliss's small face light up at the sight of him; good to receive his mother's warm embrace; good to grasp his uncle's hand, to see his smile. Caroline had some supper ready for him and he sank gratefully into the ease and comfort of his home, knowing that he could be there without guilt, that it was where he belonged.

Later, standing at his bedroom window, looking away to the west, he watched the moon rising above the fir trees, drenching the garden in its silver light. It was hard to know that Fliss was just across the landing; to be in such close proximity – yet unable to cross that final threshold.

Hal thought: We're fools. Any other couple would have been lovers long since.

He chuckled a little mirthlessly. It wasn't quite that easy, not with his mother's room next door to his own and Fliss's rooms adjoining Uncle Theo's but, even if this hadn't been the case, he knew that they wouldn't have taken the chance. They could have made plenty of opportunities over the years but he knew – and he guessed that Fliss felt exactly as he did – that once they started a physical relationship it would be impossible to stop; it would change everything. Half measures simply weren't good enough; it must be all or nothing.

So it would be nothing – if this, indeed, were nothing: to be living legitimately together under the same roof, to give and accept affection; to walk together, to laugh or worry about the children; to share almost everything. No, it was not nothing that they had . . .

A vixen barked down in the valley and an owl was hunting in the woods. Hal took one last look before he drew the curtains. He knew that the moonlight would keep him awake and he was tired, damned tired. Turning back into the room, he switched on the bedside lamp and began to unpack his grip.

The room was still dark when Theo woke. The moon had set long since but the stars were paling in the growing light from the east. He lay for a while, allowing the dreams and shadows of the night to fade, wishing that he was waking to one of those heartachingly beautiful spring days. On this November morning he would be lucky if he saw the sun rise. The recent weather had been bone-chillingly damp, depressingly grey, but yesterday afternoon the clouds had drawn off and the sun had brightened the hours before tea.

Slowly, Theo hauled himself to the edge of the bed and sat upright. Years of habitual austerity had left its mark but now he pulled on his dressing gown and felt for his slippers before he made his careful way to his chair by the window. The curtains, as usual, were drawn back but the window was closed. In the past he'd slept with his windows open, winter and summer alike, but it was a few years now since his family had allowed him to risk the icy blasts or bitter damp which assailed this ancient hill.

Even in the grey half-light the landscape was familiar. Perhaps it was simply that his inner eye supplied what could not be seen but he felt the usual sense of peace, sitting here looking out. How many mornings, he wondered, had he watched the year turning, the seasons passing? Here, each morning, he had pondered on the mysteries of life, lifting up the problems which beset the family, giving thanks for its joys and blessings. The long pageant of family life was being played out against the backdrop of the Devonshire hills, lived amongst its lanes and beaches and moors. This latest drama was no exception to the others which had gone before and which would have its place with them in time.

Sitting in his chair, waiting for the sunrise, Theo relived memories which marked his personal history of The Keep. Silently, on the screen of his mind, he saw Freddy's arrival as Bertie's bride and once again watched her playing the piano in the drawing room; small head poised, shoulders squared . . . Scene followed scene: his brother's departure to the war; his father's funeral; the twins, Peter and John, playing in the courtyard, going off to school, bringing home pretty girls in dashing sports cars. He watched Freddy suffering beneath the blow of Johnny's death, railing against the injustices of life, turning to him for comfort. He saw the three orphaned children moving from shadow into sunlight and kneeled again in spirit with Freddy as she died. Weddings, christenings, birthdays, Christmases, turned gently before his inward vision and

180

he dwelled lovingly upon each one before letting it go and passing to the next . . .

When he opened his eyes the landscape was taking shape in the morning light. Trees, bleak as charcoal cutouts, were resuming their bulky, grainy density; the dark hills, now touched with a glowing brightness, were curving into ample roundness, their shadowy steepsided coombes revealing patchy detail: clumps of dead bracken, seamed ledges of rock. Down in the spinney, bare branches stretched twiggy fingers to the pale, pure sky and the dew-drenched fields, a patchwork of plough, grass and stubble, were washed with muted colour: terracotta, silver-grey, green-gold.

Filled with joy, Theo reached for his prayer book and began to read the Daily Office. *The night has passed and the day lies open before us. Let us pray with one heart and mind . . .*

Presently he put the book aside and closed his eyes, opening himself to the hidden, peaceful loving inflow of God. As the blessed communion filled his heart, inflaming it with love, he experienced a new depth of longing; a yearning which was soon to be fulfilled. Soon . . . Now . . . He struggled briefly but his limbs were too heavy, his mind cloudy with images. Peace dispelled the lingering anxieties and fears and he gave himself up to it, willingly.

> *. . . so I shall rejoice:*
> *you will not delay, if I do not fail to hope.*

As he bowed his head in death the sun came rolling up, a hard red ball from behind the distant hills, and bathed him in its light.

'Hal's sleeping in,' said Prue, glancing at the kitchen clock. 'He was very late last night, wasn't he? I must say that it's lovely knowing that he'll be with us so often.'

She glanced quickly at Fliss, knowing that she probably hurt her quite often with unconsidered remarks, but Fliss was finishing her toast quite calmly, writing a shopping list as she did so.

'Lovely for Jolyon, too,' Prue added hurriedly. 'He's settling down already, don't you think?'

Fliss smiled at her, still slightly preoccupied. 'I think he is,' she agreed. 'It's better to know where you stand, isn't it? He'll come to terms with it in time and, you know, it's possible that Maria may well realise how foolish she's been in turning her back on him and try to make amends.'

She didn't add 'like Miles with the twins' knowing that Prue might get bogged down in regrets and anxieties and that all sorts

181

of explanations would be necessary. Fliss was well aware that Prue was torn between her joy at having Hal and Jolyon at The Keep permanently and her anxiety lest she, Fliss, was affected by Hal's presence.

Fliss thought: Well, I *am* affected by it. And sometimes it's painful and frustrating but it's worth all that to have him near.

'That's quite possible,' Prue was saying. 'At least she lets Hal see Edward although I gather that it's not working terribly well.'

'It'll probably be more successful when Edward's older,' said Fliss. 'It's very difficult for him, caught in the middle. When he's grown up he'll make his own decisions. Jolyon won't let him go.'

'Darling Jolyon. Theo and Hal are rather taken with that idea of his, you know. It would be rather fun, wouldn't it? Jolyon's very excited about it, according to Theo, but I should think that it would take a long time before it could work properly.'

'I think it's a terrific idea,' said Fliss. 'They've suggested that the best way would be to make a serious start in the kitchen garden and expand it slowly. See how it goes. He'll have to take it very seriously and approach it in a very sensible businesslike way, of course, but . . .'

'Sugar,' said Caroline, appearing suddenly from the larder. 'Brown. And coffee. I think that's it. Have you got it all down?'

'I think so.' Fliss added the items to her list. 'Any library books to go back?'

'I haven't finished mine yet,' said Prue. 'Theo's a bit late, isn't he? It's nearly half-past nine.'

An uneasy silence dropped into the peaceful ordinariness of the morning and the three women paused in their small tasks. A glance ran between them and a feeling, beginning in anxiety and turning to fear, seized them.

'I'll go up.' Fliss pushed back her chair, her list forgotten.

'I'll come with you,' said Prue. 'Could he have slept late, too?'

Nobody answered her and Caroline closed the larder door and followed them up the stairs. They stood in silence whilst Fliss knocked at the door, quietly at first and then more loudly.

'Uncle Theo,' she called. 'Uncle Theo, are you OK?'

Prue stood quite still, her knuckles to her lips, her eyes fixed on the unyielding door. Above her head, Caroline and Fliss exchanged another glance. Caroline gave an almost imperceptible nod and, with another quick knock, Fliss opened the door and went in, the others crowding behind her. Seeing him sitting there by the window, peaceful and relaxed, chin on chest, they hesitated. It was Caroline who went to his side and gently took his hand. She felt for his pulse and then bent to put her head on his silent breast. Straightening up she looked at them, shaking her head, and Prue gave a tiny cry.

'I'll call John Halliday,' said Caroline – and hesitated, as if suddenly remembering that she was not a member of the family. 'Shall I?'

'Yes,' said Fliss. 'Yes, that's the proper thing to do. Just so as to be . . . absolutely sure. I suppose he might just be . . . ?'

Caroline shook her head. 'I don't think so,' she said gently. 'But I'll go and telephone.'

She glanced anxiously at Prue, as if uncertain whether she should take her along, too, but Prue shook her head. She settled herself on the window seat and took Theo's hand in her own.

'I shall wait with him,' she said simply. 'I'd like to.' She smiled at the two of them. Her eyes were full of tears but her face was calm. 'I've known him for fifty years,' she said. 'He's been like a father to me. The dearest friend I've ever had. I've loved him more than anyone except Johnny and I'd like to have a moment or two alone with him now.'

'Yes, of course,' said Fliss, touched by the simplicity of Prue's little speech. 'We'll be back in a moment.'

She closed the door quietly behind them and Caroline put an arm about her shoulders and gave her a little hug.

'Go and talk to Hal,' she said. 'I'm going downstairs to telephone the surgery.'

Fliss stood quite still, trying to adjust to a world that had no Uncle Theo in it; no wise and calming presence; no undemanding love; no strong arm between her and the world . . .

The bathroom door opened and Hal came out on to the landing. His hair was rumpled and damp, some of his shirt buttons were undone and his feet were bare. He stopped, surprised at her stillness, brows drawing together.

'What is it?' he asked sharply. 'What's the matter?' He stretched out his arms to her and spoke more gently. 'Oh, Flissy. Has something happened?'

She stumbled across the landing towards him, her face crumpling, her composure disintegrating, and burrowed into his embrace.

'Uncle Theo's dead,' she said. 'Oh, Hal. He's dead. What shall we do without him?' – and he held her tightly whilst she sobbed, his chin on her head, his face sombre with shock and grief.

'I never realised,' said Susanna, a few days after the funeral, 'that Uncle Theo knew so many people. They were standing in the churchyard because the church was full.'

183

'He touched people's lives,' said Gus. 'There were people there who'd heard him preach years ago when he used to stand in for the clergy in the surrounding parishes. They said that they could never quite forget him.'

'And there others who said that he'd helped them. From his time in the Navy.' Susanna shook her head. 'It's so odd. He was so quiet. So unassuming.'

'He changed all our lives,' said Prue. She seemed to have lost weight and she was pale but composed. 'In one way or another.'

There were only a few members of the family still at The Keep. Most had returned to their places of employment or education. Hal had been obliged to return to London for an important meeting but Mole had remained for a few days, going with Fliss to visit Miles – who had taken the news surprisingly badly – and helping out where he could.

Now he put his cup and saucer on the low table and went to join Fliss at the window where she stood looking out into the courtyard.

'OK?' he asked.

She smiled warmly at him, glad of his unobtrusive support. He'd been such a comfort during the last week.

'I think so,' she said. 'I'm tired of losing people I love.'

'You and me both,' he said. 'I rather liked that psalm you asked me to read at the funeral. It's a coincidence, actually, because I was thinking about it quite recently in connection with Uncle Theo. That bit about his faithfulness being a shield and a buckler always made me think about him. What made you decide on it?'

'I picked up his book, you know, when John Halliday came. It was lying on the window seat. It's got the Daily Office services in it and he used to read them each morning and each evening. I took it back to my room and opened it at one of the markers. It was that psalm. When I read it I just thought it was so fitting. I know it almost by heart now. Thanks for reading it, Mole. You were just great. I'd have been in tears by the second verse.'

'That's OK. I was proud to do it. Like old Hal reading the lesson. Not much to repay him for everything he did for us.'

He saw that she was trying not to cry and sought for some means of comfort.

'I'll get you another cup of tea, shall I?' he asked – and she nodded gratefully, not daring herself to speak.

As she waited, her back to the others, she watched the rain drumming on the cobbles, dripping from the gutters, and the words from the psalm repeated themselves in her head:

184

He who dwells in the shelter of the Most High, abides under
the shadow of the Almighty.
He shall say to the Lord, 'You are my refuge and my
stronghold, my God in whom I put my trust . . .

She thought that the last verses of the psalm, too, seemed particularly apt; the words of God to his servant:

Because he is bound to me in love therefore will I deliver him:
I will protect him, because he knows my name.
He shall call upon me and I will answer him; I am with him
in trouble; I will rescue him and bring him to honour.
With long life will I satisfy him, and show him my
salvation.

It was as if Theo's hand were upon her shoulder, strengthening her, and Mole's smile, as he handed her the tea, was Theo's own; reassuring, loving. She wiped away her tears, smiling back at him, and was comforted.

Chapter Twenty-five

The church was decorated for Christmas. The tall tree soared upwards into the shadowy arches, its tiny coloured lights twinkling and glancing from the glass baubles and the coloured tinsel which decorated its branches. On the bronze cover of the font the Nativity scene was set out: tiny carved figures grouped about the Holy family, which sheltered in an open-fronted barn borrowed from somebody's toy farmyard. At this moment, however, the congregation's attention was concentrated towards the front of the church where, in the wide space before the lady chapel, a live performance of this small scene was about to be enacted. Perched on the rows of chairs, anxious mothers, one or two busy fathers, proud grandparents and fidgety siblings were preparing to watch the first of the three celebrations of the annual Nativity play.

The Chadwicks were there in force to see Lulu make her début as an actress. True, she was only to be the little shepherd boy, but she had all the responsibility of carrying the lamb which was to be presented to the Infant Jesus, and nerves were stretched. Fliss, Caroline and Prue were ready to be entertained but Susanna was slightly more concerned lest her small daughter should trip up the step, unbalancing the Virgin Mary and knocking over the crib in the process, as she had done at the dress rehearsal. A wailing Lulu had been comforted, the lamb dusted down; nevertheless the unfortunate accident had made her nervous. Susanna was tense with trepidation, clutching her hymn sheet in one hand whilst, with the other, she forcibly restrained her elder daughter from rushing out to organise the entire proceedings.

Podger watched, legs swinging, arms folded, chin on chest, deeply frustrated. In her youth – Podger was properly conscious of her seniority – she had played a splendid Innkeeper at one of these kindergarten plays and she was bursting with advice for the small boy who now waited nervously in the shadow of the pulpit. Susanna, smiling to herself, also remembered the occasion. Arms akimbo, Podger had gazed with haughty impatience upon the intimidated

187

Joseph as he'd stammeringly requested shelter. The Virgin Mary, giving a creditable performance on a push-along dog on wheels, had flinched tearfully at Podger's sharply derisive reply and Joseph had instinctively ducked as she'd suddenly leaned forward to twitch his turban into its proper place. In later years she'd moved on to the part of Herod and had been so sinister in the role that one or two of the smallest children had had to be removed, screaming in terror.

The choir had now been assembled, sitting cross-legged to the left of the steps and, to the opening chords of 'Once in royal David's city', Joseph now appeared, pushing a weary Mary on her 'donkey'. By the end of the hymn they had reached the stage, the Innkeeper was stepping out from behind the pulpit and the play had begun. Mary and Joseph were shown to the stable and, whilst the choir sang 'Away in a manager', the Baby Jesus was laid carefully in the manger.

Watching Mary tucking her baby tenderly amongst the straw, Fliss felt the usual desire to weep. There was something so evocative, so full of memories, about this simple scene: the children dressed in cut-down sheets, tea-towels wound about their heads, rattling monotonously through their lines or attacking them with all the verve of future Peggy Ashcrofts; the enthusiasm of the choir getting the better of its ability to stay in tune; the shy beamings at relatives in the audience. She thought of Mole and Susanna taking part in Nativity plays, here in this very church thirty years ago, and of her own twinnies playing these same roles at various naval Christmas parties. Young Fred and Podger had followed in their footsteps and now it was Lulu's turn.

Fliss thought: If only Uncle Theo could have been here to see her.

Though she was just as strong-willed as her older sister, Lulu did not have Podger's powers of organisation and it was to be hoped that she would not find it necessary to sort out the cast in between her own scenes. Podger simply could not rest whilst any form of untidiness, slackness or disobedience was evident and, even at the tender age of four, had found it necessary to attend to such deficiencies in her fellow thespians to the amusement of the audience and the embarrassment of her family.

Fliss, thinking of just such an occasion, remembered how Uncle Theo had leaned near to her, murmuring, 'She'd make a splendid colour sergeant, don't you think? Even the Angel Gabriel is looking apprehensive, poor fellow,' and they'd chuckled quietly together whilst Susanna had watched her small daughter with dismay and Gus had covered his eyes with his hand. The memory was enough to make Fliss swallow hard, the pain in her heart still fresh as ever as she tried to concentrate on the arrival of the shepherds. Lulu came last, carrying the woolly lamb whose dangling back legs were almost as long as her own, and positioned herself carefully at the bottom of the long step below the Holy family. Her burnous, made from a large bath towel in fetching blue and pink stripes, had been shortened a little since the accident and her Conker shoes – a cheerful note of green and red leather – showed beneath its hem. Having got her bearings and heaving the lamb more securely into her arms, she looked about her. The choir were singing lustily now – 'Whilst shepherds watched their flocks by night' – but Lulu was more interested in picking out her own family in the audience. Singing tunelessly and randomly she peered about until she caught her mother's eye and beamed widely, hoisting the lamb aloft to show that it had not been left in the vestry which was doubling as a dressing room. Susanna nodded back, restraining the urge to grin broadly, and gestured sternly with a nod of her head towards the proceedings.

As the carol came to an end her relatives watched with bated breath as Lulu stepped forward to make her gift. Joseph, a sensible little boy who had sustained a nasty bruise in the previous encounter with the presentation of the lamb, reached to help her and together they laid her offering at the foot of the manger. The Virgin Mary smiled sweetly at them both and, gasping with relief, rolling her eyes dramatically, Lulu stepped triumphantly back into her place. The family relaxed as the three Wise Men paced solemnly up the aisle and, under the cover of a spirited rendition of 'We three kings of Orient are', Susanna whispered, 'Thank heaven for that. One down, two to go.'

'She was great,' answered Fliss. 'Terrific. I'm so glad that the twinnies and Jo will be home in time to see her tomorrow.'

'Gus is coming to the last one. Remember when Fred was Joseph, and Mary had a fit of nerves and dropped the Baby Jesus?'

Fliss began to laugh but, before she could reply, Podger peered along the row to frown upon the whisperers and the sisters hastily picked up their hymn sheets and joined in the singing.

Back at The Keep preparations were being made, not only for Christmas but for Miles's return from the hospital. As she made up the beds ready for the children's arrival later, Fliss hoped that he'd begun to feel more excited about coming home. His quarters were quite ready and she'd spent many visiting hours describing exactly where his room was, how the furniture had been arranged and how the cloakroom had been converted to give him maximum accessibility so that when he'd come out for his day's trial it had gone very smoothly. She'd long since discovered how easy it was to tip over the narrow line which lay between encouragement and insensitivity. In attempting enthusiasm it was only too easy to make it sound as if Miles were extraordinarily lucky to be in his position; as if he should be envied and that he should be grateful to have the benefits The Keep could afford him. At these moments Fliss would cringe inwardly, confused and ashamed, and would somehow change the subject. She was still puzzled by the change in Miles since Uncle Theo's death. She'd told him gently, holding his hand tightly, guessing that he would feel frustrated at being unable to comfort her in her sorrow. Instead, his hand had become quite limp and a shudder had passed over his frame. Tears had flowed from beneath his closed lids – he wept easily since his stroke – and his mouth had trembled as he tried to frame words. Anxiously she had assured him of Theo's easy passing and painless death but he was not to be comforted.

Continuing to hold his hand, trying to distract him from his distress, she'd been eventually forced to speak plainly.

'I'm so sorry, darling,' she'd said. 'I knew you were fond of him but I had no idea that you'd be so upset.'

He'd squeezed her hand, let it go and, reaching for his handkerchief, he'd wiped his face roughly. He'd rummaged for his writing pad amongst the muddle on his tray table and scribbled a few words. When he'd thrust the pad towards her she saw the scrawled sentence running unevenly across the page: 'We were going to play backgammon together.'

Reading the words, Fliss had felt an uprush of grief. She could remember talking to her uncle about how they would manage when Miles came home. She'd been brittle, nervous, and her uncle had reassured her, saying that he would read to him.

'*We shall have a whale of a time together,*' he'd said. '*It's a challenge. We shall play backgammon. Miles won't let a thing like this destroy him . . .*'

Clearly Theo had somehow invested Miles with the same courage and hope which he'd instilled in them all, at one time or another, through the past years and Miles, too, would feel the loss. This thought had enabled Fliss to square her shoulders and smile at Miles as she'd returned his pad.

'You'll just have to make do with me,' she'd said, with an attempt at cheerfulness, and he'd tried to smile back at her with that lopsided grimace which made her want to weep afresh. Nevertheless, a melancholy had descended upon him which was difficult to alleviate.

Now, as she finished making up beds for the twinnies, Fliss hoped that the actual homecoming would do the trick: that a houseful of people would distract Miles. Mole was delaying the beginning of his leave so as to be able to collect Bess; Hal was picking up Jolyon and Jamie on his way from London; Kit and Clarrie would be arriving late on Christmas Eve. Trying not to think about how different it would be without Uncle Theo, Fliss crossed the passage to the big walk-in cupboard and went inside to find the decorations for the Christmas tree.

A few days later everyone except Kit and Clarrie had arrived and the celebrations were under way. Caroline and Prue seemed to have been cooking for weeks and were only too ready to let Hal make a fuss of them whilst they, in turn, made a fuss of Miles. It seemed that Fliss's hopes were to be realised and to be at last in his own quarters, to be able to get himself about the ground floor – albeit slowly with the aid of a stick – had certainly lifted his spirits. It was Mole, however, who elected to be his right hand; the one who unobtrusively anticipated his needs and sat with him, patiently making sense of his garbled speech. The twinnies and Jolyon disappeared on shopping jaunts to Totnes whilst Hal inspected the remains of the wine cellar and Prue and Caroline sat in the hall by the fire with their feet up, wondering what Hal might produce to tickle their palates.

One afternoon, coming out of her bedroom, Fliss received a tiny shock to see Hal, through the open door, bending over Theo's desk. He glanced up and beckoned to her.

'Ma and Caroline insist I move in here,' he said, almost embarrassed. 'It makes sense, I suppose, but it feels like sacrilege somehow.'

She knew that it was an apology and she hastened to reassure him.

'I felt exactly the same about using Grandmother's rooms,' she said. 'I know it's silly but, after all, the rooms can't be left empty. Anyway, you'll be glad of the extra space now you're here for good.'

He smiled. 'I hope it's for good,' he said, 'with all that it implies. I shan't change the room much, though. I like being in here. I feel the old boy's with me and there's a wonderfully peaceful atmosphere.'

She looked about her, at the battered leather-topped desk and the

191

bookcase still full of Theo's books. It seemed impossible that he should not appear, strolling in from his bedroom, the familiar smile crinkling his eyes . . .

Hal was watching her. 'I know,' he said sadly. 'It's the terrible finality of it, isn't it?'

She nodded, lips pressed firmly together, and he slipped an arm about her shoulders.

'The twinnies and Jo are back from Totnes,' he said, 'and we're going out on to the hill to cut holly. Put on a warm jacket and come with us.'

'Yes,' she said. 'Yes, that sounds like fun.'

'Go on, then,' he said. 'If we crack on we'll be back in time for tea' – but he still held her within his arm, as if reluctant to let her go.

They looked at one another for a long moment and then the twinnies came tumbling down the nursery stairs and he gave her a quick hug before releasing her.

'Hurry,' he said. 'See you downstairs in a few minutes,' – and the twinnies gathered her along with them as they raced on down the stairs to the kitchen where Jolyon was waiting for them.

The Christmas Eve market was busy as usual and Gus, strolling over from the studio, watched the activity with pleasure and a sense of belonging. He was thinking of earlier years, when he and Susanna had lived in the little flat above the studio where they'd been so happy and where their own Christmas traditions had come to birth. Because they lived over the studio, they'd always spend some of Christmas Eve morning tidying up before pottering around the market, listening to the carols. Afterwards they'd have lunch at the Kingsbridge Inn and much later they'd attend the midnight service at St Mary's. When they got back to the flat they'd have coffee and mince pies, before falling into the big, saggy bed, and in the morning they'd open their presents before going to The Keep for lunch.

Gus smiled reminiscently. What fun they'd had. Since the move to the barn and the arrival of three children some of those traditions had given way to others but there was one tradition which Gus had always managed to preserve.

From her place in the market square the woman, well-wrapped up against the cold, watched him cross the road. For the last fourteen years he'd bought a pot of Christmas hyacinths for his pretty wife which he collected at the last minute, lest they should be discovered. Now, he had two little girls exactly like their mother

192

and a son the spit of himself – but he never forgot the Christmas hyacinths.

'The dear of him,' the woman murmured to herself as he approached, and she bent to lift a pot containing three bulbs from a hidden stock beneath the trestle table. Bright, green, swordlike leaves thrust up from the crumbly rich earth but as yet there was no sign of flowers.

'Good morning.' He smiled at her. 'Have you seen my family about?'

'They were in much earlier, buying some hyacinths for their Aunt Prue, so they told me.' Her mittened fingers fumbled for change. 'There was some dispute as to who was to carry it. Blue is her colour, it seems. Not like your lady, sir.' She passed the pot to him. 'Pink as usual.'

'Pink as usual,' he agreed. 'Thank you so much.'

She watched him put the pot carefully into a large bag and then he dug into his pocket.

'You've brought us so much pleasure over the years,' he said, 'that I hoped you might like to share in it with us.'

She opened the envelope cautiously. It contained a Christmas card and a photograph had been stuck inside on the page opposite the greetings. Susanna smiled out at her, the children grouped about her, and beside them on a table was a pot of beautiful pink hyacinths in full, glorious flower. Underneath the printed good wishes someone had written carefully: 'With love to our hyacinth lady.'

She saw that all the names had been signed each by his or her owner and, when she looked up at him, her eyes were very bright. For some reason she seemed to find it difficult to speak, so Gus leaned across and kissed her lightly on the cheek.

'Happy Christmas,' he said. 'Many blessings. See you next year.'

Book Three
Winter 1994

Chapter Twenty-six

The puppy lay half in, half out of the enormous dog basket, his huge front paws and floppy ears resting almost on the kitchen floor. He was Jolyon's birthday present and he'd been named Rufus. His fluffy coat was a dark rich gold with a reddish tint and Jolyon had named him at once which, as Kit pointed out, was the very best way to name a dog. All his toys – as well as various other items – were in the basket with him: a tea-towel tugged from the Aga's rail; one of Jolyon's shoes; a gardening glove. No matter how heavy or unwieldy an article, Rufus would tug it and drag it until he had gained the basket with his new acquisition. Here he would worry it and play with it or sometimes merely sit on top of it triumphantly. One had to be hard-hearted indeed to deprive him of any of his treasures.

Sitting at the kitchen table, Jolyon watched him. Presently he would reclaim his shoe but first he would find another, older, one with which to replace it. At eight weeks old Rufus was not likely to do the thick leather a great deal of harm but it was a rather favourite pair which Jolyon didn't want ruined. He still missed Rex but he was feeling all the pride and delight of ownership in the old dog's successor; revelling in the thought of the years of companionship ahead. It would be fun when Rufus was old enough to be with him in the garden but as yet he would simply be in the way.

Jolyon reached for a biscuit, feeling at ease. It was odd to have the kitchen to himself at this time of the morning. Usually Caroline and Granny were bustling about, or Miles might be reading the newspaper whilst Fliss made coffee, so it was unusual to find himself alone. Just occasionally, however, it was good to sit in silence, thinking about things and reviewing the last six months since he'd left school. His project was going splendidly. It was just over three years now since he'd first had the idea of making The Keep's land pay for itself, and he still had a long way to go, but he'd made a very promising start. During the holidays he'd visited all the nurseries and grocery shops in the area, making a survey –

he'd called it rather grandly 'market research' – and discovering what would be the best things to grow. He'd found that many of these outlets bought in their shrubs, rather than raising their own stock, and that the demand for organic vegetables was growing.

He hadn't realised that all his own vegetables were grown organically anyway but he'd decided to make a determined start in these two areas and, even whilst he was still at school, he'd begun to build up a respectable little business. Without Caroline he couldn't have done it. She'd looked after the greenhouses and worked in the vegetable garden whilst he fretted at school but during the holidays he'd worked long and hard. He had no desire to go to university, and no one had pressed him, although his mother had been contemptuous when she'd heard his plans.

'A gardener?' She'd laughed in disbelief, her eyes unfriendly, and he'd had to brace himself against her scorn. He still longed for her to love him as she loved Ed, to win her approval, but he was old enough now to know that this was a vain hope. Yet she still had the power to hurt him, to make his precious plans look ridiculous even in his own eyes. He'd tried to explain that it was a proper business, that the Trust had given him a loan to set him up and that everything had been costed out. He had planned it thoroughly and knew exactly where he was going. Miles and Fliss had bought him a poly-tunnel for his eighteenth birthday and he was hoping to become part of the Riverford Farm Co-operative, selling them his organic vegetables. Apart from this he spent a great deal of time looking after The Keep, maintaining it, caring for it. These duties were costed in and offset against his loan.

'Wasn't that what Fox used to do?' Maria had asked, her lip curling in disdain. 'Well, if that's the extent to which your ambitions stretch . . .'

She'd shrugged, turning away from him, and after that he didn't have the courage to tell her his ideas for renovating the rooms in the gatehouse so that he could be independent.

'Go for it,' Ed had said to him privately, later. 'Sounds like fun.'

It was as if they were two separate families now: Ed and Mum and Adam; himself and Dad. He had no intention of letting Ed be swallowed up completely, however. He wrote to him at school, telephoned him and bullied him down to The Keep for holidays. Casual outings with Dad simply didn't work. Dad was edgy with the prospect of having to see Mum and Adam; Ed was confused by his sense of loyalty. Down here in Devon they were both more relaxed and this last summer had been really good.

Of course, he'd come to accept that The Keep wasn't really Ed's scene, any more than it was the twinnies' or Kit's; they liked to come for brief visits and then vanish away again. Well, that was fine. The point was that it was here waiting for them if they needed it. At least he'd given up on his dream that somehow Mum and Dad would get together again. All through those last years at Blundell's he'd lived with a variation on that theme, prayed for it, hoped for it, but now he knew it would never happen. Part of him no longer wanted it to happen – it was too late – but he was still angry and hurt by the way he'd been sacrificed and used as a kind of scapegoat. There had been some very black moments during those final sixth form years when he'd shut himself in his study, listening to Pearl Jam or Pink Floyd, remembering the past and wishing that they were still a happy family unit.

Whichever way you looked at it, the fact of the matter was that his mother didn't love him and was prepared to hurt and ignore him and didn't give a damn whether she ever saw him again. If only he could understand why. How could you not love your own child? She loved Ed, which showed that it must be some fault in himself, something that he'd done or what he was . . . Dad had once said that it wasn't anything to do with that; that it was because he and Dad were so alike and that by hurting him, Jo, she was able to get at Dad and punish him for letting her down. When he'd asked Dad how he'd let her down he'd looked kind of bleak.

'The trouble was, old son, that we shouldn't have married in the first place,' he'd said at last. 'She was very young and I . . . well, I was away at sea a great deal . . .'

He'd floundered about and it had been awful to watch him, so Jolyon had said that it didn't really matter anyway and they'd talked about something else. It did matter, though; it mattered one hell of a lot. He could see now why Mole and Kit had never married, had never taken the chance. Some grown-ups seemed to think that children had no feelings and could be pushed around and neglected for their own selfish ends. You couldn't stop loving someone to order. Just because Mum had stopped loving Dad she'd been cross that he, Jo, had stayed loyal to him. Dad had tried, he'd tried very hard, and Jo sometimes wished that he could forget about Mum and Ed and just concentrate on the family at The Keep. It was better now that he'd finished school and could get on with his own life. Dad was down quite often, which was great, and he just knew that he was going to make a go of the garden and his plans for the other land. What did it matter if Mum thought he was a loser . . . ?

Rufus was stirring, his small pink mouth yawning widely, wriggling and stretching. He'd be awake any moment and he mustn't suspect that his shoe had been swapped. Remembering a rather battered pair of trainers that he'd left in the scullery, Jolyon slipped out quietly.

In Totnes, Caroline and Prue were having coffee and delicious lemon sponge in the Anne of Cleves café in Fore Street. Shopping had been done, books returned to the library and they'd met up again, chilled to the bone and ready for a warming drink. Prue, unable to resist a treat, had stared so longingly at the cakes displayed in the window that Caroline had relented and agreed that one slice apiece couldn't do much harm. Prue was on a permanent diet which was always going to begin after the next meal.

Caroline thought: We're like a cartoon. Me, tall and stringy. Prue, short and round. The more I eat the thinner I grow but poor old Prue only has to look at a square of chocolate to put on weight.

For a while, in the months after Theo's death, Prue had lost weight. She had mourned him deeply and only Miles's return from hospital had distracted her from her very genuine grief. The sight of Miles, trying to come to terms with his disability, had shocked her out of herself. To everyone's surprise she had reacted with a very positive approach. She neither fussed nor commiserated with him but, instead, treated him with a cheerful affection which seemed to bring an answering response. Although she could sympathise with him for having to give up smoking, she refused to allow him any concessions but almost bullied him into fighting his disability.

'Nearly got it,' she'd say, listening to his stumbling speech. 'No, don't write it down. Have another go. Garment? No? Cardigan, is it? Are you cold? No, no—' as Miles shook his head, frustratedly – 'sorry. Try again. Garden? Yes? Right? *Garden*. Good. Good. So what about the garden?'

They'd go on for hours while the others would be almost desperate for them to stop, to give up and allow Miles to write it down on his pad, but Prue was adamant.

'I can see that it was better for him at the beginning,' she'd agreed, 'when it was all new and frightening. It would have been too cruel, then, to make him fight. But he needs to work at it now.'

It seemed that she'd been right. Miles had risen to the challenge and his apathy had gradually disappeared.

'It's because it's easier for us,' Fliss had admitted to Caroline, 'that we give him his pad to write on. Sometimes I just want to scream with frustration. It's like being with a very small child –

but a child who doesn't learn and develop naturally. When I think of all those mothers coping with autistic children I feel very small and ashamed.'

'To be honest,' Caroline had answered, 'I think that Prue is enjoying herself. She's good at it and she feels useful. That sounds patronising but I don't mean it to be. Over the last few years she's been very low and Theo's death was a frightful blow. It's as if Miles has given her a new purpose. You don't mind, do you?'

'I'm only too thankful.' Fliss had laughed ruefully. 'I've discovered that I'm not as patient as I thought I was. It's very humbling to admit it but I need all the help I can get.'

Now, watching Prue tucking into her sponge, Caroline saw that there was a new serenity about her. The anxious, introspective frown had disappeared and, although she was now in her seventies, there was an odd youthfulness about her. Her short pretty hair was like smoke curling round her head and her blue eyes looked dreamily out at the passers-by.

'What are you thinking about?' Caroline asked suddenly.

'I was thinking about Freddy.' Prue licked her fingers and wiped them on the paper napkin. 'Blessing her for inviting me to come home to The Keep. I suppose I might have made the move eventually but she'll never know what she did for me by actually asking me to make my home there. It made all the difference, you see. She was so sweet at the end.'

'Fliss is very like her,' said Caroline. 'I know how you feel, though. I often thank my lucky stars that I've been able to stay on. I sometimes wonder where I'd be now if things hadn't worked out this way.'

'It's odd, isn't it,' said Prue slowly, 'that none of us has come from a proper family?'

'How do you mean?' Caroline looked startled.

'Well, my parents never functioned properly and you'd lost yours before you were out of your teens. My twins never really knew their father and that awful business with Peter and Alison in Kenya left three orphans. Now Hal's marriage has broken up and there were all those problems between Fliss and Miles. Only Susanna and Gus have really made it. Mole will probably never marry and I've given up hopes of Kit. I just feel glad that she's got old Clarrie. And there's another one who had a tragic life, with his wife and child dying so young. I sometimes think that Kit has become his surrogate daughter. And I do worry about dear Jolyon.'

'I know.' Caroline looked sad. 'He's such a dear. I simply

201

cannot understand Maria. Never mind. We'll all muddle through somehow.'

Prue began to laugh. 'I've just remembered something. A Sunday lunch – oh, years and years ago – and Susanna saying something like: "How will we know how to be husbands and wives when we haven't got anyone to copy?" or something like that. Perhaps she had a point, after all?'

'At least she's managed it.' Caroline finished her coffee. 'Thank heavens that Fred won that scholarship to King's.'

'And Lulu off to Herongate in the autumn. Podger will be delighted to show her the ropes.'

'It'll be odd with no little ones around.' Caroline rummaged for her purse. 'Hurry up with that coffee or the car will be out of time and we'll get a ticket.'

Chapter Twenty-seven

Miles stood for some moments on the steps, surveying the scene before him. The courtyard had a desolate appearance on this chill winter morning but he had set himself certain disciplines and it was no use being discouraged by the weather. Thrusting his stick between his legs, Miles turned up the collar of his British Warm and carefully settled his tweed cap more firmly on his head. He had already put a glove on to his numbed hand but his other glove was ready in his pocket so that he could simply push his hand into it. Organised at last, he took his stick in his left hand and set off across the courtyard. The daily walk was part of his routine and, during these short winter days, it was best to get it over with as early as possible. He'd learned how easy it was to put it off until it was too dark or he was simply too tired to manage it. This had happened quite often in those dispiriting months immediately after the stroke but, as the spring of that following year had drawn on, so his courage had increased. Now, his walk had become as natural a part of the day as shaving or eating – and he preferred to do it on his own. To begin with he'd been glad of a companion – there was always the fear he might be struck down again or that he might simply stumble and fall – but as the weeks passed he'd discovered a need to be alone.

There had been so much to relearn. Doing everything with one hand – and the left one at that – was so time-consuming and tiring. Dressing, eating, washing, every simple action had needed to be learned again. He'd chafed at his lack of independence, becoming quickly frustrated at being treated as if he were a child, but he'd tried hard not to take it out on those who were trying to help him. Theo's words about blackmail were rarely from his mind during those early days when he'd begun to see how tyrannical the sick can become; how easy it would be to use his disability as a weapon.

Passing between the gatehouses Miles looked ahead down the long drive with the usual mix of apprehension and pleasure. There was always the tiny nagging fear that he might never get back to

203

the safety and warmth of The Keep but, at the same time, there was the promise of achievement and the freedom of being alone. At first, just out of hospital, he'd needed to know that there were people around, near at hand, keeping him company. He'd hated being by himself – depression and despair waiting to pounce – and it had been a tremendous comfort to know that at least one of the three women was somewhere close, always within call. Later, much later, he'd felt this need for solitude developing, a requirement to take stock, as it were, and to consider his new situation. It was as if physical movement encouraged a corresponding mental progression and, as his walks extended further, his thoughts flowed forward, too, sorting, filing, discarding, helping him to keep calm and balanced. This had slowly become a necessary part of the healing process until he arrived at the point where he no longer had need of company. Soon it began to irk him to have someone chattering away, feeling the need to point out various flora and fauna, or making banal comments on the changing seasons so as to distract attention from his slow progress and dragging gait.

During those early months, when they'd been too anxious to let him out of sight, one of the three had accompanied him whenever he took any outdoor exercise but, when this latent irritability soon threatened to make its presence more obvious, he'd decided to tell them exactly how he felt about his need for solitude combined with exercise. Rather to his surprise they'd been remarkably understanding so that he'd felt guilty and ungrateful, wondering if he should retract or be more flexible. Finally, he'd decided to stick to his guns and, gradually, his walk had become part of the daily round. Since his naval career had been dominated by drills and routines, by rules and regulations, he'd had little difficulty in disciplining himself and he'd concentrated hard on stretching his body to its limits; testing himself, comparing results, judging his progress.

Today, as he passed slowly, painfully, between the stone walls, he could see now how introverted he'd been; how obsessed by his health and by the possibility of recovery. The shock of the stroke, the disintegration of his life, the frightening awareness of his own mortality, all these had changed him and he could never be the same again. No longer could he live with that innocent carelessness with which his former life had been invested.

The blow had fallen and with it the loss of a whole way of life. Even so, he knew how lucky he was, and he'd begun to find certain compensations. Forced into a slower pace he was becoming gradually aware of other people, of their needs and fears. He noticed the underlying currents in sudden silences and saw raw emotions hidden beneath a cheerful exterior. His heightened emotional state often embarrassed him. The sight of Fliss, curled in a chair, absorbed in a book, could reduce him to tears. The small, serious, downturned face, the thin fingers absently looping away a strand of hair, the tucked-up feet, all these things comprising a whole sweet picture made him weep. Other things affected him, too: Prue playing dominoes with Lulu beside the fire in the hall; Caroline making a cake and listening to *Woman's Hour*, a frown of concentration on her face. These three women had become so important and so very dear to him . . .

At the end of the drive Miles paused, testing himself, before turning into the lane. Although he continually pushed against his limitations, he wasn't a fool and on some days he could do more than on others. Today he knew that he could go further than his minimum distance and, anyway, Prue and Caroline would now be on their way home from Totnes and could pick him up if his energy flagged. He limped on, thinking now of Jolyon. He'd developed a tremendous fondness for the boy, admiring the dogged way he'd stuck to his plans despite – according to Prue – derision and discouraging remarks from his mother. Slowly, through the fog of his own despair, he'd become aware of Jolyon's silent suffering. Each holiday he'd taken to studying him, seeing the misery when the boy thought himself unobserved, the dejection and, sometimes, the anger.

Plodding along, Miles felt an echo of shame. He'd had to ask Fliss what the boy's situation was; why he was spending all his holidays at The Keep and rarely seeing his mother and brother. He'd seen the flash of surprise in her eyes, quickly quenched, and knew that he should have been aware of Jolyon's rejection by his mother. Before his stroke he would have shrugged it off with some crass remark . . . Miles stopped and raised his eyes to the sullen pewter sky. That faint echo of shame was nothing to the horror which now pierced his heart when he thought of his past insensitivity: his treatment of Fliss, especially over the Hong Kong job; the years of indifference to his own children; his stubborn selfishness. It was Theo who had turned him round, shown him how he could change and grow, given him courage. The good old man hadn't judged and condemned; he'd just shown him what could be attained. What a blow his death had been . . .

'*You'll come through this,*' he'd said. '*You've shown that you're able to change and grow . . . Mind you give it everything you've got.*'

Tears on his cheeks, Miles stumbled on to the verge as a delivery van chugged by. Those words were a talisman, a prayer, a motto. Whenever he wanted to throw in the towel he saw Theo bending over to kiss him goodbye, saw his smile and felt the strength in the pressure of his hand,

'*Mind you give it everything you've got.*' Well, he was trying to do just that. It was through Theo that Fliss had come back to him, and that alone was worth every effort he could make, but he wanted to do more if he could. His relationship with his own children was good, and getting better. Jamie was doing splendidly at King's College and had decided to try for the Foreign Office. Bess was at Trinity College, planning to teach music, whilst at the same time promoting the small jazz quartet in which she played the clarinet, which was her second instrument. They were happy, confident, secure: just as he had been at their age. He gave them his love, approved their independence, delighted in their achievements. When he looked at Jolyon, however, he saw how easily his own indifference to the twins might have caused them the anguish he saw in Jolyon's eyes. It was odd that he should have been given the ability to suffer with the boy and, rather than avoiding it, he welcomed it with a new, painful humility. He saw it as a gift – though he would never have admitted it to anyone – and he hoped that he might make good use of it.

Pausing to catch his breath, he realised that he was tiring. As he stopped to rest beside the field gate he heard the sound of an engine. Looking down the lane he saw the car; Caroline and Prue returning home. With relief he stepped out, waving his stick, feeling a rush of affection at the sight of them, dear and familiar, sitting side by side.

Caroline wound down the window. 'I don't usually pick up hitchhikers,' she said, 'but in your case I'll make an exception.'

He got the door open and edged himself inside, pleased that they made no attempt to fuss over him, and then they were off again, heading for home and lunch.

Fliss had spent the morning writing letters and catching up on small neglected tasks. From her window she'd watched Miles set out for his walk and then had settled at her grandmother's bureau to deal with the growing pile of correspondence. She was happier writing letters than talking on the telephone and, anyway, some of her naval friends were abroad and it was too expensive to make long-distance calls. She wrote quickly and neatly, describing the twinnies' twenty-first birthday party and enclosing photographs.

Pausing to search for her address book, leafing through it, she wondered how her friends would react. It was only a few days since she'd received photographs of a christening party. Looking at the pretty girl proudly holding her baby, she'd suffered a jolting sense of *déjà vu*. Suddenly she was thrust back in time, nearly twenty-five years before, when this girl had been the baby and her mother had looked exactly like her daughter did now. Fliss had stared intently at her old friend, rather portly and with greying hair, laughing at something beyond the camera, and it had been a shock to realise that she, Fliss, was old enough to be a grandmother, too. Where had all the years gone? She'd sat for some while, lost in memories, reliving the past, still holding the photograph.

Now, checking the address – some of her naval friends had as many as five or six addresses after their names – she knew that a few of her friends would be just as surprised to see Bess and Jamie so grown up, although none of them would see the young Fliss in Bess. Jamie and Miles, however, were very alike and it was particularly poignant to compare them. Miles's stroke, and the subsequent years, had taken their toll and Miles looked older than his sixty-three years. Despite his cheerful smile, his glass raised high in his good hand, the contrast with Jamie's young dark vitality was painful.

Fliss pushed the photograph along with the thin blue folded sheets into the air mail envelope. The photograph was a fact, a record, and the lines on Miles's face and the whiteness of his hair bore witness to courage and fortitude as well as to suffering. She, too, was looking all of her forty-seven years. She knew that she was too thin; knew that the little frown which she'd inherited from her mother had settled into a deep line between her brows. It was difficult to believe that she was now eight years older than Alison had been when she'd died out in Kenya; much more difficult to imagine this than to see herself as a grandmother. Life seemed to move so slowly whilst it was being lived, yet suddenly chunks of it had passed: frittered hours, wasted days, making up the sum of the lost years . . .

She tried to shrug off these depressing thoughts, fighting a desire to panic. Now that the twinnies were settled so happily into their London lives she rarely saw them and her horizon had narrowed into the four walls of The Keep. Once this was all that she had desired and imagined but, in her imaginings, Miles had not been partially paralysed and the twinnies had still been children – and Uncle Theo had definitely been part of the scene . . .

Fliss thought: I'm missing Hal. I'd got used to having him

207

around. Coming down from London every weekend and cheering me up.

She rested her elbows on the desk, chin in hands. Knowing that Hal loved her was the thing that held her together, enabled her to continue to bear the frustrations and the restrictions of her life. Staring out across the tree-tops, watching the sharp, black filigree of twigs motionless against the cold grey sky, she wondered where Hal was at this particular moment. For the last year he'd been captain of HMS *Exeter*, which was leader of the Third Destroyer Squadron, and he'd been away for the several weeks since Christmas. She knew that he'd been delighted to go back to sea after more than four years ashore and she'd managed to hide her own feelings of dismay when she'd heard about the posting. After all, the squadron was based in Devonport and he would be home whenever *Exeter* was in port. Nevertheless, whilst he was away there was a permanent ache in her heart, an emptiness in her life which no one else had ever been able to fill.

Overcoming a weak impulse to lay her head on the desk and burst into tears, Fliss stood up and went across to the table which held the radio. She switched it on and immediately the music of Sibelius's Seventh Symphony filled the room. As usual, at the sound of it, she was swept back into the past – but now it was a more recent past. Now it was the last four years she was remembering: escaping out on to the hill or up on to the moor with Hal at her side; walking along deserted winter beaches with the surf pounding on the shoreline and the gulls screaming overhead, her hand warmly held in Hal's. She could feel the wind in her face, the warmth and roughness of his jersey as he put his arms about her and she burrowed into his warmth, the taste of the salt on his lips as they kissed. She relived precious moments travelling alone together in the car or sitting in half-empty pubs by roaring fires. It was possible that, had they been married, they would now be indifferent to each other, sitting in dull silence together, relying on the television to create some kind of communication between them. Yet she couldn't quite believe it. Deep down she knew that she and Hal belonged together, two halves of the same whole, and a lifetime together would not have diminished their need of one another or the contented, quiet joy of their companionship.

If Caroline and Prue guessed at the depth of the love between them they made no sign of it. Perhaps they realised that indirectly this love nourished them all, even Miles – especially Miles – and, because it was neither selfish nor destructive, it was tacitly accepted. They had come through those early days of adjustment

208

more cheerfully, more hopefully, because of it. Listening to the last movement of the symphony, Fliss remembered the final days of her grandmother's life. Fliss had been sitting beside her as she lay in bed, barely conscious, and Hal had come in. They'd whispered quietly together for a minute or so and then Grandmother had opened her eyes and looked them. She'd smiled at them and made an effort to speak. Fliss could remember the words quite clearly.

'Be happy, my children,' she'd said, as if she were at last giving them her blessing on their love and, whenever Fliss felt anxious about her love for Hal, or guilty, those remembered words laid a balm upon her unquiet spirit.

The music was finished and the car was coming into the court-yard. From her window Fliss watched Caroline and Prue climbing out, talking to one another, gesticulating, leaning back in to collect shopping bags. Miles slowly emerged from the back seat, delib-erately balancing himself as he stood upright, tucking his cap carefully under the numb, useless arm. Through her tears she watched him look about and then instinctively glance up at her window. She saw the pleasure which lightened his expression and, letting the car take his weight, he waved his stick cheerfully. She waved back, full of affection for him, and now Prue was beaming up at her whilst Caroline mimed collapse beneath the weight of the shopping bags . . .

Oh, the different kinds of love.

Chapter Twenty-eight

A week or two later, in his small galley on board *Dorcas*, Mole was preparing a late Sunday breakfast. Several people had been surprised at his decision to live on the narrowboat when he'd been posted to the Ministry of Defence, after two years as the Captain in HMS *Tireless*, but he'd survived aboard very happily so far. Once again it had become rather fashionable amongst his friends to wander down to the *Dorcas* for drinks, or, last year, for an occasional impromptu party on long hot evenings, but it was possible that he might not have remained on board through the winter if he hadn't begun his affair with Samantha towards the end of the summer. He'd met her at a house-warming party – 'Watch out,' a friend had murmured, 'Daddy's a general' – and had been instantly captivated by her youth, attractiveness and utter openness.

'Hi,' she'd said, long, dark red-brown hair tumbling over grey eyes. 'I'm Sam.'

He'd taken her outstretched hand and held it briefly. 'So am I,' he'd said.

'Cool,' she'd said, 'if a tad confusing.'

'I expect we'll manage,' he'd answered lightly.

She'd grinned at him and his heart had done strange and unfamiliar things in his chest.

'I think we could do better than that,' she'd murmured – and so they had; a great deal better.

From the beginning she'd set the pace. She turned up at unlikely moments, telephoned at all the wrong times and had an army of friends who were half his age.

'We can't,' he'd said, suddenly panicky, when they were alone together for the first time and she'd made it quite clear what she had in mind. 'I'm twice your age.'

She'd chuckled, winding her arms about him. 'I expect I'll catch up, I'm a quick learner,' she promised. 'You lead and I'll follow.'

It was impossible to resist her but he knew she was out of his league. In some ways she reminded him of Sin – she did her own

211

thing, in her own way, and was answerable only to herself – but she was more independent than Sin had ever been and the generation gap frightened him. The modern young were light years away from his own experience and he was puzzled that Sam should be so generous yet ask for nothing in return. Her parents lived in Wiltshire, she had a brother at Marlborough College and shared a flat with three other girls. Since leaving school she'd spent each winter as a chalet girl – she had a passion for skiing – then, as spring drew on, she'd try to find summer jobs in the sun. It was clear that she was as reluctant to commit herself to anything permanent as he was, yet the stronger his love grew the more difficult it was to reconcile himself to her desire for freedom. As the winter approached he'd dreaded that she should set off for the ski slopes, leaving him alone, but, to his enormous relief, she took a job helping out a friend who'd just opened a gallery in Chelsea and it was at this point that he'd decided to overwinter on the *Dorcas*.

The houseboat provided privacy and, as she began to spend more and more time with him aboard, Mole began to feel that some positive action was required. He tried to imagine himself being introduced to her father – whom she referred to as the Aged Parent – and failed utterly. Once or twice he wondered whether he should invite her down to The Keep but at the last moment his courage deserted him. Nevertheless he talked to her about his home. She seemed to be fascinated by everything relating to him – although he couldn't understand why – and, whilst he cooked supper for them both, or did the washing-up, he'd describe the way The Keep was run and its inhabitants.

Sometimes she'd ask questions, as if she wanted to get everything really clear in her mind, trying to work out the relationships. At other times she'd sit in one of her favourite positions, arms folded on the table, head resting on her crossed wrists whilst he talked.

'Cool,' she'd murmur, or, 'That's kind of spooky,' and he'd glance through from the galley to smile at her. Invariably dressed in a huge jersey and leggings, she looked so young that his heart would beat with terror at the thought of damaging her. How could he expect a girl of twenty-two to throw in her lot with a man old enough to be her father?

'The dear old AP is over sixty,' she'd told him calmly, when he'd used those words in reference to the age gap between them. 'He married when he was in his forties, too. Mummy's half his age.'

There was a small silence after this remark. The 'too' seemed to hang in the air between them and he'd wondered with a ridiculous surge of joy whether she was dropping him a hint. He hesitated, hardly daring to believe it, and she'd picked up the wine bottle so as to refill their glasses.

'I'd ask you down to meet them,' she'd said casually, 'but I simply don't trust Ma. Or you, come to that. *She's* very thin and glamorous, and *you're* a bit of a dark horse, if you ask me.'

He'd protested, but the moment had passed, and afterwards he'd cursed himself. Later, though, he'd felt a small measure of relief. She'd told him that her mother played the field and he had a sudden vision of his own future; of himself, ageing and dull, watching Sam having affairs with younger men. He'd convinced himself that she hadn't meant that 'too', that it was a slip of the tongue, but he wished that he was much younger. In the private world of the narrowboat it was easy to pretend that marriage between them might work but, when he pictured himself introducing her to his family or imagined the surprised faces of her parents, he knew that reality was very different. In any event, he suspected that he'd never have the necessary courage to propose. Marriage was now an out-of-date institution amongst the young and he couldn't see Sam in the stereotypical role of mistress. She seemed content with his friendship, with their lovemaking, with this casual arrangement, but he was beginning to find it difficult not to be possessive, not to want more of her.

On this Sunday morning, as he tipped sausages and bacon on to a plate, he was counting the days since he'd seen her; twelve, was it? Thirteen? It was longer than usual, apart from at Christmas when she'd gone abroad with a party of friends, but he was in no position to question or complain. Mole smiled wryly as he poured his coffee. It was typical that now, when he felt ready for the first time in his life to risk a commitment, it was the other person who was cautious. Sliding on to the bench seat behind the table, opening the newspaper, he began to eat his breakfast.

He was on his second mug of coffee when he heard footsteps hurrying along the pontoon. Heart jumping in anticipation, without waiting for the familiar double knock, he went aft and opened the door to the stern deck. Standing together, expressions of surprise on their faces, stood Bess and an unknown young man.

'That was quick,' she said, grinning at him. 'I expect you heard us crashing down the gangplank or whatever you call it. I told Matt to be quiet but he doesn't know how.'

The young man smiled down at her and then at Mole. 'I hope we're not disturbing anything,' he said. 'Bess said it would be OK.'

Mole pulled himself together. 'Of course it's OK,' he said,

leading them below. 'It's just that I rarely see any of my family before lunch at the weekend. This is a delightful surprise . . . Matt.'

'Sorry.' Bess was divesting herself of a thick woollen wrap whose fringed ends reached nearly to her booted heels. 'I should have introduced you properly but he knows who you are already. Matt plays the French horn with the LSO. Impressive or what?'

'Very impressive.' Mole filled the kettle. 'Have you had breakfast?'

'We're fine,' Bess assured him. 'Coffee would be great, though, if that's OK?' She sat down on the sofa, which could be pulled out to make a double bed, and looked about her. 'It's really cosy, isn't it? Gosh, I do envy you having this, Mole. She's such a sweet boat.'

'It's amazing.' Matt was examining *Dorcas* with delight. 'Look, Bess. These doors close across the passage or shut off the bathroom. Isn't it clever?'

'It comes in useful if there are people sleeping in the saloon while I'm in the aft cabin.' Mole was amused at Matt's almost childlike glee as he opened cupboards and peered into lockers. 'Gives everyone a bit of privacy. You must come on a cruise in the summer.'

He was too busy pouring coffee and parrying Matt's questions about how the solid fuel stove worked to hear more footsteps on the pontoon. Sam's double knock had hardly registered before she'd put her head in at the door. There was a sudden silence as she stood, suddenly confused, in the doorway whilst Bess and Matt gazed at her and Mole leaned out of the galley to see what was happening. Pleasure, embarrassment and several other emotions battled together in his breast as he went quickly to greet her. He took her hands, holding them tightly for a moment, his back to the others. She raised her eyebrows, grimacing comically, and he smiled reassuringly, wondering how she'd want him to play it.

'Come and meet Bess and Matt,' he said cheerfully, knowing that she would recognise the name of his niece. 'Have you had a good holiday? I didn't know you were back.'

She made vague noises as she followed him into the saloon. He made introductions and, as he put the kettle on the hob and the three young ones chatted, he racked his brain to think of some innocuous excuse for her visit. He was careful not to treat Sam as anything other than a casual visitor and she made no attempt to hint at any intimacy between them. Presently she turned to him with an easy friendliness.

'I told David I'd drop by,' she said. 'He wants to know if it's still OK for Wednesday. He's got lots of people coming and he said to say that he's counting on you.' She turned to Bess. 'Do you know the Brandons? They're a naval family. I was at school with Emily.'

'I don't think so.' Bess was wrinkling her brow. 'Brandon . . . No. It doesn't ring a bell.'

'Oh, well, just a thought. Hell, is that the time?' She set down her mug. 'I'm meeting friends and I'm late already. I'll tell David, then, shall I, Mole? You'll be there?'

'Wednesday,' agreed Mole, utterly confused, but realising that she was putting on a show for the others. 'No problem. Eight-ish, isn't it?'

'Eight for half-past. Must dash. See you, Mole. Great to meet you, Bess. Matt. No, don't get up. Bye.'

She'd gone before he could say another word and he saw her shadow fly past the window. He turned to the others with an apologetic smile, biting back frustration.

'Sorry about that . . .' – but they were clearly unconcerned, unsuspicious, trying to persuade him to come with them for a drink.

Mole refused and waved them off at last with promises that they should meet up again soon. He glanced at his watch, hoping that Sam would reappear now that Bess and Matt had gone. Guessing that the Brandon business was a kind of private message, he felt nearly certain that she would come down to the *Dorcas* on Wednesday evening – but that was another three whole days off and he needed to see her before then. Mole cleared away the coffee mugs, mulling things over. He knew of nobody called David Brandon and was impressed by Sam's quick thinking. Nevertheless, he also felt depressed. As he'd watched the three young ones together it had become even clearer that he stood no real chance with Sam. He wondered what Bess and Matt would have thought if he'd behaved as if he and Sam were lovers; slipped an arm round her, let his love show on his face. At the mere thought of it he shook his head. Long ago, Sin had taught him the rules governing an affair and he knew that discretion was one of the most sacred of those rules. He had no right to behave in any way which might embarrass Sam and she had made it clear that she had no intention of publicly crossing the line between friendship and intimacy.

His coffee was cold in its mug and he threw it away, glancing at his watch, now, with an almost nervous insistency, but there was no sign of her. It didn't occur to him that she might have taken her lead from his or that she might be wondering if she'd embarrassed him. He was unaware that his age and experience, accompanied by his tall good looks, might prove both daunting and irresistible to a girl of Sam's age. He only knew, as he watched the short winter day draw on, that he would have given anything to be Matt's age again, to have that careless confidence of modern youth.

Mole thought: When I was young I longed to be sophisticated and adult. Now I can see that it's all a big con. I feel just as nervous and insecure as I did when I was twenty. Yet Bess and Sam are so confident, so sure of themselves. And Matt was so at ease with me, despite the age gap between us. It was as if we were old friends.

He glanced at his watch again, cursing himself for being a fool, but still she did not come.

It was dark and he was dozing in front of the small television screen when he was roused by footsteps on the pontoon. He stumbled aft and had the door open before she could beat her familiar tattoo. He pulled her inside, out of the drifting, icy rain, and led her along to the warm saloon without saying a word.

'Sorry,' she said, letting him take her coat. 'About this morning, I mean. I've got a bit complacent about just wandering in. It was quite scary to see two complete strangers looking at me and I lost my cool. Sorry if it was difficult.'

He sat down beside her on the sofa, holding her cold hands, wondering why she was so tense.

'You were quite brilliant,' he said. 'Have you ever thought of taking up acting as a career?' He began to smile. 'And who the devil is David Brandon?'

She began to laugh, relaxing at last, leaning close to him.

'They *are* a naval family, actually,' she told him. 'My mother always says, "If you're going to lie make certain that there's a grain of truth in it," so I thought I'd follow her advice for once. Actually, they're out in Washington so I thought I was quite safe.'

'And Emily?' he teased. 'It *was* Emily, wasn't it?'

'Oh, Mole.' She flung her arms about him suddenly, clinging to him. 'Did you miss me?'

'Of course I missed you.' He held her closely, rubbing his face in the soft, flying hair, puzzled by her intensity. 'Daft woman! You know I miss you.'

'So they didn't guess?' she mumbled against his shoulder. 'Bess and Matt?'

So that was what was worrying her. He could imagine that she wouldn't want two young people to suspect that she was having an affair with a middle-aged man. No doubt it would ruin her street cred. At least he could reassure her on that point.

'Of course not,' he said gently. 'They didn't suspect a thing. Be reasonable. Do you honestly think that Bess would think that I could trap someone like you? Darling Sam, you're shivering. I think we need a drink and then we'll think about some supper. You haven't got to rush off?'

He managed to conceal the anxiety in his voice and she shook her head so that her beech-brown hair swung about her face and he couldn't see the tears in her grey eyes.

'No,' she said lightly, 'I haven't got to rush off. But don't go just yet. I need to be warmed up much more than I need a drink. Stay here and make me warm.'

He pulled her back into his arms and she clung to him as he began to kiss her, while the television droned unattended and the rain beat with increasing insistence on the cabin roof.

Chapter Twenty-nine

The plans which Kit and Clarrie discussed with such enthusiasm had never materialised and now, more than three years later, they were still at the house in Hampstead. There had been some changes, however. When Sin and Andrew had returned from Italy, to be met with details of houses for sale in Oxford and Bristol, they'd been horrified.

'You can't go,' they'd cried. 'It would be like breaking up a family.'

Shocked out of their preoccupation with each other they'd settled down to discover the reasons for this upheaval. By this time the excitement was wearing off a little and Kit and Clarrie were beginning to see certain disadvantages in their brave new world. However, neither wished to disappoint the other and it was almost a relief when Sin reacted so strongly.

'You simply can't go,' she'd said firmly. 'It's a crazy idea. You'd regret it in six months. Settle for a good holiday, a really long one, and get it out of your system that way.'

Kit was only too ready to agree with her but she couldn't simply leave it at that.

'It's not just a question of being in a rut,' she'd said to Sin privately. 'Don't think we're not delighted for you and Andrew but it has been quite a change, you know. And on top of that, remember, Fozzy died. Poor old Clarrie misses him terribly and it's no good saying "Get another dog" because he simply can't cope with one up on the top floor. He hates complaining but his arthritis is pretty bad, although he tries to hide it. Getting up all those stairs is becoming impossible.'

'Well you don't have to move house because of that,' Sin had said impatiently. 'Good grief! You should have said so before. Why don't we just switch round with him? Swap flats?'

Kit had stared at her in surprise. 'It never really occurred to me as a solution,' she'd said slowly. 'Andrew's been entrenched in the garden flat for ever. Do you honestly think he'd move upstairs?'

219

'If he thinks that you and Clarrie are leaving because of Clarrie's arthritis, he'll move like a shot. Honestly!' Sin had given a snort of disgust. 'I can't believe you seriously thought of going. We're a family, aren't we?'

At this point, Kit had felt a strange desire to weep. 'It's not easy adjusting,' she'd mumbled, 'after all those years together. Clarrie and I needed to think we weren't . . . well, superfluous to requirements.'

'Silly cow.' Sin's quick hug had belied her dispassionate tone. 'I'll talk to Andrew. I can't see any reason why we shouldn't move up. The flat's exactly the same size and we all share the garden anyway. Clarrie can have another dog and he won't have to worry about the stairs. So that's settled. Now what about you?'

'Me?'

'Oh, don't do that wide-eyed bit. We're too long in the tooth for girlish innocence. What about that married man? You were having a fling just before we went away. Don't prevaricate. I know you too well. Do I know him?'

There had been a silence.

'It was Jake,' Kit had admitted at last. 'I met him again and I felt just the same about him. But he wasn't having any. He said it was too late and he's got kids and so on. We had a couple of weeks of "just good friends" stuff and then he went back to Madeleine. Again.'

'Oh, Kit.'

'I'm perfectly OK now,' Kit had said quickly. 'It's just that, what with that, and you and Andrew living on cloud nine, and Clarrie hobbling about, we decided something drastic was needed in our drab lives.'

'Changing flats won't be drastic as far as you're concerned, will it? You'll just stay put.'

'To be honest I shall be quite glad to retire from this scheme gracefully.' Kit had shaken her head doubtfully. 'We got a bit carried away, to tell you the truth. Let's start with Clarrie and the dog and see where we go from there.'

Clarrie, too, had been relieved to shelve the idea of a brand-new life. It hadn't been too long before he, like Kit, had begun to think of all the advantages of his staying in Hampstead, and Sin's new plan held all the excitement he required. When he'd seen that Kit was perfectly happy to agree he'd sighed with relief and they'd begun the difficult job of moving. By the time Clarrie was established in the ground-floor flat and he and Kit had managed to find a replacement for Fozzy – a large, rough-haired wheaten dachshund puppy whom

220

he named Lucifer – spring had been almost over. Bess, having been given a place at Trinity College starting in the autumn, had asked if she could stay with her godmother for a while, just until she found her feet, and Kit had been plunged into student life again. Young people came and went at all hours and various instruments could be heard, being played in Bess's bedroom.

'They haven't got anywhere to practise,' she'd plead, 'and their landlord's making a fuss. You don't mind, do you?'

Andrew was delighted to have musicians in the house and, whilst he pretended to suffer, Clarrie was enjoying himself immensely, too.

'I sometimes have the feeling that I'm back in Scarsdale Villas,' Kit had said to Sin. 'Nothing changes, does it?'

'*You* haven't,' Sin had replied, grinning. 'You've never grown up, that's your problem.'

'I fear that you might be right.' Kit had shrugged cheerfully. 'But who cares?'

Because Kit made her friends so welcome, Bess had elected to stay on at the house in Hampstead and now, in her last year, was still entrenched, usually with another music student bedding down temporarily in the spare bedroom.

'Are you sure she isn't driving you mad?' Fliss would enquire anxiously from time to time. 'She should be standing on her own feet by now.'

'I love it,' Kit would say. 'And it's so difficult for these poor kids to practise without being chucked out of their digs or the neighbours complaining. Don't fuss, little coz. I am her godmother, after all.'

She knew that, in her heart, Fliss was relieved that Bess was safe. It just seemed odd that a young girl would want to live in a house with older people.

'She's a funny girl, our Bess,' Kit said to Fliss, during one of their long telephone conversations. 'She gets on very well with our generation. She sorts us all out and takes us in hand but in another way she's rather insecure. She's got plenty of friends of her own age, though, I promise. And I should know. They spend half their lives in my kitchen.'

They also spent a great deal of time with Clarrie. Without mentioning it to Kit, he and Bess had gone out one day during her second year and chosen a piano – a very nice Steinway – and when it had arrived in Hampstead it had been installed in one of his spare rooms.

'You shouldn't have done it,' Kit had said, shocked. 'It must have cost the earth. Oh, honestly Clarrie. This is very naughty of Bess.'

'I'll do what I like with my own money,' he'd retorted. 'And it was all my idea. I love to hear her play and you haven't got the room in your flat for a piano. I had to twist her arm, I can tell you, so don't you go on at her, mind.'

It was a rather shamefaced Bess who'd appeared that evening.

'I couldn't stop him,' she'd said defensively, before Kit could speak. 'And he said that if I didn't help him choose he'd buy a grand piano. I kept the price as low as I could. Well, as low as was possible without buying rubbish. Honestly, Kit. He was absolutely determined.'

'I believe you.' Kit had smiled unwillingly at an expression of suppressed joy struggling with the anxiety on Bess's face. 'So spit it out. What else?'

'I've been asked to accompany someone,' she'd said proudly. 'She's an up-and-coming soprano and she's giving a recital for charity. She's really good and her accompanist is ill so someone suggested me. Now we'll be able to rehearse properly together. Oh, Kit, isn't it terrific?'

Now, on this February morning almost a year later, as Clarrie and Lucifer dried themselves off in the kitchen after being caught in a shower on the Heath, he was remembering Bess's face when she'd introduced him to Matt the previous weekend.

'She's in love,' he murmured to Lucifer as he towelled his thick rough coat. 'Our Bess has got it bad.'

Lucifer groaned politely, longing for his basket by the radiator. He was of a placid disposition and, though he enjoyed the fuss made of him by the stream of young people who passed through his home, he liked a quiet life.

'He's a nice chap. Steady and reliable, I'd say, and just as much in love as she is.'

Clarrie finished the rubbing down and Lucifer shook himself vigorously, if briefly, and headed for his basket. Clarrie straightened up painfully and looked about him. He missed his views of the Heath and of the huddled rooftops but these were a fair exchange for the convenience of the garden – especially whilst Lucifer had been a puppy – and the freedom from climbing stairs. He knew now that he would have missed so many things if he and Kit had moved away: the spring beauty of the chestnut trees along Well Road; the summer evening concerts at Fenton House; reading the Sunday paper in the back bar of the Holly Bush; watching the kite-flying from Parliament Hill.

He thought: We'd have missed Andrew and Sin, too. Much more than we were prepared to admit. It's worked out splendidly. Kit's been happier than I've ever seen her. Funny old thing, life . . .

*   *   *

222

With one or two last snips of the secateurs, Fliss finished pruning the clematis which climbed the wall behind the herbaceous border and stepped back carefully on to the lawn. She shivered a little, glancing up at the sky. The thin high canopy was tinged with a glowing pale gold but she suspected that the best of the day was past. There was a new chill in the air. The robin, who had been singing from the branches of the japonica bush, fell silent as Fliss gathered up her clippings. No riotous growth filled the long border and the exposed black earth lay cold and bare. The garden looked desolate on this raw afternoon but Fliss was reluctant to go indoors. Just as she had understood Miles's need for solitary walks so she knew that her own moments alone were important to her.

She wandered across the lawn, past the rhododendrons to the bonfire, and dropped the clippings on the cold ashes. Now that Jolyon worked about the place full time the grounds had that well-cared-for look which had been missing since Fox's day.

She thought: Dear Jo. How hard he works. It's so uncanny that he looks exactly like Hal did at that age . . . Oh, Hal, I do miss you so.

She was glad that Jo had his puppy. They'd all missed Rex when he'd died but Jolyon had been inconsolable; red-eyed and uncommunicative, he'd spent hours in his room until the whole family had begun to be seriously worried. Fliss had suspected that all his hurt from the divorce and Maria's indifference to him was released into this grief and in some ways she'd almost welcomed it. She'd persuaded the others to leave him alone and slowly he'd recovered and had seemed the better for his catharsis. They'd been surprised when he'd refused to consider having a puppy – he'd said that he'd rather wait awhile – but as soon as he'd left school he'd begun to show an interest again in that direction. He'd obtained details from the Kennel Club regarding local breeders and gone to look at prospective parents.

'I wanted to be around for him,' he'd told Fliss later. 'I know we all share him but I think it's better for a puppy to have one particular person in charge of him. I'd have hated going back to school and leaving him.'

Looking across the kitchen garden, dug over and mulched with manure, strange mounds of boxes and other contraptions protecting the rhubarb roots, Fliss could see Jolyon moving about in the long greenhouse. Passing along the grassy paths where snowdrops grew under the wall, she stopped suddenly as a tiny shrew scurried out of a broken flowerpot and disappeared into a hole behind the slates. Thrusting her hands into her pockets she moved on again, hunching against the cold, listening to the noisy chatter of the rooks as they rebuilt their nests in the rookery which had been their home for more than a hundred years.

Beyond the glass, Jolyon raised a hand and she opened the door and stood inside, looking about her. The warm, earthy, pungent smell spun her back more than thirty years in time, to the garden room and to the memory of her grandmother, arranging roses, working amongst the paraphernalia of her gardening. The serious work had been done here in the greenhouse but in the garden room there would have been trays of seedlings basking in the sun; jars and vases crowded on the shelves with her reference books. The trug always stood ready with a pair of secateurs and her gloves; her old straw hat would have been cast down in one of the wicker chairs . . .

Fliss realised that Jolyon was watching her curiously and she sighed.

'How evocative smells are,' she said. 'Like music. It takes you right back in a single second.'

'I know what you mean,' he said. 'Are you OK?'

She nodded. 'I was just remembering Grandmother and being in the garden room with her just after we came back from Kenya.'

'It must have been terrible, dealing with something like that.' Fear clutched his heart at the thought of his father dying suddenly, violently. 'I can't think how you coped with it.'

'Neither can I. The thing is that you simply deal with things as they happen. If you don't have a choice you just get on with it.' She hesitated, knowing that they were on sensitive ground. 'Wouldn't you agree?'

He finished his potting up and wiped his hands on a piece of old towel.

'Yes,' he said, 'yes, you're right.'

He turned away to fetch the watering can and began gently to water the seeds in their row of plastic pots which stood on long trestle tables.

'Bess is coming down next weekend.' She changed the subject. 'She's bringing someone called Matt with her. He's another musician. French horn, I think she said. I understand that he's rather special.'

Jolyon grinned. 'How brave of her. I feel sorry for him, though. Poor chap. What an ordeal.'

'Nonsense,' protested Fliss. 'He can hardly be intimidated by any of us. We shall be perfectly charming to him.'

'It's a bit of a change, isn't it? Bess has always been so wrapped up in her music that she's never really noticed men. He *must* be special.'

'Well, Clarrie and Kit think so. We'll have to wait and see . . . Ready for some tea?'

'I certainly am.'

He finished tidying up and they went out together, along the paths which led to the back yard. Jolyon kicked off his gumboots whilst Fliss scraped leaf mould and mud from her shoes. Prue met them at the scullery door.

'I was coming to look for you,' she said. 'Susanna's popped in. She's just picked Lulu up from school and she thought she'd see how we are.'

Fliss looked at Jolyon solemnly. 'And how are we?'

Jolyon considered for a moment. 'As well as can be expected under the circumstances?' he suggested.

Lulu came bustling out. 'Mummy says it's going to snow,' she said. 'I wish it would. Rufus has eaten one of Miles's socks and Caroline's in a state.'

In the kitchen Caroline was remonstrating with Rufus who sat with his head on one side, tail wagging.

'I daren't leave anything on the Aga's rail,' she said crossly, 'in case this wretched puppy pulls it off and eats it.'

'He's only little.' Lulu kneeled beside him and gave him a hug. 'He doesn't understand yet, do you, Rufus?'

'He'll understand by the time I've finished with him,' said Caroline grimly. 'That's the third thing this week. I've hardly any tea-towels left.'

'Sorry,' said Jolyon, trying not to grin. 'Next time I go into Totnes I'll buy you lots of new ones.'

'And a new pair of socks for Miles,' added Lulu. 'Can Rufus come into the hall for tea?'

'*May* he, darling,' corrected Prue, automatically. 'I don't see why he shouldn't, not if you keep an eye on him. What do you think, Jolyon?'

'Why not?' Jolyon smiled at Lulu. 'He can't be expected to know how to behave if he never goes into company. No feeding him, mind.'

'Of course not.' Lulu looked shocked at such a suggestion. 'Come on, Rufus. Teatime.'

She picked him up in her arms and lugged him off to the hall, followed by Jolyon and Prue.

Fliss grinned at Caroline. 'Eating socks,' she said in her Ellen voice. 'Whatever next, I wonder.'

Chapter Thirty

Susanna was right about the snow, although it lasted barely forty-eight hours before westerly winds brought warmer weather and a thaw. Nevertheless, its novelty lent a glow of excitement to the drab winter days. Jolyon unearthed the sledge and Miles went out on the hill with him to watch him toboggan down the uneven slopes. He pushed off in great spirits, the toboggan bumping dangerously as he gathered speed, until it tipped suddenly sideways, silencing his cries of triumph.

'Not as easy as it looks,' he shouted, wiping snow from his face. 'There was a dirty great tussock halfway down. There's not enough snow, that's the trouble. I'll have another go.'

This time the sledge hit some buried obstruction, slewing round, and Jolyon got to his knees, laughing, shaking back his blond hair. Miles waved back, feeling a great affection for this boy who looked just like Hal when he'd first arrived at Dartmouth. His parents' unhappy marriage had robbed Jolyon of the confidence Hal had inherited but physically they were tremendously alike. Miles remembered those Dartmouth days: parties, Ladies' Nights, Summer Balls.

He thought: I was in love with the whole lot of them, even old Mrs Chadwick. As for dear old Theo . . .

It was strange that, although he'd been so deeply affected by Theo's death, yet slowly he'd begun to feel that he had never left them. By the time Miles had come to terms with Theo's physical absence it was as if he had gradually become present in his heart and mind. At last, half fearing ridicule, he'd said as much – or rather, written as much – to Fliss.

'I feel the same,' she'd said, returning his pad, smiling at him. 'It's as if he's left us a spiritual blueprint to help us, so that we can call on him whenever we need him. It's a great comfort.'

That had summed it up rather well and Miles had felt pleased that they were in accord. It was so easy to feel isolated, trapped inside his inability to articulate properly, inside his slow, unwieldy body. As he watched Jolyon brushing himself down and turning to trudge back up the hill, Miles was remembering what it felt like to be young and strong, although he'd never had Jolyon's sensitivities or his awareness of others. For Miles these qualities had come late, but not *too* late, and a bond was forming between them. With Hal so much at sea, Jolyon had got into the habit of sitting with Miles during the long winter evenings, talking about his new ideas and sharing his thoughts. When he'd seen that they were taken seriously, he'd expanded. He'd outlined his plans for the acres to the south of The Keep and explained his reasons for wanting to develop them into a nursery and so create a garden centre. As he'd warmed to his theme he'd become excited, drawing on Miles's pad, showing how the stables could be converted into a shop with a small tearoom.

'We could have a farm shop and do Pick Your Own,' he'd said, his eyes wide with visions. He'd looked at Miles anxiously then, coming back to earth. 'What do you think?'

Miles had grabbed his pad and written 'BLOODY GOOD IDEA' in big straggling capitals and then turned it so that Jolyon could see. He'd read it and then burst out laughing and suddenly they were holding hands, rocking to and fro, cheering. When they'd calmed down a little, Miles had made him see that the scheme must be costed out sensibly so that a business plan could be presented to the Trust. Miles was more than happy to tackle it and, between them, they were preparing the facts and figures to show Hal when he came back from sea. Fliss knew all about it and was as excited as they were . . .

'I'm getting the hang of it.' Jolyon was beside him again. 'Isn't it odd how it all looks so different when it snows?'

They stood together, staring out over a landscape made mysterious and unfamiliar. In the distance clumps of trees stood black and stark against the dazzling white purity, casting ink-blue shadows, whilst, closer at hand, a few early catkins trembled in the sharp air.

'Wonderful,' Miles said – and Jolyon nodded to show that he'd understood.

Going carefully they went back through the door in the wall, scattering the birds which were feeding on the bird table, and into the kitchen. Miles limped away to his own quarters and Jolyon went into the kitchen. Rufus was still asleep, exhausted by his earlier activities in the snow, and Jolyon left him to his slumbers and let himself out quietly. His hand was still on the door knob when he heard a cry and the front door slam. He hurried along the passage and into the hall. His father and Fliss were standing together, their arms about each other, and, although Fliss's face was turned away from him, Hal's expression was one of great tenderness. For a moment Jolyon was confused, almost frightened by the suggestion of some deep current of emotion, but his father, seeing him standing there neither moved nor did his expression immediately change.

'Hi, Jo,' he said, easily and naturally, his arms still round Fliss. 'If I'd realised that I'd get this sort of reaction I'd come home unexpectedly more often.'

Fliss unwound herself and looked at Jolyon with a self-mocking grimace of embarrassment.

'Sorry,' she said. 'It was just the shock of seeing him there. Oh, what a lovely surprise. Prue will be thrilled. I'll go and find her and put the kettle on.'

She passed Jolyon in the doorway and Hal took off his coat and dropped it on a chair.

'We docked a day early,' he said. 'Someone was coming this way and offered me a lift, so I didn't bother to wait to telephone. The lane was in a pretty bad way and I decided to walk up the drive in case we got stuck.' He strolled across to the fire and leaned down, warming his hands. 'Poor old Fliss. I gave her the most terrific fright. She's much more emotional since old Miles had his stroke, don't you think?' He glanced at Jolyon, smiling. 'You look as if you've seen a ghost, too. I can see that I'd better telephone if I get in earlier in future.' Hal's voice was calm, unperturbed, his smile free of guilt or anxiety. 'I suppose that now you're grown up I don't get a hug?'

Confidence restored, fears subdued, Jolyon flung his arms round his father and held him tightly.

'It was such a surprise,' he muttered. He didn't explain whether it was his father's appearance or the embrace which was the surprise and Hal did not ask him to elaborate.

'You're looking well.' His father held him at arm's length and then let him go. 'Everyone OK?'

'Fine.' Jolyon suddenly realised that he would be able to tell him all his splendid plans and excitement surged up, utterly drowning that formless, frightening suspicion. 'There's lots to tell you.'

'Good. That's good.' Hal was watching his son thoughtfully. 'At least, I hope it is.'

'Oh, it is,' Jolyon reassured him. 'It's a bit complicated, though . . .'

Voices were loud in the passage from the kitchen and Hal raised his eyebrows.

'It looks like it'll have to wait for a moment. That sounds like Ma, if I'm not mistaken. Stand by for more hysterics.'

229

Jolyon chuckled as his grandmother surged through the door, arms outstretched.

'Oh, Hal,' she cried. 'Oh, darling, how lovely to see you . . .'

Hal winked at Jolyon over her head as he took her into his arms, embracing her warmly, and, completely reassured, Jolyon winked back.

Fliss was alone in the drawing room, playing a Chopin prelude, when Hal found her. It was the first moment during the last three days that they'd been alone. Jolyon had gone to Exeter to stay with friends for the weekend, Prue and Miles were sleeping off Sunday lunch and Caroline was out on the hill, revelling in a wild west wind.

He came in quietly enough, prepared to sit and listen but, glancing over her shoulder, she stopped playing abruptly and swung round on the stool, her hands in her lap.

'It's OK,' he said, correctly reading her expression. 'Nothing to worry about.'

'I keep thinking about it,' she said wretchedly. 'His expression was so shocked, just for a moment, as if he'd guessed.'

Hal sighed and sat down in an armchair. 'Part of me wishes he had,' he said grimly. 'It's so hard, sometimes, to keep pretending.'

'Don't,' said Fliss fiercely. 'Just . . . don't, Hal. Not at the moment.'

He looked at her sharply and she tried to smile as he swore savagely under his breath.

'We can't *not* keep trying, that's the trouble,' she said desperately. 'It's not just Jo. It's Miles, too. It would be bad enough if we'd both suddenly fallen in love, but if either of them guessed that it went back so far . . .'

'That's certainly my fear with Jo.' Hal leaned into the cushions and folded his arms behind his head. 'I don't want him to think that it was because of us that my marriage didn't work with Maria. I'd hate it if anything spoiled the relationship between him and you.'

'And the other thing is that he and Miles are becoming close.' Fliss looked troubled. 'The young can be so puritanical, can't they? So unforgiving. I have this horrid feeling that Jo would feel much more sympathy for Miles and Maria than he would for us. And in a way, he's right. It's like we've always said, isn't it? We didn't have to marry them – but we did and we have to stick by it. Jo is still terribly hurt by Maria's behaviour but he can't stop loving her and longing for her approval.'

230

'He's young. Nineteen's a tricky age . . . Oh, my darling, what a bloody mess.'

'It's not too bad for most of the time but just occasionally I feel like chucking it all up and asking you to run away with me.'

'Oh, Flissy.' He stood up and went across to the piano, pulling her to her feet and holding her close. 'You and me, both. But how could we live with ourselves? Poor old Miles . . .'

'Don't.' She rested against him. 'I know we can't. Of course I do. But every now and again I feel so rebellious. It's dangerous when we're both feeling like it at the same time. When I saw you so unexpectedly, coming into the hall, I just forgot everything.'

'So did I. It seemed so natural, somehow. Coming home and finding you waiting for me.'

He kissed her long and hard and then, still holding her close, glanced at his watch.

'Why don't we go out for a potter round in the car? Up on the moor, perhaps, or over to Bigbury. The sea should be magnificent today.'

'Do you think we could?' She put her arms round him again. 'It would be wonderful.'

He stood quite still, his cheek against her hair, thinking.

'Ma and Miles are out for the count,' he said, 'and Caroline's communing with nature. I'll leave a note on the kitchen table saying that we're going over to see Susanna and Gus. We always feel relaxed there, don't we? They do us good. But we'll have a drive about first. How does that sound?'

'Sounds like heaven,' she said. 'Jo isn't coming back till tomorrow so we needn't feel guilty. At least, no more than usual.'

He cupped her face in his hands and kissed her again.

'Go and grab a coat. We'll have a good brisk walk somewhere to get rid of the glooms. I'll write a note. See you in the courtyard in five minutes.'

Later in the evening, back in her room, Fliss sat by the window looking down into the courtyard. The evenings were beginning to draw out and it was not yet quite dark. In Fox's old quarters in the gatehouse the lights were on, streaming out into the dusk. She knew that Hal had gone to have a look around, to assess the cost of making it habitable again. Jolyon hoped to make it his own little pad and Hal wanted to size up the work required without Jolyon's excited interruptions. Watching the lights gleaming on the wet paving stones, she wondered how often her grandmother had sat here, knowing that Fox was pottering happily across the courtyard.

231

Maybe, in due course, she would see Jolyon's lights shining out and feel comforted to know that he was there.

The drive with Hal had been wonderful. Content, relaxed, revelling in each other's company, they'd driven through the deep, secret lanes where snowdrops glowed with pale luminosity whilst above them the downy white balls of the goat willow and the alder's red catkins lent colour to the bare hedgerows. In the distance the moors rose, lion-coloured beneath a watery lemon sun, patched with brilliant, new-minted gorse blossom. They'd talked quietly together – or remained silent – with the ease of good friends, laughing at old jokes, reminiscing about past outings. Now, apart from him again, Fliss longed for him with a sudden terrible intensity; an intensity which she rarely let him see.

She thought: We never talk about what would happen if Miles were to die. I wonder if Hal ever thinks of it? Perhaps he'd be shocked if I said that I sometimes imagine it.

She drew her feet up on the window seat, wrapping her arms about her knees. As long as no one was hurt and she did not allow such imaginings to weaken her, was it wrong to think about it occasionally? The trouble was how much damage did such daydreaming do? Was it a kind of safety valve? Or did it simply make the situation worse? It was at moments like these that she missed Theo most. It was the sort of question one could ask him without fearing that he would be shocked, yet she'd always wanted to try her best for him. It was odd, that, because he'd never remonstrated or preached; never pontificated or been holier-than-thou. Nevertheless there had always been a kind of horror at the thought of disappointing him or letting him down. Dropping her head on her knees, she longed for him as she sat there; longed to see that familiar smile, to feel his hand on her shoulder and his strength communicated, flowing into her . . .

Quietly a memory slid into her mind: the day, nearly eight years before, when she'd agreed to go back to Miles. He'd come to The Keep for lunch and on the drive back to Dartmouth she'd asked him if he'd felt like Daniel in the lion's den. It was supposed to be a joke but Miles had spoken quite seriously about Theo, then.

'*If you let him down,*' he'd said, '*you'd be endangering something far more precious than your skin or your pride. In fact you know that you'd be letting down this vital thing inside yourself, not him at all, and he'd be alongside you in the gutter, holding your hand while you wept with the grief and the pain of it.*'

He'd said something like that and she'd been so surprised and impressed by Miles being capable of such insight that she'd never

232

quite forgotten his words. It was at that moment that she'd known that she must give her marriage a second chance.

Now, looking back, she could remember how confident she'd been, so full of new zeal, but, all too soon, weakness had edged in, tarnishing her bright new resolutions. Her love for Hal was unchanging, yet she knew that Uncle Theo had never disapproved of it. She knew that he'd known she'd married Miles as a shield against the pain of Hal's engagement to Maria, but at least he had tried to make certain that she'd gone into the second round of her marriage with her eyes open.

'*I want it only if it is the right thing for you and for Miles, because you love each other enough to care about each other's happiness,*' he'd said. He'd warned her against the use of power and she'd told him that it was all too easy to follow one's baser instincts.

Remembering, Fliss straightened up and reached for Theo's Daily Office book which she kept on the window seat. Opening it, she carefully took out a loose sheet of paper. It was much folded, yellowing, creased with age and use. She'd found it some weeks after his death and could remember him reciting it to her once.

Who can free himself from his meanness and limitations,
if you do not lift him to yourself, my God, in purity of love?
How will a person
brought to birth and nurtured in a world of small horizons,
rise up to you, Lord,
if you do not raise him by your hand which made him?

How indeed? Closing her eyes, her hand clenched upon the paper, Fliss drew slowly back from the edge of the abyss. Her horizon must continue to contain Miles and Jolyon; her love for Hal must not be inflamed by wild imaginings and corroding resentment. His love could continue to be her strength or her weakness, depending on her limitations. It could nourish – or it could destroy. There, in the winter twilight, Fliss knew that it was something which would never be absolutely resolved either way. It was a minute-to-minute battle as her weakness muscled within her, waiting to throw her. She tried to pray but only the word 'Help' came to mind. Yet it seemed to be enough to bring her a measure of peace.

She raised her head and looked out into the darkness. The lights in the gatehouse had been switched off but she did not feel alone. She could remember the last words of the prayer without looking at the paper; see in her mind Theo's small clear writing:

233

so I will rejoice:
You will not delay, if I do not fail to hope.

It was some kind of promise and she clung to it. There was enough love to go round, much to be thankful for – and, next weekend, Bess was coming home.

Chapter Thirty-one

'This is so much fun,' said Sam. 'It's really fab, just puttering along and doing your own thing. It must seem a bit odd after submarines, though?'

'At least you can see where you're going.' Mole hunched his shoulders against the cold breeze. 'That's a nice change. And I was never much of a sailor. All that leaping about and hauling on bits of string is too much like hard work. This is much more my style. I like being able to see the countryside as I go along. Or the city, in this case. And the pubs.'

'It's strange how different things look from the water, isn't it?' She stared up at tall warehouses, towering above their reflections in the water. 'It's the same with trains. All the secret places you'd never see from roads. It all feels quite different. Even the city has a magic quality from the water.'

'I wish we could have made it into the countryside,' he said, 'but it takes too long at three miles an hour. It would be dark before we got anywhere. Just wait till summer comes and then we'll really extend ourselves. If you're good I might take you as far afield as Oxford.'

She looked at him, standing easily on the chequer plates which concealed the engine beneath his feet, his hand resting lightly on the tiller, and smiled to herself as she perched on the deck-locker which doubled as a seat. He caught the edge of the smile as she pushed the long hair away from her face.

'Warm enough?' he asked – and cursed himself. He knew she hated being cosseted or fussed over. 'The one disadvantage with narrowboats,' he was hoping to cover his lapse, 'is that you can't steer from inside. It's not a problem in the summer but not so good in February. Any chance of some coffee?'

'Only if you let me steer later on.'

She kissed him quickly before she slipped below and he felt the exhilarating up-swoop of spirits that these sudden, rare, tokens of affection always produced. If he were her contemporary he could shout with pleasure, seize her and kiss her in return, do all the mad wild things that would be forgiven him simply because he was young, but at his age such behaviour would be simply ridiculous. She would despise him. It wouldn't be cool; one of her favourite words. Surely it was his maturity that must be the attraction? If he started to behave like a student, it might undermine whatever it was that she saw in him. He simply couldn't risk it. How he envied Bess and Matt their open delight in one another, their readiness to demonstrate their love, oblivious to the reaction of other people. He couldn't afford that 'out in the street with no clothes on' kind of infatuation. In Matt and Bess it was charming; at his age it was pathetic. Anyway, Sam gave no sign that she would welcome such unsophisticated passion.

He raised a hand to a cyclist on the towpath, feeling a thrill of gratitude that she'd responded so readily to his idle suggestion that they should take the *Dorcas* off for a weekend. As they passed beneath a footbridge, he wondered how the relationship would have flourished if he'd been stuck in a flat somewhere, probably sharing with an oppo, unable to make the most of these moments of utter privacy and freedom. On board, it was as if they were right out of the world, cocooned in a small sphere of time and space all their own. He knew that this wasn't good, not if there were to be a future for them. It was like a romance that flowered on holiday or aboard ship; only rarely could it survive the rough and tumble of daily life or bear the harsh light of reality without fading. For Bess and Matt it was easier: their love was rooted in their shared passion for music and encouraged by their friends. Jamie thoroughly approved of Matt, and had sung his praises to the family, but how would Jamie respond if he were introduced to Sam?

Mole shuddered inwardly as he imagined the raised eyebrows which would indicate silent approbation, faint surprise and an unspoken respect for his uncle's ability still to be able to score. Would Jamie – or anyone else for that matter – react in the same way if the woman involved were in her thirties and not so devastatingly pretty? He knew that he was being morbidly sensitive but he was unable to crush this fear. Perhaps, as time went on, he might find the courage to overcome his insecurity – but so much depended on Sam. She was still cautious, shying away from commitment, happiest at times like these when they were alone. Since the unexpected visit from Bess and Matt, the boat had ceased to feel quite the refuge it had been previously, nevertheless there were periods of time when they both knew that they were safe from intrusion.

This weekend was proving a tremendous success and Mole could imagine the spring stretching ahead into summer, providing months of delight. They could spend weekends – and all his leave if she agreed to it – cruising the canals and, perhaps by next autumn, they might both feel more confident, assuming that she stayed around that long . . .

'Coffee.' She was smiling up at him, passing him his mug, before climbing on to the stern deck.

'I want to moor up before it gets dark,' he said. 'Preferably at the Black Horse at Greenford. It's nearly two hundred years old and the food's delicious. You take the tiller while I just check the map.'

'This is kind of scary,' she said. 'I push it away from me if I want to go left and pull it towards me if I want to go right. Is that it?'

'Something like that.' He grinned at her. 'I imagine you don't want to learn the technicalities? Like port and starboard, for instance?'

'Certainly not,' she said. 'I work on the "kiss" method?'

'Kiss method?'

'Keep It Simple, Stupid.' She shivered and gulped back some coffee. 'It's getting chilly.'

'Don't worry. We'll stop soon and batten down the hatches for the night. After we've been to the pub.'

'Cool,' she said. 'I'm starving.'

Half an hour later, as the dusk closed in, the *Dorcas* was moored safely beside the tow path, not far from the brightly lit comfort of the Black Horse.

In Kit's kitchen, Bess and Jamie were sharing an Indian takeaway which Jamie had brought with him.

'So the weekend was a great success,' Jamie was saying. 'And Matt was welcomed with open arms.'

'It was fantastic.' Bess was eating chicken korma hungrily. 'He was really good with Dad. You know, kind of confident and relaxed, even when he couldn't really understand him. And Dad was brilliant. I know it sounds awful but I couldn't help wondering how it would have been before . . . you know?'

'I know what you mean. I must say he's much easier these days. More sort of mellow.'

'That's it,' agreed Bess eagerly. 'If only he could have been like that when we were little . . . Mum looked a bit washed out, I thought, but she was great with Matt.' She hesitated. 'Matt sort of officially asked for my hand.' She glared at him. 'Don't you dare laugh!'

'I'm not laughing. Would I dare? But how do you mean, "officially"?'

'We want to get married,' she said gruffly, not looking at him.

'*Married?*' He stared at her, food forgotten. 'But why? Isn't it a bit early for that? Can't you just live together for a bit?'

'I don't want to just live with him,' said Bess, crossly. 'Nor does he. Want to live with me, I mean. We want to get married. Why not?'

Jamie shrugged. 'No reason at all, I suppose. It's just that you're so young. And you haven't had much experience yet.'

'I'm not much younger than Susanna was when she got married,' protested Bess. She sighed deeply. 'I want us to be like them. She and Gus are still in love after all these years and Matt and I are going to be just the same.'

'If you say so.' Jamie raised the can of beer he'd had the foresight to bring with him. 'I'll drink to that. Is it too crude to ask how you intend to support yourselves?'

'We'll manage,' she said airily. 'We can't get married until I've finished at Trinity, and we've got to get a few things sorted out, but we can wait.'

'I'm glad to hear it.' He grinned at her. 'As for me, I intend to play the field for a while yet.'

She laughed. 'Do I take this to mean that you've finished with Karen?'

'She's ditched me,' he said ruefully, 'but I am rising above it. Got any nice friends who are unattached?'

She shook her head and then paused, frowning.

'Yes?' He was watching her encouragingly.

'I was thinking of the girl we met on Mole's boat,' she said slowly. 'She was really nice and terribly pretty. Long, reddish brown hair and about our age . . .'

'Don't stop there,' he said. 'My mouth is watering. Are you suggesting that Mole's been hiding this private passion from us? Cunning old devil.'

'Don't be silly,' she said impatiently. 'You're as bad as Matt. He said exactly the same sort of thing afterwards. She just dropped by to bring him a message about some party being given by the Brandons. Some naval thing, I gathered. Do you remember the Brandons?'

He frowned thoughtfully. 'Rings a bell. Anyway, what's her name? When can you introduce us?'

'She's called Sam. Samantha Something. Oh hell, I can't remember.'

'You're useless,' he said severely. 'Hopeless. Too wrapped up in love's young dream.'

'Sorry,' she said cheerfully. 'You'll have to ask Mole. He'll introduce you.'

'I'll do that,' he said. 'Anyway, I need to speak to him . . .'

'Speak to him about what?' she asked, as his voice trailed off vaguely.

'Oh, nothing important. Just . . . nothing.'

'Yes it is,' she said, her curiosity aroused. 'Come on. Spit it out.'

'It's only that . . . Well, don't say a word, not even to Matt. Promise?'

She nodded, surprised. 'Whatever is it?'

'Well, I'm thinking of having a try at . . . a government job. Not the Foreign Office, if you see what I mean, but something I thought about a while ago.'

'Oh, Jamie. You're not going to try for MI6 after all?'

She'd instinctively lowered her voice but he scowled at her. 'If you breathe a word I'll murder you,' he said – and she was suddenly reminded of their childhood and the endless games of make-believe. 'I shouldn't have told you but . . . Well, I suppose I just wanted some encouragement from someone I can absolutely trust. I'm not telling another soul, not even Mum and Dad, see?'

'But you said you needed to speak to Mole?'

'Yes, well, Mole's different . . .' He looked angry with himself. 'Look, just forget it, OK?'

'I swear I won't breathe a word to anyone, not even to Matt. I absolutely swear.' She might have been six years old again, crossing her heart and hoping to die if she should break her promise. 'Honestly, Jamie, I'm not stupid. I know how important it is.'

'I know you do.' Her face relaxed a little as he looked at her, his faithful lieutenant of bygone years. 'OK. Anyway, it'll probably come to nothing.'

Later, after Jamie had gone, Bess went downstairs to see Clarrie. Lucifer came wagging to meet her and she crouched to pat him.

'He knows your knock.' Clarrie was beaming at her. 'Never barks at you, does he? Come to do some practising?'

He loved it when she played. Keeping quiet as a mouse, he'd listen from some other room of the flat, door wide open, and creep in with some tea at discreet intervals. Now, watching her murmuring to Lucifer, her brown hair, shiny as seaweed, falling across the dog's rough coat, he tried to swallow down the lump in his throat. She was so young, so gifted, and he had been given the privilege of encouraging her. How glad he was that Kit and he had not moved away to some far-off city, so missing this precious development. He knew that he'd been lucky to have some part in the lives of Kit and Sin; now it was extending to the next generation and he was grateful for it. Kit had, to some extent, filled the empty space in his heart left by the death of his wife and daughter – and now, as he grew old, here was Bess sharing the vitality of her youth and strength with him.

'How's Matt?' he asked when she stood up and slipped an arm about his shoulders, casual and easy as she might be with any of her friends. 'Have you eaten? Kit's out tonight, isn't she?'

'She's not back yet but Jamie brought an Indian takeaway with him.' She wandered ahead of him into the kitchen, her brow furrowed. 'Matt's OK except that he's got a bit of a problem with his landlord. One of the tenants has complained about him practising so he's been given a warning. It's a new tenant, apparently, so it looks as if there might be problems ahead.'

'Like some tea?' He knew she never drank coffee.

'Love some. That Korma was quite spicy and I'm really thirsty.'

She sat at the table, chin in hands, and he watched her covertly as he bustled about. During these last fifteen years he'd grown experienced in the devious ways of women and he had a strong suspicion that there was more to come. Bess, however, had learned the value of silence and continued to dream into space, her grey eyes looking on things he could not see.

He cleared his throat. 'I thought Matt did his practising during the day.'

'So he does. That's why it's been OK before. All the other tenants are out at work. But this old bat has just retired and she's finding it irritating. I suppose,' said Bess generously, 'that you can't absolutely blame her. Listening to the French horn isn't everyone's idea of fun but poor old Matt has to practise some time. I expect he'll have to look for somewhere else.'

Clarrie looked at her innocent face suspiciously and she beamed at him as she put sugar in her tea.

'I'm so lucky to have you,' she said. 'It was good of Kit to let me stay with her. Not that Trinity has accommodation, anyway, so I couldn't have lived in, even if I'd wanted to, but I'm really glad I came here. And then you buying me the piano and everything. I really do appreciate it, you know. Musicians have so many problems to deal with.'

'Artists have to suffer for their art,' said Clarrie severely. 'It's a well-known fact.'

'Probably,' she agreed amiably, 'but not to the extent that they can't perform or earn a living. Bit counterproductive then, isn't it?'

'Possibly.' Clarrie had a feeling that he was being outmanoeuvred. 'But if we're talking about Matt, I don't see any great signs of suffering.'

'Not *yet*,' said Bess severely. 'But we don't know how bad it might get if he's not allowed to practise. It would just be such a relief if we knew he had somewhere to go if things got really bad. If you see what I mean . . . ?'

'I know exactly what you mean. You're thinking of the several empty bedrooms I have in this flat.'

'Well . . .' She grinned at him, colouring slightly. 'It was just a thought.'

'I doubt we'll allow Matt to be homeless,' he said, 'but I should have to speak to Kit first. *If*,' he bent a stern look upon her, 'such an emergency occurs.'

She stood up so as to hug him, swallowed the last of her tea and banged the mug back on the table.

'And now I shall go and practise,' she announced. 'Any requests before I get down to business?'

'Yes, please,' he said at once. 'That thing you were playing last time.'

He hummed a few bars and she laughed.

'Chopin,' she said. 'It's one of the *Ballades*. And there was I thinking I'd got you on to Szymanowski. Ah well.'

She disappeared in the direction of the music room and Clarrie sat on at the table, listening to her playing, his mind busy with ideas, whilst Lucifer lay sleeping at his feet.

Chapter Thirty-two

'I didn't think that I could cope with dear old David Attenborough this evening,' said Prue. 'Nature is so violent, isn't it? It's so . . . so *wasteful*. Those baby turtles trying to make their way down to the sea before all the predators get to them and those foolish ducks who lay their eggs in trees and then disappear, so that when their young are born they have to *launch* themselves to the ground into the jaws of the waiting animals. It's so utterly senseless. And it's exhausting to watch. I sit there, egging them on, positively *willing* them to reach safety. And then there's the lions. Dear old cuddly-looking things, until you see them taking over other lions' prides and killing all the darling little cubs . . . Oh, I know that nature has its own laws but there's something so depressing about so much murder and mayhem. Though with all this terrible news from Bosnia, man seems hardly any better. Worse, if anything. I can hardly bear to watch the news and I get so muddled with Bosnians and Serbs and Croats . . .'

Miles was understood to say that he preferred a good old-fashioned war film and Prue agreed that at least you knew whose side you were on. She leaned forward to fit another piece into the jigsaw puzzle and stood up to put some logs on to the dying fire. The flames licked eagerly at the dry wood, crackling and leaping up the wide chimney, and Prue settled back on the sofa beside Miles.

'I'm rather anxious,' she admitted, 'about that telephone call from Edward. I know it's no good crossing bridges and so on but I have this *premonition*, just here.' She placed her hand on her heart and looked at him distressfully. 'I know that Caroline says I'm fussing, and that there's no earthly reason why Edward shouldn't come down for the rest of half term if his friend's been taken suddenly ill, but I smell a rat. Where is Maria? And why isn't she with Adam? Why can't Adam look after Edward? . . . Yes I know that Edward's old enough to look after himself. That's what you're trying to say, isn't it? Well, I agree with you. He's seventeen, and a very self-sufficient sort of boy, but that's my point, you see. Why, quite suddenly, is he determined to come down to The Keep after all this time? It's not as if Hal is at home . . . Oh yes, I agree that I'm here, and Jolyon, and it's sweet of you to think that he wants to see me – but why now? . . . I'm quite sure that this piece fits here. It's such an odd colour, isn't it? Now, in you go . . . Well, perhaps not, after all. You know I quite thought that it was right . . . A drop more Scotch? A tiny one? Good. I'll join you . . . There we are. Yes, here's to us . . . You must be so pleased that darling Bess has found such a nice boy. We liked him, didn't we? . . . Yes, I know she's young but so was I when I married Johnny. No point in waiting if you find the right person, is there? . . . Oh, I know what you're saying but I think you *do* know, even if you're very young. And Bess knows her own mind. Just like you when you met darling Fliss. Look how you waited for her. So faithful and loyal. Anyway, they can't marry just yet so there's no need for you to worry about them . . . There! I've found that tricky piece at last. *Quite* a different colour than I thought it would be. Goodness, you've done splendidly. I feel quite ashamed of my poor little effort. I need Jolyon to help me. He's so quick at jigsaws . . . Oh, Miles, I know I've said all this before but I simply can't help saying it again. I am *so* grateful for your generous offer to dear Jolyon. It is so terribly sweet of you to back him. I know the Trust is doing all they can for his garden centre but to pay to have Fox's quarters modernised for him is just *so* kind. Hal explained that the nursery project must take precedence, and naturally Jolyon quite understood, but your offer is just breathtaking. He's over there now, you know. Measuring up and pacing things out. He's quite beside himself. And you have your own two to think about . . . Yes, I know that you've taken out insurances and so on. Fliss explained it all very carefully but even so . . . Now, could this be the piece you're looking for? Oh, well done. That's the whole of that corner finished. I think we deserve another little drink for that. Just a splash? Splendid . . . You see, I'm so worried that it might unsettle Jolyon if Edward's having problems. He's just beginning to accept the situation and to stop playing that very dismal, dreary music to himself and he's stopped that terrible thing of looking so *utterly* wretched when he doesn't think anyone's watching and . . . where was I? . . . Oh, yes, that's right. Edward. I'm certain that Maria is at the bottom of this and I shall be so angry if they upset Jolyon all over again when he's just so happy . . . Oh, look! Here's the outside piece we've been searching for. I must have knocked it on the floor when I stood up to do the fire. There. In it goes. Dear Miles. It is *such* a comfort to be able to have these chats with you . . .'

*   *   *

244

In the studio below the castle wall Gus was busy designing brochures for the coming season. The recession had hit Devon hard and several of his clients were now bankrupt. Banks, which had lent money so readily in the past against so little security, had called in loans and mortgages, and even those businesses which were surviving were having difficulty in meeting their bills. There was no question of the studio employing any staff now and Gus had been relieved to find a tenant for the flat who seemed capable of paying the rent.

'It would be more sensible at the moment,' Susanna had said, 'if I could get a job which earned money.'

Well, in a way she was right – he could just about manage alone – but it was so good to have her back in the studio with him. She was so capable, so completely *au fait* with the business, so good with clients. He loved having her around, humming to herself, dashing out to Harberton Art Workshop to buy odd bits and pieces and coming back to tell him whom she'd seen and what was happening in the town. It was just like the early days of their marriage all over again, even down to the struggle with cash flow, and Gus was enjoying it. He swung round in his chair to look at Susanna, standing at the light box, spotting negs. In her rugby shirt, worn loose over leggings, her dark hair pushed back impatiently behind her ears, she even looked the same. As if she was aware of his scrutiny, she glanced up at him.

'How's it going? Like some coffee?'

'It might help the inspiration to flow,' he said. 'In twenty years I think I've said all that there is to be said about hotels.'

'You need Podger.' She went into the small kitchen and filled the kettle. 'You must admit she has a way with a turn of phrase.'

'She certainly does. If you combine it with her insistence on absolute truth the whole leisure industry in south Devon could be ruined almost overnight.'

Susanna leaned in the doorway. 'She wants to take over the business when she leaves Herongate.'

'Don't remind me,' groaned Gus. 'She wouldn't have a client left within a year. I, Gus, prophesy it. Take note.'

'She's young yet,' said Podger's mother soothingly. 'Give her time.'

'*Time*?' His voice rose alarmingly. 'If she's this bossy at eleven can you imagine her at twenty?'

Susanna chuckled. 'She'll mellow,' she said. 'She'll tone down, you'll see.'

'Promise?' asked Gus grimly. 'When she comes in here to work during the holidays I have to send out the equivalent of a government health warning to the clients.'

'Odd, isn't it? That she's so bossy.' Susanna went back into the kitchen but her voice floated out to him. 'Fred's such a sweet-natured chap . . .'

'Like his father,' said Gus with satisfaction. 'Quiet, considerate, charming . . .'

'That'll be quite enough of that. And Lulu is much more biddable. It's so odd that three children can be so different.'

'It's the same with all families. Look at you three. It's difficult to believe that you and Fliss are sisters. You certainly don't look alike. Of course, you share the Chadwick determination to get your own way . . .'

He ducked as she stood his coffee on his desk and aimed a blow at his head.

'Talking of which,' she said, settling on a stool with her own mug of coffee, 'I wonder how things are going at The Keep.'

Gus glanced up at the clock. 'Will Edward have arrived yet?'

'An hour ago. Prue came over all grandmotherly and forbade Jo to fetch him. She was afraid of them being alone together before anyone else could discover what was going on.'

'She's quite right, of course.' Gus leaned back, stretching, reaching for his coffee. 'It would be so easy for Edward to bind Jo to some kind of secrecy which would be bad for both of them. There mustn't be any going into huddles. Jo's always tried to protect Edward and the last thing he needs now is to be enjoined into any conspiracies.'

'It's a good thing that Caroline took the call. She said that Edward was very cagey and evasive and that's what started everyone panicking. Caroline's so down-to-earth that if *she* thinks that something's odd we all take notice.'

'It's a pity that this has happened now when old Jo seems to be getting his act together. I think it's very good of Miles to offer to pay to convert the gatehouse.'

Susanna looked thoughtful. 'I think he's trying to repay the Trust for all the benefits he's able to enjoy. I know he pays his way and all that but Miles is the sort of person who finds it hard to be passive. He's encouraged Jo about his garden centre plans, and it would be wonderful to make The Keep start to pay for itself, but I think that Miles sees the gatehouse as his very own baby. A kind of legacy, if you see what I mean. So that people will say, "Oh, yes, Miles was responsible for that gatehouse conversion" and he'll have done his bit.'

'I think you could be right.' Gus doodled with his pencil. 'He's

246

certainly got his head screwed on when it comes to business. That was a very competent plan he drew up for Jo to show the trustees. Very impressive. It'll take time but it's a brilliant idea.' He laughed suddenly. 'Your grandmother would have a fit to think of The Keep becoming a garden centre.'

'She'd've called it a nursery.' Susanna smiled reminiscently, affectionately. 'Anyway, it's not quite like that, is it? The entrance will come in from down the lane and it's separate from the grounds. Still, we have to move with the times and I'm sure Grandmother would have agreed with that. The trouble is that we all have to make money to survive.'

'I'm sure she would.' Gus sighed and finished his coffee. 'And talking of which, I've got to go over to Hope Cove this afternoon to look at a hotel. It's just been taken over by new owners. Want to come?'

She looked at him quickly, eyes sparkling, lips pressed together – and his heart jumped oddly in his breast.

'Do you think we should leave the office unmanned?'

'Yes,' he said. 'Yes, I do. The sun's shining and spring's nearly here. We deserve an afternoon out together.'

'As long as we're back in time for Lulu . . .'

Gus sighed. 'Story of my life. If I'd known about the hardships of fatherhood . . .'

'Shut up and get on with it,' said Susanna. 'We'll find a pub and have a sandwich on the way. Oh, Gus. I do love you.'

'Ditto, Sooz,' he said. 'Oh, blast. Can you answer that?'

She grinned at him mischievously as she stretched across to lift the receiver and, with a fair imitation of Podger's voice, she said: 'Studio Graphics. *Who's* speaking, please?'

The two boys stood on the hill, staring across the dun fields, shivering a little in the strong, cold wind. Rooks wheeled, calling hoarsely, and, higher still, seagulls floated, leaning on the wind, yellow eyes turned earthwards. On a distant slope a tractor moved slowly, churning the mud which glowed crimson in a sudden downslant of sunshine.

Edward was delving into the pocket of his shirt beneath the thick jersey, dragging out a battered packet of cigarettes, which he offered to Jolyon as he shook one from the packet.

'No,' said Jolyon, staring. 'No, thanks. I didn't know you smoked, Ed.'

Edward shrugged, found his lighter, and turned his back to the wind, making his own shelter.

'Just don't tell Granny,' he said, inhaling, turning back. 'Or Miles. Nothing worse than reformed smokers.'

Watching him, Jolyon felt a terrible ache of pity.

He thought: It's queer that it should make him look even younger. Like a kid aping the grown-ups . . .

To his critical eye, Edward looked thin and strangely unkempt, in a glittery, bright sort of way. His skin was pale and he was reluctant to meet your eye. He moved all the time, continually twitching, jerking his shoulders, tapping a foot. Now he flicked nonexistent ash before taking another drag at his cigarette. Jolyon was filled with fear.

'Does Mum know you smoke?' He tried to sound casual. 'Of course, she smokes, doesn't she?'

'She knows I have the odd one,' he said indifferently. 'It's not a crime, Jo. I'm seventeen, you know.'

'Yes, I know.' Jolyon set off down the sheep track, wondering what to say to this brother who had suddenly become a stranger, glad that their father was at sea. 'I'm sorry that Mum . . . that Mum's got problems with Adam.'

Last evening, beneath their grandmother's relentless questioning, Edward had caved in and admitted that Maria had gone away with another man and Adam was staying with friends.

'It was just for half term,' he'd mumbled, sitting at the kitchen table, his hands twisting and tearing at a linen table napkin. 'Mum's fed up with Adam. They argue all the time and then she tells me about it. She's found this other guy – I think he's an estate agent – and she'd planned to go off for a few days while I was with Dan. I knew about it but I didn't know where she'd gone. And then Dan got this stomach thing and his mum was afraid I might catch it and that's when I found that Adam had gone, too. I could've just gone home, I s'pose, but I didn't want to be all on my own for a week.'

His lips had twisted, as if he was trying not to cry, and Jo had looked at his grandmother in horror. Luckily everyone else had tactfully left them to it but he could see that Granny was upset, although there was a kind of strength, a determination, which he'd never noticed in her before.

She'd taken Edward's restless, tearing, crumpling fingers in her own hands and was now holding them tightly.

'Why should you be all alone for a week,' she'd asked reasonably enough, 'when you've got your family here, longing to see you? Did Mummy give you a telephone number in case of emergencies?'

It was odd that: Granny saying 'Mummy' as if Ed was a little boy, but then Granny was pretty old – at least seventy – so perhaps he seemed like it to her. Ed was shaking his head, still biting his lips, staring at the table, and Granny had looked at him, Jo, again as if she was counting on him, as if he was an adult in her eyes and not a little kid, like Ed.

'I'll make some tea,' he'd said, very calm, very casual – and she'd smiled at him with such sweetness that for a minute he'd feared that he might blub, too, and he'd realised just how difficult all this grown-up stuff was.

'Have you met this other man?' Granny was asking, and Ed was shaking his head again.

'She wanted me to,' he'd muttered, 'but I wouldn't. It seemed so sort of disloyal to Adam. And I didn't want to encourage her and stuff. She was a bit like a kid about it, like she wasn't married and she'd just met this new guy and I ought to be as excited as she was. She'd come home late in the evening when Adam was in bed or down the pub and she'd dance about and sing.'

That's when Jo had felt really sick inside. He could remember that happening to him, when he'd thought she'd been out at meetings, but, much later, when he'd grown up a bit, he'd realised that she'd been with Adam. Now poor old Ed was going through it. He'd been ashamed to feel relief, the lifting of a weight from his heart because Mum was behaving to Ed as she'd behaved to him. That needn't mean she didn't love Ed, he'd told his conscience quickly, only that they were on equal terms now.

'Does Adam know about him?' Granny had asked.

There had been a long silence; long enough to pour the tea and put the milk and sugar in and pass the mugs round.

'Does he, darling?' Granny wasn't going to give in.

'Yes,' Ed had admitted reluctantly. 'They row about it.'

'Oh, darling . . .'

'It doesn't matter,' Ed had said fiercely. It looked as if he was glad to have to pick up his mug and let go of Granny's hands. You could see he didn't want her sympathy. 'I don't care. I'm finishing school next year and going to the States.'

'To *America*?'

He'd wanted to smile at the expression on Granny's face, like America was somewhere out in space, but he couldn't smile while Ed looked so miserable.

'Granny Keene's got relations out there and they've invited me over for a year, before I go to university. It's only eighteen months away and I've got Dan . . .'

Out on the hill, turning to see if Ed was following him, Jo called: 'Going to the States sounds fun.'

'Perhaps I'll stay there if I like it.' Ed caught him up and they went on together. 'Your plans sound good, too, Jo. Especially the gatehouse. Nice to have your own pad.'

'Mmm.' He tried to hide his pride. It seemed a bit mean in the circumstances. 'I don't think Mum approves, though.'

'Who cares what she thinks?' Ed sounded violent, bitter, and Jolyon felt another familiar nerve touched. 'I'm fed up with the way she tries to manipulate me all the time. She's so bloody good at emotional blackmail. When I tried to be a bit . . . well, stuffy, I suppose, about this new guy, she went all weepy. She said that all her problems went back to the fact that Dad and Fliss were lovers years and years ago and that Dad pretended it was over when it wasn't. She said he broke her heart and ruined her confidence. Do you think it's true?'

He couldn't answer Ed, he simply couldn't. He just shook his head, looking away, trying not to remember that scene in the hall and the expression on his father's face as he'd held Fliss in his arms.

'Well, I didn't believe it anyway,' Ed was saying. 'It's just another excuse. Nothing's ever her fault. First Dad and now Adam. I like old Adam, actually. Oh, shit, who cares? Bloody hell, it's freezing. Come on, Jo, I'll race you round the spinney.'

Chapter Thirty-three

'We were never lovers,' said Fliss quietly. 'We never went to bed or anything remotely like it. Nothing more than a few kisses and lots of hugs. Oh, Jo, it was all over by the time I was eighteen and Hal was twenty-one . . .'

'But you were in love?'

He was a stranger, standing across the room, head lowered, fists in pockets; a stranger – and yet so terribly like Hal.

'Yes,' she said wearily. 'We were in love.'

'You still are, aren't you? I saw you in the hall.'

'I know you did. Yes, we love each other but you simply have to believe that all those years ago, after we agreed that we mustn't be together, we never looked or showed any love to each other. Hal fell genuinely in love with Maria. It's only now, just occasionally, with Hal divorced from your mother, and Miles . . . and Miles ill, that we share a moment of affection.'

'Do you mean . . . ?' He couldn't look at her. 'Have you ever . . . been together?'

'No,' she said strongly.

Silence fell between them. He'd been brave enough to come to her room, to confront her in her own quarters rather than on neutral ground, and she was grateful for her familiar surroundings. The atmosphere of this room, her grandmother's sitting room, comforted her as she looked at Jo. She could feel his pain but that was all; his affection for her had been switched off and she struggled not to panic. It wasn't just his love for her that was at stake here; it was his trust in his father, his love for him, that she might put at risk.

The wind raged about the house, buffeting the granite walls. Somewhere downstairs a door slammed and they heard the high yelping cry of the puppy. Even this helpless, insistent sound did not distract Jolyon. As she watched him, the years rolled back and it was Hal, standing across the room: head bent, face closed, all his thoughts inward. Somehow she must make him understand, take him with her, so that he could enter into the world she and Hal had shared.

'Listen,' she said. 'Try to picture how it was thirty years ago. We were together a great deal but we didn't have the freedom young people have now. It wasn't the norm to have sex before you got engaged, and especially not in this household, anyway. Ours was a very romantic kind of love. Hal was at Dartmouth and there were parties and lots of outings and just ordinary fun. The world has changed, Jo, in thirty years. We lived in the shadow of the bomb but there was a deep-down security. Your generation lives with the spectre of AIDS and the breaking-up of family life. These days the world changes from minute to minute. Technology is out of date the moment it's been invented, and values we took for granted are rapidly disappearing. I have the feeling that our generation educated its children for a world that was already passing.' She paused. 'We had fun, and Hal and I were very good friends in an innocent way which probably wouldn't be possible now. It was a tremendous shock when he told me that our love had no future. He explained that he thought that I was too young to make such a commitment and that, our fathers being identical twins, there was a danger to any children we might have.'

He was looking at her now, but there was no friendliness in his eyes, merely a kind of patient watchfulness. She felt a terrible fear at the thought of losing his affection and part of her considered how she might draw him back to her. She might, for instance, mention the murder of her brother Jamie and the transference of her love for him to Hal; she could tell of the comfort Hal had given his younger cousin, of her need for him in her despair, her whole life dislocated. From there it would be a short step to the painful little tale of her heartbreak . . .

For a brief moment it seemed that Uncle Theo and Grandmother were both in the room with them and their faint presence strengthened her against her momentary weakness and injected steel into her spine. She straightened her shoulders, lifting her chin, trying to smile into Jolyon's unresponsive face.

'You mustn't think that we were some kind of star-crossed lovers,' she said. 'Hal was a little older than you are now and about to set out on his career. He loved pretty girls, fast cars and excitement, and when he met Maria he fell absolutely in love with her. He was so proud of her. Please don't imagine that she was some kind of second best and that secretly he was pining for me. It wasn't like that. Try to see it how it was . . .'

She thought: But how was it? I've always loved him and there

252

was always that small magic between us. I don't want to lie or cheat but how can I make him understand?

'And was it like that for you and Miles?'

She stared at him. There was danger here. His respect and affection for Miles were not to be taken lightly – but could she risk the absolute truth?

'No,' she said baldly. 'He loved me but I'd never seen him as anything else but a good friend.'

'And when did you fall in love with him?'

How cool he was, how precise; rather like a young judge . . .

'I never fell in love with Miles,' she answered – and felt a huge wave of relief engulf her. She would stand by the truth whatever it might cost her, yet she had no right to influence or damage his love and trust for his father – or for Miles. 'Falling in love is a febrile, exhausting, passionate business,' she said reflectively. 'It's romantic and emotional and wonderful – and if you're terribly lucky it settles down into a good working relationship. Otherwise it burns itself out or dies in the face of the boredom and routine of the daily round. I was already very fond of Miles when he proposed to me and I grew to love him slowly. My love for Miles is based on the qualities I've discovered in him. That is why there was never any risk that I should betray him with Hal. I honour Miles too much, especially now.'

'But when you were with Dad in the hall,' he insisted, 'I had a feeling then, some kind of intuition, but afterwards I thought I must be wrong. But you still love each other, don't you? Whatever you may say, it's always been there underneath, hasn't it?'

He did not add the words 'undermining your other relationships' but they were implicit in his questioning and they seemed to echo in the silence.

'Yes,' she said at last, 'it's always been there. Subconsciously I've felt it, as one might be aware of any abstract comfort, like warmth, for instance. But for years neither of us spoke or thought of it. We were too busy holding on to what we had. Remember that as soon as we were married – all four of us, I mean, – Miles and I went to Hong Kong for two years and Hal and I hardly saw each other for the next ten years. Please try to get an absolutely unbiased picture, Jolyon. I was moving about with Miles and the twinnies and Hal was at sea a great deal. We were too busy, too preoccupied, to entertain sickly notions of unrequited love.'

'But if it was there underneath,' he insisted, 'mightn't it be possible that your other relationships were suffering.'

'Oh, Jo,' she said sadly, 'how can I answer you truthfully? I don't

253

know, you see. I don't know what it might have been like otherwise. But answer some of these questions yourself. You were neither blind nor deaf. Were your parents happy together? Was your father unloving, indifferent? Did he make efforts to make you all happy? Did he seem like someone who wanted an excuse to get out?'

She waited. Footsteps passed overhead and a flurry of rain was dashed against the window.

'No,' he said at last, unwillingly. 'He was always trying to calm things down. Mum was . . . moody at times, irritable. I was always waiting for him to come home. She missed him . . .'

'I know she did,' Fliss said gently. 'Maria should never have been a naval wife. She needed to have her husband with her. And why not? That's not a criticism. It's a most unnatural life, after all. She was . . . insecure.'

'She would be,' he said fiercely, 'if she thought that Dad was still in love with you.'

Well, she had put the weapon into his hands; it wasn't surprising that he should use it.

'Hal told her that there had been a romantic attachment between us.' She shrugged. 'Perhaps it was foolish of him but I expect that he feared that some joke might be made of it to her by some member of the family. The silly thing was that most of the family never even knew about it until much later. They thought that our affection was purely the brother-and-sister variety. Susanna and Mole still do. I think that Hal, knowing that she's a jealous person, wanted to remove any danger of such insecurity by telling her that it was quite unimportant. Confessions are always silly. They might be wonderful for the confessor but they don't do a lot for the confessee. However, I think Hal wouldn't have believed for a moment that the admission of some boy and girl affair with his cousin would affect his marriage permanently. If it had been a full-blown love affair lasting years that might be different but she knew that it wasn't like that—'

'How did she know?' he interrupted.

She folded her arms beneath her breasts, clenching her fists. 'Jo,' she said quietly, 'please try to think. I know you can't know how things were before you were born but apply what you *do* know to this situation and see things straight. Think back. Remember as much as you can. If the love between me and Hal was so intrusive why didn't we pack it in and get together? Was it Hal who left Maria? Can you remember anything that can prove that he didn't give everything he'd got to keeping his marriage going? Even if she felt jealous of me in those early days can you think of anything – anything at all – in Hal's

254

behaviour which gave Maria any ongoing rational reasons for insecurity?'

'Then why?' he cried angrily. 'Why did she leave us? If it wasn't insecurity because of you and Dad then why did she go? Why did she stop loving us?'

His hurt was almost palpable. To prevent herself from reaching out to him, she hugged herself tightly. There was danger here; not for herself or Hal but for Jolyon himself. If only Theo were beside her; how terribly she needed him now . . .

'I tried to think it out,' he was saying. 'She knew Adam when she was young, did you know that? I thought that perhaps it was she who couldn't get over her first love and that she was just trying to put it on to Dad. If she'd been in love with Adam all the time then I could understand it a bit. But now there's this other chap.' He stared at her almost accusingly, as if she were deliberately refusing to understand him. 'I don't want to think that my mother is an uncaring, selfish bitch,' he shouted.

'You would rather think that your father is a lying adulterer?'

He jerked back, as if she had administered a physical blow, his face wrenched with shock.

'You'll have to make up your mind,' she said coolly. 'You see, Jolyon, what you really want is for both your parents to be perfect. Because we're all thirty years older than you are you expect us to be without sin, free of faults or weaknesses. It's a nice thought, isn't it? But unrealistic. It's hard to live with the knowledge that we are not loved, especially by those whom we think owe us love. It diminishes us so we search about for reasons to help us live with it. Of course we can lie to ourselves and cheat ourselves, and we can let it be a splendid reason for letting ourselves off the hook when we need an excuse for our own failures. You can go ahead if you want to, with this hanging round your neck like some monstrous pet. You can take it out and look at it, stroke it, encourage it, so that it saps your energy and your common sense and finally brings you down into the dust. Or you can put it at a distance and look at it with clear eyes. You can think, "OK, so this is how it is because my mother had certain weaknesses and couldn't cope and I'm one of the victims of her inadequacy. On the other hand there are all these other people who know and love me. They want me to live with them, to work for them and are trusting me. I can make do with this, not least because it's one hell of a lot more than most people ever have."

'You can do that, Jolyon, or you can be like Maria who, despite the love of her husband and sons, preferred to submit to her

255

weakness until it took her over. Everyone must feed her need. Hal first, then you, then Adam and now Edward, and because it is insatiable the list will be endless. You don't have to find reasons for other people's weaknesses, just accept that they have them and love them anyway. Don't try to judge and condemn. It's bad enough coping with one's own failures and attempting to change and grow. You see we all have crossroads: choices, decisions to make, and then it's up to us. When you get to your crossroad, Jolyon, I hope you don't turn aside with excuses that you weren't loved by your mother . . .'

The door closed quietly behind him and she was alone. Trembling, she made her way to her chair and sat down. Each muscle ached with the effort of hiding her fear and she was icy cold. She closed her eyes.

She thought: I got it utterly and absolutely wrong. I've destroyed whatever he had to hold on to and given him nothing in its place.

Presently she stood up again, moving clumsily about the room, unable to think clearly, not knowing what to do. She bumped against a small table and put out her hand to steady the jar which stood upon it. It was the ginger jar, given to her when she left Hong Kong by the twinnies' amah, Rennie. When Miles had been posted to Northwood, the jar had been left at the house in Dartmouth and one of the tenants had broken it. It had been cleverly repaired but she'd felt sadness and shame that she'd risked this token of loyalty and friendship to careless strangers. Afterwards she'd taken it with her as a talisman, a reminder of those particular qualities. As she stood there, her finger running over the cracks, thinking back over the long years, the door opened behind her.

'Sorry.' It was Jolyon's voice. 'I . . . just needed to be on my own for a minute.'

She did not turn round and he came across to her, bending to look at her. She steeled herself to meet his eyes, preparing herself for the expression she might find there. He was smiling at her, animosity replaced with a new peace, but there was concern, too, and shame.

'It needed to be said,' he told her, recognising her apprehension, reassuring her. 'It'll take a bit of getting used to but it's all there, if you see what I mean. I just need to assemble it and get used to having it about . . . you know? It's just . . . I'm really sorry I said things. Implied . . .' He hesitated and then tried again, anxiously. 'I had no right . . .'

She held the jar towards him and he put out his hands for it, puzzled, so that they held it between them.

'Feel the cracks?' she asked. 'It got broken but it hasn't really hurt it. Not really. We all get it wrong, you see, and then there's damage. But it can be put right and, though it might not be the same afterwards, sometimes it can be better. It's very special to me, this jar, and now I'd like you to have it, Jolyon. Your first present for your new home.'

He took it from her, setting it down gently on the table, and she went into his outstretched arms and they stood together in silence, holding each other tightly.

Chapter Thirty-four

Lulu had a loose tooth. Lying on her back in the dog basket with Rufus, she wobbled the tooth with her tongue, rocking it to and fro, feeling how soon it might suddenly give way. She wondered what would happen if she swallowed it by mistake and, just to be on the safe side, she put her tongue firmly in the other cheek. It was nice here in the kitchen, looking at the dresser which went up and up into the shadows with all the pretty, shiny bits of china, and listening to something just quietly gurgling away in its saucepan on the Aga. She'd wakened that morning with a tickly throat and a shivery feeling and Mummy had dithered about whether she should go to school. It was a bit tricky because Mummy was supposed to be going to the studio. Daddy had already gone off to meet someone and there wouldn't be anyone to answer the telephone, and she'd been talking to herself while she'd made the Ready Brek. She'd said things like, 'Oh, dear, I wonder if it's anything serious,' and, 'Of course, there's that bug going round.' Then she'd said, 'I suppose you could come into the studio with me,' but Lulu had known that it was a kind of test because of the way she said it, as if she was thinking about it a bit but not as if it was actually settled. Lulu knew that if she'd said, 'Oh, yes, please,' then Mummy would have guessed that she wasn't as ill as all that, so she hadn't said it. Instead, she'd just put some sugar on her Ready Brek and pushed at it with her spoon as if she didn't much want it. Mummy had said, 'Aren't you hungry?' and she'd rested her elbow on the table and leaned her head on it, as if she was very tired and a bit miserable, so she didn't have to answer. Mummy had sighed and said, 'Well, it's Friday, so I suppose one day off won't matter,' and she'd telephoned The Keep.

Now, lying in the dog basket with Rufus asleep on her tummy, Lulu swallowed carefully so as to feel how her throat was doing. Caroline had given her something to gargle with which had tasted really yucky but she'd enjoyed making the noise with her head right back and her eyes screwed up. It still felt tickly so it hadn't absolutely been a lie but she could have managed at school,

259

which made her feel a bit uncomfortable inside. She'd wakened up knowing that she wanted a holiday, and not a holiday like the weekend or proper school holidays, but a holiday when everyone else was working. One of her favourite treats was being able to do holiday things when other people couldn't. It was nice to think that all her friends were busy in school while she lay here in the dog basket with Rufus. She wobbled her tooth again and turned her head a little, so that she could smell the clean wool rug beneath her cheek. She knew it was clean because Fliss had said so earlier. Aunt Prue had said, 'Should she be in the dog basket if she's got a cold coming?' and Fliss had said, 'It's a clean rug. I put it on this morning,' and then they'd gone off to the market in Totnes.

She stroked Rufus's soft, fluffy coat, liking the weight of him, warm and heavy on her tummy. Jo had winked at her as he'd gone out to his work in the garden. Jo was her favourite person at The Keep and she'd decided that when she was grown up she would marry him and live with him in his dear little house by the gate. It wasn't quite ready yet but you could see how it was going to be when it was all finished. She would help him in the garden and they would have several dogs. She pushed at her tooth again with her tongue, rocking it quite hard. Although it hurt a bit she couldn't seem to stop it but she couldn't quite bring herself to give it a tug and pull it right out either. She wished she could because then the tooth fairy would come and give her fifty pence. When she'd said that to Caroline and Miles earlier, Miles had said something in his funny voice and Caroline had said, 'Quite right. Sixpence was the going rate, wasn't it? I can just imagine Ellen's face. "Ten shillings for a tooth," she'd've said. "Whatever next, I wonder,"' and Miles had laughed.

Lulu wriggled, shifting Rufus higher and drawing up her knees. The door opened and Caroline came in. She waggled a hand and said, 'You're like Kit. She was happiest in the dog basket,' and then she began to do things which sounded as if lunch might happen soon. It was funny, because as soon as Caroline was there, moving to and fro, Lulu felt all kind of drowsy and happy and safe and she rubbed her cheek against Rufus's warm coat. Pictures started to form inside her head and, after a bit, she closed her eyes so that she could see them better.

'She's been asleep for the last half an hour,' said Caroline. 'It will do her good.'

'I'm sure it can't be good for her to sleep in a dog basket.' Prue was still in her coat, her arms full of shopping. 'Do you think she's got that flu-y thing coming, Caroline? Susanna says half her class is away with it.'

'She's probably just a bit overtired. We all need a small unofficial holiday now and then.' Caroline refused to fuss. 'As for being in the dog basket, well all I can say is that it never did Kit much harm.'

'Except that she never grew out of it,' said Prue sadly. 'Oh, I know you think I'm foolish but I sometimes wonder about it. Even when she was grown up there was always someone older for her to turn to, who treated her as if she were still a child. Ellen and Fox did, of course. Even Jake did. And then there was Clarrie.'

'If you ask me,' said Caroline, stirring the soup, 'Kit is perfectly happy as she is, especially since she's had Bess to look after. I know that she hasn't married and had her own children but there can be just as much happiness found in looking after other people's – as I ought to know.'

'Oh, Caroline,' said Prue remorsefully, 'I wasn't implying . . . You know I don't mean . . .'

'Kit is probably a better godmother than she would have been as a mother. What do you think, Fliss?'

Fliss, who had just come in, dumped some carrier bags on the edge of the table.

'All I can say is that she's a brilliant godmother,' she said, beginning to unpack the bags. 'The twinnies treat her as if she's part of their own generation and she's never mumsy and panicky with them. Old Clarrie's more motherly than she is. She'd never notice if they weren't eating properly or whether their clothes were clean but they'll tell her things they'd never tell me and they value her judgement. I worry about them far less knowing that she's there and that they look upon her as a friend. Especially Bess. Jamie's much more confident and he's finding his feet now, but it's been wonderful for Bess to have Kit around. She's been very good to her.'

Prue was looking happier. 'Maybe you're right,' she said. 'Perhaps it is better for her to be one removed from parenthood.'

Caroline smiled. 'I can just see her, head in a book, no shopping done, and the baby in the dog basket. Dear old Kit.'

Before Prue could protest, Jolyon came in. 'It's really dank out there this morning,' he said. 'What's for lunch. Soup? Oh, great. Did you find any curtain material for my new bedroom, Granny?'

At the sound of his voice, Rufus woke and struggled up, disturbing Lulu in the process. There was a brief tangle of paws and arms and Rufus's head caught Lulu's jaw a sharp bang. She gave a cry of pain, not quite knowing where she was and feeling frightened for a

261

moment. Confused, seeing everyone looking at her, she wondered whether it was a good moment to burst into tears to cover her embarrassment and excite sympathy. As she opened her mouth, she stopped quite suddenly, eyes widening. Carefully she put her fingers into her mouth and drew out a small white tooth.

'Look,' she said, tears forgotten. 'Look. Rufus has knocked my tooth out.'

There was a general cry of praise and, beaming now, she scrambled out of the dog basket, holding the tooth aloft.

'Keep it safe,' advised Jolyon. 'The tooth fairy will be along tonight.'

'Fifty pence is the going rate,' said Caroline, giving the soup a final stir. 'She told us so earlier. Miles was shocked at the rate of inflation. And, talking of Miles, will someone go and find him and tell him that lunch is ready?'

Much later, in the quiet hour before dinner, Miles sat in the hall with Fliss. Lulu had been collected long since and had gone home clutching the tooth in a small paper bag. The prospect of the tooth fairy was, apparently, a sovereign cure for any lingering flu symptoms and she'd gone off with her mother, chattering cheerfully, completely recovered.

'Well, why shouldn't she have a day off?' Fliss had asked, as she and Miles waved them out of the courtyard and turned back into the warmth of the hall. 'It can't do any harm just now and again . . .'

She'd fallen silent and, glancing at her, he'd been surprised at her expression. She'd looked faintly confused, awkward, and he'd suddenly realised that she was thinking of the occasional dissensions they'd had in the past as a result of their different opinions regarding the twinnies' upbringing. He knew that he'd often been too strict, too concerned that they should grow up reliable, responsible adults to allow any licence. Also, to his shame, he also knew that he'd never looked forward to having them about, that he'd thought holidays were plentiful enough without granting bonuses.

As she went to build up the fire and he sat down on the sofa, he was remembering a particular argument they'd had over the children's birthday. Fliss had wanted to drive them down to The Keep a day early and he'd balked at the idea of the twins missing a day at school. He sighed to himself, recalling that he'd given her a little lecture on discipline. What a prosy bore he must have seemed to her. He was glad, now, that on those small matters she'd rarely given in to him. When it affected the children, she'd

262

exercised her own judgement, thought the matter through and acted accordingly. For herself, she'd allowed him to guide their lives until that cataclysmic moment when she'd refused to go with him to Hong Kong. Even now he could feel the echo of that particular fusion of anger, hurt and astonishment. Looking back, he wondered how he'd managed to leave her; how he'd imagined that a job in Hong Kong would be more important to him than his wife. Of course, he'd secretly believed that she'd give in and come out to join him. What a fool he'd been and how little he had known her . . .

She smiled at him as she sat down beside him, slipping her hand into his, leaning against his shoulder, curling her legs beneath her. Jolyon came wandering in, nodded smilingly to both of them and, sitting down, reached for the newspaper and shook it open. Looking at him, Miles was aware that there was a change. Attempting to define it, he decided that Jolyon had the relaxed yet quietly alert air of someone who has recognised and accepted the solution to a problem even if he has not yet totally come to terms with it.

Miles thought: Perhaps young Edward made Jo see that it's that wretched Maria who's the weak one. Not him. It's clear that she doesn't love anyone except herself and it's about time Jo realised it.

The force of his own good fortune suddenly engulfed him: things might so easily have been different. The easy tears which were now his bane, rose into his eyes and he swallowed defiantly, blinking them back, holding Fliss's hand tightly. Her quick, warm response made him feel even more emotional and he began to rummage for his handkerchief. Fortunately, Jolyon was engrossed in the news of the IRA's mortar attack at Heathrow. Nevertheless, aware of Miles's embarrassment, Fliss uncurled her legs and smiled at him.

'Would you like me to play for you?' she asked – and he nodded gratefully, preparing to rise. They went out together.

After they'd gone, Jolyon put down the paper and stared thoughtfully at the flames. When he saw Fliss and Miles together like that, peaceful and really close, he felt an absolute bastard after the things he'd said to her. After Ed had said that about Fliss and Dad, out on the hill, the only thing he'd been able to think about was that scene in the hall, with the two of them hugging, and he'd known then that his instinct had been right. He'd been so obsessed, so sure that this was the cause of all his pain, that he hadn't thought it through at all. He'd just gone at her, bull-headed, forgetting all the love and kindness she'd shown him ever since he was little. Yet she seemed to have forgiven him utterly; understanding how he was feeling and giving him the vase. She'd made him think, though. It was like she'd slapped his face when she'd said that he'd rather think Dad was a lying adulterer – but she'd been right when she'd told him that he wanted to think that his parents were perfect. He'd been confused, wanting to put the blame on anyone but himself or his parents, hitting out illogically at anything. It was simply that he couldn't face the idea that Mum didn't love him. Now, he could see the truth. It was funny that Ed had already recognised it. Nothing had to be her fault, he'd said, and that she didn't love anyone except herself.

He leaned forward to reach for a log, tossing it well back on the fire. It was the truth – but it was still going to take time coming to terms with it. He couldn't just write her off, pretend she didn't exist, but he no longer felt like he was carrying a heavy weight in his heart. The odd thing was that he didn't mind about Dad and Fliss. He was glad she'd been honest with him, although he felt badly for forcing her to admit all those private things, but he felt really sad for them. It would have been so easy for them to get together; just as easy as it had been for Mum and Adam . . . Instead they'd struggled on. Dad had tried really hard, he knew that, and you could see that Fliss had made Miles happy, you only had to see the way he looked at her to know that. She and Dad hadn't only loved each other, that was the point. It was very complicated but he didn't have to get uptight about it any more, not if he didn't want to; it was his choice.

Picking up *The Times* again, he settled back to read the leader.

'All the same,' Prue was saying in the kitchen, 'perhaps we shouldn't encourage Lulu to get into the dog basket quite so often. I know Kit is very happy, and I don't mind any more about her not marrying and having babies, but I wouldn't like to think that darling Lulu might be . . . well, you know, affected in the same way.'

'I think Kit missed having a father around,' said Caroline gently. 'All those boyfriends were a kind of safety net and she needed to feel secure.'

'Darling Johnny.' Prue wiped her eyes with the tea-towel. 'If only he could have lived to see them all. Jolyon reminds me of him so much. It's wonderful and painful all at the same time.'

'What about a glass of that nice sherry?' suggested Caroline, taking the potato peeler from Prue's hand and guiding her towards the larder. 'Wouldn't that be a good idea?'

'Perhaps it would steady me,' agreed Prue, looking a little brighter. 'You'll join me, Caroline?'

'It would be quite wrong to let you drink alone,' said Caroline solemnly. 'And while we're about it, you never showed me the curtain material you bought this morning for Jolyon's bedroom over in the gatehouse. Go and get it while I pour out and then we'll raise our glasses to the tooth fairy.'

Chapter Thirty-five

Travelling back to London, Mole felt a sense of exhilaration, of intense expectation, which was unlike anything he'd experienced previously when leaving The Keep. It was odd that, although he'd done this journey so many times during his life, there was usually a faint depression, a sinking of the spirits as he started up the car or climbed into the train. He'd never been very good at saying goodbye to his family. The last day was such a misery to him that it was almost a relief to make the final farewells and hurry away. He hated it if anyone accompanied him on to the platform; dreaded the awful ritual of standing about, glancing at watches, making banal small talk. He wished that he could be like his cousin, whose easy, outgoing nature never balked at such things. Hal bore courteously with his mother going with him to the station, chattering to him on the platform, waving until the last carriage had vanished. He happily took the children in his car to the end of the lane – before turning them out to walk back home – so that they might eke out the longest possible time with him. Hal's last day was as cheerful as his first and Mole envied him. The family, however, understood his own theories regarding departures and respected them.

This time, Mole was travelling by train. He'd told his family that his car was playing up but the truth of the matter was that he'd lent it to Sam. Her father was very ill and she'd decided to go home for several days. Since she was having trouble with her own small car – combined with a few financial hiccups – he'd suggested that she should borrow his. He'd been ridiculously pleased when she'd agreed. She was so independent, so prickly where her pride was concerned, that he rarely made such gestures. This time, however, she'd accepted gratefully. Tomorrow he would see her again . . .

It was probably foolish but he looked upon the borrowing of the car as a positive step forward; as a breaking down of the barrier of her fierce independence. Looking out of the window as the train ran alongside the river at Teignmouth, Mole knew that this was the source of his exhilaration, the root of his expectation. This sensation of a barrier had persisted during those early days with Sin except that, in an indefinable but very positive way, Sin had, from the very beginning, held him at arm's length. There had never been any question of a permanent commitment. She'd always made it quite clear that, though they might have a great deal of fun together, it would never develop into anything more serious. In that case, too, there had been the age gap problem and he could quite see that Sin had no wish to be officially attached to someone seven or eight years younger than she was. It had been a terrific time for him, an amazing experience, and he'd been deeply fond of her but, even with Sin, there hadn't been this deep down, gut-twisting excitement; nor the terrible heart-rending tenderness.

Despite Sam's independence, he'd never considered it impossible that they might have a future together. If only he could be more sure of her. Although he'd met one of her flatmates – Lizzie, was it? – at that first party, Sam never invited him back to the flat. She always gave him the same reason that she used when the conversation edged round to meeting her parents – and her mother in particular; that he was too attractive, too much of a dark horse, that she couldn't trust her girlfriends. Was it a reason – or an excuse? He suspected that she feared, as he did, that her friends and family would be horrified by the age disparity. This weekend, at The Keep, he'd promised himself that, if an opening should occur, he would mention Sam. On the journey down he'd rehearsed a few casual sentences: 'I've been seeing this rather fun girl, lately . . .' Or: 'I met a rather nice girl at a party recently . . .' Even he had to admit that these words sounded so pedestrian, so completely inadequate, as to be almost insulting – and he knew he'd have to struggle to prevent himself from adding, '. . . but the trouble is she's only half my age.' Part of him hoped that Bess had mentioned Sam; that he would be catapulted into explaining; forced out of his procrastination. Of course, the moment had never arisen.

One of the reasons he'd made the visit this weekend was because he was hoping to take Sam cruising during Easter and after that it would be a while before he managed to get down to The Keep. The visit to Greenford had been an unexpected success. He'd feared that the three-hour trip might prove cold and uncomfortable but the mild February weather had been kind and he'd made certain that they'd stopped often, to go below for hot coffee or soup. She'd loved the Black Horse, been enchanted by mooring overnight by the landing stage outside the pub gardens, had acknowledged how much more delightful it would be in the spring and summer. An Easter cruise was more or less settled . . .

He leaned back more comfortably in his seat, giving himself up to pleasant dreams. Watching the calm, quiet waters of the Exe estuary gleaming softly in the early sunshine, the waders running in the mud before the advancing tide, he remembered other journeys: journeys back to *Dolphin*, back to Blundell's, back to Herongate. In those very early days Susanna would have been with him. Peering from the window, chattering ceaselessly, begging him to open the sandwiches, talking to strangers. He chuckled inside himself. What a terror she'd been to him; what anxiety he'd suffered on her behalf. Yet she had come through college, marriage, childbirth, and managed to remain the cheerful, happy girl he'd always known and whom he loved so much. Podger and Lulu were very like her and, now that they were past those first, fragile years, his fears for them were abating. He sometimes wondered if he should worry more about Fred, who had a dreamy, quiet gentleness which might easily invite bullying. Oddly, though, there was a kind of armour which protected Fred, as if his innocence were its own protection.

Mole thought: He reminds me of Uncle Theo.

He sometimes tried to imagine how he might have talked to Uncle Theo about Sam: tried to imagine those wise, thoughtful eyes fixed upon him; tried to hear the words he would have spoken. When he thought about his uncle, however, only fragments of scripture came to his mind, like the bit about the shield and a buckler which he'd told Fliss about at the funeral . . . How dear she was to him. Fliss had come through, too. Her marriage had not been easy, and Miles's stroke had been a ghastly shock; nevertheless Fliss had struggled on, dealing with it, making the relationship work. Uncle Theo's death had been a shattering blow for her. Perhaps only he, Mole, knew how very deeply she'd rested against their uncle's strength and how much she missed him. At least she had Caroline and Prue to bear her company and share the load. How right their grandmother had been to make every attempt to hold on to The Keep as a place of refuge. He wondered if it would survive into the new century or whether subsequent generations would be obliged to let it go. At least Jolyon was making every effort to maintain it for the future.

As the train drew out of Exeter he gave himself up to thinking about Sam. He'd known her now for several months, yet it seemed as if she'd always been around. He could hardly remember what his life had been like without her or how he had existed. Paradoxically, it was this that prevented him from speaking out. How lonely it would be without the prospect of the sound of her footsteps along the pontoon; how he would miss watching her at the table in the saloon. Arms crossed, head on wrists, eyes closed, she'd listen while he talked to her, as a child might listen whilst being told a story. She never tired of the tales of his childhood and he wondered if it were the stability of his life as a small boy at The Keep which appealed to her. He knew that being an Army child she'd moved about – which he suspected accounted for her restlessness – but she'd also let certain things slip regarding her mother; odd remarks which led him to believe that the small Sam and her little brother had spent a great deal of time alone or in the care of other Army wives. It was with fascination that she heard the stories of Ellen and Fox, of birthday teas and flying kites on the hill, of picnics on the beach and tricycling round the courtyard. She knew about Susanna and Fliss and their families; of Hal's divorce and of Kit's doomed love for Jake. This particularly interested her and he'd had to explain why, through misunderstandings and an inability to commit, the relationship had foundered.

'Sounds familiar,' she'd murmured – and he'd paused, wondering if he'd heard her correctly, tempted to take her up on it. Did she mean that he and she were like Kit and Jake, or was she thinking of other people? He'd left it too late, though, and the moment passed. It was strange that he, so private, so self-contained, should be ready to talk about himself and all those who were so dear to him. Sometimes, after she'd gone, he'd curse himself for being boring, conceited, self-centred, and vow that he'd never mention his family again. Yet it was she who would start it: 'Go on then,' she'd say. 'You were telling me about your little house in the orchard' or 'So what happened, then, when Mrs Pooter died and Ellen wouldn't let Fox have another dog . . . ?' and he'd try to distract her, turn the conversation towards her own concerns and interests, but she'd insist with such an authentic longing and intensity that he'd eventually give in to her. Slowly, through these months with her, it was as if he'd relived his whole life – but even Sam did not know of his nightmares, his fear of the assassin, of death striking, suddenly, unexpectedly, out of a bright summer day. It was long, now, since he'd thought of them, or been plagued by nightmares, but he wondered if this might be the test. When he knew he could talk of these things to her, then this might be the sign for which he was waiting. The thought of it made him self-conscious. He was, after all, forty years old. Did he really feel it was necessary to maunder on about his childish terrors and psychological problems to a girl of Sam's age?

He clenched his fists in frustration. Why must the whole question come back to her age? He knew he was afraid of looking pathetic in her young, clear eyes. An older woman, with broken relationships behind her and other emotional baggage collected during the years, might be more tolerant of a partner who woke up shouting in his sleep. The young could be so cynical, so tough; how could he dare to risk her pity? Yet how could he live without her? It was surprising that he should feel so low, that life should look so dull, when he imagined being without her.

Forcing back these negative thoughts he imagined, instead, Sam driving his car, listening to the radio or to one of his tapes. His warm Aran jersey – begged for the occasion and lent with foolish pleasure – tied carelessly by its sleeves around her shoulders. She was a first-rate driver and always loved to have music playing in the car.

'Not Brahms again,' she'd say teasingly. 'Oh, well, if we must, we must,' but he saw that she often clicked one of his tapes into the cassette player, especially the piano concertos, and then she'd put her hand on his thigh so that he could hold it whilst he drove.

He remembered how she'd sat beside him – long hair, the colour of beech mast, falling forward; her face intent; grey-green eyes inward-looking – and he'd wondered where the music was carrying her . . .

'I love you,' he'd said, impulsively, instinctively, recklessly.

She'd grinned up at him, eyes bright. 'Ditto,' she'd said. Just that: 'Ditto' – and he'd wanted to shout, 'Marry me. Live with me and have my babies. Let me look after you' – and had said instead, 'There's a good pub round here somewhere . . .'

Mole stirred restlessly, staring out at sunlit fields and small grey villages. Was he missing endless opportunities – or was there wisdom in waiting? Might she be waiting for him to make the first move, afraid of rejection? Supposing she should meet some other man whilst he was prevaricating? Slowly a resolve began to harden within him. Even losing her might be preferable to this agony of indecision. She would be back in London tomorrow and then they would plan the Easter weekend together. Easter; the time of new birth and resurrection. This would be the time to break out of the stifling bond of indecision, to cast away fear and worry. Joy broke through him in a wave of cleansing light and quite suddenly he remembered Uncle Theo's words: '*You mustn't worry too much, Mole . . . It can be terrible . . . Suffocating and enfeebling . . .*' It was as if his uncle were briefly beside him, his hand on his shoulder, filling him with strength.

Mole thought: I shall do it.

The trembling exultation which followed in the wake of his decision carried him from the train, into a taxi and down to Lisson

271

Grove. The late morning sun shone brightly and, as he passed through the gate, he felt almost weightless with relief and happiness. The man coming towards him raised his hand towards the brim of his cap and Mole returned the salute cheerfully. Subconsciously he recognised the white overalls with the scarlet logo as the uniform of the engineer who came down to service boats from time to time and owned a key to the gate, but there was something else – something unpleasant – which nibbled at his memory as he strode along the towpath and stepped on to the pontoon.

As he swung himself aboard the answer struck into his mind. The engineer's face was familiar because it was the assassin's face: eyes wide and blind, smiling with closed lips . . . Death striking suddenly, unexpectedly, out of a bright sunny day. It was his last thought as he stepped into the stern and the engine exploded beneath his feet.

Driving up from Hampshire the next day, Sam stopped at a village shop for some chocolate. Her father's health had deteriorated further and, although she was exhausted from lack of sleep and anxiety, the headline caught her eye and she turned the newspaper on the counter towards her.

'What . . . ? What's this?'

'Didn't you see the news last night, love?' The shop owner was pleased to be able to be first-hand with such appalling news, almost cosy in her terrible ghoulishness. 'IRA it was, apparently. A revenge killing, they said. The naval officer who died had been working behind the scenes, it says, and because of him the murderer's brother had gone to jail. Something to do with gun-running. They planted the bomb on the engine of his narrowboat. Killed outright, he was. Terrible, isn't it?'

Back in the car Sam read the article through carefully until, seeing the woman's curious glances from the window, she started the engine with a trembling hand and drove very slowly until she found a lay-by. Clutching Mole's jersey around her shoulders, his favourite Brahms filling her ears, she began to weep.

Book Four
Spring 1998

Chapter Thirty-six

On Easter morning Fliss sat on the bench in the courtyard in the April sunshine, Rufus stretched at her feet, listening to the robin. Slowly, with the passing years and the changing seasons, this wooden seat had become a special place for her. It was here, in the shelter of the courtyard wall, hung about with wisteria and clematis, that she found it easiest to meditate; to clear her thoughts and arrange ideas. Here, with the robin as company, she felt a measure of peace during even the stormiest passages of life; here, she felt closest to those she could no longer see. Her grandmother had worked here, moving slowly along the path beneath the wall, dead-heading the roses which clung and draped about the branches so that in spring and summer the stone was hidden by a living tapestry of texture and colour. She, too, had talked to the robin as she'd worked, listening to his song as she'd rested for a moment on the bench, her secateurs in the basket beside her. If she half closed her eyes, Fliss could almost visualise her: elegant even in old tweeds, a linen hat tilted over her eyes, her arms bare and brown from hours of working in her beloved garden. How comforting the mere sight of her had been; how valuable her gift of imparting courage with love. Although her physical presence was withdrawn, yet the gift remained: a point of reference which had the power to square the shoulders and straighten the spine. Hers had been no empty preaching, no sterile, textbook advice. The passing on of courage flowed from her own experience and had been wrought out of loss and pain – and joy. Her grandmother had been no stranger to grief, yet she had been able to accept the precious moments of happiness, too. Fliss, looking back, wondered how much of her grandmother's acceptance, her apparent lack of bitterness, had been the result of living with Uncle Theo. His gift was a different one which moved you to a different level and offered you a wider horizon . . .

'*We are as big or as small as the objects of our love . . .*'

Here, Uncle Theo had sat, hands clasped on his walking stick, his face peaceful. He had not come to find comfort here – Theo had carried the source of his strength within him – yet he was often to be found, sitting in the sun, in the shelter of the wall. Fliss wondered if perhaps he, too, had been remembering the others who had lived and worked at The Keep. It was odd, considering how reluctant he'd been to give advice, how much she'd relied upon him. Now, when she looked through the books he'd used, it was as if she heard his voice so that her anxieties were distilled into a kind of prayer. His particular, unique legacy sustained her.

The robin had a nest, high up in a hole in the wall. Earlier in the season he had vigorously contested his territory with an upstart invader and had emerged victorious. Each morning, during this cold sweet spring, Fliss wakened to his song of triumph piped from the highest vantage point whilst his mate sat on the nest, concealed by the spiny branches and bricky-red flowers of the *Chaenomeles japonica*. Fliss had watched her building the nest, flying in and out with twigs and moss, and now she was sitting on a clutch of speckled eggs whilst her mate, beady eye cocked, scarlet breast puffed with self-importance, strutted on the flagstones looking for grubs.

'I don't know what you've got to crow about,' Fliss said, as he hopped near her shoe. 'She's the one doing all the work.'

As he trilled his plaintive song, she leaned to look into the carrycot which rested beside her on the bench. Her grandchild, Bess's daughter, Paula, was fast asleep. Here was the reason that Fliss was at home on Easter morning while the family was at church. She didn't mind. She'd gone to the early service and was very happy now to spend a quiet hour with her tiny, three-month-old granddaughter in the shelter of the courtyard. Perhaps it was this peaceful, precious companionship which had brought back so many memories on this warm spring morning.

Fliss thought: I can't really believe that I am a grandmother. I'm fifty-one years old but inside I feel just as I always did.

She tucked the soft blanket gently round the sleeping form and wished – not for the first time – that Miles could have seen his grandchild. It was not yet a year since he'd had the final massive stroke which killed him. Several small, warning strokes had preceded that final blow, and at least it had been mercifully quick, but Fliss wished that he could have been spared to see Bess so radiantly pregnant, Matt's touching pride, and, ultimately, their darling baby girl.

At least he had taken his part in the wedding celebrations; he'd known that they were happily married and settled in the house in Hampstead. Once the date for the wedding had been fixed Kit suggested that she should move downstairs to share with Clarrie so that Matt and Bess could take over her flat. Matt was still with the LSO but Bess had taken up teaching, although she still performed with the jazz quartet which had been formed whilst she was still a student. She and Matt were overwhelmed at the generosity of such an offer but Fliss was anxious that her daughter's happiness might be taken at Kit's expense.

'It's best for all of us,' Kit hastened to reassure her. 'Clarrie's getting on now and I shall be glad to be closer at hand for him. And Bess needs to be able to pursue her own career when Matt's touring round the world. She'll make a super teacher, which isn't surprising, is it? You were, too. And we're just so delighted that they want to stay. It's fantastic to have young people around, and if Andrew wants to adjust the rent to help them whilst they're starting out, well, that's his decision. He can afford it. Anyway, he looks upon it as his contribution towards the musicians of the future.'

So Bess gave piano lessons whilst Paula slept peacefully through scales and arpeggios, or was entertained by Kit and Clarrie in the flat below.

Rufus shifted, groaning gently as he stretched luxuriously in the warmth, resting his heavy head on Fliss's foot. Sitting quietly, hands in her lap, her face turned towards the sun, Fliss thought about Miles. In some way the first stroke had prepared her to manage without him. Then, their lives had altered so cataclysmically, their married relationship changed so drastically, that this final adjustment was far less painful than it might have been. She did not feel that she'd lost a husband so much as a very dear friend. Sometimes, guiltily, she wondered if this might be because of her love for Hal, yet she suspected that she missed the Miles who had become her companion much more than she'd have missed the husband of those early years. Despite his disabilities, she'd found him a great comfort, especially during those terrible months following Mole's death.

Instinctively her hands twined together and she frowned, her eyes still shut against the gentle sunlight. Even now, four years later, his death was shocking; as unacceptable to her as the deaths of her parents and older brother. There was something so unfinished about his life, so violently sudden about the ending of it, which made it difficult to come to terms with it. She guessed that anyone mourning a young life, suddenly cut off, must feel the same. At least Mole had achieved his ambition within the Service. He'd overcome the fear which dogged his childhood to the extent that he'd risked his life beyond anything demanded by his career, yet Fliss could never attain the acceptance, however reluctant, which informed her thoughts and memories of the other members of her family who had died. It was just like living through the terrible loss of her brother Jamie all over again. Death, striking suddenly out of a bright sunny day, bringing horror and grief, leaving no opportunity to tie up loose ends.

Paula stirred and Fliss became alert, waiting for small cries or the waving of fists but there was silence and she relaxed again. It was odd to have a tiny baby in her charge. It seemed so long since she'd had the responsibility of such a terrifyingly frail, small person that she was occasionally seized with fear lest she should inadvertently harm her.

'Don't be daft, Mum,' Bess would say, confident with youth. 'She's as tough as old boots, really.'

Even Jolyon was at ease with his goddaughter, holding her as if he'd been doing it all his life, unfazed by shrieks or messes. Just so had Hal been with his boys: firm, tender, natural. Jo had the same instincts, scooping Paula out of her pram, holding her in his arm whilst he ate with one hand or read the paper. He seemed infinitely experienced and she always seemed relaxed with him, as if some sixth sense told her that she was safe. Of course, Jo was so much happier now. He was coming to terms with his private pain, the nursery was doing well and his plans were slowly taking shape and becoming realities. Jolyon had taken his life into his own possession and was making it work. Fliss smoothed the cot blanket pensively, remembering how desolate Jo had been after Miles had died.

'He was my friend,' he'd said, almost defensively, as if excusing the weakness of tears. 'He's been such a terrific help.'

They'd comforted each other, their own relationship made stronger since the confrontation four years earlier. Jolyon kept the ginger jar on a low shelf in his living room in the gatehouse, a reminder to them both, and as he'd grown older Fliss knew that she had nothing more to fear from him. He'd come to terms with the fact of her love for his father, realising, at last, that it did not diminish or deprive Miles. She wondered if he'd realised that it was her love for Hal, or – even more important – his love for her, which enabled her to function. Through her grief for Miles and her attempt to deal with Mole's tragic death, Hal's love had been as unchanging, as unyielding as granite. He'd told her as much as he was allowed, and she and Susanna had guessed the rest. Susanna had been oddly resigned, accepting it with far less anguish than Fliss could have believed possible. She and Mole had been so close, had shared so much . . .

'It was as if there was an inevitability about it,' Susanna had said months afterwards. 'There was that dark core. Those "black dog" moods that seemed to weigh on him. I can't put it very well but I almost felt that he was courting death if only to prove to himself that he wasn't afraid of it. Like a child shadow-boxing or whistling in the dark.'

'That's terrible,' Fliss had said, shocked. 'I begin to wonder if he was ever happy. Oh, Sooz . . .'

'I know.' Susanna had smiled sadly. 'He never completely recovered from Kenya, did he? Not in a way so that he could deal with it. I'm sure that's why he never got married. He was afraid to risk himself.'

'I can't bear to think of it,' Fliss had answered. 'That terrible loneliness which must have been inside him . . .'

She'd cried, then, and Susanna had comforted her, but Fliss had never managed to accept his death as final. She had to believe that there was some way of going forward which embraced him gently and quietly, drawing him into the pattern . . . if only she could find it. Her childhood, here at The Keep with her family and with Ellen and Fox, had reconciled her at last to the deaths of her parents; watching Hal growing up had eased the pain caused by the loss of her brother. Yet in her grief for Mole there was no true relief. He was still alone. As he had been in life so he was in death: hovering on the fringe, unable to commit. It was impossible to accept that he must be abandoned in isolation. So she waited, calmer now, but still waiting for the formula which would enable him to take his place . . .

Perhaps it was because he had died not long before Easter that she always thought about him particularly during the spring; or perhaps it was because it was naturally a season of aching sweetness, of the promise of new beginnings. Melancholy accompanied the cold light evenings; restlessness invaded the soul. The words of the Easter anthem, fresh in her memory from the early service at church, echoed in her mind.

For since by man came death: by man came also the resur-
*   rection of the dead.*
For as in Adam all die: even so in Christ shall all be made
*   alive . . .*

Paula woke and began to murmur. Presently she grew more active. Her small mewling cries disturbed Rufus, who raised his head, watching Fliss to see how she would react. She glanced at her watch, remembered the lunch, and stood up.

'Come along,' she said, touching Paula's cheek with her finger.

279

'Mummy will be back soon, wanting her lunch. Sounds as if you want yours, too.'

Picking up the carrycot, and followed by Rufus, she crossed the courtyard and disappeared into the hall.

The robin hopped down, inspected the path for any edible evidence of human occupation and, abandoning the search, flew to the topmost branch of the wisteria and began to sing.

Chapter Thirty-seven

At lunch the conversation turned to the tearoom which was being built in part of the converted stable and which would soon be ready. It had been Prue who had conceived the idea – 'So relaxing to sit down with a cup of coffee and think about all the nice things you'd like to buy' – and Miles had costed it into his business plan. It had never been regarded as a priority but Jolyon, eager now to see the whole project up and running, was beginning to pursue a plan of his own.

'After all,' said Hal, who was carving, 'just because the place is nearly ready to be used doesn't mean that it has to be opened just yet, does it? We have to think about staff and so on. Perhaps you could experiment during the summer holidays? We mustn't run before we can walk. It's sensible to get the tearoom building done at the same time as everything else but we can put the setting-up on hold for a bit.'

'It's a pity Podger hasn't finished school,' said Bess, helping herself to potatoes. 'She'd be brilliant. I can just see her, can't you? She'd run it single-handed. Are you going to have a proper shop, eventually, Jo?'

'It *is* a proper shop,' said Jolyon indignantly. 'You can buy anything you need for the garden. We've even got pots and tubs, now.'

Hal and Fliss exchanged smiles: Jo was very defensive when it came to his business.

'It's very professional,' agreed Caroline pacifically. 'After all, Jo isn't trying to attract the tourists. It's good solid regular clients he needs. The nursery is coming on very nicely but I agree with Hal about the tearoom. It's nice to get the work done so that it's all ready to go – no point in bringing the builders back in again later – but I think it's a bit early to open it.'

'It's going to be so pretty,' said Prue rather wistfully. She could visualise it clearly and was longing to see the small square room with its exposed beams and irregularly shaped windows in action; bright

281

cotton tablecloths on the tables, Bryan Hayes' lovely, evocative watercolours of local scenes for sale on the stone walls, delicious home-made cakes displayed on the counter, cheerful, hard-wearing rugs on the slate-flagged floors. The china would be simple – white with perhaps a gold edging – not too delicate but not coarse and thick either . . .

'It's the staff that's the problem.' Hal sat down at last with his own plate. 'Once it's opened you can't mess about. There have to be set hours otherwise people will be disappointed and it will get off on the wrong foot. It's very difficult to judge how many customers would actually stop for tea and coffee. Don't forget that locals are never very far from home and might not want to pay for things that they can get for free ten minutes away.'

'Well, that's why I was asking about the shop,' said Bess, passing the vegetable dishes down the table towards him. 'If you sell other things apart from the gardening stuff it would bring in tourists as well, wouldn't it? And locals from further afield if it's worth coming for.'

'I must say that it sounds rather fun.' Prue was struck by the idea. 'I suppose you could expand it into other areas, couldn't you, Jolyon?'

'If you're imagining a kind of Dartington Cider Press out there in the stableyard, Ma, you can forget it,' said Hal, before Jolyon could answer. 'Apart from anything else we haven't got a hope in hell of getting planning permission. The lane isn't big enough to cope with the traffic. Anyway, I don't think it's what Jo has in mind for the future.'

Jolyon, who was enjoying his lunch, beamed at them. He was quite used to his family – jointly and severally – discussing his business and making plans for it. He didn't mind; after all, they were all part of it really. Nevertheless, he had acquired the happy knack of going along with them, discussing, agreeing – and then quietly doing exactly as he'd decided long since.

'I think Granny has the right of it,' he said, spearing some carrot with his fork. 'If people have the chance to sit down and mull things over a bit then they'll probably buy a few other items afterwards. Especially if they're drinking good coffee and eating lovely sponge cake. Puts 'em in a good mood.'

'So what's the problem?' asked Matt. 'Is it simply premature? You need to make more money on the nursery side to pay the staff in the café, is that it?'

'More or less.' Hal reached for the gravy. 'It's a bit chicken and egg. We don't know how it will go until we do it and then it's a bit

282

late to draw back if it doesn't work too well. I like the idea of trying it in the summer with a few students. Then we don't have to take on permanent staff and get bogged down before we're ready.'

'Such a shame to have to wait,' said Prue. 'I'm sure it would work quite splendidly.'

Hal glanced at her sardonically, about to point out that not everyone was possessed of her capacity for coffee and cakes, but Jolyon spoke first.

'I think so, too, Granny. I was hoping to have a trial run at Whitsun, actually. It's the start of half term so there will be lots of people about. I had an idea but I don't know whether it would work . . .' He shook his head, sighing a little and she looked at him sympathetically.

'What sort of idea, darling?'

'Well, I was wondering . . .' He took his time, pretending that he was thinking it through as he spoke. 'Supposing we tried it between ourselves? I agree with Dad about taking on staff – it's too risky – but supposing we did it all ourselves? You and Caroline make wonderful cakes and stuff, and I'm sure you could cope with serving the coffee and tea, couldn't you, Granny? Just for the holiday weekend, that's all . . .'

'Oh, darling,' Prue looked alarmed. 'I don't think I could. Not actually serving people and taking money.'

'But you'd be terrific with people,' he exclaimed encouragingly. 'You'd chat to them about their gardens and their children and they'd love it. It's only a tiny tearoom, after all. Four tables at most. You can write the order down just to be on the safe side and Caroline could take the money if it makes you nervous.'

'Thank you,' said Caroline politely, inclining her head. 'How kind of you to think of me. Would that be between helping out in the shop and making the cakes? I only ask because I want to know.'

He grinned at her. 'I was going to ask Alison if she'd help me in the shop so you could be with Granny. She'll be home for half term.'

'Alison?' queried Bess, frowning. 'Oh, you mean Podger. I'd almost forgotten that her name is Alison.'

'Well, you shouldn't.' Jolyon sounded neither cross nor censorious, merely quietly firm. 'She's nearly sixteen and it's not a very kind nickname.'

There was a tiny silence; Hal and Fliss exchanged glances again. He raised his eyebrows; she gave an almost imperceptible shrug.

'It was never meant to be unkind,' Prue was protesting. 'It was because she was so *cuddly*, if you see what I mean. And

283

now, of course, it's become a habit and everyone knows her as Podger.'

'She's not called Podger at school,' said Jolyon calmly. 'Her friends call her Alison . . . Is there any more meat, Dad?'

'Well, she'd be quite perfect in any situation which requires organisation.' Caroline passed her plate, too. 'I thought she was considering going into the Navy?'

'Should we warn the First Sea Lord?' wondered Hal. '"England sleep, your Navy is awake." Well, it certainly would be with Podger in the ranks. Thank God I shall be retiring next year.'

'Only if you don't get promoted,' Prue reminded him. She disapproved of Hal's assumption that he would not be made up to Rear Admiral. 'Anyway, Podg – Alison always said that she was going into the business with Gus.'

Hal, piling meat on to his son's plate, was about to observe that, this being so, it was probably Gus who had suggested the Navy but the expression on Jo's face stopped him.

'Well, she's very young,' he said instead. 'Plenty of time to think about a career.'

'So what about it, Granny?' Jolyon embarked on his second helping enthusiastically. 'It'll be fun. Fliss'll help, won't you, Fliss? It'll be a real family enterprise . . .'

'What about fitting the place out?' Hal sat down again and picked up his knife and fork. 'It's one thing having the building done but what about all the furniture to go in it?'

'It's only a few tables and chairs,' argued Jolyon. 'The builders have put in the loo and there's a sink and things, and the counter is built in. We could make do to begin with, couldn't we, Granny?'

Prue, torn between her anxiety at the prospect of being so publicly involved and the prospect of disappointing her beloved grandson, wavered visibly.

'Oh, darling . . .'

'It's like market research,' said Bess. 'You'll get an idea about how it would work and whether it's worth starting it properly.'

'Exactly.' Jolyon sent her a grateful glance. 'And it won't cost anything . . .'

'I think you should go for it.' Bess was now as excited as Jolyon. 'You don't have to buy expensive tables to begin with, do you? Anything would do and you could cover them with pretty cloths. You could buy some really great stuff in Salago, lovely Indian material, and make them up . . .'

'And are you going to be around for the bank holiday?' asked

284

Caroline sweetly. 'Do we gather that you'll be down, lending a hand . . . ?'

'When you say "it won't cost anything",' murmured Hal, 'do you mean that Salago is going to *give* us this material? And I'd like to remind you that tables and chairs might initially grow on trees but in their finished state—'

'There's loads of time,' cried Bess. 'It's six weeks away. Plenty of time to find some old second-hand stuff. And if you don't want to go to the expense of cloths you could paint them if they're too scruffy. Hey, that would be really cool, Jo. Brightly painted chairs and tables. None of this old-fashioned scrubbed pine stuff. It could look really fab by the time you've finished . . .'

Caroline rose and began to collect plates. 'I won't say, "Whatever next, I wonder",' she said resignedly, 'although I feel the words hovering in the air about us. Just settle it between yourselves and then give us our orders. Meanwhile I shall get the pudding. But remember, Jolyon, we're talking about tea and coffee and cakes and *nothing* else.'

'So what's all this about Podger being called Alison?' asked Hal later, as he and Fliss walked on the hill before tea. 'Or am I making a mountain out of a molehill?'

'I was as surprised as you were,' admitted Fliss. 'They've spent a lot of time together this holiday and I have to say that she is the most enterprising child. I think that Jo's enjoyed having her around but it's probably nothing more than a passing phase.'

They were silent, both oddly reluctant to pursue the matter further, content simply to be together. Out here, on the hill, the chancy breeze was chill and Fliss turned up the collar of her jacket as she looked out upon the familiar scene. Beneath the wall primroses bloomed, their delicate pale gold glowing against the powdery stone, whilst a tiny wren, hidden in the ivy above them, scolded crossly. On the lower slopes sheep grazed, lambs pressed against their woolly flanks, their plaintive cries echoing in the quiet air. The chequered fields were patched with sharply brilliant gorse-blossom and the bare hedgerows were cloudy with drifts of bridal blackthorn. Fliss leading, they began the descent to the river, but presently Hal caught up with her, reaching for her hand.

'Do we not want to talk about Jo and Podger because we feel it's too close for comfort?' he asked. 'That it might be us all over again?'

She smiled, knowing that it was exactly that possibility which had

285

made her sheer off. It was strange that Miles's death had made the situation between them even more difficult. The bars of the prison had disappeared but she seemed incapable of enjoying the freedom. She'd told herself that it was simply a matter of time, and Hal had made no attempt to hustle her, yet she seemed caught in a kind of limbo from which she could not quite free herself. For the last year Hal had been at Faslane, Commodore of the submarine base, and at such a distance it was not difficult to postpone any discussion about the future.

She thought: We've waited thirty-five years. One more won't make too much difference.

Hal's question, however, threatened to bring the subject more immediately into the open. She held his hand tightly, ashamed of her fears.

'I'm being silly,' she said lightly. 'You're quite right, of course. Just for a moment I *did* wonder about Jo and Podger. I caught myself trying to decide how we'd all react if they . . . if they . . .'

'If they fell in love like we did,' Hal supplied. 'And how *would* we react? Did you get that far?'

'Not really,' she said. 'That is to say, *I* wouldn't have any objections but I couldn't quite imagine how everyone else might feel. Sooz, for instance, or you, come to that.'

'I could hardly object, could I?' He laughed softly. 'Do you take me for a hypocrite?'

'Of course not but . . . Well, you never know how people might react, do you?' She hesitated and then plunged on. 'Look at me, for instance. I've loved you for thirty-five years and now that we're both free I feel . . .' She shook her head. 'I don't know what I feel. I can't describe it.'

'It's a bit of a shock, I suppose. I feel it, too, in a way. We've kept it all battened down for so long that it's almost frightening to think we don't have to any more.'

She looked at him with relief. 'I might have known you'd understand. But it's so silly, isn't it? Good grief, we're not children. This is no silly infatuation or teenage lust. Why can't we simply . . . *do* it?'

'It would be a great deal easier if we weren't surrounded by family. If we could appear one day and say, "Oh, by the way everybody, we got married last week," and then hurry away again, it would be simpler. I don't think anyone would actually throw a fit though, do you?'

'No. No, I don't. And it wouldn't look too heartless, would it? After all, Miles has been gone for nearly a year.' She looked at him anxiously. 'Oh, Hal, I don't know what's wrong with me. I love you, though. That never changes.'

'So I should hope.' He kissed her tenderly. 'Don't worry. There's no rush. It might be best to wait until I've finished at Faslane, anyway. I can't imagine that you'd want to make your first appearance as my wife in a submarine base. There's only one more year to go and then we'll make a whole new start.'

She held him tightly, relieved yet feeling the usual terror that something might happen to him before they could be together.

'I'm being an utter fool,' she said. 'Only there's something . . . I don't know what it is . . .'

'I've got a fortnight's leave,' he said. 'Let's not spoil it by worrying. We'll have lots of time for talking things through. The right moment will present itself. Come on. Let's go round the spinney and then I'll know that I'm really on leave.'

Chapter Thirty-eight

Later in the week, Fliss and Caroline agreed that it was time for a party; the first for many months. With so many of the family home for Easter, the moment was at hand to make up for the sad first Christmas following Miles's death. After a great deal of discussion it was decided that the excuse should be Prue's seventy-fifth birthday, which had taken place some weeks before but had not been properly celebrated.

'Not that we need an excuse,' said Caroline, 'but it gives it a point. Something to revolve round. And it's especially nice with Hal home. No chance of tracking Edward down, I suppose?'

Fliss stood the iron at the end of the board, frowning. 'We could ask Jolyon. I know he keeps up with him as best he can but otherwise I wouldn't have a clue.'

'Such a pity, isn't it? Poor Edward has had a bit of a rough deal.'

Caroline sat down on the bed and glanced about her. It was Fliss who had moved the ironing board into Mole's bedroom. The aired washing, ready to be pressed, was piled on the end of his bed but otherwise it had all the appearance of a room which might be occupied at any moment. Mole's old teddy, which had accompanied him to school, sat in the ancient wicker chair with the golliwog which Ellen had knitted; his Arthur Ransome collection stood on the oak chest between carved bookends made by Fox for his tenth birthday; framed photographs of submarines hung on the walls. It was certainly more the bedroom of the child rather than the man – but then there had been nothing returned to them that could be kept as a memorial to him. Nothing had survived the blast. Only the things which had been found in the car, parked a few streets away, had been returned. The police were obliged to force the door – his keys would have been in his pocket – but there was nothing personal to be found: one or two old cassettes, some documents in the glove compartment pertaining to the car, a pair of wellingtons in the boot. Since Mole generally travelled with a library of cassettes, several current paperbacks and an odd jersey or jacket, it had been surprising – and disappointing – to find the car so bare of his presence . . .

Fliss was watching her and Caroline tried to smile.

'Sorry,' she said. 'Woolgathering. We were talking about Edward . . .'

'And thinking about Mole.' Fliss set the iron down and began to fold one of Hal's shirts. 'You probably think it's morbid of me to do the ironing here,' – 'Of *course*, I don't,' Caroline said quickly – 'but I'm trying to . . . keep him with us. No, no. Don't misunderstand me. I'm not talking about refusing to accept that he's dead. It's simply that all the others, Grandmother, Uncle Theo, Fox, Ellen and now Miles, have been drawn into the pattern. We can talk about them easily and happily and they're still a part of our lives in a way. Have you noticed that we never talk about Mole? Not really, do we? Not in the way that we do about the others. Why is it?'

Caroline studied her carefully. She'd guessed that something more than Miles's death was destroying Fliss's peace of mind but she had not guessed that this was at the root of it; not four years on . . .

'Flissy, dear,' she said gently, 'I utterly agree with you. It hasn't been the same. I don't think it can be, you know, when a life is cut off so abruptly. Mole was still quite young. Oh, I know he was forty but in this present age that's nothing. It was the same for your grandmother, you know, when the tragedy happened in Kenya . . .'

'I think of that often,' said Fliss, almost eagerly, it was such a relief to talk. 'How did she manage?'

'She was a very strong woman,' said Caroline slowly, 'but you mustn't forget that she had Theo. There is no question that he was a great support and comfort to her. Nevertheless she had many very bad moments. It must have been a comfort to have the three of you to concentrate on. Children are demanding but you have less time to despair. Perhaps now, with Miles gone, you have too much time to brood . . . ?'

'It's possible.' Fliss reached for the next item and spread it over the board. 'I sometimes feel guilty that I think less about Miles than I do about Mole but it's really because Miles has been . . . *absorbed*. You and Prue talk about him quite naturally and so does Jolyon. He belongs. I have this awful feeling that Mole is still on the edge. There's a terrible feeling of . . . of unfinished business.'

She bit her lip and began to push the iron over the pillowcase. Caroline watched her anxiously. Fliss had always been maternal with her siblings – another legacy from the death of her parents and big brother – but Caroline simply did not know how to comfort her now.

She thought: We need Theo.

'Have you talked to Hal about it?' she asked.

'Quite a lot at the beginning. Of course, the whole thing was hampered with secrecy and silence and Hal was away at sea, anyway. Susanna has come to terms with it far better than I have, which almost makes it worse. They were so much closer, being nearer in age, and yet she is able to accept it.'

'Susanna is blessed with a happy disposition,' said Caroline gently. 'I'm not implying that she's insensitive or shallow but she takes things as they are. And she was also very busy with three children and helping Gus with the business. You were here, looking after Miles, with plenty of time to think and Prue bursting into tears every time we mentioned it. And as for feeling guilty about not grieving as much for Miles as for Mole, well, that's nonsense. He had all those years here with us and his death was signalled, wasn't it, so it was quite different? Added to which, Miles was in his late sixties. No great age, I admit, but a lot older than Mole was when he died.'

'I know.' Fliss smiled at her gratefully. 'But I still wish I could accept it. Draw him in and let it go . . . if you see what I mean. Anyway, let's forget it and talk about the party. Edward. No, I don't know where he is at the moment. He's another one who's slipped away. I think Jolyon said something about going back to his relatives in the States.'

'All that business at university,' sighed Caroline. 'Drugs and shoplifting. Poor Edward. He lost his way for a while. Well, never mind. Let's concentrate on happier things. Bess and Matt are staying another week, and Kit says that she and Clarrie could come down for the weekend, which would be rather fun. They could drive down on Saturday morning but she has to be back in London for Tuesday. We could have the party on Saturday or Sunday.'

'Then let's make it Sunday,' said Fliss, 'then it won't be a problem for Gus and Susanna or Jolyon. Now what have you got in mind? Is it to be a lunch? Or dinner? Or an enormous tea?'

'We'll start with tea,' said Caroline thoughtfully, 'and drift on into dinner.'

'There will be fourteen of us,' warned Fliss, laughing. 'Sure we can manage tea *and* dinner?'

'Quite sure,' said Caroline contentedly. 'We'll use the dining room for dinner, don't you think? Do it in style. Podger will give us a hand . . .'

'Alison,' Fliss reminded her. 'Remember what Jolyon said.'

Caroline looked as if she might speak but changed her mind. She stood up, stretched a little and gathered up the neatly ironed pile.

'Nearly coffee time,' she said. 'Come on down presently and we'll make a list while Prue and Hal are in Totnes. I think it should be a surprise party, don't you? All Prue's favourite things. What fun! I feel quite excited already.'

After Caroline had gone, Fliss switched off the iron and wandered over to the window. Mole's bedroom looked north, across the hillside, and she kneeled on the window seat, resting her arms on the bar of the sash window. It had been a relief to talk to Caroline, to take comfort from her, but in the end the problem still remained. Deep down inside she still felt alone. No one felt quite as she did about Mole – and no one could advise her as to what she should do about the situation between herself and Hal. Everyone was too used to them both to give it much thought. Perhaps it was assumed that she and Hal had agreed to continue with the present status quo; that it was too late and they were both too old to want to change it.

Chin on her arms, Fliss watched the cloud shadows pouring over the land like smoke. Light and shade, chasing each other, gave the impression that the hillside was rolling away beneath her. The ground dropped steeply here, at the back of the house, and she looked down upon glossy-backed rooks who drifted below her, riding the wind. Memories passed across her mind as swiftly as the shadows over the earth; memories of earlier days: their arrival at Staverton station and their first night when Ellen had let Mole take the puppy to bed with him: the way he hated to let her out of his sight and his terrible dumbness. The years rolled forward and she remembered Mole at his passing-out parade, and his surprise and pride when she'd asked him to give her away at her wedding.

'No problem,' he'd said with studied carelessness. 'Nothing to it. You can always rely on me, you know.'

Confused by her own emotions about Miles and the way she still felt about Hal, she'd wept and Mole had comforted her with the clumsy, awkward caring of youth. 'Emotional things, weddings,' he'd said. 'I expect you'd like a drink . . .' He'd never fussed or probed but through the years he'd been there: quiet, dependable, compassionate. In the house in Dartmouth; when Grandmother died; at Uncle Theo's funeral . . . She'd loved him so much, so anxiously . . .

292

The scene blurred before her eyes as she wept again, for him, for herself and because of the empty aching inside her.

Presently, wiping her eyes, she thought about Hal. She and Hal were wasting time. She knew it but could do nothing about it. There seemed no bridge from the past to the future, only this timeless limbo inside which they both now existed. There was no means at hand to carry them forward. Since Miles died Hal had had two weeks' leave – apart from coming home for the funeral – and his leave had been too soon after Miles's death to even consider planning for the future. Christmas had been so short a time – barely six days – and this lack of time together was one of the reasons why it was so easy to let drift all that was between them. Perhaps if they could have simply gone to bed the barrier might have broken down naturally and easily, but how was it to be done? It seemed impossible that she should go to him as he lay in Uncle Theo's narrow bed and just as difficult to feel relaxed in Grandmother's room.

Even the idea of the two of them going away for a holiday seemed too orchestrated, too self-conscious to take seriously. Hal was away so much that he looked forward to his leaves at home and she had never bothered with holidays. As a family, they'd never been the sort of people who went abroad, who longed to lay in the sun or study ancient architecture. No doubt they could be considered insular and dull but the fact remained that, should either she or Hal suggest a holiday together, the other would know that it was simply a device, a means of getting away from the family; and then what? She could imagine the embarrassment, the contrivances hidden by casual behaviour which would fool neither of them. They didn't need to go away to enjoy each other's company, to be easy and happy together, so in the end it came back to sex. They would be going away so as to deal with the physical problem which lay between them. If they were different characters, light-hearted, careless, it might work, but then, if they had been such people, no doubt the problem would not still exist. They would have succumbed to their desires long since.

She suspected that Hal was less inhibited than she was, more ready to move forward, yet he felt her anxiety and was afraid to act. He probably thought that it was too soon after Miles, that she would feel disloyal, or that she was not yet ready to face the reaction of the family. Meanwhile the days slipped past.

Fliss thought: Perhaps it's already too late. Thirty-three years too late.

She felt fear pluck at her throat. Life was too precious to be wasted – she, of all people, should know it. Death might come at any moment, striking out of a clear, bright day . . . She felt

293

that if she turned suddenly she would see Mole standing behind her: hands in pockets, head lowered thoughtfully. He would smile at her, Uncle Theo's sweet smile which crinkled up his eyes before it touched his mouth . . .

The room was quite empty; peaceful, cool. Fliss stood up, pushing her handkerchief into her sleeve, pausing to settle the teddy bear more comfortably before she went out, closing the door gently behind her.

Chapter Thirty-nine

'Will you drop me off at The Keep this morning, Dad?' Podger spread butter with a generous hand and reached for the marmalade. 'I've said I'll go and help Jo so that Caroline can get on with things for Aunt Prue's party.'

Gus lowered his newspaper. 'Does this mean,' he asked, trying to keep the eagerness out of his voice, 'that you won't be coming to the studio today?'

Podger eyed him shrewdly. 'You just want a day off so you can laze about,' she said. 'Drinking coffee all day and chatting to all your old mates who drop in.'

'Spending time with people is an important part of business,' Gus told her somewhat speciously. He knew quite well that many of his friends would never require his particular services. 'It's not just harrying clients, you know, and frightening them into paying their bills.'

Podger snorted contemptuously. 'You're as bad as Jo,' she said. 'Sometimes people need a push, especially when it comes to parting with money. And they need someone to make up their minds when they're dithering and stuff. Jo's hopeless.'

Gus regarded his elder daughter affectionately but with his usual puzzlement. Years of living with three women had not yet accustomed him to their peculiarities. Why, for instance, had Podger cut off her long hair but now insisted on scraping back the short ends into various combs and clips, one of which looked like the bulldog clips he used in the studio except that it was bright green plastic? Why did she wear boots of a size and weight which would have done sterling work during an eighteen-hour-a-day shift in a quarry? Why were the nails of her fingers painted with at least three different colours?

'Jo's nice,' said Lulu, defending her big cousin. 'He's training me to be a gardener and I'm going into business with him when I leave school.'

Gus thought: At least she's stopped embarrassing poor old Jo by telling his friends that she's going to live in the gatehouse with him. We must be grateful for small mercies.

'I might run the administrative side for him,' said Podger casually, 'while I'm sorting out the studio. It'll probably be big enough by then to need a proper office and stuff.'

Gus laid his newspaper aside. 'I thought you had ideas of joining the Navy,' he said anxiously. 'You were going to be the first woman to drive a submarine.'

'Gone off it,' said Podger laconically. 'Anyway, you need me. It's time Mum had a break.'

'Sounds good to me,' said Susanna, appearing with fresh coffee. 'When's this happy day to be?'

'Brace up,' said Gus, offering his mug. 'You've got three more years of slavery before you are to be released from the treadmill.'

'Can I go with Podger?' asked Lulu. 'I want to help, too.'

'You've got the dentist,' said Susanna firmly, 'as well you know. We'll go round afterwards and see how they're doing. But you'll be able to help me here. I'm doing lots of cooking so that Aunt Prue doesn't suspect what's going on. We'll buy her a present while we're in Totnes.'

'Didn't you buy her a present for her proper birthday?' Podger was shocked at such callous indifference.

'Of course we did,' said Susanna. 'But there's no harm in buying her another one, is there? A seventy-fifth birthday is rather special, after all.'

> '*Now, of my threescore years and ten,*' sang Gus,
> *Twenty will not come again,*
> *And take from seventy springs a score,*
> *It only leaves me fifty more.*
>
> *And since to look at things in bloom*
> *Fifty springs are little room,*
> *About the woodlands I will go*
> *To see the cherry hung with snow.*'

Podger rolled her eyes at the eccentricity of her parent but Lulu looked thoughtful.

'What is it?' she asked. 'It's nice. But if it's spring why is there snow?'

'It's a Housman poem,' answered her father, 'set to music by Butterworth. And snow is another word for the white blossom. Three score years and ten is the lifespan allotted to man. Seventy years in all. So you see your Aunt Prue is doing rather well. What's Fred doing today?'

'We shan't know that until he gets up,' said Susanna, sugaring her coffee. 'Very little, I suspect.'

'A bit of a rest won't hurt him,' said Gus, who had a soft spot for his son. He never tried to organise him or tell him what he should be doing and he was delighted that Fred wanted to follow his grandfather and great-uncle into the ministry. 'He's been working hard and he needs to be refreshed ready for his A levels next term.'

'Hurry up with that coffee, Dad,' said Podger, pushing back her chair. 'Don't forget you've got to take me to The Keep. You'll be late if you don't get a move on.'

She disappeared in the direction of her bedroom and Gus, breathing deeply through his nose, looked at Susanna. She grinned at him.

'Look at it this way,' she said cheerfully. 'You've got a whole day to yourself. Can't be bad.'

'I'll try to concentrate on it during the journey,' he promised grimly.

Podger reappeared. 'Not ready yet?' she asked genially. 'Never mind. Where are the keys? I'll go and start the car.'

'You'll do nothing of the sort,' he said, rising hastily, abandoning his coffee. 'You just leave my car alone. I'm ready now, anyway.'

He kissed Susanna and Lulu and hurried out after Podger.

'Just remember,' they heard her saying, 'that in eighteen months' time I'll be able to apply for a driving licence and then I'll be able to drive you everywhere . . .'

By the time Kit and Clarrie arrived, the preparations were well under way. Prue, who'd been told that they were simply wanting to get out of London for a few days, was delighted to see them. She took Clarrie off to his quarters – Miles's old rooms so as to save Clarrie the pain of climbing stairs – telling him that she was looking forward to a gossip about Sin and Andrew as well as an update on Jamie. Fliss never interfered with her son's activities, relying on Bess to keep her informed if a problem arose. She knew that Jamie was happy working with his 'think-tank' and if she suspected that there might be other, more secret, activities involved she never mentioned it. Prue, however, was more interested in his social life, especially regarding the continual succession of pretty girlfriends, and Clarrie was happy to settle down with her in the hall, a bottle of Scotch and two glasses between them, whilst they waited for dinner on Saturday evening.

Leaving Fliss and Caroline in the kitchen, Hal and Kit strolled in the garden together. The air was sweet and cold, and a thrush was singing in the orchard. The rain had drawn off at last, leaving a tender blue-green sky, and the western hills were washed in luminous golden light. Sparkling raindrops showered over her hands as Kit broke off a spray of Freddy's favourite *Ribes odoratum* and inhaled the fragrance of its yellow flowers.

'Ma hasn't got a clue what's going on,' she said. 'I've brought her masses of freesias and smuggled them into Fliss's bathroom. She's looking a bit stressed out, I thought. Fliss, that is. Not Ma. It occurs to me, little brother, that you two still haven't got your act together.'

He frowned, not looking at her, and she glanced at him sharply.

'Don't tell me you're both still doing the "just good friends bit"? Oh, I don't *believe* it! Honestly, Hal. I don't want to sound callous but Miles has been dead for nearly a year. What the hell are you both waiting for now? Some divine intervention? Authorisation from the Pope?'

'Oh, shut up!' he said angrily. 'It's not funny. And it's not that bloody simple, either.'

She watched him, eyebrows raised, lightly brushing the spray of *Ribes* to and fro across her lips.

'Sorry,' he said presently. 'It's just . . . not a joking matter.'

'No,' she said. 'No, I can see it wouldn't be. Not for you two, anyway. But it's getting silly, Hal. Fliss has got that end-of-tether look about her. That little frown is back and her jaw is all clenched. She's too thin, too. What's going on?'

'We can't seem to take the plunge,' he said slowly. 'I know it seems as if it should be easy. We've loved each other all our lives, and we've been under the same roof for years, but now we're both free at last we can't seem to break out. I honestly think that none of the family would give a damn. After all, we're not going to have children so the old fears don't apply, but even so . . .'

'It's sex,' said Kit cheerfully. 'Amazing how it always comes back to it, isn't it? That's what's blocking it. Well, there's nothing to stop you both now, is there? For heaven's sake just get on and do it.'

'You make it sound so easy,' he said irritably. 'Just think about it. The whole family has got used to our situation. They take us for granted now. How passionate would you feel if you knew that Ma was likely to come wandering into your bedroom at midnight with an attack of insomnia? Or that Jolyon might burst in with some brilliant new idea for his damned nursery? And how do we behave the next morning? Do we subtly imply with loving gestures and caresses that the Rubicon has been crossed and that we are now the equivalent of a married couple? I'm sure *you'd* manage splendidly but Fliss and I are very conventional people and we don't get too much time together to iron out the problem. The other thing is that she's never really recovered properly from Mole. I thought she was coming to terms with it but just lately she's been rather odd.'

'I know that's been a nightmare for her.' Kit looked grave. 'Like her parents and Jamie all over again. It was a terrible thing, appalling, but I thought she was more or less over it. Maybe this new peace agreement has brought it all back again. It's rather bitter to think that such people might be walking about free in a few months' time, isn't it?'

'I don't think it's that.' Hal shook his head. 'I can't describe it but she's . . . oh, I don't know. Abstracted. Not quite with me.'

Kit stopped quite still so that Hal was obliged to pause, too. He looked at her, surprised at the serious look on her face.

'You've got to do something,' she said urgently. 'It's gone on too long, Hal, and soon it will be too late. You can't expect Fliss to make the running. Like you said, she's too conventional and she might be anxious about the family's reaction, especially Ma's and Jo's. Just do it, Hal. No, I don't mean the great seduction scene. I agree you're both a bit too old for creeping along landings or going away for the weekend. It's too ridiculous and undignified. You've just got to tell them. Don't even ask Fliss. Just do it. There are times when a man needs to take the initiative, never mind about how emancipated we women are or how high our consciousnesses have been raised.'

He was staring at her. 'But how can I not tell Fliss? She'll be a bit miffed, won't she?'

'Of course she won't,' she said impatiently. 'She might be embarrassed, anxious, surprised, but she won't be angry. Take my word for it. She'll feel an overwhelming relief. Poor old Flissy has had a rotten deal. She's loved you all her life, Hal, but if you're not careful her love will pass its sell-by date and go bad on her and she could finish up bitter and miserable. Just trust me and do it. Tell the family that you're getting married, set a date for it and afterwards go away for a few days together. Then come home and settle down. It will be so simple, I promise you, if you'll just *do* it. You were the one who told her first time round. You took the responsibility and made the final decision. Now you've got to do it again.'

'You're right.' He was looking past her and she knew that he was thinking back to a spring over thirty years before. 'You're absolutely right.'

'There's one other thing,' she told him. 'You took my advice then, little brother, so take it now. It's the same advice but for different reasons. When you've told them don't stay around. It'll be embarrassing and mawkish and you'll both find it hard to handle. Say your piece and say it loud and clear. Name the day, tell Flissy you love her and then clear out. Ma and Caroline will be delighted, and Fliss'll have quite enough on her plate without you hanging about like a star-struck lover.'

'I've been a bloody fool,' he said. 'Bless you, Kit. You're so right and I just couldn't see it.'

'You're too close to it,' she told him, 'and it's gone on so long. She looked after Miles for all those years and now he's dead and for the first time she's free. She doesn't know how to handle it. She's lost her bearings and I suspect that deep down she's scared stiff. The poor girl's all at sea . . .'

'Very nautical.' He was grinning at her, relief and excitement in his eyes. 'I'll go and polish up my anchor.'

'Oh, shut up.' She aimed a blow at him and dropped her spray of flowers.

'What are you two up to?' Fliss was coming across the lawn. 'Dinner's nearly ready and I wondered if you'd like a drink.'

'An unnecessary question, little coz.' Kit found the *Ribes* and picked it up. 'Just lead us to it. I was telling Hal about Ma's freesias and he was trying to persuade me to let him in on it. He's forgotten to get anything, as usual.'

'I gave her a present on her birthday,' he said, unperturbed by his sister's aspersions. He slipped an arm about Fliss's shoulders and gave her a hug and she smiled up at him. Remembering Kit's words he felt a thrill of fear. How terrible if he should lose her now through procrastination. 'Play to us?' he suggested. 'Play to us until dinner's ready,' and they crossed the grass together and went through the French doors into the drawing room.

300

Chapter Forty

After lunch the next day, feeling pleasantly sleepy, Prue settled herself on the sofa in the hall. For one reason or another everyone had disappeared but she was quite content to rest by the fire, pretending to read the newspaper but actually dozing, with her head against a cushion. Even Clarrie had gone off, mumbling about finding a book he wanted to show her. It was so good to see Clarrie again, and she was enjoying the weekend enormously. Saturday had been such fun, what with Kit and Clarrie arriving and a lovely morning in Totnes with Hal. It was Caroline who'd reminded her that she had an appointment at Town and Country, although she'd quite forgotten about it herself. Even now she couldn't quite work out how she'd got so muddled but Caroline had been very firm and Hal had said, 'Come on, Ma. I'll drive you in now and we'll have coffee in the Quaker House before you have your hair done,' and one way and another she'd found herself in the car and whisked away. It was always a treat to spend an hour in the salon up in the Narrows. She'd known Sheila, for . . . oh, it must be at least twenty years now, probably longer . . . yet she was still just as slender and vivacious as she'd been when her salon had first opened. Her sharp humour had enlivened many a morning and the glint in her brown eyes was as mischievous as ever. Then there was fair-haired Jill, with her sweet face and warm smile, and young Claire, tall and dark and pretty, who was just beginning her apprenticeship. It was such a happy atmosphere, sharing in their dramas and excitements, and telling them her latest news.

Still, it was not like her to forget an appointment, although they'd clearly been expecting her. Afterwards she'd met Hal in Rumour. She knew that he and Jolyon felt less at ease in the tea-shop than in the wine bar and, anyway, Hal often preferred a pint or a glass of claret late in the morning. She always hoped that tall Cris, the bar manager, would be there whenever she went in; he was so welcoming and friendly and made the most delicious hot chocolate. Hal had been waiting for her, leaning at the bar with his pint, chatting to Cris about a rare edition of a book he'd just found in the Pedlar's Pack, and they'd made a fuss of her and she'd had a Danish pastry with her chocolate. They'd both been so sweet. If only Hal could be at home more. Really, this modern feminist anti-men fashion was quite extraordinary . . .

Prue thought: I miss Miles. He was such a dear. So brave. It was nice to have a man about again, especially after darling Theo died.

She began to feel pleasantly sentimental, just a gentle sadness which eased the heart and enabled her to embrace all the people whom she'd loved and lost. Darling Johnny . . . Eyes closed, she saw him again. Impossible to imagine that someone who'd been so warmly, vitally alive could submit to the cold hand of death. Hal was like him and so was dear Jolyon, although Jolyon was quieter, more thoughtful than Johnny had been at his age. It was quite incredible to think that Jolyon was twenty-three. Twenty-three and doing splendidly after such a shaky start following the divorce. How Maria had hurt him. She'd left Adam for another man and then left him, too. Even her parents had despaired of her and lost sympathy. Edward would be celebrating his twenty-first birthday in a few weeks' time and none of them knew where to send cards or presents. Poor, poor Edward. It was more than a year since she'd seen him. He'd come down to The Keep for the weekend, although he'd spent most of it with his brother in the gatehouse and Jolyon had done his best to cope. Only afterwards had he told them that Edward had been sent down from university for taking drugs and something to do with shoplifting.

Prue pulled the old tartan rug across her knees. The draught that slid under the front door was creeping round her ankles and she let the rug fall comfortingly over her legs. She settled herself again, closing her eyes. Of course, none of them had wanted her to know, they'd wanted to protect her but she'd been able to tell at once that something was wrong. The thing was that, during the time she'd managed to spend with Edward, she'd felt that he was almost a stranger, he'd looked like no one she knew, and she'd recognised none of his mannerisms. She hadn't quite known how to approach him and he'd been wary, restless, relieved to get away. She'd felt helpless and inadequate, and known that Hal had felt the same, yet Edward continued to refuse any overtures of love or assistance except those made by his brother. It wasn't as if Edward looked like Maria. That might have been painful but it would have been a start, something to work on . . .

She thought: The thing about families is that if we're lucky we all recognise certain things in one another and then we know how to react.

Hal and Jolyon were like Johnny, with bits of Freddy jumbled in, and Kit was like herself, Prue, and Prue's own mother; there was a certain instability combined with a reckless love of life which could be hazardous. Kit had turned to darling old Clarrie but there had been moments when Prue had feared that her daughter might go off the rails, especially after that terrible business with Jake.

Now Fliss was an interesting combination of Freddy and Fliss's own mother, Alison. She had a very straight glance, a trick of lifting her chin and squaring her shoulders which made her look terribly like her grandmother. On the other hand there was Alison's anxiety, her little worried frown and the tendency to take life just a bit too seriously. Not that poor darling Flissy had had much to laugh about in those last years with Miles . . .

Prue smoothed the soft wool with a rhythmic, stroking movement. Of course, Fliss had her twinnies and now there was dear little Paula to bring her comfort. It was odd that Jamie should look exactly like Miles when they'd first known him and yet in character should be just like his Chadwick grandfather. Peter had had that confidence, that decisive air, that witty, light touch which charmed the girls. Nevertheless Jamie – like Peter before him – kept his own counsel and, like Kipling's cat, he walked by himself. He was fond of his family but tended to find them slightly overwhelming en masse and was not given to sharing confidences, except perhaps with Bess. She was another odd mix, bless her. She was serious, not overconfident, yet full of courage, which was exactly like Fliss, but she didn't look like either of her parents. Miles always said that she looked like his mother and she certainly wasn't a Chadwick, neither the dark nor fair variety. Now Jolyon was a typically fair Chadwick but how sad it was that there was no one to carry on Theo's and Mole's dark good looks. Poor Mole. What a terrible, terrible thing to happen. He'd been such a funny little boy, hiding under rugs . . . under this very rug that she was holding. He'd lie along the sofa and cover himself with it, no matter how warm the weather.

Prue fidgeted a little, finding that she was trying to turn her mind away from that first meeting with him after Kenya, but she couldn't quite block it out. The images persisted, growing clearer . . . It was midsummer, and she and Kit and Hal were coming down to The Keep for the annual holiday. It had been hot, terribly hot, and the three of them had travelled down on the train from Bristol. Fox had collected them from Staverton station and, as they'd arrived in the courtyard and were getting out of the car, Mole had come out of the

303

front door. She could see him, in her mind's eye: a small figure in the bright sunshine, rubbing his eyes as if he'd been asleep. 'Mummy!' he'd screamed. 'Mummy! Jamie!' and he'd run down the steps and across the grass and flung his arms round Hal's waist . . .

Prue tried to swallow her tears as the memories flooded back. She remembered how Hal had been frozen into immobility, shocked and horrified by such a reception. No one had told him that he was the image of his cousin Jamie, no one could have imagined that at the sight of him Mole would believe that the Kenya massacre had been simply a nightmare and that his big brother was back from the dead. How strange those following weeks had been. At least the shock had restored Mole's voice and then there had been the slow climb back from grief . . . and to what end?

The gentle pleasant sentimentality was giving way before the authentic pain of loss. Prue pushed the rug aside, determined to find company. Before she could lever herself to her feet, however, the door to the back of the house opened and she could hear singing. Before her amazed eyes a long procession wound into the hall with Lulu at its head. They were all singing 'Happy Birthday' to her and Jolyon was bringing up the rear carrying a perfectly enormous cake with candles on it. They crowded round her, showering presents upon her, laughing, bending to kiss her. Kit slipped an arm round her neck and whispered, 'Many, many more, honey,' and engulfed her in a scented shower of glorious freesias whilst Lulu climbed on to her lap crying, 'It's a surprise. We parked round at the stables so you wouldn't hear us come in.'

'Oh,' she gasped, tears dried as if by magic, happiness lighting her face. 'Oh, my darlings. However did you manage this without my suspecting anything?'

'Happy birthday, Ma,' said Hal. 'Champagne with the cake but only for those who've eaten their bread and butter.'

She stared up at them: Hal sending her a tiny wink; Clarrie beaming; Caroline fussing over the best silver teapot, Fliss made room for scones and clotted cream on the low table. Susanna sat down beside her, Gus and Fred placed extra chairs and Podger hurried about organising the proceedings. Bess came to perch on her other side, with baby Paula in her arms, and Matt leaned on the back of the sofa.

She thought: So that explains the hair appointment. I was being got out of the way. Oh, what darlings they are . . .

Hugging Lulu, smiling at her loved ones, Prue began to open her presents.

*　　*　　*

By the end of the week the holidays were over. Kit and Clarrie, followed a few days later by Bess, Matt and baby Paula, returned to London; Podger, Lulu and Fred were dispatched to their respective schools. Only Hal remained, not due back in Faslane until the following Monday.

All through the last few days of his leave he waited for an opportunity to follow Kit's advice. Looking at Fliss with new eyes, he saw the lines of strain about her mouth, the tiny frown between her feathery brows. There was a tense, coiled look about her, as if she were waiting, wound as tight as a spring. Anxiety washed through him, leaving fear in its wake. Supposing she had ceased to love him? He knew that she was deeply fond of him, no question of that, but supposing her love for him had already begun to go bad on her and she was dreading the question she was expecting him to ask? It might explain her prevarication, her reluctance to discuss the future.

As soon as he'd identified his fear he acted upon it and took her up on to the moor. As he drove through Buckfast, towards Holne, he saw how her thin hands clasped and unclasped on her knees, noted her introspection. He set himself the task of relaxing her, talking idly, pointing out small indications of spring's arrival: a chiffchaff swinging on a branch of budding crab apple; a clump of early purple orchis on a grassy bank; two painted ladies fluttering above a patch of violets which clung in the crevice of a dry-stone wall. The moor showed a placid, smiling face: fold on fold of blue distant hills, smooth grey stone, wooded valleys misting into a new tender green. Venford Reservoir was a dazzling shield of water, blue as the sky which overarched it; a secret shining jewel set deep within the surrounding ink-black pines.

They walked out to Bench Tor and stood together looking down into White Wood; seeing the gleam of water far below between the branches of the trees which clung to the coombe's steep sides; listening to the river thundering through the narrow rocky chasm. Sheep scrambled, sure-footed on the piled granite, watching them with narrow yellow eyes whilst ponies grazed undisturbed on the lower slopes.

Across the valley a cuckoo called and suddenly they saw him, unmistakable with his pointed wings and long tail, they watched his dipping flight as he dropped down towards Meltor Wood and disappeared from sight. They laughed, delighted, hugging each other.

'Odd, isn't it?' said Fliss. 'He's such a rogue and yet we love him.'

305

Looking down at her, Hal saw that the signs of strain were gone and her face was as carefree as a child's. He pushed back the fair strands of hair that blew about her face and bent to kiss her. Her arms tightened about him and her response told him all that he needed to know. In his relief he clasped her closely to him but before he could speak there was the sound of yelping and thudding feet. A dog appeared over the rocks, sheep scattering before him, and behind him came a young man, shouting threats, brandishing a lead, gasping for breath.

'Sorry,' he cried when he saw them. 'He's only a puppy, really, but I should have kept him on the lead. A sheep broke right in front of him . . .'

They acknowledged his dilemma, sympathised, agreed that the puppy must be controlled, but by the time the fuss was over, the moment had passed. Once or twice, on the journey home, Hal attempted to find appropriate words, to warn her of his intention to tell the family, but each time he opened his mouth, Fliss began to speak and he was forestalled. Nevertheless, Hal no longer doubted that Kit's advice was sound; it was simply a matter of timing, of finding the right moment.

It came on Sunday afternoon, hours before he was due to leave for the station. He'd been down in the stableyard with Jolyon and when he came back into the hall, Jolyon on his heels, they were sitting by the fire: Caroline and his mother; Fliss and Susanna. Tea was in progress and they were laughing about something Podger had said to Gus. Fliss glanced round at him and he saw that the old expression was back; a kind of patient resignation which was worlds away from the happy face which had laughed into his, up on Bench Tor in the warm spring sunshine. He clenched his fists, pushing them into his pockets and walked into the circle of firelight and warmth. They all looked at him now and he smiled at them, swallowing down a ridiculous spasm of terror.

'There's something I want to say,' he said. 'It might come as a shock but it shouldn't, not after all this time.' They were all silent now, watching him. 'Fliss and I are going to get married. You all know that we've loved each other since we were children and now there's nothing to prevent us being properly together. I think it's best if we have a registry office ceremony as soon as possible and then Fliss and I will have a few days away somewhere. We don't want a huge fuss . . .'

The echoing surprised silence crashed into a noisy hubbub of words and laughter. Prue was in tears, Caroline was hugging Fliss, Susanna sat in open-mouthed amazement. Hal stood quite

306

still feeling almost foolish, undecided as to what he should do next, trying to gauge Fliss's reaction. It was Jolyon who carried him through. Hal felt his arm seized in a fierce grip and then his son was hugging him, thumping him on the back with his free fist, congratulating him. Hal had barely time to register his gratitude before Jo released him and turned to Fliss, opening both arms to her. Her eyes met Hal's at last and, in that brief moment before she was engulfed by Jolyon's embrace, he saw that they were bright with pure joy, shining with unutterable relief.

Chapter Forty-one

Several weeks later Fliss wandered in the orchard, Rufus at her heels. She'd wakened this morning with a sensation of restless excitement fluttering in the pit of her stomach; an odd impression of anticipation. For days after Hal's announcement she'd wakened with a similar feeling, except that a tremendous relief had been mixed in with the happy brew of sensations. It was as if a burden had been lifted from her heart, a nameless weight from her back, and she'd been surprised at how completely different she'd felt. She even breathed more deeply, more freely, and her overwhelming happiness and contentment informed every aspect of her life. Now that the act was done she couldn't imagine why she and Hal had hesitated so long. The family had been so wholehearted in their generous delight that she could see now that she'd built up an edifice consisting of entirely unnecessary anxieties and imaginary difficulties which had threatened to become insurmountable. She had been at the point of despair, which was numbing into indifference. No wonder that she felt lighter than air, weightless, now that the yoke had been thrown off.

As she passed beneath the bent branches of the ancient apple trees, whose blossom was now fading, she relived those earlier emotions. How grateful she'd been for Hal's tact in making the announcement just before he went away: how difficult it would have been to have him around whilst Prue wept with joy at regular intervals, trying to convince both herself and Fliss that it was worth waiting over thirty years for such happiness, and Caroline dealt pragmatically with the Registry Office at Newton Abbot and planned a small reception. Jolyon's quiet pleasure, his complicit smiles and amused winks in the face of Prue's and Caroline's euphoria, were comforting. He'd kept her steady. Despite numerous suggestions and attempted persuasions, she'd held firm to the plan which Hal had outlined.

'We must keep it simple,' he'd said later, on that momentous

Sunday evening when she'd driven him to Plymouth to catch the night train. 'Ma will turn it into a circus if she can.'

They'd sat together in the car park, turned toward each other, his hands cupping her face. She'd been utterly silent yet possessed of a strange trembling, a kind of nervous teeth-chattering reaction which she'd hardly been able to hide.

'I don't much care what we do,' she'd muttered. 'Only I don't want to hurt their feelings.'

'Damn their feelings,' he'd said. 'For the first time I'm considering *our* feelings, Fliss, and I'm sure this is the right way to do it. We'll have a church blessing later on but just now I want to get it over and done with.' He'd held her tightly then, her head buried against his shoulder, and she'd heard him chuckling softly. 'Sounds rather brutal, doesn't it? I don't mean it to. I just want us to be together. I'll give you a buzz as soon as I get hold of my diary and let you know how soon I can get down again. It'll take a bit of organising since I've just had leave but it'll be as soon as I can. I'll take a few extra days and we'll go away. Wherever you like, I don't mind, but we need to do that . . . Hell, is that the time. Come and wave me goodbye, my darling . . .'

Once he'd gone she'd been possessed with the terror that she would never see him again; that the train would crash, or a terrorist would attack the base . . .

Rufus came wagging up with a dead branch which he laid invitingly at her feet and she bent to smooth his head. He'd already had a long early morning walk on the hill but he enjoyed a game in the orchard, which had been out of bounds to him during its weeks of springtime beauty. The crocuses and squills were over now but the grass, which was never cut until the bulbs had died back naturally, was long and wet, and her shoes were soaked. She flung the branch between the rough-barked trunks and, as Rufus plunged after it, sending up sparkling drops of water, her thoughts returned readily to the recent past.

The ceremony had been as brief and down-to-earth as could be expected and she'd been almost glad that Susanna's children were away at school and that Matt had a concert which prevented him from coming down. Bess, Jamie and Kit had travelled from London together, leaving Paula in Sin's care with Clarrie and Andrew in attendance, and Susanna and Gus accompanied Prue, Caroline and Jo. Only Edward's absence had cast a shadow. Hal had been deeply distressed that he'd been unable to contact his younger son and all his guilt and sorrow had surfaced so that she'd needed all her tact to reassure him that he was not to blame for the rift that had

310

developed, to encourage him to believe that one day Edward would come back to them. She'd taken pains to remind him that Jamie, too, was engrossed in his own life now; independent, travelling far afield, committed to his research post which, both she and Hal knew, fronted other, more sinister, activities about which nobody questioned him. She'd comforted Hal by reminding him that they were lucky to have Jo around, that Bess was such a frequent visitor, and that they must put aside any sorrows and anxieties so as to enjoy this happy day thoroughly with their family.

Neither she nor Hal had wanted any fuss, especially in public, but it had been lovely to come back to The Keep for a celebration lunch with them all before driving away to Cornwall.

'It's nice to be called Chadwick again,' she'd said dreamily, on the drive down, and he'd smiled, not looking at her, and reached out for her hand.

Now Fliss smiled too, remembering, as she paused beneath a tree, touching the warm, grainy wood, feeling the powdery lichen crumbling beneath her fingers. The hotel had been charming: a small country house with pleasant owners and an old-world atmosphere. There had been no difficulties, no embarrassments. They were too old to be taken for honeymooners; too easy and relaxed to be suspected of enjoying an illicit weekend. In fact, nobody really noticed them at all. There, in the shadowy room which looked across the bay to St Michael's Mount, she and Hal had resolved the tensions and denials of thirty years.

It had been a shock to find that his lovemaking resulted in such a physical release. Afterwards, as they'd clung together, she'd suddenly begun to cry. The tears had welled out, unstoppable, gently washing away the accumulation of fear and loneliness, bringing an exquisite relief which had remained with her. They'd returned to a simple homecoming, natural as if they'd been doing it for ever, and had moved into their new quarters. Their bedroom, which had been Theo's study, had windows looking east over the hill and south into the courtyard. The bedroom had become Hal's dressing room. Fliss's bedroom was left as a spare room, but she and Hal continued to use the sitting room – her grandmother's favourite room – as a refuge.

The family had been wonderful. All the things she'd feared – antagonism from Jo and Prue, shock and resentment on their father's behalf from the twinnies – had never materialised. She suspected that Caroline had talked it through many times with Prue and guessed that Kit had been doing the same thing with Jamie and Bess. However the transition had been effected she did not quite

311

know, she was only glad that it had been so painless. Surprisingly, it was Susanna who had been the most affected.

'I never knew,' she'd said over and over. 'Why didn't you tell me?'

Fliss had explained that she and Hal had parted whilst Susanna was still a child at school, that they'd made certain that their feelings were hidden, that they'd never let them affect their marriages, but Susanna had not yet quite recovered from the shock. Her feelings were complex: hurt that Fliss had not shared this secret with her, yes, but, more importantly, shame that she'd never guessed it for herself. Fliss knew that there was still a little way to go before Susanna's sunny spirits were restored to normal but this was the only cloud in her perfect sky; that and the fact that Mole had not been there to share in her happiness.

As she bent to look into the small stone house which he and Susanna had used for so many of their childhood games, she was aware once more of the strange feeling of expectation rising inside her; a renewal of the sensation which had been with her since early morning. The inability to find peace or come to terms with his death had been muffled beneath the layers of her recent experiences but now, this morning, it was surfacing again, a part of this other faintly disturbing emotion. Surely, now, she could accept the fact of his death, quietly and naturally, and let it go?

She crossed the lawn, Rufus trotting ahead, passed through the garden room, pausing to give him a biscuit, and out into the courtyard. It was warm here, the scent of the wisteria blossom drifting in the soft air, and Fliss sat down on the bench, Rufus settling gratefully in the shade behind her, his head on his paws. The robin was singing from the top of the wall and, somewhere closer at hand, a bumble bee lumbered amongst the blue pendant flowers of the wisteria, droning somnolently. The sun was hot and she leaned back with a sigh of pleasure. Several minutes passed as she let these sounds and scents lull her into a peaceful drowsiness yet she knew that a part of her was poised; still, alert, waiting . . .

She heard the car's engine as it approached up the drive and frowned a little, puzzled. Caroline and Prue were having a Dartington day, walking in the gardens and lunching at the White Hart, and Jolyon wouldn't be back until much later. The engine was switched off and she heard a door slam. Another door was opened and she heard a voice before this door was closed, too. There were footsteps on the drive and she opened her eyes, sitting quite still, staring across the courtyard.

A figure was entering through the gateway between the gate-houses. It was a small boy, hardly more than three or four years old. He came running in, looking eagerly about him, unafraid and full of life. From behind him a woman called and he paused, waiting, gazing beyond the sunny rectangle of grass to where Fliss sat watching him. The woman had caught up with him now, taking his hand, looking around.

Fliss climbed slowly to her feet, her heart hammering so hard in her side that she could hardly breathe. The woman caught the movement and made a small gesture of acknowledgement. Still holding the child's hand, she approached slowly, almost reluctantly.

'Hello,' she said awkwardly. 'I was looking for some people called Chadwick.' She laughed a little, an embarrassed little sound, as she nodded towards the grey stone castellated house. 'No need to ask if this is The Keep.'

Her anxiety was tangible but Fliss did not glance at her. She continued to stare down at the small boy who, head tilted back, gazed up at her unwaveringly. The girl – now that she looked at her at last, Fliss could see that she was not much more than a girl – was trying to master her apprehension. She was patently nervous, self-conscious, and her greeny-blue eyes met Fliss's own with an expression which was almost pleading. Fliss saw that she was fair-haired, well built and guessed that, in almost any other circumstance, she was a confident person.

'My name's Lizzie Fairbanks,' she said. 'Are you . . . ?' She let go of the child and plunged her hands distressfully through her long fair hair. 'Look, I don't know how to handle this now I've seen you. It seemed OK while we were driving down and last night at the hotel in Totnes. But now that I'm here . . .'

Fliss was looking at the boy again.

'My name's Fliss Chadwick,' she said to him. 'What's yours?'

'Sam,' he said cheerfully. 'My name's Sam Chadwick . . .'

Liz caught Fliss by the arm, steadying her.

'Hang on,' she said anxiously. 'I'm sorry. I'm really sorry. Oh hell, I should have written after all but I needed to see you. Look, sit down again . . .'

The boy stood at her knee, watching her curiously with Mole's eyes, and she smiled at him with shaking lips, swallowing hard, trying to smile at him.

'I've been waiting for you,' she told him – and realised suddenly that it was the truth.

Rufus struggled up, wakened from his deep sleep, coming out

313

from behind the bench, and the boy crouched to stroke his head, murmuring to him, Fliss momentarily forgotten.

Lizzie subsided beside her. 'Sorry,' she said again – but it was clear that she was deeply relieved at Fliss's reaction. 'Look, I can see now that this was stupid. Anna and Laura said it would be but any other way seemed all wrong. I wanted to see you face to face. Are you OK?'

Fliss gazed at her, frowning so as to get a better look. 'Are you . . . ?'

'No,' said Lizzie quickly. 'That's the trouble. Oh dear. I'll say it quickly and then we'll go through it slowly afterwards.' She lowered her voice, her eyes on the boy who was now sitting beside Rufus on the paving stones. 'Sam's mother died a few weeks ago in a skiing accident. Until then we'd managed between us with Sam. There are four of us. *Were* four of us. So there was always someone around for him. Her name was Sam, too. Samantha. When Mole died . . .' She hesitated, glancing quickly at Fliss, her eyes full of tears. 'She loved him so terribly, you know. It was almost painful to see her. We teased her so much but she didn't care. Only she was so much younger, you see, and she was afraid that he was worried about the age gap. "I know he loves me," she used to say over and over again. "I know it. But he won't commit himself." She drove us all mad. And then they went off on his boat together for a weekend and when they came back it was like it had all changed. I think that's when she knew for sure that he really loved her. She was so happy . . .'

Sam came back to them. 'Dog,' he said triumphantly, pointing. 'It's a dog.'

Fliss instinctively put out her hands to him – and drew them back quickly. Lizzie watched them both warily, blowing her nose.

'His name is Rufus.' Fliss's voice was under control, her smile steady. 'Do you see the door over there? The one into the garden room? That's what we call it. There's a box on the chair inside the door with some of Rufus's biscuits in it. He's had one already this morning but another one won't hurt. Would you like to take him over there and give him one?'

The boy was already urging Rufus across the grass, running beside him with promises of the treat to come. Fliss watched him go inside, looking round with that lively curiosity.

'Tell me quickly,' she said.

'Sam's father was ill.' Lizzie spoke swiftly, quietly. 'She went down to see him for a week. Mole lent her his car and she was like a kid about it. She used to wear his jersey and play his cassettes. It

314

was . . . Well, it was rather touching really but we used to send her up rotten about it.' She swallowed and cleared her throat. 'Sorry. Anyway, it was while she was away that the . . . that the boat was blown up. When she got back to the flat she was like she was drugged or something. She'd heard the news on the way up from Hampshire and she left the car in a back street somewhere and came straight home. She'd got his jersey on and an old jacket and carrying all his Brahms cassettes and she was shivering so much she could hardly stand up. Her face was puffy with crying. Sodden. It was later she told us she was pregnant. She said that she'd done it quite deliberately because she knew that although Mole loved her he might never have the courage to commit himself. She knew he'd marry her once he knew about the baby. "I would have made him so happy," she kept saying, "and now he'll never know about the baby." It was terrible . . . Sorry. Are you all right? Oh God . . .'

'I'm OK.' Fliss took her face out of her hands and bit her lip. 'Go on. If you can . . .'

'Her father died a few weeks later, and her mother . . . well, her mother is a bit of a cow. She was much younger than Sam's father and she was always having affairs. Anyway, she wasn't interested in Sam or the baby and Sam was determined to do it all on her own. She was a great mother, she really was. I know it wasn't terribly conventional but we all looked after him. Anna's a nurse and Laura works in a pub so we all did different hours which meant he was never alone. He started kindergarten last autumn and he was just fantastic. He's a friendly little chap and very confident. Sam only went on the skiing holiday because she'd decided he was old enough to leave for a week. It was the first time she'd been since before . . . Anyway, we just couldn't believe it when we heard. It's just tragic.' Her voice wavered but she ploughed on. 'Sam's been OK about it but, to be honest, I think it's because he's been brought up by us all, if you see what I mean, rather than just her. We all love him. Oh, shit. I don't know if I'm doing this right.'

'You're doing wonderfully.' Fliss took Lizzie's hand and squeezed it hard. 'I'm trying to take it all in but it's a bit . . . sudden.'

Lizzie laughed mirthlessly. 'What an understatement. The trouble is we didn't know how to do it. Laura thought we ought to write and Anna was all for telephoning. But apart from the shock it would have been for you I wanted to see you face to face. I needed to see your reaction to him. I felt I knew you a bit because Sam told us so much about you all, you see. Mole must have spent hours talking to her about his home because she'd repeat it all to us later. She had a rather unstable childhood, poor old Sam, and for some reason it appealed to her. You'll find that she's told it all to young Sam. All about Ellen and Fox, was it? And Uncle Theo and Aunt Prue. There's another sister isn't there? Susie, is it?'

'Susanna.' Fliss shut her eyes. 'Why didn't she come to us at the time? It would have been such a relief.'

'We said that. We tried to persuade her but she wouldn't have it. "He'd have taken me down to meet them if he'd wanted to," she'd say. She was terribly stubborn but I think it was that, deep down, she didn't think you'd believe her and she couldn't have borne it if you'd thrown her out or told her to prove it.' Lizzie glanced at her curiously. 'You didn't have a problem, did you?'

Fliss smiled sadly. 'He's exactly as Mole was at that age. It's . . . it's quite devastating.'

'It must be.' Lizzie sighed frustratedly. 'I wish she'd come earlier.'

'At least you've come now,' said Fliss. 'I shall want to hear it all over again, of course, all the details if you can bear it. I hope you've got some photographs of her.'

'I brought masses,' said Lizzie. 'And I brought Mole's things, too, just in case you . . . Well, you know. And some photographs she took of him. And lots of young Sam, of course. They're in the car.'

'I think we need some coffee,' said Fliss. She smiled at Lizzie, trying to come to grips with this astounding event. 'Would you like to find the photographs while I get the kettle on? I'm so sorry to hear about Sam. Is that why you decided to come and find us at last?'

Liz was on her feet, stretching with relief, looking about her, but at Fliss's words she looked down at her quickly.

'I should have said earlier,' she said, tension returning. 'It's not quite that simple, you see. With Sam gone and Laura moving in with her chap next month it's impossible for Anna and me to keep young Sam any more. We'll have to get new people in to help with the rent or move to a smaller place. We'll miss him terribly – well, I will – but we just can't manage. It wouldn't be fair to him, you see. We're hoping that you'll take him. After all, this is where he belongs isn't it? With his own people? That's why I've come.'

Chapter Forty-two

Fliss was alone again. Lizzie and Sam had returned to Totnes in
her small Fiat, Sam twisting as far round as he could in his small
seat, his hand fluttering at the back window. He hadn't wanted to
leave, although this was mainly due to the friendship he'd made
with Rufus.

'You could stay,' Fliss had said at the last moment. 'Stay here.
There's plenty of room.'

'No.' Lizzie had answered quickly, almost abruptly. 'Give yourself a break. There's lots to think about. And it might be better to
give the others a bit of a warning.'

'You're probably right.' Standing there beside the car in the
sunshine, Lizzie half inside, she'd thought about the shock to
Caroline and Prue. Confused, anxious that she should show her
gratitude, she'd said, 'Come back soon, though.'

Lizzie had smiled at her. 'I've got two weeks off,' she'd said. 'I
need time to adjust too, you know.'

Behind the bright smile and brave words, Fliss guessed that it
wouldn't be easy for Lizzie. They'd talked more comfortably over
coffee in the hall and Fliss had been able to pull herself together a
little. Sam had come scrambling along the sofa, settling himself on
Lizzie's lap, and she'd held him naturally, easily, smoothing back
the dark hair as he slept.

'She was my best friend,' she'd said. 'We were at school together
and neither of us wanted to settle down. We both temped rather than
be tied to one job. She adored skiing and that winter with Mole was
the first time she didn't go abroad. I met him at that same party, you
know. He was drop-dead sexy, wasn't he? I was really impressed that
she'd made it with him. After that she wouldn't let us near him. "Bring
him round," we'd say but there was no chance. It was the same reason
she never took him home, I think. Her mother was deadly. Couldn't
resist any man, according to Sam, and she and Mole were much the
same age, you see. She's remarried now and lives in Provence and
she doesn't want to know. She wouldn't want anyone to know she's

317

old enough to be a grandmother. It's pathetic. Charlie's cool, though. That's Sam's younger brother. He's in the Army and couldn't do anything about looking after young Sam but he'll want to stay in touch. You'll like Charlie . . .'

She'd talked on, holding the sleeping child, brushing back her blonde hair, reaching for her coffee. In her jeans and oversize sweatshirt she'd looked hardly more than a child herself, and Fliss had watched and listened as four years came slowly to life before her eyes. Mole's Aran jersey, knitted by Caroline, his old tweed jacket and a pile of cassettes lay on the sofa and from time to time, as Lizzie talked, Fliss's eyes had drifted to the photograph she'd held in her hand. The girl was so young, dark hair swinging forward, a mischievous smile on her lips; with Mole's jersey slung about her shoulders, perching on the stern, she looked happy and relaxed.

'Mole took that one on the trip to Greenford on the boat,' Lizzie had told her. 'It was that weekend which changed everything for her. She really knew he loved her after that. She never forgave herself for going home when she did. If she hadn't, you see, Mole wouldn't have been on the boat just then . . .'

'But he'd've gone aboard later,' Fliss had said gently, as Lizzie mopped her streaming eyes. 'It could have been worse. If it had happened after he'd got back in the evening Sam might have been with him and there would certainly have been other casualties.'

Lizzie had held the child tightly as she'd rummaged in her sleeve for a tissue. 'She couldn't bear it that he didn't know he was going to be a father.' Her voice had been shaky. 'Sam was so sure at the end. "It's all he needs," she said. "It'll give him the confidence to commit and it'll be fab." It was really great to see her so happy after all her uncertainty. I miss her terribly. Sorry. Honestly, I'm not usually like this . . .'

Fliss had poured her some more coffee, knowing that Lizzie was grieving for her friend, and talked inconsequentially whilst she recovered.

'Come back in the morning,' she'd said, as they stood together by the car. 'Come and get to know us properly. I want you to feel at home here.'

Lizzie had hugged her quickly, before climbing into the car and driving away, and Fliss had stood for some time staring after them.

She went back into the hall and began to clear the coffee things, moving slowly, stiffly and clumsily, as if she had aged suddenly. She couldn't get the child out of her mind. Watching him sleeping on Lizzie's lap she'd been swung back forty years in time to Staverton station: the three of them, standing together, waiting; Mole, clinging to her skirt, watching her with his brown eyes. Sam was just like him physically, but he had a cheerful confidence, a lively curiosity, which Mole had never possessed, not even before the tragedy in Kenya. He'd been a quiet, passive little boy and she guessed that young Sam's bright, out-going quality was inherited from his mother. She, too, had had an unhappy childhood, according to Lizzie, but she'd made up for it at school and afterwards. How good she must have been for Mole; how happy she must have made him.

Fliss paused in her clearing up and selected a photograph from the pile on the sofa. Mole grinned out at her. Standing at the tiller of the *Dorcas*, his hair blowing about, he looked happier than she'd ever seen him. There was a positive self-possession in his stance, an assertion which must have always been present – how else could he have done so well in his career? – but seen rarely in his private life.

Fliss felt a surge of gratitude to the unknown girl, and a sense of relief. She knew now that a great deal of her own grief was centred in the knowledge that Mole had never loved or been loved except by his family. She'd imagined that he'd never known that special happiness of a close relationship, of being loved simply for oneself, and this new knowledge was a balm to her pain. She was not surprised that he'd never brought Sam to The Keep. The age difference would have been a huge barrier to him; probably as big a problem as his own reluctance to commit himself.

Still holding the photographs, one in each hand, she sat down and looked at them both: the two Sams. She tried to recall the details of that last weekend he'd spent with them. He'd told them he'd got a problem with the car and he'd travelled by train. Well, that was clear now. Sam had been lent the car so as to visit her sick father. It also explained why there were none of the usual bits and pieces which Mole generally left lying about in his car. Putting down the photographs, Fliss reached out and picked up the car keys – they'd assumed these must have been in Mole's pocket when he died – and held them, turning them over in her fingers. It was Susanna who'd had the silver dolphin made specially for him just after he'd passed Perisher and had been given his first command.

Quite suddenly she remembered how she and Susanna had driven down to the dockyard to see HMS *Opportune* all those years ago. He'd shown his sisters over the submarine, trying to hide his pride, introducing them to his first lieutenant. Afterwards, sitting in the car, both sisters had been near tears . . .

The sound of the car jolting into the courtyard recalled her to the present. Standing up quickly she saw that Prue and Caroline were back. She glanced at her watch, shocked to see how late it was, how unprepared she was. Gathering up the photographs with unsteady hands, snatching up Mole's jersey and jacket, she ran upstairs.

'I can't believe it,' said Prue for the fifth time. 'Poor Fliss. What a shock for you.'

They were still sitting at the kitchen table although it was getting on for five o'clock. Jolyon had come in for a late sandwich. He'd heard the news with delight but had hurried away again, taking Rufus with him, whilst the three women sat on together. The shock united them so that the whole world seemed centred on the table between them. The photographs, produced once Fliss had carefully broken the news, were passed from hand to hand, now one, now another. Caroline had held his jersey in her arms for some while, patting it from time to time, her eyes thoughtful; Prue had shed tears over the key-ring, remembering Susanna's delight in Mole's pleasure. Twice Fliss had stood up to make tea, moving quietly between the Aga and table, but the room seemed held in a kind of spell, a bubble which contained the three of them. Their movements were slow, almost languid; their speech hushed, gentle.

'I'm getting used to it now.' Fliss crossed her arms on the table and smiled at her aunt. 'It's a wonderful shock, after all. Terrible about his mother, of course – I don't mean that – but to know there's a tiny piece of Mole still with us is.' She took a deep breath, shaking her head. 'It's such a relief.'

'And this poor child, this Lizzie . . .'

'She's being very brave,' said Fliss. 'It took tremendous courage to come all this way to find us but she's an intelligent girl. Once Sam had died she knew that she must find young Sam's legal guardians although I don't quite know what she might have done if she'd disapproved of us. His grandmother has moved to Provence and refuses to take any responsibility and his uncle is in the Army and incommunicado at the moment. Anyway, he's far too young to be able to cope with a small boy. Lizzie was Sam's best friend and she loves little Sam, you can see that. It'll be a terrible wrench for both of them but what alternative is there?'

'He can't be left with two young girls.' Prue was firm about this. Fliss had been obliged to explain the situation to her several times and at first she'd been shocked that the child had been brought up in such a haphazard fashion. Slowly she'd been reconciled to the idea but it was clear that, with his mother dead, Sam should be introduced to a more conventional upbringing.

'It's not quite that simple, is it?' Caroline was trying to remember that she wasn't actually a member of the family, yet she knew she must speak out. 'He's used to it and those girls are his family. Oh, I know that we . . . you are his blood relations but even so . . .'

Fliss smiled at her gratefully. 'This is the big stumbling block as far as I can see,' she agreed. 'Sam is used to a flat full of young people. Lots of bustle and friends coming and going. It's clear that he's very adaptable, he's had to be and that's good, but it will be a tremendous shock to find himself here with his mother dead and only an elderly household to replace his friends.'

'Your grandmother said much the same thing when she interviewed me.' Caroline looked at Prue. 'Remember how worried she was that the children were surrounded by such old people after their own young family?'

'Of course Freddy was in her sixties and so were Ellen and Fox . . .' Prue paused. 'But I don't see that there is any other option. Do you?'

'He's a darling,' said Fliss. 'I can't wait for you to see him. But, my goodness, a three-year-old . . .'

She thought: I wonder if that's the sort of thing Grandmother said to Ellen? 'They're darlings, of course, but how on earth shall I manage with three small children at my age?' She must have been as frightened as I am now.

'Three and a half,' Caroline was saying thoughtfully. 'He'll be able to go to play school, of course, but it's an exhausting age.'

'There's the three of us.' Prue was being persuasive. 'We'll share the load. And Jolyon will be such a help, being so young. Surely we can manage between us?'

'We can *manage*,' said Caroline. 'Of course we can *manage* but it's Sam I'm thinking of, Prue. Fliss and Mole and Susanna had each other. There was a continuity from their past in Kenya to their future here—'

'And I knew Grandmother,' broke in Fliss. 'And Ellen and Fox. As well as you, Prue, and Kit and Hal. We weren't coming to strangers, remember.'

'No.' Prue agreed rather unwillingly. 'No, I see that. But he's so young, isn't he? In a few months he'll hardly remember London.'

'Prue's got a point,' said Caroline. 'He's not much older than Susanna was and she can't remember anything about Kenya, can she, Fliss?'

'Not really. She certainly can't *remember* Daddy and Mummy

or Jamie, but the thing is that I'm not certain that I'd *want* Sam to forget. It's been such an important part of his life. Susanna knows all about her life in Kenya because I've told her. I've filled in the spaces and made it real for her. She knows that Jamie and Hal were so alike that they might have been twins, and that Hal and Jo look just like Daddy. She knows things that Mummy said and the way she thought and the things we all did together. It's part of her history and now she knows it just as well as if she *can* remember it. The past is important. It's part of what we are and I don't want Sam to lose his small bit of it.'

There was silence.

'Supposing,' said Prue, after a moment, 'supposing one of us took him back from time to time? We could stay with Kit and take Sam to visit these girls. If nothing else it would be good for him to be with a young family like Bess and Matt and dear little Paula.'

She looked at them eagerly, anxious to provide a solution. It was unthinkable to her that the child, Mole's son, should be left with two young girls in London – even if they were prepared to have him.

'It's a good idea,' said Fliss cautiously, 'but it doesn't answer the problem of him being here with three women who are so much older. I know Jo's great with children but I'm not sure that that's quite enough.'

Caroline was watching her sympathetically.

She thought: Poor Fliss. She's just come through the lean years and now she's faced with this. Prue's seventy-five. I'm not far off seventy. She knows she's got her work cut out. So much for settling down with Hal . . .

'I need to speak to Hal.' It was as if Fliss had read her thoughts. 'It's been such a shock that I haven't told him yet.'

'I don't know how the family would feel about it,' said Caroline carefully, 'but Mrs Chadwick also saw the importance of having a younger person for the three of you, Fliss. That's where I came in, forty years ago.'

Fliss laughed. 'Don't think I haven't been considering it. Between us all, I'm terrified at the thought of the upheaval, specially now when Hal and I were contemplating a peaceful retirement together. Oh, I know we're still young for retirement, only in our fifties, but it was a nice idea, all the same.' She looked at them and they saw tears in her eyes. 'But this is Mole's son. Oh, I can't *wait* for you to see him.' She pushed back her chair. 'I'm going to telephone. I want to speak to Hal and then Susanna.'

There was a silence after she'd gone; the mood was broken,

the bubble burst. Caroline stood up and collected the mugs; Prue glanced at the clock.

'Jolyon will be in any moment,' she said vaguely. 'We must think about some supper. Oh, Caroline, I don't know whether to laugh or cry.'

'I should do both,' replied Caroline cheerfully. 'The occasion seems to call for it. You wash up and I'll peel some vegetables.'

'Fliss will need a drink when she comes back.' Prue looked happier. 'Speaking to Hal will be good for her. Oh dear. Just when they were going to be together after all these years. It's a tremendous responsibility, of course, but we simply must resolve it somehow.'

'We all need a drink,' said Caroline firmly, 'but first things first. Washing-up, prepare supper. Then we'll go through it all again. It's going to take quite a bit of getting used to.'

Chapter Forty-three

'I've lost my good opinion of myself,' said Susanna, 'and it's very depressing. I've been trying very hard to adapt to the idea that Fliss and Hal have been in love all their lives and now, out of the blue there's this new shock. It seems that Mole not only had a girlfriend but he also had a son. I'm . . . gob-smacked. It's so totally unbelievable that I didn't suspect something. We were so close, we shared everything. I can't believe that he felt he couldn't mention this girl to me.'

Sitting beside her in their small courtyard as the shadows lengthened and the house martins darted above them, Gus knew how hurt she was.

'I think there are areas of our lives which we all tend to keep utterly private,' he said gently. 'And especially someone like Mole. He was such a natural oyster, wasn't he? You were the closest he let anyone get to him but this would have been difficult to handle for him, even with you. And remember that he didn't know about the child. As for the girl, like Fliss said, it was probably the age gap that was holding him back. Perhaps he thought we might pull his leg a bit. It's the sort of thing that any man might feel the least bit sensitive about. A pretty girl, young enough to be your daughter, is bound to arouse certain reactions and Mole would have hated anything which really mattered to him getting off on the wrong foot, wouldn't he? It took the dear old boy so long to work up to things. I'm just so pleased that he *had* such a close relationship, aren't you? I always feared that he'd missed out.'

'It's all so sad,' she murmured, shivering a little in the cool air, dragging her soft woollen shawl more closely round her. 'So tragic. First Mole and then that poor young girl. An avalanche, Fliss said. What a series of disasters. And now this little boy . . . I can't wait to see him. Fliss says he's a dark Chadwick, just like Mole and Uncle Theo.'

'And you, too,' said Gus, smiling a little. 'You and the girls are dark Chadwicks, too.'

325

'I know.' Susanna tried to throw off her depression. 'I'm being a bit silly. I'm not really surprised that Fliss never told me about her and Hal – she's very self-contained and it wasn't just her secret – but I feel badly that I never suspected anything. Or if I did I didn't do much about it. I never noticed that she wasn't particularly happy or anything except when poor old Miles had his stroke and that was different. It makes me feel so selfish. I'm sure *she* would have known if our situations had been reversed.'

'It's probably the difference between being the eldest and the youngest of a family,' he said. They'd talked this over several times but he knew that it was necessary so that she could get it out of her system. 'Fliss was so much older than you. Eight years is quite a gap, especially in a case like yours where she had to be a little mother to you and Mole. She was always on the alert for you both but she wouldn't have wanted you to be worrying about her. It must have been a relief that you didn't know about Hal. She could relax with you and be herself. Don't underestimate the value of that. As for Mole, you were terribly important to him, you know that, Sooz. Don't let this spoil it for you. That would certainly be tragic.'

'I know.' She smiled at him. 'I told you, I'm being silly. The trouble is it makes you feel nervous. I don't know now whether Fliss is feeling delighted or terrified about Mole's little Sam. She *sounded* absolutely thrilled but it must be an enormous shock. I don't know whether to rejoice with her or to sympathise. I don't know how to be natural any more in case she's hiding things and I'm getting it wrong.'

'For a start,' he said, trying not to smile at her earnestness, 'it's not one thing or the other. Nothing is ever that cut and dried. It'll be both. So you can sympathise and rejoice in turn quite confidently. Of course she's pleased that Mole's still with us, so to speak, but it's a tremendous responsibility to come out of the blue with no warning.'

'Especially when she's all set to make up for that lost time with Hal. It's rotten timing and a daunting prospect. She's fifty-one, after all, and three is such a busy, demanding age.'

'I imagine your grandmother must have felt much the same,' said Gus. 'She would have wanted you all, no doubt about it, but she must have quailed at the thought of it.'

'I hadn't looked at it quite like that,' mused Susanna. 'There were Ellen and Fox, of course. And Caroline. I'm sure she couldn't have managed without Caroline.'

'Caroline was the bridge between you all. The missing genera-tion. If young Sam stays they'll have to do something along those lines. Even if they could manage physically there would be a huge gap age-wise.'

'Fliss says that Hal is already saying the same thing. She spoke to him before she phoned us. He's pleased, of course, but very firm, apparently, about having help. Good for him. He'll make sure it's done properly but it'll be tricky. The Keep's a big enough place but living with strangers isn't easy and, on top of that, poor little Sam will have someone else he'll have to get used to. Poor little chap. Oh, Gus, I *am* looking forward to seeing him. Mole's son.' She shook her head. 'It's so weird. Spooky, as Podger would say. How proud Mole would have been, wouldn't he? He'll never know about him. Isn't life cruel?'

'He knows,' said Gus. 'He knows all about young Sam.'

'But I can't see him doing it,' muttered Susanna. 'It's not the same.'

'Tell you what,' said Gus. 'Why don't we go over to The Keep? They'll have finished supper and we can have a chat and look at the photographs this girl – Lizzie, is it? – has brought. I know we were going tomorrow morning but why shouldn't we go now? They'll probably be glad to have a bit of a diversion themselves.'

'Oh, yes.' She looked at him with relief: the old Sooz, eyes bright and excited, and his heart moved in his breast in the odd, familiar way. 'That's a brilliant idea.' She was getting up, hauling him to his feet. 'Telephone them, Gus, while I get myself organised.'

She paused in the doorway, turning back to him, slipping her arms round him, hugging him. He smiled down at her.

'Thanks,' she said. 'Thanks, Gus.'

'I love you,' he said. 'And everything's going to be OK. We've got ourselves a new nephew. A new Mole without any of the dear chap's hang-ups. Let's be happy about it, shall we?'

They stood together for a long moment, holding each other, and presently they went inside hand in hand.

Fliss stood at the bedroom window looking out into the night. There was no moon but the stars twinkled softly in the soft dense darkness and a mist was rising above the river, flowing and curling across the fields where the sheep huddled in the shelter of the trees. The plaintive musical mewing of the little owl echoed over the hill, answered by its mate further up the valley, and she heard the nervous rustling of small birds which roosted in the ivy below the window.

Thoughts and ideas jangled and jostled in her head and she felt very tired but quite unrelaxed. This whirlwind, in the shape of

327

Lizzie and Sam, had burst upon her private world and she was flattened by it. At this moment she felt utterly unable to deal with the new situation. Shock, delight, relief; all these sensations had carried her forward, bearing her up until she'd been able to shut the bedroom door and find herself alone. Here she could slough off any requirement to be strong, to appear controlled and in charge.

She groaned aloud and sank down on to the window seat, drawing up her knees and lacing her fingers about them. The family was bearing up splendidly under the circumstances but she knew that the final decisions and responsibilities were hers – and Hal's. At the mere thought of him she relaxed a little, slumping forward so that her forehead rested on her knees. His voice had been comfortingly calm when she'd spoken to him earlier. He'd assimilated the news quickly, not needing to be told over and over, grasping the facts easily. She'd been so grateful for that. By then, with the excitement flagging and all the ramifications of this event bearing in upon her, she'd needed that ready, intelligent reaction.

'It's really splendid news, Fliss,' he'd said. 'It's what we needed' – she'd blessed him for that generous 'we' – 'to come to terms with Mole's death, isn't it? It softens the blow. She must have been quite a girl to go it alone without telling anyone. How sad that none of us met her. It must have been such a shock, Flissy. You poor darling. Rather like a ghost appearing if he looks as much like Mole as all that. And how brave of Lizzie to come down and beard the lion in his den. If his mother was her best friend she must be feeling pretty distraught herself. What a bloody awful thing to happen. I remember reading about that avalanche in the newspaper. Do you want me to come down, Fliss?'

She'd hastened to reassure him. At the moment there was little he could do and she knew that he was very busy and had just taken extra leave, too. It was unfair to drag him back simply to hold her hand. At the same time she was glad now that they'd agreed that she would not return with him to Scotland.

'I'm sure we can manage,' she'd said, 'although I'd love you to see him. It's probably best just to take it slowly at the moment. Of course I'd love to see you, you know that . . .'

They'd talked quietly together for a few precious moments before returning to the new situation.

'We'll have to check the legal side,' he'd said. 'We might have to adopt him. It could be that his grandmother is his next of kin and that could cause problems later on. Have a word with Michael about that, will you?' He'd chuckled softly, that dear, familiar intimate chuckle, and, shutting her eyes, she'd longed for him so fiercely that she could barely stand upright. 'Odd, isn't it, Fliss? History repeating itself like this. Let's hope we make as good a job of it as Grandmother did . . . Let me know how things go and start looking into finding some kind of help. We shall need it, Fliss. Don't even begin to imagine that you can manage alone. I agree that we don't particularly want to start our married life on a submarine base but we don't quite know what the future holds for us and wherever I go after this I shall want you with me. Young Sam simply must have continuity, apart from the obvious need for a young person about the place for him, and Ma and Caroline are too old for that kind of responsibility . . . Right, then.' His voice had changed and she'd guessed that someone else was now in his office with him. 'Speak soon? Love you. God bless.'

The brief time with him had steadied her but now she felt lonely and afraid. Never before had she realised quite what a burden their arrival from Kenya must have been to her grandmother. If this supposition were true, it had in no way detracted from her love for her grandchildren, there had never been any question about that, nevertheless she must have been unnerved by the prospect.

Raising her head, gazing out into the night, she wondered how the small Sam was dealing with the loss of his mother. At least he'd been used to being shared around; he'd become a social, adaptable child, but there had been one or two moments when he'd turned to Lizzie with a questioning look on his bright little face and he'd asked, 'Mummy coming soon?'

She'd heard Lizzie swallow audibly before saying quickly, 'She simply can't come, Sam. She's had to go a long way off,' and he'd continued to frown. She'd hugged him, distracting him, controlling her own grief, and Fliss had been overwhelmed with admiration for her.

'I wish we'd known her,' she'd said to Lizzie later. 'It would have been such a comfort.'

Now, listening to the owl, watching the steadily flashing lights of an aircraft, she realised that it would also have been a tremendous help. Sam looked far too much like Mole to seem a stranger to her, nevertheless it would have given them a working knowledge of this small person if they'd been acquainted with his mother. Perhaps, during the fortnight which Lizzie could spare them, they could learn as much as possible from her so as to give them a guide to the future. Here, her grandmother had been at an advantage. She'd already known Fliss and Mole had been very close to their mother, Alison. It must have assisted her in those moments when some kind of recognition is important . . . Fliss closed her eyes, almost light-headed with weariness.

Quite suddenly it seemed as if the room were full of people. The shades of all those whom she'd loved seemed to throng about her and, deep inside herself, she felt a faint echo of courage, as if in response. She opened her eyes and looked around her, remembering the many different occasions when she'd sat here with Uncle Theo, resting on his strength, listening to his wisdom. Hal had put the old battered desk in his dressing room but he'd left the armchair by the window, and the bookshelves with their contents were untouched. Despite redecoration and different furnishings, Fliss felt Theo's presence and was comforted. Somehow she would come through . . .

As she slipped into sleep, relaxed at last between the cool sheets, she thought she heard his voice. He was in the chair by the window, reading aloud, and the quiet words dropped gently into her consciousness, soothing her. The words were familiar and she tried to remember which psalm it was; she recognised it because it was Mole's favourite: the shield and the buckler one that he'd read at Theo's funeral.

'He who dwells in the shelter of the most High, abides under the shadow of the Almighty . . .'

Mole: holding her skirt, afraid to let her out of his sight.

'He shall say to the Lord, "You are my refuge and my stronghold, my God, in whom I put my trust . . ."'

Mole: cycling round the courtyard, on the swing under the oak tree, playing cricket on the lawn.

'He shall cover you with his pinions and you shall find refuge under his wings: his faithfulness and truth shall be a shield and buckler . . .'

Mole: going off to school, running round the spinney.

'You shall not be afraid of any terror by night: nor of the arrow that flies by day . . .'

Mole: at his passing-out parade at Dartmouth, taking command of his first submarine.

'He shall call upon me and I will answer him; I am with him in trouble, I will rescue him and bring him to honour . . .'

She was dreaming now, watching the photographs changing into reality, seeing Mole and Sam together, laughing, free, happy. She knew that she was weeping but it no longer mattered. She took her farewell of him, peacefully at last, and, turning her cheek upon the pillow, she slept.

Chapter Forty-four

A few days later, Lizzie and Sam moved their few belongings out of the hotel and into The Keep. Everyone agreed that it was important that Sam should begin to feel at home, to settle in rather than to be merely a visitor, and it seemed perfectly natural that he should be given his father's bedroom. He was enchanted by the residents who waited for him in the old wicker chair and to whose ranks he added his own well-worn teddy bear. Some of Mole's books which, over the years, had found their way down to the study were re-established in the small white-painted bookcase and a few toys were selected and carried up to his new quarters. One of his own treasured possessions was a bright red photograph wallet containing, on one side, a picture of his mother and, on the other, the original of the photograph of Mole on *Dorcas*. He showed them proudly to Fliss.

'Daddy,' he said cheerfully. 'Daddy on his boat. That's Mummy.'

Fliss's eyes met Lizzie's above his dark head as he stood the wallet carefully on the cupboard beside his bed but, for once, neither of them was capable of a response. Sam didn't notice their silence, he was too busy setting out his toys and arranging his books. He was quite resigned to the fact that Daddy had gone away for some time, and that Mummy had now joined him, but he was very excited to be given the bedroom his father had used when he was a little boy and to have his books and toys as his own. Whilst he was settling in and unpacking his small case, Fliss wandered across the landing to see how Lizzie was managing.

She was more than happy to use Jolyon's old bedroom which, since his removal to the gatehouse, had remained quite empty of any personal belongings. Lizzie seemed to live out of a rucksack although she also carried a portable set of photographs in a leather holder. These were standing on the chest of drawers and Fliss bent to look at them. A middle-aged couple, accompanied by two springer spaniels, beamed happily out at her.

331

'My parents,' said Lizzie, flinging clothes into drawers. 'We were an army family which is why I bonded with Sam at boarding school I suppose. Dad's retired now and they live at Pin Mill in Suffolk. The other one is a photograph of my brothers. Simon is a medical student and Nick starts university in the autumn. They're not bad, as brothers go. They're all mad about sailing, hence Pin Mill.'

'They look fun.' Fliss straightened up. 'I didn't mean to pry. It's just that I feel I know you very well already, I suppose, and I can't resist photographs. I hope you've got everything you need. Caroline's room is next door and there's a little kitchen next to the bathroom, just in case.'

'It's a fantastic place.' Lizzie finished her unpacking, slung her empty rucksack under the chair and looked about her. 'It's so roomy and old but it's not all done up and smart, is it?'

Fliss snorted derisively. 'It certainly isn't smart,' she agreed. 'We've never been able to afford smart. Just keeping the old place going takes all we've got. Everything's run by a trust. My grandmother wanted The Keep maintained as a place for the whole family, not just one part of it. It's a wonderful idea but very complicated. At times like this, however, you realise that her vision was a good one. I hope that the next generation can keep it going. Jolyon's doing his best to make the place pay for itself . . .'

'And now there's Sam,' said Lizzie lightly, as Fliss fell silent. 'Perhaps he'll go into the Navy like his father. It's a bit of a Chadwick tradition, isn't it?'

'It is indeed. I must say that he was taking great interest in those photographs of submarines on the walls in his room.' Fliss laughed. 'I'll have to make sure that he's not indoctrinated too young.'

They went together into his room and Fliss watched as he seized Lizzie's hand, showing her his new treasures. He was such an easy, friendly little boy but she was already panicking at the thought of looking after him without Lizzie. He had taken to them all readily enough but Lizzie was the person to whom he turned quite naturally in happiness or anxiety. She was his anchorstone, his friend, and Fliss's heart failed each time she imagined the scene when he learned that she was to leave them. She knew that Lizzie was worrying about it, too.

'I want what's best for him,' she'd told Fliss anxiously one evening, just before bedtime. Sam was saying good night to Rufus before going upstairs for his bedtime story. He'd had his bath and had come downstairs for his supper in the kitchen. They watched him kneeling beside Rufus, stroking him, talking to him, and, glancing at Lizzie, Fliss was shocked to see the naked misery on her face.

'I shall miss him so much,' she'd muttered wretchedly, 'but I want what's best for him. I owe it to Sam. She would have relied on me, you see.'

Now, as Lizzie swung him up so that he could see the submarine photographs more closely, Fliss felt her heart contract with anxiety.

She thought: I wonder if I could persuade her to stay a bit longer. Just an extra week or two while I look about for someone else. Oh hell . . .

Next morning, as she watched Sam cycling round the courtyard on the small tricycle, which had last been used by Lulu, and dragged out of retirement by Jolyon, Fliss made a new discovery. Sam pedalled furiously, head bent low over the handlebars, pausing at intervals to rest and to talk to Jo who strolled beside him. As he talked, his flushed face turned earnestly to Jolyon, who now balanced, crouching on his heels, beside him, it occurred to Fliss that it was Susanna whom he resembled. She and Mole had always been physically alike but it was Susanna's vivacity manifest in this small boy: her energy and friendliness; her ability to adapt and her love for adventure. The realisation comforted her. She had no wish to play down Sam's inheritance from his mother, far from it, but if these qualities resembled those belonging to her own sister it made everything just a little easier.

It was at this moment that Susanna herself wandered in to the courtyard, waved to Jo and Sam and crossed to the bench where Fliss sat.

'I was just thinking about you,' Fliss told her. 'I've made a discovery. I think Sam is like you as well as Mole. He's got your friendliness and sunny nature. I can't tell you how pleased that makes me feel.'

'I can't say that I've been feeling too sunny just lately,' said Susanna, 'but I'm glad if you're pleased.'

'Of course I'm pleased,' said Fliss, surprised. 'Don't forget that you're the only true success of our generation when it comes to ordinary down-to-earth happiness. You and Gus are our icons. I have to say that I've always found your calm, optimistic outlook terribly comforting. I shall be delighted if Sam looks like Mole and is exactly like you.'

'Thanks,' said Susanna, after a minute. 'That's . . . really nice. Thanks. So how's he settling in?'

333

'He fine. That's what I mean. He has your happy, easy nature.' She sighed. 'But the test will come when Lizzie goes. He's just lost his mother and I really don't know how he's going to take losing Lizzie, too. We'll stay in close touch with her, of course. She's his godmother, did I tell you? Poor Lizzie. I think she'll find it just as awful as he will.'

Sam made another circuit, pausing to beam at them as he drew level, and Rufus pottered out of the garden room and lay down on the grass in the sun. Sam slipped off the tricycle, unable to resist a quick chat to his friend, and Rufus licked his face enthusiastically. Susanna laughed as Sam set off again, pedalling vigorously, watching to make certain that Jolyon was keeping up with him, and then stretched out her legs, frowning a little.

'I'm sure you've thought of this and it's been rejected,' she said, 'but isn't it at all possible that Lizzie could stay on?'

'Don't think I haven't thought of it,' said Fliss. 'She's got another week with us but she has to think about her job in London and there's a possibility that she'll have to move, so I don't like to impose on her. If I really pressed her she might stay another week but the trouble is we don't know how long it might take for Sam to adjust, do we? Will another week make much difference, anyway? Or will it just make it harder than ever to make the break?'

'I didn't mean that.' Susanna looked at her sister. 'She's told you that she temps and that she's going to have to move out of her flat. So she's not terribly settled, is she? We know she was Sam's best friend and the boy's godmother and she loves him dearly. I'm probably stating the obvious and you've done this already but have you actually suggested that she should remain as his nanny?'

There was a very long silence. A fluffy, speckled baby robin hopped along the path and Rufus yawned mightily, snapping at a fly. Sam and Jolyon had reached the gatehouse and, after some persuasion, Jo was allowing him to venture out a short way on to the drive.

'I didn't think of it,' said Fliss at last. 'None of us did. It sounds crazy, doesn't it, now you've said it, but we were so fixated on her life being in London. It's the most obvious and wonderful solution. I can't imagine why none us thought of it except that we've been too close to the situation to see clearly. It's brilliant. Oh hell! I almost wish you hadn't thought of it, Sooz. I don't think I could bear it now if she refuses.'

'Well, she hasn't refused yet,' said Susanna, the pragmatist. 'Try it and see. Where is she?'

'Caroline took her into Totnes with her. We thought she needed a break from us all and it seemed a good idea to wean Sam away in small doses. But do you really think she might stay? We're so dull, down here. She's used to London, remember. There's not much to offer her, is there?'

'There wasn't much to offer Caroline, was there, but she seems to have been perfectly happy.'

'Oh, Sooz!' Fliss began to laugh. 'What a comfort you are. It would be simply perfect. But I must talk to the others first. I'm quite certain that Prue and Caroline would be thrilled to bits and I can't see Hal making a fuss about it. As for Jo, he's rather taken with her already . . .'

'Then don't tell Lulu,' said Susanna. 'She covets his gatehouse and won't welcome another female muscling in on her pitch.'

'I wondered if it might be Podger,' ventured Fliss. 'They got on so well this last holiday.'

Susanna shook her head, amused. 'No chance, I'm afraid. She's very fond of him but only as another person to be organised. She sees him as a challenge and dear old Jo is very sweet to her. No need to worry.'

Fliss smiled. 'I'm glad to hear it,' she said.

Susanna glanced at her. 'It must have been awful,' she said awkwardly. 'You and Hal all those years . . . I'm sorry. I wish I'd noticed . . .'

'I'm glad you didn't,' said Fliss roundly. 'It was bad enough with Prue and Caroline knowing. I felt I could never *quite* relax when Hal was around. With you we could be utterly natural and it was such a relief, especially during these last years when Miles was ill. Surely you noticed how often Hal and I turned up for a few hours of relaxation together. You and Gus were like a little haven for us.'

'Really? That's great then.' Susanna gave a great gasp of relief. 'I've been a bit low about it, to be honest. And when all this happened . . . Do you feel a bit hurt that Mole never mentioned her?'

'We know now that Mole had learned to keep a great deal secret.' Fliss shrugged. 'He was naturally self-contained, wasn't he? I think that the other part of his career, which none of us knew about, must have made him more so. He'd have wanted to be utterly sure of Sam before he told anyone how he felt. As far as I can tell, he hadn't even told *her*. She'd guessed it but the baby was her way of pushing him over the edge. Poor old Mole . . .'

'I hadn't seen it quite like that.' Susanna sat up straighter. 'Thank goodness Lizzie was around to throw some light on it all. You must try to persuade her to stay, Fliss. Poor kid. It could be just what she needs, too.'

'It's a brilliant idea.' Fliss glanced at her watch, distracted. 'Look, I'm going to try and catch Hal before he goes to lunch. I'll clear it with him and then, when the moment is right I'll talk to Lizzie. Keep an eye on Sam for me.'

Fliss disappeared into the house and Susanna got up and strolled across the grass. She felt happier than she'd felt for several weeks; her normal cheerful spirits revived, her humour restored. As she passed between the gatehouses she began to hum aloud.

Sam sat on the swing, a rope clenched firmly in either hand whilst Lizzie pushed him. Higher and higher he flew in the dappled shade beneath the oak tree and Fliss's mind swung back, as it did so often now, to the past and her own childhood. She was becoming used to seeing Sam in the garden, on the stairs, up in the nursery wing. Part of the family; part of life at The Keep.

Fliss thought: Mole's not on the edge any more. He's moved in. Right inside. He's part of the pattern, part of the past and the future. Oh, thank God. Oh, Mole . . .

Now, watching them – Lizzie laughing, shaking back the mane of hair from her eyes, protesting that she was hot whilst Sam shouted gleefully, urging for 'More! More!' – Fliss suddenly felt that this was the moment for which she'd been waiting since yesterday's talk with Susanna. Hal, Prue, Caroline, Jolyon; each of them had been delighted with the idea, equally amazed that none of them had thought of it before.

'Come and have some juice,' Fliss said, as the swinging slowed down a little. 'Look, Rufus is ready for his biscuit and poor Lizzie is tired out. She needs a drink, too. Have a rest and then we'll have another swing later.'

Sam gave in without too much of a struggle, always ready to move on to the next exciting event in his small life, and they went inside. For once the kitchen was empty and, lifting Sam into the highchair which had seen so many years of service, Fliss supplied him with some toys and a picture book while she fetched his juice. Whilst she made coffee, talking quietly to Lizzie, they watched him begin to nod. He had great energy which was renewed at regular intervals by catnaps. He would sleep deeply for twenty minutes at unscheduled moments and they were learning to make the most of these brief respites. Lizzie carried him into the hall, laid him on the sofa, and then sat down opposite with Fliss, who had brought their coffee.

'I suppose,' began Fliss, trying to hide her nervousness, encouraged by the memory of the family's enthusiasm, 'that you *do* have to go back next Sunday?'

336

Lizzie grimaced. 'Don't talk about it,' she said. 'They'd manage without me, of course. I'm not indispensable, I take care of that, but I don't like to let people down.'

'I'm beginning to believe that you *are* indispensable to Sam,' said Fliss, quietly. 'He's going to miss you terribly.'

'Don't,' groaned Lizzie. 'Please don't. Can't you see I've been worrying about it, too? I shall miss him so much. I've thought and thought about it but now I've seen this place I know it would be utterly selfish to keep him in London, even if we could sort it out between us. And we can't. Anna's always had the least to do with him, you see, so with Sam gone and Laura moving out it's just not on. I've racked my brains, I promise you. Perhaps you'll bring him up to see me sometimes?'

Fliss looked into the pleading blue-green eyes. 'I was looking at it the other way round,' she murmured. 'I suppose you wouldn't consider staying here with us? If you like temping couldn't you look at this in the same way? A temporary job with us until Sam is older.'

Lizzie's eyes were round with surprise. 'Live here with you, d'you mean? As a nanny? But I haven't been trained for it. I haven't got a clue.'

'My dear girl.' Fliss shook her head, 'if that's the only problem we're on velvet. I've watched you with him and you're as capable as any mother, believe me, and a great deal more loving than many . . . What d'you think?'

Behind the surprise and confusion, joy was breaking like the dawn over Lizzie's face.

'It's just unbelievable. It's really cool. I mean, do you really think I could do it? I've never thought of myself as a nanny. We mucked in with Sam, and I probably did more than Anna or Laura, but even so . . .'

'We've got Caroline. She'd be a tremendous tower of strength,' said Fliss carefully. She hesitated; wondering whether Lizzie would accept this, waiting for pitfalls, but Lizzie's reaction was one of obvious relief.

'That's true,' she said. 'She must have been through all the childhood diseases and stuff with all of you – but even so . . .'

'Think about it,' suggested Fliss, overwhelmed by relief that she hadn't been turned down flat. 'Just think about it, Lizzie. We needn't be too hard and fast about it. It might take twelve months, or twelve years, but if you think you could put up with us we'd be so very grateful.'

'I'd love it,' she said seriously. 'Oh, I can't really take this in,

Fliss. Now you've said it, it's . . . it's so exactly right. But I'd have to talk to Anna and things. I couldn't let her down. She'd have to get someone else in my place and I'd have to talk to the girl at my agency.'

'Of course you must do everything properly,' said Fliss at once. 'I quite understand that. Only it would be such a relief if I thought we weren't going to lose you, Lizzie.'

The girl beamed at her, all her natural confidence and enthusiasm swinging round to deal with this new challenge. 'Don't worry,' she said. 'The more I think about it the more I can see that this is an offer I can't refuse. Anna will understand and the agency won't care one way or another. Honestly. Oh, Fliss, if you're really sure . . . ?'

'You're the bridge,' said Fliss, 'between Sam's past and his future, and I have this feeling that, without you, we might all come tumbling down. Yes, Lizzie, I'm really sure. We all are. Think it through carefully. Telephone your parents, if you like, and tell them about it. Give yourself time to consider it carefully and then we'll talk again. Meanwhile, my coffee's cold. I'm going to make some more.'

In the kitchen she stood quite still for some moments, gripping the back of a chair, head bent, weak with relief and happiness. Presently she pushed the kettle on to the hotplate and began to make the coffee with trembling hands.

Chapter Forty-five

At the end of the week, Lizzie returned to London to sort out her affairs and collect her belongings. She intended to take the opportunity to make a quick dash to Suffolk to see her parents but promised that she would be back within three days. Fliss had already spoken to Mrs Fairbanks on the telephone. She'd mooted this suggestion as tactfully as she could, knowing that Lizzie, at twenty-four, considered herself quite independent, and had been relieved when Lizzie had cheerfully agreed to it.

'Mum's not given to flights of fancies,' she said – looking again at the photograph Fliss could readily believe it – 'but it's probably sensible. She's terribly fond of young Sam and he's been down to Pin Mill quite often. The boys adore him. They can't wait to teach him to sail. I must admit that they were all devastated when Sam died so Mum'll be really pleased to know that we won't lose touch.'

Armed with this information, Fliss had no hesitation in inviting the Fairbankses to The Keep and promised that Sam should continue to visit Pin Mill with Lizzie. Mrs Fairbanks sounded a jolly, sensible woman and, as two service wives, she and Fliss had much in common. She was delighted to think that Lizzie would be settling down with the Chadwicks in Devon and clearly had no doubts of her daughter's abilities as a nanny.

'She was wonderful with the boys,' she told Fliss. 'Very sensible but very loving. Of course, she can be a bit bossy from time to time. Can't think who she gets it from . . .'

From the sound of bass rumblings in the background, combined with Mrs Fairbanks's chuckle, Fliss suspected that Colonel Fairbanks was offering his wife a solution.

'Dad'll be even more relieved than Mum,' Lizzie said later. 'He's more of a worrier. He'll like to think that I'm settling down a bit. By the way, I've been thinking about Charlie. He's away on exercise in Norway for a few weeks but I'd like you to meet him. He's rather special to me, just like another brother, and he *is* Sam's uncle. Now that we know that his grandmother is happy to let you keep him

339

and doesn't really want to know, it's even more important that we stay in touch with Charlie.'

Slowly things were falling into place, all the knots unravelling smoothly, and when Lizzie went off to London it was with the feeling that she was going to sort out the last of the immediate problems.

'Lizzie gone,' said Sam thoughtfully as he and Fliss waved her goodbye. The little Fiat jolted down the drive, Lizzie's arm flailing wildly from the window, and, when the car had finally disappeared, he sat for a while astride Fliss's hip staring after it. 'Back soon?' He ducked his head so as to look closely into her face. 'Back for tea?'

Her heart sank a little. She was braced for these three days to be difficult but she smiled bravely into his eyes and gave him a quick kiss.

'Not for tea,' she said cheerfully, 'but she'll be back as soon as she can.'

She knew he would not understand how long three days might be but recognised that he needed to be reassured that Lizzie would not disappear completely. It was difficult to know what might comfort him, under the circumstances. At three and a half, Sam had already experienced loss and her only hope was to keep him as occupied as possible.

'We're going to the seaside,' she told him. 'Jo's coming with us. And Rufus. Rufus loves swimming and you can paddle. We shall take a picnic to eat on the beach. Let's go in and see what Aunt Prue has packed up for us, shall we?'

Turning his thoughts away from his anxieties, talking to him about the delights ahead, they went back into the house whilst she silently blessed his naturally resilient and optimistic nature.

That evening another little thread presented itself to be woven into the emerging pattern. When Sam was safely in bed, tired out with the excitements of the day, Fliss telephoned Kit to tell her the latest news. It had been agreed that the London contingent would wait until Sam was properly settled at The Keep before they descended but Fliss kept them all posted with each new development.

'The really nice thing is that we seem to be getting a whole new family along with Sam,' she told Kit. 'We've got Lizzie and her parents, as well as her two brothers. And then there's Sam's brother, Charlie. I know we're a rather insular lot, as you've often told us, but now it seems that we're being swept along on a new tide of events which is going to carry us all into the millennium. It's rather exciting, isn't it? Of course, it's just fantastic that

Lizzie can stay with us. It's an absolute miracle. Just like Sam himself.'

'I'm delighted to hear it, honey.' Fliss could hear that Kit was smiling. 'It was your turn, believe me. By the way, Bess has just come in and she's got something to tell you. I'll say goodbye for now. Give my old ma a kiss, won't you? Honestly, little coz, I'm so thrilled for you.'

There was barely time to rehearse mentally her usual anxious catalogue of the disasters which might have befallen her daughter before Bess was on the line.

'Oh, Mum,' she said excitedly, 'you'll never believe this. Honestly, you won't. It was Matt who thought of it, actually. Mum, we met Sam. We met her on Mole's boat. Are you still there? Listen. She came on board one Sunday morning when I'd taken Matt down to meet Mole. Isn't it utterly amazing? It was Matt who reminded me of it. She was really nice and terribly pretty. Easy and friendly and great fun. I remember that, afterwards, Matt said something about Mole doing well and I jumped on him. Only because of her age, though. They were really nice together. And later, when I told Jamie about her because he'd just broken off with some girlfriend or other, he made the same remark. About Mole being a dark horse or something. I just wish I'd taken notice of them. Isn't it amazing, Mum? But it's nice, isn't it? That we actually met her, I mean. Are you still there . . . ?'

'I can't think why I'm so pleased about it,' Fliss said to Prue later. Caroline was upstairs, pottering about within earshot lest Sam should disturb and be frightened. 'It's silly, really, but I'm just so thrilled. Bess can't wait until Sam's old enough so that she can tell him that she met his mother.'

'That's the reason, darling, isn't it?' Prue smiled at her. 'It's a connection with her through one of us. It's important. Bess will tell us about it, over and over again, and, soon, we shall come to think that we knew her, too. We'll be able to imagine the scene and fit her into it and gradually she'll become real to us. Mole's dear love, and darling little Sam's mother. Of *course* it's important.'

Fliss looked at her gratefully.

'Kit sent you a kiss,' she said, 'and I think I shall deliver it in person.' She did so. 'Isn't it nice to think that Hal will be home for the weekend? He's going to stay on long enough to meet Lizzie but I can't tell you how relieved I shall be to see him.'

Prue looked into her glowing face and then took her in her arms, holding her, rocking Fliss as if she were a child.

'I'm so happy, my darling,' she murmured. 'So very happy for

341

you both. Do you forgive us for keeping you apart? Me and Freddy, I mean. We truly thought it was for the best. We were so frightened about the babies, you see, and we knew how important children would be for you, Fliss.'

'It's in the past.' Fliss hugged her tightly. 'And we've got my twinnies and dear old Jolyon. And we all loved Miles in the end, didn't we? He was very special. We've all come through in one way or another, haven't we? Let's not look back. Not now, when there's so much to look forward to.'

'What's going on here?' asked Jolyon, coming into the kitchen. 'Is this a private love-in or can anyone join?'

'Oh, darling.' Prue released Fliss and beamed upon him. 'Is it supper time already? Let's have a little drink while I get myself organised and Fliss will tell you some exciting news she's just heard.'

Up in the nursery wing, Caroline set down the iron and trod softly across the landing into Sam's room. Had she heard a cry? Sam lay sleeping peacefully, one arm flung wide, the other wrapped about Mole's teddy. She stood looking down at him, as she had looked down upon Mole, so many years before. The soft, rounded cheek, flushed by the sunshine; the dark shiny hair tumbled on the pillow; these were familiar to her. So had Mole looked – and Susanna – forty years before. She thought of Ellen and of Fox – and felt that Mrs Chadwick was standing at her shoulder, as she had so often stood, looking down upon a sleeping child. She remembered Theo's words, used whenever he'd heard the children's prayers.

'The Lord grant us a quiet night and a perfect end.'

Gently she touched the curling fingers and chubby wrist, lightly smoothed the dark hair from the untroubled brow, and went quietly away.

The afternoon was hot. Cows stood knee-deep in the shallows beneath the pollarded willows and swallows skimmed low above the surface of the water, where the midges executed their tireless dance. Across the valley, grass was being cut for silage, the machines moving slowly, so that the fields were striped, regular as corduroy, with green and pale gold. Fliss could hear the lark singing somewhere high above her, the notes of his song cascading, falling, through the quiet air. From the edge of the spinney she could see the glowing blue flood which lit its shadowy interior: bluebells spreading from trunk to trunk, rippling against the smooth boles, flowing over the earthy floor. Fliss felt happiness bubbling inside her. Soon Hal would be home.

'I might give you a buzz from the station,' he'd said. 'Or I might grab a taxi. Either way I should be home in time for tea . . .'

Instinctively she glanced at her watch, knowing that it was too early yet. She'd left Prue listening for the telephone – just in case – and watching Sam as he slept, stretched on the sofa in the hall, and she'd come out on the hill because she simply couldn't sit still. She longed to see Hal; longed to see him, to talk to him, to share everything with him; could hardly wait to see his face as he looked at Sam. Before that, however, she wanted to go round the spinney.

Memories crowded in upon her as she stepped back into the sunshine from the leafy protection of the trees and began to walk round the spinney. It had become a symbol long since and she'd wanted to do it alone as a gesture to the future. She'd done it as a child and as a girl; before she'd set out for Hong Kong with Miles, frightened at the prospect of having her baby so far from home, and years later, with Hal, on an afternoon just like this one. Today, quite suddenly, she'd known that this was the time. It was significant; a kind of brief stopping place between past and future where she could pause for a moment and catch her breath.

Fliss thought: I'm being a twit. Dramatising myself. But now I can see that those moments *were* important ones. Tiny staging posts where I could look back and review the journey so as to get my bearings for the future.

The future looked good. As she skirted the edge of the tall beeches she thought with pleasure of all that lay ahead; so much to do; so much to share. As she shaded her eyes to watch the buzzard circling over the hill, listened to the lambs crying in the fields across the river, she saw other shadows moving on the edge of memory: Fox, pausing to light a cigarette whilst Mrs Pooter ran ahead: Mole and Susanna singing breathlessly as they climbed the hill behind Kit and Hal, going home to tea after an afternoon by the river; Jolyon and the twinnies playing in the snow. Grandmother and Uncle Theo would have been sitting in the hall and Ellen would have been busy in the kitchen with Caroline, piling scones on to a plate, putting bramble jelly into a dish, making tea in the silver teapot.

Tomorrow, she and Hal would bring Sam out on to this ancient hill; they would take him down to the river and round the spinney and he would ride back home on Hal's shoulders. Tomorrow there would be birthdays and Christmases, schooldays and holidays. Life would go on for the next forty years as it had for the last, ever since she and Mole and Sooz had arrived at Staverton Station and Grandmother had met them and brought them back to The Keep.

*   *   *

343

In the hall Sam was still asleep whilst Prue sat opposite, knitting some small fleecy garment, probably for baby Paula.

'Did he ring?' Fliss leaned beside her on the back of the chair, whispering so as not to disturb Sam.

Prue shook her head and held up her knitting, showing Fliss that she was nearly at the end of her wool, gesturing that she might now go upstairs and find some more. Fliss nodded and she slipped quietly away. Sam stirred and murmured, 'Mummy?' and Fliss watched him, her heart moved by compassion. As she hesitated beside him, she heard the engine of a car. It approached the gatehouse, idled outside in the drive, and then a door slammed and it pulled away. Sam came fully awake and sat up, flushed and rumpled with sleep. He looked about for his teddy and slid to the floor, pattering across the hall to where Fliss stood at the window.

Hal came into the courtyard, carrying his grip, his coat slung over his shoulder. He paused for a moment, looking up at the old house as if saluting it, and then approached across the grass.

Sam pulled at Fliss's hand, standing on tiptoe, trying to see out of the window.

'It's Hal,' she said, smiling with secret delight. 'He's early. Come and say "Hello" to him.'

She swung him up in her arms, settling him astride her hip, and together they went down the steps and out into the sunshine to meet him.